Enid Blyton

Malory Towers
Collection 3

3 BOOKS IN 1

Written by Pamela Cox

Hodder
Children's
Books

HODDER CHILDREN'S BOOKS

New Term first published in Great Britain in 2009 by Mammoth
Summer Term first published in Great Britain in 2009 by Mammoth
Winter Term first published in Great Britain in 2009 by Mammoth
This edition published in 2016 by Hodder & Stoughton

1 3 5 7 9 10 8 6 4 2

Enid Blyton ® and Enid Blyton's signature are Registered Trademarks
of Hodder & Stoughton Limited
Text © Hodder & Stoughton Limited
Cover illustration © Hodder & Stoughton Limited
No trademark or copyrighted material may be reproduced without the express
written permission of the trademark and copyright owner
The moral right of the author has been asserted.

A CIP catalogue record for this book
is available from the British Library.

ISBN 978-1-444-94993-3

Printed and bound in Great Britain by Clays Ltd, Elcograf S.p.A.

The paper and board used in this book are from wood from responsible sources.

MIX
Paper from
responsible sources
FSC® C104740

Hodder Children's Books
An imprint of
Hachette Children's Group
Part of Hodder and Stoughton
Carmelite House
50 Victoria Embankment
London EC4Y 0DZ

An Hachette UK Company
www.hachette.co.uk
www.hachettechildrens.co.uk

Malory Towers
Collection 3

Other Enid Blyton School Stories Collections

The St Clare's Collection 1:
The Twins • The O'Sullivan Twins • Summer Term

The St Clare's Collection 2:
Second Form • Third Form • Kitty

The St Clare's Collection 3:
Claudine • Fifth Formers • Sixth Form

The Malory Towers Collection 1:
First Term • Second Form • Third Year

The Malory Towers Collection 2:
Upper Fourth • In the Fifth • Last Term

The Malory Towers Collection 3:
New Term • Summer Term • Winter Term

The Malory Towers Collection 4:
Fun and Games • Secrets • Goodbye

The Naughtiest Girl Collection 1:
In the School • Again • Is a Monitor

The Naughtiest Girl Collection 2:
Here's … • Keeps a Secret • Helps a Friend • Saves the Day

The Naughtiest Girl Collection 3:
Well Done • Wants to Win • Marches On

Contents

New Term   1

Summer Term   203

Winter Term   407

Malory Towers

New Term

Written by Pamela Cox

Contents

1 Back to Malory Towers 1

2 New friends and an old enemy 15

3 The first night 27

4 The new head-girl 38

5 A shock for Felicity 51

6 The new girls settle in 62

7 A dirty trick 74

8 Secrets and tricks 88

9 Vanishing cream 99

10 Half-term 109

11 Trouble in the third form 120

12 A shock for Amy 133

13 Mrs Dale springs a surprise 144

14 A bad time for Felicity 154

15 Veronica in trouble 166

16 Veronica gets a chance 177

17 A happy end to the term 191

Back to Malory Towers

'Darrell, are you and Sally absolutely sure that you don't want to come with Daddy and me when we drive Felicity to school?' asked Mrs Rivers as she buttered a slice of toast.

'Absolutely sure,' said Darrell firmly. 'I think that seeing dear old Malory Towers and knowing that I don't belong there any more would make me burst into tears, to be honest. Do you feel the same, Sally?'

Darrell's friend, Sally Hope, who was staying with the Rivers family for a few days, nodded. 'Exactly the same. I would like to go back and see the old place one day, but not yet. The memories of all the fun we shared and the friends we made are just too fresh.' Sally sighed heavily. 'I can't believe that our schooldays are over and we shall never go back to Malory Towers again.'

'You poor old things,' said Mr Rivers, looking up from his newspaper. 'Really, anyone would think that the two of you had nothing left to look forward to. But you're both off to university soon and a whole new chapter is beginning for you.'

'I know, and I'm really looking forward to starting university,' said Darrell. 'But it won't be as much fun as school.'

'I expect it *will* be fun, but in a different way,' put in her younger sister, Felicity. 'Just think, you'll have your own rooms, and no lights-out, and I bet you'll both be invited to lots of parties and dances, and –'

'And, who knows, we may even get a little studying done,' said Sally, with a laugh. 'It's going to be jolly hard work as well, young Felicity, so there's no need to sound quite so envious.'

'Oh, I'm not envious, Sally,' Felicity assured her, pushing her porridge bowl away. 'I absolutely *love* being at Malory Towers, and I can't wait to get back there.'

'And I suppose your eagerness to return to school has nothing to do with the fact that you'll be able to shake off Bonnie Meadows at last?' said Darrell slyly. 'My word, the poor girl won't know what to do with herself when you're gone.'

'Latch on to somebody else, hopefully,' said Felicity, with a groan. 'That girl has absolutely ruined my holiday. With all the towns in the country to choose from, why did her parents have to move here?'

'Felicity!' protested Mrs Rivers. 'That's not very nice. Especially as the poor girl obviously thinks the world of you.'

Felicity, who was getting a little tired of hearing the new neighbours' daughter referred to as a 'poor girl', rolled her eyes and said, 'No, she doesn't. Not really. She's just grateful to have some company of her own age, for a change. I'm sure she would have been just the same with anyone who had been kind to her.'

'That's the trouble, Felicity – you were *too* kind to

her,' said Darrell. 'You need to be firm with people like Bonnie.'

'I know,' said Felicity with a sigh, thinking that downright Darrell would have had no trouble in brushing Bonnie off. 'But I just couldn't bring myself to be unkind to her – in spite of the fact that she's such a drip!'

'That's what comes of wrapping children in cotton-wool,' remarked Mr Rivers. 'It would do young Bonnie the world of good to be sent to a school like Malory Towers, where she could mix with other girls and learn to stand on her own two feet.'

'But I thought that Bonnie was too sickly and delicate to go to school?' said Mrs Rivers.

'She may have been when she was younger,' said Mr Rivers, folding up his newspaper. 'But there's absolutely nothing wrong with her now – apart from an over-anxious mother, of course.'

'And Daddy ought to know,' said Darrell, referring to the fact that Mr Rivers was a highly respected member of the medical profession.

'Of course,' said Mrs Rivers. 'But I can't help feeling a little sorry for Mrs Meadows. It must have been dreadfully worrying for her when Bonnie was ill, especially with Mr Meadows being away so much. I suppose it's only natural that she's got into the habit of being over-protective.'

'Mother, do we *have* to spend my last precious moments at home talking about Boring Bonnie?' asked Felicity plaintively. 'Isn't it bad enough that she's been my shadow for the last few weeks?'

'All right, dear, we shan't mention her again,' said Mrs Rivers. 'Now, are you absolutely sure that you haven't left anything out of your trunk? And is your night case all packed and ready?'

'Yes, I've double-checked and I haven't forgotten anything,' answered Felicity.

'Good,' said Mr Rivers, pushing his chair back and getting to his feet. 'In that case, I shall go and start loading up the car and we'll be off.'

'I suppose *I* shall have to learn to stand on my own two feet as well,' said Felicity with a sigh. 'Now that I shan't have my big sister at school to look out for me. I shall be so lonely!'

Darrell laughed. 'Somehow I think you'll learn to stand on your own two feet very well. And as for being lonely – well, every time I tried to speak to you at school you were surrounded by your friends, so I daresay you'll be fine.'

'I'm so looking forward to seeing the others again,' Felicity said. 'Susan, and Pam, and Julie . . .'

'And June?' asked Sally with a quizzical look.

'Yes, even June,' laughed Felicity. 'I know that she can be troublesome, and outspoken, and downright wicked at times – but she's jolly good fun and she does make me laugh.'

Just like her cousin, Alicia, thought Darrell. 'Well,' she said. 'So long as she doesn't involve you in any of her crazy schemes, and get you into trouble.'

'I really think that June is beginning to change,' said Felicity thoughtfully. 'Remember how she knuckled down to games practice last term? And don't forget that she saved Amanda's life!'

'Yes, June proved that she has good stuff in her,' said Sally. 'And no one could doubt her bravery. But she's one of those people who will always work hard if something interests her, or if she wants to prove a point to someone else. Once she loses interest, or has made her point and doesn't need to try any more – then watch out! Because when June is bored or has nothing to focus her attention on, that's when she starts stirring things up!'

Exactly like Alicia, thought Darrell, grinning to herself as she remembered some of her friend's more outrageous pranks.

Felicity laughed. 'Yes, you're right, Sally. Actually, I hope June doesn't change *too* much. I couldn't bear it if she went all goody-goody on us!'

'I don't think there's much danger of that,' said Darrell drily.

'June sounds a very strange girl, I must say,' said Mrs Rivers, who had been listening with interest. 'But it does seem that she has many good qualities – and Malory Towers is certainly the place to bring them to the fore.'

All three girls agreed heartily with that, but there was no time to discuss the matter any further, for Mr Rivers appeared in the doorway and said, 'Felicity, I've put your trunk and night case in the car. All I need now is you and your mother, and we can leave.'

Felicity leaped up excitedly to get her hat and coat, then Darrell and Sally walked with her and Mrs Rivers to the door. But, alas for Felicity, as they stepped outside, Bonnie Meadows was walking up the garden path, determined not to let her new friend go without saying goodbye. She was a pretty girl, small and very dainty, with enormous, soft brown eyes, brown curly hair and a little rosebud mouth. She also had an air of fragility and helplessness – or, as Felicity liked to call it, goofiness – about her.

'Oh, Felicity, I'm so glad that you haven't left yet!' she cried in her lisping, little-girl voice. 'I know that we said goodbye yesterday, but I *did* so want to come and see you off, and Mummy knew that I wouldn't be able to rest if I didn't get my way, so here I am!'

A snort from behind her made Felicity turn, to see her sister and Sally standing there with idiotic grins on their faces. She glared fiercely at them, then turned back to Bonnie and, in a rather too-bright voice, said, 'Yes, here you are! Well, Bonnie, it's been simply lovely spending the hols with you, but Daddy's waiting and . . . Oh, Bonnie, please don't cry!'

But it was too late. Tears had already welled up in Bonnie's big eyes, her bottom lip jutted out and, to Felicity's great embarrassment, she began to sob loudly. An expression of horror on her face, Felicity looked round at Darrell, who at once took charge of the situation. She came forward and put an arm round Bonnie's shoulders, saying briskly, but kindly, 'Come along now, Bonnie, there's really no need for all these tears. Before you know it the holidays will be here and Felicity will be home again. And I'm sure she'll write to you, often, won't you, Felicity?'

'What? Oh, er – yes, of course. Every week,' said Felicity, casting an anxious look towards the car, where her father was impatiently drumming his fingers on the steering wheel. 'Now, I really must go, Bonnie, or I shall be late on my first day back.'

She gave the girl a pat on the shoulder, then turned to her sister and said, 'I'll write to you, as well, Darrell. You will write back, won't you, and tell me all about how you're getting on at university?'

'Of course,' promised Darrell with a smile. 'Now off you go, or poor Daddy will simply explode! Say hello to dear old Malory Towers from Sally and me, won't you?'

Felicity ran to the car, Darrell's and Sally's goodbyes and Bonnie's cry of, 'I shall miss you so much, Felicity!' following her.

'Goodbye, Darrell! Goodbye, Sally!' called Felicity, sticking her head through the open window as her father started the car. 'Goodbye, Bonnie! I'll write to you soon.'

Then they were off – back to Malory Towers.

The journey was a long one, and to Felicity, eager to be back with her friends, it seemed to go on forever. Mrs Rivers had packed a picnic lunch and they found a pleasant spot overlooking the sea to stop and eat, but Felicity was so excited, and so impatient to resume the journey, that she could only manage a couple of sandwiches.

They drove on for another hour, then the car rounded a bend in the road and Felicity cried, 'There it is – Malory Towers! I can see it!'

Felicity felt a warm glow of pride as she looked at the

school – *her* school. Standing at the top of a cliff, Malory Towers was certainly a magnificent building, its four towers – one at each corner – making it look almost like a castle. Mr Rivers drove on, along a steep, narrow road and through a big, open gateway into the grounds of the school, which was thronged with excited, chattering girls and groups of parents. He had hardly brought the car to a stop before Felicity had the door open and was off, racing across the lawn.

'Felicity!' called her mother. 'You haven't got your night case. Felicity, come back!'

But it was no use. Felicity was now part of a group of laughing, gossiping third formers, all of them busy exchanging greetings and catching up on news.

'Look everyone, it's Felicity! Did you have good hols?'

'Hallo, Nora! Goodness, don't you look brown?'

'I say, isn't that Pam over there, with her people? Pam, come and join us!'

'Have the train girls arrived yet? My word, isn't it super to be back?'

It certainly was super, thought Felicity happily, looking round at all her friends. There was the big, good-natured Pam, the scatterbrained but humorous Nora, and horse-mad Julie, who had brought her pony, Jack Horner, to school with her. And now a slim girl, with short, light-brown hair and a turned-up nose, joined the third formers – Felicity's best friend, Susan. She slipped her arm through Felicity's and said, 'Shall we take our health certificates to Matron and find our dormy? Then perhaps we'll have time to go down and take a look at the pool before supper.'

'Good idea,' said Felicity. 'I say, where *is* my night case? Oh goodness, I've left it in the car. And I'd completely forgotten about Mother and Daddy! Wait here a moment, Susan, while I just go and say goodbye to them.'

With that, Felicity dashed off, back to where she had left her parents.

'Ah, so you've finally remembered us,' said her father, a humorous twinkle in his eye as she raced over to them.

'Sorry, Daddy, I was just *so* excited to see the others again,' gabbled Felicity, her words tumbling out. 'Susan's here, and Nora, and Julie's back, and she's brought her pony, and –'

'We quite understand, dear,' said Mrs Rivers, with a smile. 'I'm just glad that you like life at school so much.'

'Like it? I *love* it!' said Felicity ecstatically, hugging her mother.

Mrs Rivers hugged her back and said, 'Now, you will write once you've settled in, won't you? Just to let us know how you're getting on. And we'll be over to see you at half-term, of course.'

Having finished her goodbyes, Felicity grabbed her night case, and she and her friends entered the North Tower and made their way to Matron's room. Each tower at the school was like a separate house, each with its own dormitories, dining-room and Matron, and the girls came together in the main building for lessons. The girls from the different towers generally got along very well with each other, but there was a good deal of friendly rivalry, and every girl was intensely proud of her own tower, convinced that it was quite the best in the school.

There was a strange girl in Matron's room, handing over her health certificate, and the others looked at her curiously. She was striking, rather than pretty, with a long, aquiline nose, very straight, shiny fair hair and grey eyes, which were fringed with thick dark lashes that contrasted starkly with her pale hair. She would have been very attractive, but for her haughty, slightly disdainful expression. 'As though she has a bad smell under her nose,' as Susan remarked later. The third formers wondered who she was, but before their curiosity could be satisfied, Matron turned to greet them, saying with her beaming smile, 'Ah, more third formers! Well, girls, it's very good to see you all back again and I hope none of you is going to give me any trouble this term. I don't want any of you falling ill or having accidents. And, above all – *no* midnight feasts.'

'As if we would, Matron,' said Nora, with an innocent, wide-eyed look. 'We're going to be the best-behaved third form in the history of Malory Towers.'

'Apart from June, perhaps,' said Julie, with a laugh. 'I say, where *is* June? Have you seen her yet, Matron?'

'No, but I've no doubt she'll turn up, just like a bad penny,' replied Matron wryly. 'It's a wonder she and her cousin, Alicia, haven't turned my hair grey between them. Now, girls, let me have your health certificates – and woe betide anyone who has forgotten hers!'

But, fortunately, no one had, and as, one by one, the

third formers gave them in to Matron, the new girl stood to one side, watching them, Felicity thought, rather as one might watch animals in a zoo.

When Matron had finished, she seemed to remember the girl, for she said, 'I've a new girl here who will be joining your form, so you may as well take her with you and show her round a bit.' She put her hand on the girl's arm and drew her forward. 'This is Amy Ryder-Cochrane.'

Pam, who had been head of the form last term, took the lead and said in her friendly way, 'Pleased to meet you, Amy. I'm Pam Bateman, and this lot are Felicity Rivers, Susan Blake, Nora Woods and Julie Adamson.'

'Hallo, Amy,' chorused the third formers. 'Welcome to Malory Towers.'

The girl inclined her head in a way that was almost regal, and Felicity had to stop herself giggling. She didn't much like the look of Amy, but was determined to give her a chance. Being the new girl in a form where all the others had known each other for a while must be quite daunting, and perhaps Amy was just a little shy. So she smiled at the girl and said, 'If you come with us, we'll show you to your dormy. Matron, are we all in together?'

Matron picked a piece of paper up from her desk and said, 'Yes, you're all in dormitory number nine, along with June, another new girl called Winifred Holmes and Veronica Sharpe.'

Then she moved away to greet two second formers, while the third formers looked at one another in dismay, and Nora gave a groan. 'Veronica Sharpe! Don't say that *she* is staying on in the third for another term!'

'She must be, if she's sharing our dormy,' said Susan gloomily. 'Rotten luck for us.'

'Now, that's enough, girls!' said Matron crisply. 'Off you go now to unpack your things – and make sure that you put everything away tidily.'

'Yes, Matron,' chorused the girls, and they trooped out obediently, taking their night cases with them.

'I expect you must find all this rather strange, Amy,' said Susan kindly, as they made their way upstairs. 'But don't worry, you'll soon settle in. Have you been to boarding school before?'

'Of course,' answered Amy in rather an affected tone. 'I went to Highcliffe Hall, and it was simply first-class. One of the best schools in the country, and frightfully exclusive.'

The listening third formers, who thought that there was no better school in the country than their own beloved Malory Towers, raised their eyebrows at this and, pushing open the door of the dormitory, Felicity said coolly, 'If it's so marvellous, what made you leave and come here?'

Amy thought quickly. She couldn't tell the truth, of course – which was that her father had decided that she had become far too conceited and stuck-up for her own good since she started at Highcliffe Hall! And that the only way to bring her down to earth was for her to attend a good, sensible school, whose pupils learned the things that mattered. Instead she said, 'Oh, the school was so far away from my home that it was difficult for Mummy and Daddy to visit at half-term. Malory Towers is much nearer for them, so I suppose that's *one* advantage it has over my old school, anyway.' Amy followed the others into the dormitory as she spoke and looked round, wrinkling her nose in distaste. 'Goodness, it's awfully cramped in here,' she complained, putting her night case on one of the beds. 'At Highcliffe there were only four girls to a dormitory, so we had plenty of space to put our things. And I don't think much of the way this room has been decorated.'

And the girls didn't think much of Amy! They wanted to like her, and to make her feel welcome at Malory Towers, but, really, she was making it terribly difficult. Didn't she realise that it simply wasn't done for a new girl to criticise everything like this?

'Well, I'm sorry if our standards don't match up to those of Highcliffe Hall,' Felicity spoke up, looking coldly at the new girl. 'But I, for one, think it's a very nice room!'

'Hear, hear!' chorused the others.

And indeed it *was* a very nice dormitory. Despite Amy's scornful words, there was plenty of room for all the girls. Each one had a little cabinet beside her bed, in which she could keep all her personal belongings, as well as a small wardrobe. The beds had pretty green, floral patterned bedspreads, which matched the curtains at the big window, from where there was a splendid view of the beautiful gardens. One of the beds already had a pair of slippers placed neatly beside it, and there was a book on top of the little cabinet. The girls guessed that they belonged to Veronica, and wondered where she was.

'How I hate unpacking,' sighed Nora, opening her night

case. 'Thank goodness our trunks aren't brought up until tomorrow, because I simply couldn't face having to put everything away tidily on my first day back.'

A frown crossed Amy's haughty little face as she said, 'Don't tell me that we actually have to unpack our trunks ourselves? Why, at Highcliffe Hall each dormitory had a maid, who did all our unpacking, and looked after our clothes, and made our beds.'

Pam, who was bending over her night case, looked up and said, 'Well, I'm afraid there are no maids to unpack for you here, Amy. We have to do *everything* ourselves.'

'That's right,' said Nora, nodding solemnly. 'It's a hard life, but you'll soon get used to it. The dressing-bell goes at five o'clock sharp, and after we've washed – in cold water, of course – we must sweep the floor and make sure that everything is spick and span in here.'

The girls had to force down a laugh as they watched poor Amy, who looked as if she was about to faint! Then Felicity, with a very serious expression indeed, went on, 'After that, Matron comes in to do her inspection, and if everything isn't exactly right it's bread and water for breakfast. If we're lucky!'

This was too much for Nora, who gave one of her explosive snorts of laughter and Amy, realising at last that she was being teased, flushed bright red and glared furiously at the third formers. But she had no time to retort, for the door was pushed open, and a girl with wicked, narrow dark eyes and a cheeky expression burst in. June was back!

New friends and an old enemy

At once a perfect hubbub broke out, and the newcomer found herself surrounded. June might be stubborn, outspoken and malicious, but she also had the kind of daring and boldness that the others envied and that, along with her talent for playing the most amazing tricks and a wicked sense of humour, meant that she was extremely popular.

'June, you're back! How marvellous!'

'Did you come on the train? We wondered where you were.'

'Hope you've brought plenty of jokes and tricks with you.'

June grinned. 'You bet I have! And I've brought something else too – a new member of the third form.'

She stood aside and, for the first time, the girls realised that someone had entered the room behind her. The new girl had a short, boyish cap of pale hair, laughing blue eyes and a friendly, open face. The girls liked the look of her at once, and thought how different she was from Amy when she grinned round and said, 'Hallo everyone, I'm Freddie Holmes. Well, actually I'm Winifred Holmes, but everyone calls me Freddie, so I hope that you will too. June has been telling me all about Malory Towers, and I simply can't tell you how happy I am to be here.'

'Oh, do you two know one another, then?' asked Julie.

'We met on the train,' said June, slipping her arm through Freddie's. 'Miss Peters was there, too, and, knowing what a kind soul I am, asked me to take Freddie under my wing.'

Felicity looked sharply at June, knowing that – at times – she could be extremely *un*kind. But there was no trace of malice in the girl's expression now. She looked happy to be back at Malory Towers, and happy to have made a new friend.

Amy, meanwhile, had been very much in the background – and she wasn't happy about it! She wasn't the slightest bit interested in June and Freddie – or any of the others, for that matter. But she did like being the centre of attention, and didn't at all care to be ignored like this. She hadn't wanted to come to this stupid school, but as she was stuck with it, she meant to make everyone sit up and take notice. At Highcliffe Hall everyone had admired Amy's aristocratic looks, envied her expensive possessions and hung on her every word as she boasted about her wealthy, well-connected family. And she had thrived on their admiration and envy, for these things were extremely important to her. Although the Malory Towers girls seemed much more sensible and down-to-earth than those at Highcliffe Hall, Amy had no doubt at all that she would soon become a source of great admiration to them, too.

Eager to take centre stage, she opened her night case

and, with much groaning and sighing, began pulling things out and tossing them on to her bed. If she made enough fuss, perhaps one of the others would offer to unpack her trunk when it was brought up tomorrow! She gave a particularly loud sigh and June, who was extremely shrewd and very good at sizing people up, stared at her and said in an amused voice, 'And who have we here?'

'Oh, June, this is Amy Ryder-Cochrane,' said Felicity. 'Another new girl.'

'I'm afraid Amy is having a little trouble adjusting to our ways,' put in Susan, giving June a meaningful look. 'Her old school was *very* exclusive, you see. One of the best in the country, so she tells us.'

'Dear me,' said June smoothly, walking over to Amy. 'What a come-down for you having to rough it with us at Malory Towers.'

Amy looked at June suspiciously. Was she being sarcastic? The others were in no doubt at all, and waited with bated breath for the new girl to feel the full force of June's sharp tongue. But kind-hearted Pam didn't feel that it was fair to give Amy too hard a time on her first day, and stepped forward, asking, 'Have we time to show Amy and Freddie round a bit before tea?'

Susan looked at her watch and answered, 'There isn't time to show them everything, but perhaps we can take a quick look at the swimming-pool.'

'And the stables,' put in Julie. 'I must see how Jack has settled in.'

'Jack?' repeated Freddie, looking puzzled.

'Jack is Julie's pony,' explained Felicity. 'His full name is Jack Horner, but his friends call him Jack.'

'A pony at school!' exclaimed Freddie. 'My word, how super. I'm simply dying to see him, and the swimming-pool, and . . . oh, everything!'

'Well, buck up and get your night case unpacked,' said Felicity. 'You too, June, otherwise we shan't have time to show the new girls round at all.'

The two latecomers quickly unpacked, then June noticed that there were two spare beds.

'Someone seems to be missing,' she said.

'Well, there are normally ten to a dormitory, but there are only nine of us this year,' said Felicity. 'That's why there's a spare bed.'

'But there are only eight of us here,' said June. Then she pointed towards the bed with the slippers beside it and asked, 'Who's sleeping there?'

'Oh, of course, you won't have heard, June,' said Pam. 'We're to have the pleasure of Veronica Sharpe's company this term.'

'How lovely for us,' said June, pulling a face. 'Just what we need in the third form – a sly, spiteful little snob. I know that none of the old third formers could stand her.'

'You had better watch your step, Felicity,' said Julie, with a frown. 'Do you remember how your sister, Darrell, caught her snooping around in the sixth's common-room last term?'

'Yes, I remember,' said Felicity, with a grin. 'Darrell made her write an essay on respecting one's elders, and got her to read it out to the whole of the sixth form. But I don't see what that's got to do with me!'

'Well, Veronica was simply furious with Darrell, but was too much of a coward to try and get back at her,' said Julie. 'And if she's still holding a grudge, she might try to take it out on you.'

'Well, if she tries any of her mean tricks on Felicity, she'll have the whole of the third form to deal with,' said Susan loyally.

'She certainly will,' agreed Pam. 'But come on, let's not waste any more of our time discussing Veronica. We'll take a look in at our new common-room, then go down to the swimming-pool.'

And, chattering at the top of their voices, the girls left the dormitory and made their way downstairs.

As their voices faded away, the door of the bathroom at the end of the dormitory opened and someone stepped out – Veronica Sharpe!

Veronica hadn't meant to listen in on the others – at first. She had just finished washing her hands in the bathroom when she had heard the third formers enter, and she fully intended to make her presence known and say hallo to them. Then she had overheard Amy's remarks and been most impressed by how grand the new girl sounded. Wouldn't it be fine to have a girl like that for a friend, she thought – someone right out of the top drawer! As she listened, it quickly became clear that the others weren't impressed by Amy at all – and that suited Veronica just fine, for it meant that she would have no competition. Veronica had always found it difficult to make friends at school, but she couldn't see that it was due to her own sly, rather spiteful nature. She preferred to tell herself that none of the girls at Malory Towers were good enough to become her friend. But now, here was someone who *was* good enough.

She took a step towards the door, then stopped suddenly, as a thought occurred to her. If she joined the others now they would know that she had overheard them, and would realise that she was only trying to befriend Amy because she was grand and wealthy. No, better to stay hidden for the time being. Veronica decided that she would go all out to win Amy over at teatime, then nobody could accuse her of wanting to be friends with the new girl for the wrong reasons. Pleased with herself, the girl tiptoed across to the bathroom door, listening for all she was worth. A sneer crossed her face when she heard the others greet that horrid June. How Veronica disliked that girl – and how she would love to take her down a peg or two! Well, when Miss Peters announced that she was to be head-girl of the third form tomorrow, she would do exactly that! Veronica almost shivered with excitement at the thought. She was *sure* to be head-girl, for she had been in the third form for one term already – and wouldn't she enjoy lording it over the others! *And* she was going to have the richest girl in the form for her friend. The term was really getting off to a good start.

Then Veronica heard her own name mentioned, and pressed her ear even closer to the door. The smug smile slid from her face as she heard what the others thought of her. Sly, sneaky, spiteful and a coward. Tears of anger and self-pity sprang to her eyes and she turned red with humiliation. The mean beasts! Not for a moment did it occur to Veronica that it was her own behaviour in the past that had made the third formers despise her. Nor did it cross her mind that the girls were only speaking the truth. She *did* still bear a grudge against that high and mighty Darrell Rivers, and had spent many pleasant hours during the holidays thinking up ways to get back at her through her younger sister. The third formers' scornful words might have made another girl stop and think, and perhaps decide to change her ways. But Veronica only felt even more determined to get back at Felicity for her disgrace last term.

Part of her wanted to storm out of the bathroom and confront the third formers. But that would only end in Veronica feeling even more humiliated, for then they would know that she had been eavesdropping. And what would Amy think of her then? No, she needed to keep a cool head and not act rashly. It was a relief when she heard the others leave, and could emerge from her hiding place.

With the dormitory all to herself, Veronica was quite unable to resist the urge to do a little snooping. That must be Felicity's bed, over by the window, for there was a framed photograph on the cabinet of Felicity, Darrell and their parents. The family looked very happy, all of them smiling widely, but Veronica felt very sour indeed as she picked it up, fighting an impulse to throw it to the ground and smash it. But that would be a mistake, for the others would instantly suspect her. This was typical of Veronica, who only saw things as they affected her. She didn't think that it would be *wrong* to destroy another girl's belongings – merely that it would be a shame if she was caught out!

Carefully she replaced the photograph and walked over to the bed next to hers, wondering who the occupant was. A bottle of expensive French perfume stood on the cabinet and a very pretty pink dressing-gown had been placed, folded very carefully, on the bed. Veronica ran her hand over it, thrilled to discover that it felt like real silk. This must be Amy's bed, for surely no other third former would have such exquisite belongings. What a bit of luck that the new girl had chosen the bed next to hers! Instantly, Veronica's ill humour disappeared. There would be plenty of time for her to teach Felicity a lesson – after all, she had the whole term ahead of her. For now she meant to concentrate on making a friend of Amy.

The rest of the third form, meanwhile, were happily showing off their school to the new girls.

It was a real pleasure, thought Felicity, to show Freddie round. The new girl seemed genuinely thrilled to be at Malory Towers, and exclaimed with delight at everything, reminding Felicity very much of the way she had felt on her first day. Amy, however, turned her rather large nose up at everything.

'Don't we have our own studies here?' she asked, surprised and displeased, as they looked in at the cosy common-room. 'We did at Highcliffe Hall, and we were allowed to decorate them just as we pleased.'

'You'll have to make do with a common-room now, Amy,' said June. 'I'm sure you'll think that it suits the rest of us down to the ground – a common-room for common girls!'

The others laughed, but Amy scowled and turned away.

At the stables, Freddie went into ecstasies over Jack, making a great fuss of him and begging Julie to let her ride him one day. But Amy refused to go near him, complaining that the smell of the stables made her feel sick.

When they reached the pool, Freddie's eyes lit up and she exclaimed, 'Oh, how lovely it looks! So inviting! I could dive in right now.'

'Well, I shouldn't dive in with your clothes on, Freddie,' laughed Nora. 'Or you'll get into a row with Matron. But the weather is still quite warm for September, so you may get the chance to go for a dip later in the week.'

The Malory Towers girls were very proud of their beautiful, natural swimming-pool, which was hollowed out of rocks and filled by the sea as the tide ebbed and flowed. Amy, though, barely glanced at it, merely remarking haughtily, 'We had a magnificent indoor pool at Highcliffe Hall. It was heated, which meant that we could swim in the winter months too.'

Even good-natured Pam became exasperated with her, and muttered crossly to Felicity and June, 'She'll be going for a swim sooner than she thinks, if she doesn't shut up. I'm just itching to shove her in!'

'Be patient, Pam,' laughed June. 'I've one or two tricks up my sleeve and it won't be too long before dear Amy learns that pride comes before a fall!'

As the third formers walked back to North Tower,

they spotted two sixth formers coming towards them, and Susan said, 'Look, it's Kay Foster, the new Head Girl. And Amanda!'

Amanda Chartelow had been in the sixth form with Darrell last term. She had been a superb sportswoman, but had annoyed many of the girls with her arrogance and superior attitude. But poor Amanda had learned a hard lesson when she broke the rules of the school and went swimming in the sea. The strong current had thrown her on to the rocks, and it was thanks to June that she hadn't drowned. Sadly, though, Amanda's injuries had put paid to her hopes of representing her country in the Olympic Games, or of taking part in any sport at all for a while, and the girl had gone through a very bad time indeed. It would have been very easy for her to have moped about, or become bitter, but Amanda had proved to everyone that her character was as strong as her body. Almost overnight, she had lost her arrogance, thrown herself into coaching the younger girls, and had made up her mind that, if she couldn't pursue a career as a sportswoman, she would train as a Games Mistress. Amanda had become a much nicer person and the girls, who had once disliked her so heartily, now admired and looked up to her. And they were very pleased to see that the slight limp, which had been a result of her injuries, now seemed to have disappeared.

Amanda greeted the third formers cheerily, then gave them some news which delighted them. 'Miss Grayling has made me games captain. So I hope all you youngsters are going to work hard for me, for I shall be a real tyrant!' But there was a broad grin on Amanda's face, and the third formers knew that she would never be a tyrant again.

'Oh, Amanda, that is good news!' said Felicity. 'I must write and tell Darrell. She'll be absolutely thrilled for you.'

'How's the leg?' asked June, who had even more interest than the others in the sixth former. She, more than anyone, had clashed with the old Amanda. But June's act of bravery in saving her life had created a bond between them, and now they had a great mutual respect for one another.

'Getting better,' said Amanda. 'My parents made sure that I spent the holidays resting and, although it nearly drove me mad at the time, it really has done me good. I still shan't be playing any sport for a bit, but the doctor says that there has been no permanent damage. Anyway, that's quite enough about me – I suppose you've all heard that Kay here is the new Head Girl?'

'Yes, and I'm going to have a jolly hard time living up to the previous one,' said Kay, with a laugh. She was a tall, dark girl with warm brown eyes, a humorous face and a friendly manner. The younger girls liked her enormously and felt certain that she would be a worthy successor to Darrell.

As the third formers went on their way, Susan said to Felicity, 'Well, I think Miss Grayling has made two jolly good choices there. I wonder who will be head of the form?'

'I expect we'll find out tomorrow,' said Felicity. 'I wouldn't be surprised if it was you, Susan.'

Her friend laughed. 'That's funny, I was just about to say exactly the same about you.'

'I don't think Miss Peters will choose me,' said Felicity, feeling pleased that Susan thought she would make a good head girl, but quite certain that she wouldn't be in the running. 'I can be so indecisive sometimes – and I don't know if I would be strong enough to keep people like June in order.'

'Even the mistresses have a hard time keeping June in order!' chuckled Susan. 'I say, perhaps they will make *her* head of the form! There's no doubt that she would make a strong leader.'

'True. But she would lead us all into trouble!' said Felicity. Then she gave a sigh. 'I expect it will be Veronica. After all, she has already been in the third for a term.'

'I'd forgotten all about Veronica!' said Susan in dismay. 'Blow, we shall have a miserable time of it if she's head of the form.'

The first night

A most delicious supper had been laid out in the dining-room. Each of the long tables was set with big plates of cold meat, bowls of salad and delicious, buttery potatoes baked in their jackets. There was the most scrumptious-looking fruit salad with cream for afters and, as the girls entered, their eyes lit up.

Two people were already seated at the third-form table. One was Mam'zelle Dupont, one of the school's two French mistresses, and the other was Veronica Sharpe. The girls eyed her a little warily, but Veronica – eager to make a good impression on Amy – was on her best behaviour and greeted them with a cheery 'Hallo' and a wide smile. The third formers looked surprised but – thinking that perhaps the girl had decided to turn over a new leaf, and determined to give her a chance – smiled back. Veronica glanced at the two new girls, noting that one of them was laughing and joking with June. That must be Freddie, so the girl with the straight, shiny hair and rather aloof expression must be Amy. She was standing slightly apart from the others and, although she would never have admitted it, feeling a little lost as they all seated themselves. So when Veronica touched her arm and said in a friendly way, 'You must be new. Why don't you have the seat next to mine?' she felt extremely grateful.

'Ah, welcome back *mes petites*!' cried plump little Mam'zelle Dupont, smiling around. 'How good it is to see you all again – Felicity, Susan, Pam, Julie – ah, and the dear Nora! I see that we have some new girls, also. The good Miss Potts told me to expect you,' went on Mam'zelle. 'And she told me your names. I know that one of you is called Winifred, and that –'

'It's Freddie, Mam'zelle, not Winifred,' June corrected her, helping herself to a jacket potato.

'Always you interrupt, June,' said Mam'zelle, looking put out. 'And I know that you are pulling my foot, for Freddie is a boy's name.'

'You mean pulling your leg, Mam'zelle,' said June, with a grin, as the others giggled. 'But I'm not, honestly. She really *is* called Freddie – aren't you, Freddie?'

Freddie nodded. 'It's true, Mam'zelle. People only call me Winifred if I'm in trouble.'

It seemed very odd to Mam'zelle that this girl should want to be known by a boy's name, but she had been teaching at Malory Towers long enough to know that English girls could be very eccentric indeed. So she accepted this with a shrug and said, 'Ah well, I should not like you to think that you were in trouble, so I shall call you Freddie. And you, *ma chère*.' She turned to Amy, with a smile. 'You have an unusual name too, have you not?'

'Not really, Mam'zelle,' answered the girl, looking puzzled. 'My name is Amy.'

'Ah yes, but your surname, *he* is unusual,' said Mam'zelle. 'Miss Potts told me. Now, what was it again? Something from one of your English nursery rhymes.'

Mam'zelle frowned as she tried to remember, while the third formers looked perplexedly at one another and Amy said, 'But my surname has nothing to do with a nursery rhyme. It's Ryder –'

'Ah yes, I have it!' cried Mam'zelle, banging her hand down on the table and making everyone jump. 'It is Ryder-Cockhorse!'

The third formers simply roared with laughter at this. All except Amy, of course, who couldn't bear to be made fun of, even unwittingly, and flushed angrily. Even sourpuss Veronica had to hide a smile, but hide it she did, as she certainly didn't want Amy to think that she was laughing at her.

'*To see a fine lady on a white horse,*' murmured June, once the laughter had died down. 'Only Amy would never ride a white horse, because she wouldn't be able to stand the smell.'

Of course, this made the third-form table erupt again, the girls' laughter so noisy that Miss Potts, at the head of the first-form table, glared across at them, and Felicity said, 'We'd better keep the noise down. Potty looks annoyed.'

'Miss Potts,' explained June, seeing that the two new girls looked puzzled. 'She's the head of North Tower. Quite a decent sort, but she doesn't stand any nonsense. That's her, over at the first-form table.'

Freddie glanced across and caught the beady eye of

a rather stern-looking mistress, and looked away again hastily. No, Freddie decided, she definitely wouldn't like to get on the wrong side of Miss Potts!

'And over there,' said June, nodding towards the fourth form's table, 'is Mam'zelle Rougier, the other French mistress.'

Mam'zelle Rougier was tall, and as thin as Mam'zelle Dupont was plump. She also looked rather bad-tempered, and the fourth formers at her table seemed a little glum and subdued.

'Thank goodness we've got Mam'zelle Dupont at our table,' went on June, lowering her voice. 'She has a hot temper at times, but she's good fun and a splendid person to play tricks on. Quite unlike Mam'zelle Rougier, who has no sense of humour at all.'

Mam'zelle Dupont, meanwhile, had returned to the vexed question of Amy's surname, saying, 'It is a most unusual name, Ryder-Cockhorse. I do not think that I have heard it before.'

'Actually it's Ryder-*Cochrane*,' said Amy rather stiffly, as muffled giggles broke out again.

Seeing that Amy's feathers were seriously ruffled, Veronica seized her chance and murmured in a low tone, 'You mustn't mind Mam'zelle. She doesn't mean to offend – it's just that she gets things mixed up sometimes. As for the rest of the third formers – well, I wouldn't take much notice of them either. They have a very childish sense of humour, I'm afraid. Here –' she passed a plate of cold meat to Amy. 'Do help yourself.

The suppers here are jolly good, and I'm sure you must be hungry.'

Amy *was* hungry, and she took the plate with a word of thanks and a faint smile. Encouraged, Veronica began to engage the new girl in conversation, asking her a great many questions, showing enormous interest in her answers, and making her admiration quite clear. Pleased that there was at least one person in this horrid school who appreciated her, and delighted with the opportunity to boast about herself, Amy began to thaw and chatted quite pleasantly with Veronica.

June, on the opposite side of the table, was busily pointing out various girls and mistresses to an interested Freddie, but her sharp ears picked up snatches of the two girls' conversation. If she didn't know better, June would have felt quite certain that Veronica was sucking up to Amy because of her wealthy background. But Veronica hadn't been in the dormitory earlier and had only just met Amy, so she couldn't possibly know anything about her. Perhaps Veronica really *had* changed her ways, and was being kind and unselfish in putting Amy at her ease. But somehow June doubted it.

Mam'zelle Dupont, however, was quite taken in. Veronica had never been one of her favourites, but watching her now, as she went out of her way to make this new girl feel welcome, the French mistress began to think that she might have judged her a little harshly.

The bold, wicked June also seemed to be looking after Freddie, and Mam'zelle Dupont smiled to herself. Ah, they might be eccentric, with their jokes and tricks, and their strange names, but these English girls were good and kind at heart!

Nora, with her fluffy blonde hair and round, blue eyes, was one of her pets. When she covered her mouth suddenly to stifle a yawn, Mam'zelle Dupont cried, 'You are tired, *ma petite*! And no wonder. I am sure that you must all be fatigued, after your long journeys and the excitement of your first day back at school. As soon as you have finished your meal, you shall go straight to bed!'

There was an immediate outcry at this, of course. In fact, the girls felt pleasantly tired and wouldn't be at all sorry when bedtime came. But as for going up straight after tea, when it was so early, and there was still so much gossip to catch up on, and they wanted to make this precious first day last as long as possible – why, it was unthinkable!

'Only the first-form babies go to bed straight after tea,' said Felicity, rather loftily. 'We third formers are allowed to stay up until nine o'clock usually, although we have to go to bed at eight on the first night. And I, for one, am not going up a *second* before we have to!'

And stay up until eight they did, although many of the third formers felt their eyelids drooping, and Nora almost nodded off on the sofa in the common-room and had to be nudged awake by Julie.

'Come on, sleepyhead,' said Julie, hauling the protesting Nora to her feet. 'The bell for bedtime has just sounded, and you can't go to sleep here!'

'I say, look at those two,' said Felicity to Susan, as they

walked upstairs together. 'It seems as if they have become firm friends already.'

Ahead of them walked Amy and Veronica, still deep in conversation, and Susan laughed, saying, 'It seems right, somehow, that the two most unpopular girls in the form have teamed up with one another. Although I'm not sure whether this friendship will be good for either of them. But Veronica seems determined to stick to Amy like glue!'

'Rather like Bonnie stuck to me, during the holidays,' said Felicity, with a wry smile.

'Ah yes, dear little Bonnie,' said Susan, with a grin. 'I should think you were as glad to see the back of her as she was to see the back of me!'

Susan had come to stay with Felicity for a week in the holidays, and the visit had not been a great success. Bonnie, quite overcome with jealousy, had taken an instant dislike to Susan, and had done everything possible to make her feel unwelcome.

'As though *she* were my best friend and *you* were the one trying to come between us, instead of the other way round!' an exasperated Felicity had complained after a particularly trying afternoon, during which Bonnie had been openly rude to Susan. Luckily, the sensible Susan had refused to be drawn into a quarrel and had merely laughed at Bonnie.

'My goodness, how she disliked me!' Susan said now as they entered the dormitory. 'I couldn't help feeling a little sorry for her, though. It can't be much of a life not being able to go to school, and make friends, and share in all the happy, jolly times that most schoolgirls have.'

'Oh, Bonnie is quite well enough to come to school now,' said Felicity. 'But her mother won't let her. Honestly, Susan, I think that Mrs Meadows is quite the silliest woman I've ever met. If she didn't fuss over Bonnie, and spoil her so, she might turn out to be quite decent.'

'Well, thank goodness our parents had the sense to send us to a splendid school like Malory Towers,' said Susan. 'I simply can't imagine being anywhere else!'

Swiftly, the girls changed into their pyjamas, brushed their teeth, and climbed into their cosy beds, but June and Freddie, who were both thoroughly overexcited, continued to talk after lights-out.

'Can't you two shut up and go to sleep?' groaned a tired Nora. 'I'd just dropped off and now you've woken me up again.'

'Sorry, Nora,' said June. 'We didn't mean to disturb you.'

But, moments later, Freddie's voice could be heard again, followed by a loud snort of laughter from June's bed, and Veronica frowned to herself in the darkness. As she was to be head of the form, it was up to her to see that the two girls obeyed the rule about no talking after lights-out. It would be as well, she decided, to start as she meant to continue, and show these two that she wasn't going to stand any nonsense, so Veronica sat up in bed and said crisply, 'You two – June and Freddie! Get to sleep at once. You both know very well that no talking is allowed after lights-out, and if you disobey I shall report you to Miss Peters!'

Now, Nora wasn't the only one who had been getting a little tired of June and Freddie's chatter, for several of the girls felt annoyed at the pair for keeping them awake. In fact, Susan had been on the verge of telling them to be quiet herself. But none of the third formers intended to take orders from Veronica until it was announced that she was head-girl, and they rebelled at once.

'Sneak!' called out Julie.

'You're not head of the form,' said Susan. 'You've no right to tell us what to do.'

'Besides, I heard you whispering to Amy after lights-out!' added Felicity indignantly. 'And you only stopped because she fell asleep. Hypocrite!'

Veronica's cheeks flushed a deep angry red, and she hissed, 'Felicity Rivers, how dare you speak to me like that! I am the senior member of this form and I consider it my duty –'

'Pooh!' June interrupted her rudely, sitting bolt upright in bed. 'You don't have a sense of duty, Veronica. What you *do* have is an inflated sense of your own importance. Well, let me tell you, just because you've already spent a term in the third form, it doesn't make you senior to the rest of us, and it certainly doesn't give you the right to start dishing out orders. Only the head-girl will be able to do that, and I very much doubt that it will be you! Miss Peters knows you too well.'

Smarting, Veronica opened her mouth to make an angry retort, but just then the girls heard the sounds of footsteps on the landing, and the door opened and Miss

Potts stood silhouetted in the doorway.

'Come along now, girls, no more talking!' she commanded briskly. 'I realise that you're all excited to be back together again, but you'll be fit for nothing in the morning if you don't get your sleep. Who is head of the dormitory? Oh, no one, I suppose, as the head-girl of the form hasn't been announced yet. Well, Pam, as you were head-girl last term, I am putting you in charge for tonight, and will leave it to you to deal with anyone who breaks the rules. Goodnight, everyone.'

'Goodnight, Miss Potts,' chorused the girls, snuggling down into their beds as the door closed behind the mistress.

'All right, girls,' came Pam's low, pleasant voice. 'Miss Potts is quite right. We shall all be too woolly-minded to concentrate in class tomorrow if we don't get to sleep soon, so no more noise.'

'Whatever you say, Pam,' said June meekly, making the others grin to themselves. Apart from Veronica, who scowled fiercely. She knew what was behind this sudden – and most unusual – display of meekness on June's part, of course. It was her way of saying that she would accept Pam's leadership, but not Veronica's. For the first time, a doubt crept into the girl's mind. Could June have been right in saying that Miss Peters would not make her head of the form? It was true that Veronica had never been one of the mistress's favourites, but surely Miss Peters would not consider making one of these silly kids head of the form over her? Why, the idea was ridiculous, for none of them was fit to lead the others. Not the bold, brazen June, nor the scatterbrained Nora, that was certain. Pam had already had her turn, while Julie was so wrapped up in that horse of hers that she was quite unable to concentrate on anything else. As new girls, Amy and Freddie wouldn't be in the running, which left that cheeky little Felicity Rivers and her goody-goody friend Susan. Veronica curled her lip scornfully. As if either of *them* had the strength of character or the air of authority necessary to lead the third form!

Having ruled out her new form-mates as rivals, Veronica felt happier and settled down contentedly under the bedclothes. Miss Peters had a good deal of common sense and would not allow her personal feelings to influence her decision, Veronica was sure. The mistress would do what was best for the third form – and what was best, thought Veronica, would be for her to be made head-girl.

The new head-girl

Amy's first full day at Malory Towers did not get off to a good start. Veronica watched in admiration as the new girl brushed out her shining hair, before deftly braiding it into a thick plait, which she secured with a brown ribbon, to match the school uniform.

'You do look lovely, Amy,' gushed Veronica. 'How I wish my hair shone like yours.'

'I don't think that even *I* could look lovely in this dreadful uniform,' complained Amy, frowning at her reflection in the mirror. 'The one I had at Highcliffe Hall was so much nicer. We were allowed to wear –'

'Don't tell me,' interrupted June, who had been listening quite unashamedly. 'You were allowed to wear ball gowns and tiaras to breakfast.'

'I was talking to Veronica, not to you,' retorted Amy stiffly, scowling at June, before turning to rummage in a little jewellery box on her cabinet. From this, she selected a pretty charm bracelet.

'I say, Amy, you're not going to wear that in class, are you?' asked Veronica, frowning.

'Of course,' replied Amy. 'Why shouldn't I?'

'Well, we're not really supposed to wear fancy

jewellery,' Veronica told her. 'Miss Peters will probably make you take it off.'

The listening third formers grinned at one another, each of them thinking the same thing: that it was most unusual for Veronica to warn another girl that she was likely to get into trouble. Normally she would have held her tongue, for there was nothing that gladdened her spiteful nature more than watching someone else get into a good row. But Veronica was determined to become Amy's friend – her *best* friend – and that meant that she couldn't simply stand by and allow her to incur the wrath of Miss Peters without at least *trying* to stop her. Not that Amy seemed very grateful, for she merely shrugged and fastened the bracelet around her wrist, saying haughtily, 'What a stupid rule! I daresay Miss Peters won't even notice that I'm wearing jewellery.'

'*Rings on her fingers,*' chanted June in a sing-song voice. '*And bells on her toes. She shall be punished for wearing those!*'

The other third formers roared with laughter at June's clever rhyme, but Amy turned bright red. It would be just too humiliating if Miss Peters did send her out of class to remove her bracelet. Reluctantly, she turned away from the others and took it off, placing it back in the box.

Veronica noticed that the girl had placed a photograph on her cabinet and, in an effort to placate her, said brightly, 'Are those your parents? My goodness, isn't your mother beautiful? And how handsome your father looks.'

The woman in the photograph certainly was very beautiful, though she didn't look much like Amy, as she was dark, with a small, turned-up nose and big green eyes.

It was obvious that Amy had inherited her looks from her father, a most distinguished-looking man. His features were very similar to his daughter's and he had the same fair hair.

Amy cheered up at once at this praise of her parents and said, 'They are a good-looking couple, aren't they? You must meet them at half-term, Veronica. I say, wouldn't it be super if my parents hit it off with yours?'

Veronica listened to this with mixed feelings. On the one hand, she couldn't wait to meet Amy's beautiful mother and handsome, wealthy father. But on the other, she was quite unable to picture her own hard-working, down-to-earth parents becoming friends with the Ryder-Cochranes. Why, they had nothing in common with them at all! In fact, Veronica's parents could prove to be a bit of an embarrassment to her at half-term. Her mind working swiftly, she wondered if she could think of a way to put them off coming.

'Amy!' called Pam. 'It's almost breakfast time, so you'd better tidy your nightclothes away and make your bed before we go down.'

Amy, who had never made a bed in her life, looked rebellious, but the ever-willing Veronica was at her side in a flash, saying, 'You fold your pyjamas up neatly, Amy, and I'll make your bed for you.'

'Oh, no you won't!' said Pam firmly. 'Amy is quite capable of making her own bed, Veronica.'

'Really, Pam, I don't see what business it is of yours if I choose to help Amy,' retorted Veronica.

'It's my business because Miss Potts made me head of the dormitory – even if it is only temporary. And I don't see why Amy should get out of doing her own chores.'

Pam might be placid and good-natured, but she took her responsibilities very seriously indeed!

'But Pam, I really don't know *how* to make a bed properly,' protested Amy, looking at Pam beseechingly. 'I don't have the faintest idea how to fold the corners neatly, as the rest of you have done. Can't Veronica just show me how to do it now, then tomorrow I can do it myself?'

'Very well,' agreed Pam. 'But be quick, both of you, or we shall be late for breakfast.'

Amy turned away, so that Pam did not see the smirk on her face. Veronica had already boasted to her about how she was certain to be made head-girl, which meant that she would also be head of the dormitory. And if she chose to do Amy's chores for her, nobody would have the authority to stop her.

'Well done, Pam,' said Susan in a low voice. 'We're all going to have to sit on Amy good and hard if she's to settle down at Malory Towers.'

'Yes, but there's no point in the rest of us trying to get some sense into her if Veronica goes and undoes all our good work by running round after Amy, and telling her how wonderful she is,' said Felicity, with a frown, as she watched Veronica making Amy's bed. 'I simply can't understand it. Veronica is the very last person I'd have expected to put herself out for anyone, but she's really going out of her way to be nice to Amy.'

'Isn't it obvious?' said June, with a sneer. 'Veronica wants to be friends with the wealthy, well-connected new girl. Horrid little snob!'

'I would agree with you, June,' said Pam, thoughtfully. 'If it wasn't for the fact that Veronica struck up a friendship with Amy over tea yesterday – and she had no idea then that she is wealthy and well-connected.'

'That's right,' said Susan. 'Perhaps Veronica has genuinely taken a liking to Amy and really wants to be a true friend to her.'

'I don't believe that Veronica has ever been a true friend to anyone in her life!' declared the forthright June. 'She's only ever nice to people if it's to her advantage.'

'That's a bit harsh, June!' protested Felicity. 'I know that Veronica hasn't done much to give anyone here a good opinion of her, but she can't be *all* bad.'

June laughed. 'That's typical of you, Felicity. Always trying to see the good in people – even when there isn't any!'

And somehow June made it sound as if trying to see the good in people was a fault, and that Felicity was being rather naive and silly. Felicity felt put out, and was grateful when Susan laid a hand on her shoulder and said, 'You should be pleased about that, June, for it means that Felicity even manages to see a little good in *you*!'

June laughed at that, and went off to speak to Freddie, while Susan said in a low voice to Felicity, 'Never mind what June says – I think it's a jolly good thing that you're always willing to believe the best of people.'

'Perhaps,' said Felicity, with a wry expression. 'But it's not always easy. Especially with people like Veronica and Amy – and sometimes even June herself!'

Kay Foster approached the third-form table as the girls were finishing breakfast, and said in her friendly way, 'Hallo, kids. Freddie and Amy, can you come along to Miss Grayling's room with me, please?'

'Goodness, don't say we're in trouble already!' exclaimed Freddie, a look of dismay on her face.

'Don't worry, Freddie,' laughed Felicity. 'You're not in trouble. Miss Grayling always sees the new girls on the first day, and says a few words to them.'

'I'm sure you'll find what she has to say most inspiring,' said Veronica to a rather apprehensive-looking Amy. 'I know that her words had quite an effect on me. I'll come and wait outside the Head's room for you, Amy, so that you don't get lost on the way to class.'

As Kay marched off with Veronica and the new girls, June turned to the others and said in a low voice, 'Thank goodness Veronica's gone. Listen, everyone, I have a box of tricks in the dorm that my cousin, Alicia, gave me. I haven't opened it yet, so, as we have a little time to spare before lessons, shall we nip back up and take a look?'

'Ooh yes, let's!' cried Nora, clapping her hands together excitedly.

'That would be super,' said Felicity, pushing her chair back and getting to her feet.

'I have to go to the stables to see Jack,' said Julie,

frowning. 'Blow! I would have loved to see your tricks. Can't we go up and see them at break-time?'

'No, because I want to open the box when Veronica's not around,' said June, shaking her head. 'If she sees us all disappearing off to the dorm at break-time she's bound to guess something's up and come snooping.'

'Anyway, Julie, you saw Jack *before* breakfast!' pointed out Pam. 'I'm sure he's not going to pine away because you don't visit him *after* breakfast as well.'

'Yes, you can go and spoil him at break-time instead,' said Susan. 'Do come and see June's tricks with us now, Julie – it will be such fun!'

So Julie allowed herself to be persuaded, and the girls made their way swiftly up to the dormitory, where June pulled a cardboard box from beneath her bed.

'It's a pity Freddie can't be here,' said Felicity. 'She strikes me as the sort of girl who enjoys a good joke or trick.'

'She is,' said June, with a grin. 'Freddie was the form joker at her old school, and we're planning to team up and play all sorts of pranks this term.'

This sounded good, and the girls exchanged excited glances.

'I'll have to slip up here with her later,' said June, 'and show her what's in the box. Now, let's get the lid off and see what we have!'

The girls crowded round June, and there were a great many 'oohs' and 'aahs' as she pulled the items from the box.

'Good old Alicia!' exclaimed Felicity, as she picked up

an extremely realistic-looking rubber spider. 'My word, we can certainly give Mam'zelle Dupont a fright with this!'

But the most interesting item by far was a bar of perfectly ordinary-looking white soap, wrapped in pink tissue paper, with a label attached to it. As the others looked at it, puzzled, June began to read the writing on the label. Then she gave a crow of laughter and said, 'Listen to this! Whoever uses the soap will find that their face and hands turn a dirty, muddy brown about half an hour after they've washed. Oh, how super!'

'I should say!' chuckled Nora. 'We'll have to decide who to play it on.'

'I think I've already decided,' said June with a wicked grin. 'Can't you just picture our dear Amy walking into breakfast, completely unaware that she looks as if she's wearing a mudpack?'

The girls could picture it very well indeed, their eyes lighting up as they grinned at one another.

'Do it tomorrow, June!' begged Julie, but June shook her head.

'It's too soon. I always think it's best to save tricks until the term is a few weeks old and we're beginning to feel bored.'

'Good idea,' said Pam, as June shoved the box back under her bed. 'That will give us something to look forward to. Now, we'd better get a move on, or we'll be late and that won't impress Miss Peters at all!'

The girls made their way to one of the long buildings that connected the four towers, and found their new classroom. Amy, Freddie and Veronica were already there, as were some of the girls from the other three towers. The North Tower girls greeted them cheerily, then seated themselves. June was pleased to see that Freddie had managed to bag herself a seat in the coveted back row, and quickly took the one next to her. Felicity and Susan took the desks in front of them, while Pam, Nora and Julie found three seats together across the aisle from the others. Veronica and Amy sat next to each other, of course, at the front of the classroom, and as more girls from the South, East and West Towers came in, the desks gradually filled up. There was a babble of noise as the girls chattered away to one another, then Anne from West Tower, who was standing guard at the door, suddenly hissed, 'Shh! Miss Peters is coming.'

At once the noise ceased, the third formers getting to their feet as a mannish young woman with short hair and a rosy complexion entered.

'Good morning, girls,' she said crisply, setting the pile of books she carried down on the desk.

'Good morning, Miss Peters,' replied the girls politely as they eyed her with interest.

'Miss Peters is a good sort,' Darrell had told Felicity. 'But she has a temper. She won't stand for anyone playing the fool in her lessons, and if there's one thing that makes her angry, it's people who try to dupe or deceive her.'

She looks perfectly pleasant and friendly now, thought Felicity, as the mistress smiled round at her class.

'Sit down, girls,' she ordered in her rather deep voice.

'Now, before we get down to making timetables and giving out books, I am sure that you are all eager to know who is to be head of the form.'

A murmur of excitement rippled round the room and Veronica immediately sat up straight in her seat, a rather smug look on her face.

'Just look at Veronica,' whispered June to Freddie. 'My goodness, I'd love to see that smirk wiped off her face!'

'Quiet, please!' commanded Miss Peters, with a glare in June's direction. 'Well, this was a very difficult decision to make, but I have discussed the matter with both Miss Potts and Miss Parker, and we have decided that the head-girl of the third form is to be Felicity Rivers.'

Indeed, it had been a very difficult decision. Miss Peters and Miss Parker, who was the second-form mistress and knew the girls very well, had narrowed it down to Susan and Felicity, and found it very difficult to choose between them.

'I feel that both of them would make excellent head-girls,' Miss Parker had said. 'They are both sensible, trustworthy and kind-hearted. I really don't see how we are going to decide.'

Fortunately, at that moment, Miss Potts had entered the mistresses' common-room, and Miss Peters had asked her opinion, saying, 'As Head of North Tower, you probably know both girls far better than Miss Parker and I. What do you think?'

Miss Potts had sat down, remaining silent and thoughtful for a few moments. Then, at last, she spoke.

'There is no doubt that Susan has more confidence in herself than Felicity. However, I have always felt that young Felicity was a little overshadowed by her older sister. Darrell was so popular, and such a success at Malory Towers – especially in her last year, when she was Head Girl – that Felicity was always known as her little sister and never really came into her own. She has always been less sure of herself than Darrell, and less forthright in her opinions. Yet she is a very strong, determined little character and, now that Darrell is gone, I think that the time has come for Felicity to shine. I feel that if she was made head-girl she would certainly seize the opportunity and make the most of it. And I think that she has a great deal to offer the school. Of course,' she added, 'Susan would also make a fine head-girl, and the decision must be yours, Miss Peters.'

'I think that you are right, Miss Potts,' said Miss Parker, who had been listening to the mistress most attentively. 'With a little more confidence, I believe that Felicity could be as big a success here as Darrell was. She certainly has good stuff in her.'

'Very well,' Miss Peters said. 'Felicity Rivers it is then.'

'I'm afraid that Veronica Sharpe is going to be bitterly disappointed,' said Miss Potts drily. 'She is quite certain that the position is hers.'

'It never entered my head to make Veronica head-girl,' said Miss Peters, with a rather scornful laugh. 'I'm afraid that young lady has a lot to learn before she can ever be given a position of responsibility. She would have been a most unpopular choice!'

Felicity, however, was an extremely popular choice, and the classroom resembled a bear garden for a few moments, as the third formers congratulated her noisily.

'Well done, Felicity!'

'Jolly good show! You'll make a super head-girl.'

'My word, won't your parents be proud?'

June, delighted to see the look of horror on Veronica's face, cheered loudest of all, leaning forward and slapping Felicity on the back. 'Congratulations, Felicity! I'm so pleased for you.'

Only two girls remained silent. One, of course, was Veronica, who felt humiliated beyond words. To think that Felicity Rivers, of all people, had been given the honour that she had wanted so badly for herself. Veronica would almost have preferred that dreadful June as head-girl! And worst of all, she had actually boasted to Amy last night that she was going to be head-girl. Why hadn't she kept her mouth shut?

The other girl who was unable to speak was Felicity herself! For a moment, she thought that she had misheard Miss Peters as the mistress announced her name. Then Susan had given her a hug that almost pulled her out of her seat, the cheering and yelling had erupted, and she had realised that it was true. She, Felicity Rivers, was head of the third form! Felicity felt that she would burst with pride and happiness. She must write to her parents tonight – and Darrell, of course – and tell them the news! My goodness, how thrilled and proud they would all be! And what a super term this was going to be. Felicity vowed silently that

she would be the best head-girl any form had ever had –
even better than Darrell! Nothing would go wrong while
she was in charge, nothing bad would happen and there
would be no problems whatsoever.

But Felicity was wrong. The third form's problems were
just about to begin!

A shock for Felicity

The first week of term simply sped by. Life at Malory Towers was full, busy and happy, so that the girls scarcely had a moment in which to be bored or homesick. But there were irritations too. Amy remained aloof and stand-offish, looking down on everyone other than Veronica, whom she graciously allowed to be her friend. As for Veronica herself, she had become more sour than ever since Felicity had been made head-girl.

'The two of them seem to have formed their own exclusive little club,' remarked Nora one day.

'Yes, though I don't know why Veronica thinks she's so superior to the rest of us,' said Julie rather indignantly. 'I saw her people last half-term and they are quite ordinary.'

'Veronica has become superior by association with Amy,' drawled June. 'Or at any rate, she thinks she has. And the more time the two of them spend together, the worse it's going to get.'

Felicity was in hearty agreement with June over this, and did her best to get the two girls to mix more with the rest of the form, but her efforts were in vain. Felicity spoke to Susan about it at tea one afternoon.

'I really feel that it's my responsibility to do something

about them,' she said in a low voice. 'They're awfully bad for one another. Veronica just encourages Amy in her belief that she's a cut above the rest of us. And as long as she has Amy for her friend, Veronica won't attempt to mix with the rest of us and will become even more unpopular.'

'Yes, but what *can* you do?' asked Susan reasonably. 'You can hardly order them not to be friends.'

'No, but I shall think of something,' said Felicity, with a determined set to her chin, and Susan grinned. She didn't doubt for a minute that her friend would do whatever she set her mind to, for she had always known that Felicity was a strong character. And now that she was head of the form, it was coming to the fore.

'I say, look!' cried Nora, who was sitting opposite them. 'Miss Potts has just appeared with a new girl. A first former, by the look of her, for she's only a little scrap.'

'Poor little soul,' said Pam, sympathetically. 'It must be awfully nerve-wracking to walk into a room full of strangers. Still, the first formers are a decent bunch and I daresay they'll look after her.'

Felicity and Susan, who had their backs to the door, turned curiously to look at the newcomer. Felicity, who had just taken a bite of fruit cake, choked, while Susan gasped.

'Bonnie!' said Felicity in horror. 'Susan, it's Bonnie!'

'Yes, I can see that,' murmured Susan, sounding less than thrilled.

For the wide-eyed little girl standing next to Miss Potts was none other than Felicity's neighbour, Bonnie

Meadows. At that moment, she caught sight of Felicity, and gave a high-pitched squeal of excitement, before daintily weaving her way through the tables to join the third form.

The girls stared at her in astonishment as she cried, 'Felicity! Aren't you surprised to see me?' Then, without giving Felicity a chance to reply, she went on rapidly, 'I missed you so much that I was quite miserable, then Daddy came home from one of his trips abroad and was quite worried about me, because he could see that I wasn't my old self. So he talked Mother into letting me come here, so that I could be with you, then he telephoned Miss Grayling and fixed it all up in a trice.'

Bonnie at last stopped to take a breath and June, who had been watching with a look of wicked amusement on her face, and had noted the shocked expressions on Felicity and Susan's faces, said sweetly, 'How nice for you, Felicity, to have another friend here. Do introduce us!'

'This is Bonnie Meadows,' said Felicity, pulling herself together. 'She's a neighbour of mine at home.'

'Well, that's excellent,' said Miss Potts, who had followed Bonnie over and arrived just in time to hear this. 'Bonnie will feel quite at home with you to look after her, Felicity. I shall leave it to you to help her settle in.'

Felicity, putting her own feelings to one side for the moment, quickly introduced Bonnie to the other third formers, and to Mam'zelle Dupont, who was extremely taken with this angelic-looking little newcomer.

'Susan!' she said. 'Please will you go to the kitchen and ask them for another plate for *la petite* Bonnie. And perhaps we could have some more cake, for I see that you greedy third formers have eaten it all up so that there is none left for the poor child. Sit down, *ma chère*, for I am sure you must be tired and hungry after your journey.'

As Susan went off to do as Mam'zelle Dupont had asked, Bonnie turned her sweet smile on the French mistress and thanked her prettily. Then she slipped into the seat that Susan had just vacated, beside Felicity, while Pam poured her a cup of tea.

The others, meanwhile, were sizing her up. Nora, who, with her deceptively innocent expression, wide, blue eyes and shock of fluffy blonde hair, was a long-standing favourite of Mam'zelle's, was none too pleased to see the French mistress fussing over this new girl. Pam thought her rather sweet, while Veronica considered her to be quite silly and childish. Most of the others thought that she couldn't be too bad if she was a friend of Felicity's, and were prepared to give her a chance. Felicity and Susan, of course, were thoroughly dismayed at this turn of events, and poor Susan looked most disgruntled when she returned from the kitchen bearing a tray of cakes and sandwiches.

'Thank you so much, Susan,' said Bonnie, looking up at the girl with round, innocent eyes as she set the tray down on the table. 'Oh dear, have I taken your seat?'

'It is no matter,' said Mam'zelle Dupont, quite failing to notice the hint of spite behind the sweetness. 'Susan, there is an empty chair at the second-form table. Bring it over, and you can sit next to me, then we shall be comfortable.'

Felicity, however, looked decidedly *un*comfortable, thought June, doing her best not to laugh. She turned her attention to Bonnie and asked, 'What school did you go to before you came here?'

'Oh, I've never been to school before,' answered Bonnie, tossing back her brown curls. 'I was very ill when I was little, you see, and the doctors said that I was too delicate to go to school.'

'Ah, *la pauvre*!' exclaimed Mam'zelle, her ready sympathy stirred. 'But you are quite well now, *n'est-ce pas*?'

'Oh, yes, Mam'zelle,' said Bonnie. 'And I'm so looking forward to starting school properly, and being with Felicity again.'

'You'll be able to make up a threesome, with Felicity and Susan,' said June, looking every bit as innocent as Bonnie herself. 'Won't that be super?'

Neither Susan nor Bonnie looked particularly thrilled at this idea, while Felicity groaned inwardly. She couldn't very well throw Bonnie off altogether – especially as she was head-girl, and it was her duty to help her settle in – but she certainly didn't want the girl tagging along with her and Susan all the time. Whatever was she to do?

After tea, Felicity and Susan took Bonnie up to the dormitory to unpack her things. Amy was there, searching through her cabinet for a book, and she glanced up when the others entered.

'There's only one spare bed, Bonnie,' said Susan. 'And it's this one, next to Pam's.'

Bonnie frowned, for she had been hoping to be next to

Felicity, but she said nothing and began unpacking her trunk, which had already been brought up by the handyman. She pulled out a pretty floral-patterned dress, which she had brought to wear at weekends, and it caught Amy's eye.

'I say, what a lovely dress!' she said, coming over to take a closer look at it. 'I have a very similar one that my mother bought me when we went on holiday to Paris. Where did you get yours from?'

'I made it,' replied Bonnie, looking pleased. 'It took me simply ages, but I didn't mind because I love sewing. Look, I made this one as well.'

'My word, you are clever!' said Amy, the genuine admiration in her tone astonishing Felicity and Susan, for they had never heard it before. 'These clothes are as beautifully made as the ones Mother buys for me. It must be dreadful to have to make all your own dresses though.'

'Oh, I don't *have* to do it,' said Bonnie. 'I told you, I love sewing – and it's the one thing that I'm really good at. Besides, if I make something myself, it means that it's truly exclusive and no one else has a dress exactly like it.'

'I'd never thought of that before,' said Amy, much struck. 'I do so hate looking the same as everyone else, don't you? Come over here, Bonnie, and I'll show you some of my things.'

Eagerly, Bonnie followed Amy, and Susan tapped Felicity on the shoulder, murmuring, 'I'm not particularly interested in the latest fashions, are you? Let's leave them to it.'

Felicity nodded and, unnoticed by the other two girls, who were now in the thick of a conversation about clothes, they tiptoed out of the dormitory.

'Well!' said Susan. 'It seems that those two have an interest in common.'

'Yes,' said Felicity, thoughtfully. 'In fact they're quite alike in many ways. Bonnie's not stuck-up, and she doesn't look down on people like Amy does, but she's awfully spoilt and vain.'

'Yes,' agreed Susan. 'When I stayed with you in the hols, I noticed that she was always doing her hair, or admiring herself in the mirror, just as Amy does. I say, Felicity, what are you thinking? I do believe you have an idea!'

'I was just wondering if we couldn't push Bonnie off on to Amy,' answered Felicity, with a grin. 'That would kill two birds with one stone, so to speak, for it would stop Amy and Veronica spending so much time together –'

'And it would mean that we wouldn't have Bonnie tagging along after us all the time!' Susan finished for her. 'It's a marvellous idea, old thing, but will it work? After all, Bonnie came here because she wanted to be with *you*, not Amy. And we both know how persistent she can be.'

The two girls had reached the common-room by this time, and they sat down together on an empty sofa. Felicity bit her lip, as she always did when she was thinking hard, and at last she said, 'Susan, I've got it! How would it be if I made a point of asking Bonnie to befriend Amy, as a favour to me? I can tell her that I'm a bit concerned that Amy isn't settling in very well, and that I'm worried she's getting too close to Veronica.'

'Bonnie's bound to agree if she thinks she's doing a favour for you,' cried Susan, her eyes lighting up. 'It's simply marvellous!'

'What's marvellous?' asked June, coming over with Freddie and sitting down on the arm of the sofa.

Quickly Felicity and Susan told the two girls their plan, and June grinned. 'Poor Veronica won't be too pleased at having to share her precious Amy. And anything that annoys Veronica is fine with me! I say, I hope that Bonnie and Amy aren't going to spend too long in the dormitory. I wanted to show Freddie my box of tricks before bedtime.'

But just then the door opened, and the two girls came in, chattering nineteen to the dozen.

'Just look at Veronica's face,' whispered Freddie. 'She doesn't look too happy to see Bonnie and Amy on such friendly terms.'

Indeed she didn't! Veronica was sitting in a corner alone, reading a book, and her lips pursed as Amy, instead of coming over to join her, sat at a table with Bonnie, and the two began poring over a fashion magazine together.

'She looks as though she's been sucking on a lemon!' chuckled June. 'Blow, I'd really like to stay and see what happens next, but we'd better go up to the dorm, Freddie, if you want to take a look at those tricks before the bell goes for bedtime. Felicity, if a row breaks out do come and fetch us!'

But there was no row, for as soon as Veronica got up to

join the other two, Bonnie left the table and came over to join Felicity and Susan.

'Amy's awfully nice, isn't she?' said Bonnie, ignoring Susan and addressing her remark to Felicity.

'Er – yes, awfully nice,' agreed Felicity, exchanging a glance with Susan. Now was the time to put their plan into action. 'Actually, Bonnie, I was glad to see you getting on so well with Amy, because she's a new girl too and hasn't really got to know many people yet, so –'

'But I thought she was friendly with that Veronica girl,' interrupted Bonnie.

'Yes, she is,' said Felicity. 'And that's the problem. You see, Bonnie, Veronica is . . . well, let's just say that she isn't a very pleasant girl, and she's awfully unpopular with the rest of the form. And I'm afraid that, by spending so much time with Veronica, Amy is cutting herself off from the rest of us and missing the chance to make other friendships. So, if you could be her friend too, I really think that it would be very good for her and I would be so grateful to you.'

The thought of being able to do something to please Felicity brought a sparkling look to Bonnie's eyes, and she glanced across at Amy and Veronica. Amy saw her looking and smiled, but the scowl that Veronica gave her was most unpleasant!

'Yes, I see what you mean,' she said at once. 'Of course, I'll be happy to do that for you, Felicity. But I'm only doing it as a favour, because *you* are my real friend, and no one else could ever take your place with me – not even Amy.'

Amy, for her part, had thoroughly enjoyed her little

chat with Bonnie. If she was honest with herself, she had little in common with Veronica, and didn't even like the girl very much. Really, she had only palled up with her because there was no one else, and Veronica did so enjoy listening to Amy's tales of her grand home and family. Veronica also made no secret of her admiration, and this was very pleasant to Amy. But it would be nice to have Bonnie as a friend too, and talk about things like clothes and hair-dos, which Veronica knew very little about. Amy thought that she would get Bonnie to make her one of her exclusive dresses too, just as she had got Veronica to make her bed every morning. Felicity had ticked the two of them off about it at first, but at last she had realised that she couldn't very well force Amy to make her own bed, and that if she put her foot down the girl would probably just leave it with the sheets in a muddled heap. And that would result in an order mark for the whole form, so in the end Felicity gave up, though she wasn't happy about it, as she felt that Veronica and Amy had got one over on her.

Bonnie lost no time in getting to work, going up to Amy in the dormitory as the third formers got ready for bed and saying, 'Amy, I simply must show you a new way of braiding your hair in the morning. I learned how to do it in the holidays, and I think it would really suit you.'

'I think Amy's hair looks lovely the way it is,' interrupted Veronica rudely, looking coldly at Bonnie. But Amy brushed her aside and said, 'Oh, thank you, Bonnie. I do so hate having to tie my hair back for school, and it's always nice to find a new way of doing it.'

And soon the two of them were gabbling away about hair-dos, while Veronica stood to one side, looking so put out that Felicity felt a little sorry for her. But soon it was time for lights-out and Felicity called out, 'Come along, Bonnie, into bed now. You and Amy can carry on your conversation in the morning.'

Within moments all the girls were in bed, most of them falling asleep immediately. Felicity had expected Bonnie, who had never been separated from her mother before, to feel homesick, and had dreaded that the girl would cry herself to sleep. But there wasn't a peep out of her, much to Felicity's surprise and relief.

But it was some time before Felicity herself managed to get to sleep, for Bonnie turning up so unexpectedly had really shaken her. And what if her plan to get the girl to chum up with Amy failed? Veronica certainly wouldn't want Bonnie tagging along, and would do her best to push her out. Then Bonnie would follow Felicity around like a lost puppy, making her friendship with Susan difficult, and life at Malory Towers much less enjoyable. Felicity sighed and turned over in her bed. Blow! *Why* did Bonnie have to turn up now? Just as things seemed to be going so well!

The new girls settle in

The three new girls each settled down in their own way. Freddie had a quick brain and could have done extremely well at lessons, but she preferred to follow June's lead and put her brains to work in planning ingenious jokes and tricks. She quickly became popular with the third form, for she was sunny-natured and shared June's mischievous sense of fun. But she was not quite as bold and daring as June, nor did she have the hardness and malice that were such flaws in the other girl's character.

'I like her tremendously,' said Susan to Felicity one day, as the two of them chatted about the new girls. 'I just hope that June's don't-care-ishness doesn't rub off on her.'

'Perhaps Freddie's good-heartedness will rub off on June,' suggested Felicity. 'I must say, she's the only one of the three new girls that I'm really keen on.'

Certainly Amy was far too stuck-up to be popular, while the teachers found her extremely trying as well, for her work was far below the standard of most of the form.

'I can't decide whether she's lazy, or stupid, or both!' an exasperated Miss Peters said to Miss Potts in the mistresses' common-room, after she had struggled to mark one of Amy's essays. 'She doesn't seem to understand the basic rules of grammar, she's hopeless at maths, not the slightest bit interested in history, and – according to Miss Maxwell – won't exert herself at all when it comes to games and swimming, for she doesn't like getting red-faced and untidy! The only thing Amy is any good at is French.'

Having spent so many holidays in France, Amy did, indeed, speak the language very well, which pleased both Mam'zelles enormously.

Bonnie was not much better than Amy at lessons but, having spent most of her time with adults, she had become extremely clever at 'twisting them around her little finger', as a disgruntled Nora put it. Poor Nora had had her nose pushed very much out of joint by Bonnie's arrival. She had always taken for granted that she was Mam'zelle Dupont's favourite, making a joke of it and using her position to advantage when it suited her. But now she found that she didn't like to see another girl taking her place. Mam'zelle Dupont positively doted on Bonnie, although her French was poor, while Miss Simmons, the quiet little needlework teacher, was thrilled to find a member of the third form who could sew well. Miss Linnie, the art mistress, and Mr Young, the singing teacher, were also charmed by Bonnie, and gave her a very easy time indeed.

But not all of the teachers were fond of Bonnie. The blunt, downright Miss Peters considered her an empty-headed little creature, with far too many airs and graces, while Mam'zelle Rougier, who made it a habit to dislike those girls who were favoured by Mam'zelle Dupont, remained unmoved by either Bonnie's tears or her smiles.

As for Miss Maxwell, the games mistress, she was driven to distraction by the girl.

Bonnie had never been swimming in her life, and her shrill squeal as she entered the cold water for the first time made everyone jump, including Miss Maxwell.

'Bonnie!' she said angrily. 'I thought that you were in difficulties, judging from the noise you're making, but the water is barely up to your waist!'

Then Susan swam past and accidentally splashed water in Bonnie's face, which caused her to scream again.

'Baby!' said June scornfully to Felicity. 'Honestly, anyone would think that Susan was trying to drown her. I've a good mind to duck her – at least then she wouldn't be able to scream!'

Felicity grinned, but the smile was wiped off her face a few moments later when, as she was poised to dive into the pool, Bonnie let out an ear-splitting yell, because Veronica – whether deliberately, or by accident, nobody was sure – barged into her and almost knocked her over. Distracted, Felicity lost her balance, and instead of swallow-diving gracefully into the pool she did an undignified belly-flop and almost landed on top of a very surprised Pam!

'I have had quite enough of this!' said Miss Maxwell, losing her temper. 'Bonnie, I really can't allow you to disrupt the third form's swimming like this any longer. Please get out of the pool at once and get dressed!'

'Yes, Miss Maxwell,' said Bonnie meekly, hurrying to climb out of the pool.

Only Felicity caught the tiny little smile on the girl's face just before she turned to walk back up to the school, and she gave a gasp.

'The little monkey!' Felicity thought to herself. 'I believe that Bonnie played up deliberately to get out of swimming!'

But, as much as she exasperated the others, Bonnie did have her good points. She was extremely loyal to those she considered her friends, as Veronica found out when she made the mistake of criticising Felicity to Amy in front of her.

'I can't *think* what made Miss Peters choose Felicity Rivers as head-girl,' Veronica said, in a sneering tone. 'I don't think she's a good leader at all, for her character is far too weak. If you ask me, she only got the position because her sister was Head Girl last year.'

Amy opened her mouth to reply, but before she could speak, a furious Bonnie confronted Veronica, saying angrily, 'You take that back at once! How dare you say things like that about Felicity? I think that she's a jolly good head-girl, and she's my friend, and I won't have you making spiteful remarks about her!'

Both Veronica and Amy were quite taken aback, and since Veronica – who preferred to make her criticisms behind people's backs rather than to their faces – didn't want her remarks getting back to Felicity, she did not retaliate.

But Julie, who had been sitting nearby, had overheard the whole conversation, and had, in fact, been about to leap to Felicity's defence when Bonnie stepped in, and the new girl at once went up in her estimation.

Bonnie's loyalty came to the fore again a few days later, in the French lesson – and this time she surprised the whole form!

Mam'zelle Dupont was not in the best of tempers, for the first form, who she had just left, had played her up quite dreadfully. Which was unfortunate for June, who – feeling a little bored – had also chosen that morning to act the goat.

Lifting the lid of her desk to hide from Mam'zelle's view, she ripped a page from her exercise book and swiftly folded it into a paper aeroplane.

'Freddie,' she whispered. 'I bet I can hit the back of Amy's head from here.'

'And I bet you can't!' answered Freddie at once, with a grin. 'She's too far away.'

Bonnie, who sat across the aisle from the two girls, didn't hear this exchange, but she caught the sudden movement as June raised her hand and launched her paper aeroplane on its journey. Mam'zelle, who had turned her back to the class while she wrote something on the blackboard, remained in blissful ignorance, until a few giggles broke out as the aeroplane glided gracefully over Amy's head and, much to her surprise, landed on her desk. Amy picked the aeroplane up and Mam'zelle, who had whipped round upon hearing the giggles, glared at her furiously.

'So!' she said angrily. 'You are so good at French that you can waste the class's time in this way, Amy?'

Poor Amy looked horrified and protested, 'But Mam'zelle, I didn't throw the aeroplane! I was just –'

'Be silent!' cried Mam'zelle, her black eyes snapping coldly. 'How dare you interrupt me? You are a bad and disrespectful girl, Amy, and you will be punished. Tonight you will learn the whole of the French poem we have just started, and you will say it back to me tomorrow.'

Amy, stung by the injustice of this, longed to argue but didn't dare. When Mam'zelle was in this sort of mood, she was quite likely to make her learn *two* poems! Why didn't the mean beast who had thrown the aeroplane own up and get her out of trouble? In fact June, at the back of the class, was about to do just that. She might have her faults, but she wasn't about to allow someone else to be punished for her joke. Before she could do so, however, Bonnie got to her feet and piped up, 'Mam'zelle! It wasn't Amy who threw the aeroplane – it was June. I saw her.'

The third formers, who had very strict ideas about telling tales, gasped, looking at one another in horror, and at Bonnie in disgust. Felicity gave a groan. Of course, never having been to school before, Bonnie probably didn't realise that it wasn't done to tell on one's form-mates. And, as head-girl, it was up to Felicity to put her straight!

'June, is this true?' said Mam'zelle, looking sternly at the girl. 'And you did not have the courage to tell the truth, even when *la pauvre* Amy was about to be punished?'

'It's true that I threw the plane, Mam'zelle,' said June, going very red as she stood up. 'But I was about to own up, truly I was.'

'I don't believe you!' cried Amy, who disliked June intensely and felt very grateful to Bonnie for coming to her rescue. 'You probably did it on purpose to get me into trouble.'

'I did not!' said June indignantly. 'It was just a joke, but –'

'Enough!' shouted Mam'zelle, stamping one of her little feet crossly. 'June, *méchante fille*, you will have the punishment that I was going to give the poor, innocent Amy. You will learn that poem, and you will recite it to me tomorrow. And, as a second punishment for not owning up, you will go to bed half an hour early this evening!'

The girl was horrified, and smarted at the injustice of the second punishment. But, bold as she was, even June did not dare to argue with an angry Mam'zelle Dupont, so she said meekly, 'Yes, Mam'zelle,' and took her seat again. But she glared angrily at Bonnie, and Felicity, turning in her seat to give June a sympathetic look, saw it. 'Oh dear,' she thought. 'There's going to be trouble!'

And Felicity was quite right, for June marched up to her at break-time, a stormy expression on her face as she said, 'I say, Felicity, what are we going to do about Bonnie? She simply can't be allowed to get away with sneaking like that.'

'No, I suppose you're right and something will have to be done about her,' said Felicity. 'There's no time now, but we'll hold a form meeting in the common-room at lunchtime.'

So as soon as lunch was over, the members of the third

form trooped into the common-room. Only one person was missing, and that was Bonnie.

'Where is she?' demanded June, her eyes flashing angrily. 'I suppose the little coward doesn't have the courage to face me.'

'Actually, June, Miss Peters wanted to see Bonnie about some prep,' said Amy coldly. 'She'll be here shortly.'

Felicity, who didn't want to be too hard on Bonnie, was quite glad that the girl wasn't there yet, and she clapped her hands together for silence, before saying, 'June, I quite understand that you're angry, but please let's not forget that Bonnie hasn't been to school before and doesn't quite understand all our ways.'

'Oh, you would stick up for her, Felicity!' said June, a harsh note in her voice. 'Just wait until the little sneak shows her face! My word, won't I tell her what I think of her! The silly baby is always turning on the waterworks over something or other – and this time I'll give her something to cry about!'

This was exactly what Felicity was afraid of. June in a rage was not a pleasant sight, and little Bonnie would never be able to stand up to her.

'No, June!' said Felicity firmly. 'I am head-girl, and I am running this meeting, and Bonnie will be given a chance to have her say. Then the form as a whole will decide if she is to be punished, and how.'

Just then the door opened and Bonnie herself entered. Felicity moved forward to speak to her, but June got in first. Throwing Felicity a mocking look, she stalked up to Bonnie and said menacingly, 'What do you mean by sneaking on me to Mam'zelle Dupont, you horrid little beast?'

The third formers watched with bated breath, some of them hoping that Bonnie would get what she deserved, others hoping that June would not go too far, and *all* of them waiting for Bonnie to burst into noisy tears. A worried expression on her face, Felicity braced herself, ready to step in if the need arose.

But June had underestimated the new girl. Bonnie wasn't used to being spoken to in such a way, and she didn't like it one little bit. She didn't much like June either, and was quite shrewd enough to realise that tears would not work with her. So she met the girl's angry gaze squarely and said coldly, 'Don't be ridiculous. I did nothing of the sort.'

June gave an outraged gasp. 'So you're a liar, Bonnie, as well as a sneak! The whole form heard you tell Mam'zelle that it was I who threw that paper aeroplane.'

There were murmurs of agreement from the listening girls, but Bonnie said quite calmly, 'Yes, that's right. Amy was going to be punished for something you had done, so I stepped in and told Mam'zelle the truth. But I did *not* sneak! You see, my dear June, sneaking means just that. It means going behind someone's back, doing something sly and secretive and underhand. I spoke up in front of the whole form, so I really don't see how there was anything sneaky about it!'

Felicity stared at the girl in surprise, for what Bonnie

had said was quite true – she *had* told tales, but she had been perfectly open about it.

June swiftly recovered and said, 'Very well, perhaps "sneak" is the wrong word in this case, but you *did* tell on me!'

'Yes, to get a friend out of trouble,' retorted Bonnie, just as quickly. 'And I must say, June, I would have thought better of you if you had owned up yourself.'

There was just enough scorn in the girl's tone to throw June on the defensive and she said hotly, 'I *was* going to own up, as I tried to explain to Mam'zelle! But I didn't get the chance, thanks to you!'

'Well, how was I to know that?' said Bonnie, opening her eyes wide. 'I'm the new girl, don't forget. I don't know anything about your character, June – whether you're the kind of person who will keep quiet and let someone else take her punishment, or the kind of person who will come clean and take the consequences.'

'I'm no coward!' said June indignantly. 'I would never let anyone else take the blame for something I had done.'

'I'm very glad to hear it,' said Bonnie with a little smile. 'It's just a pity that you weren't a bit quicker in taking the blame, then all of this unpleasantness could have been avoided. I hope that this will be a lesson to you, June. Now, if you'll excuse me, I need to go and speak to Matron.'

And with that, Bonnie swept from the room with her little head held high, leaving behind her a stunned silence. Susan, who was doing her best not to smile, nudged Felicity and nodded towards June, still standing in the

71

middle of the floor, with her mouth open like a goldfish. Felicity bit her lip hard to stop herself from laughing. Pam and Julie, meanwhile, were clinging to one another as they tried to stifle their laughter, while Nora's shoulders shook uncontrollably with mirth. Even Veronica, jealous as she was of Bonnie, had relished seeing June rendered speechless, while Amy had enjoyed the scene tremendously.

Suddenly, a loud burst of laughter broke the silence, and the girls were amazed to realise that it came from June herself!

'My goodness!' she gasped, when she was able to speak. 'Who would have thought that little scrap would be able to stand up to me like that? But she did, and I must say that I admire her for it!'

And the third formers, joining in June's laughter, admired *her* for being able to admit so honestly that someone had got the better of her. You could always rely on June to do the unexpected, thought Felicity wryly, feeling quite relieved that the row was over. But, when she thought about it later, she felt a little uneasy. June had flouted her authority by refusing to allow her, Felicity, to run the meeting her way, and by confronting Bonnie when she had been told not to. And Felicity, anxious to avoid a row, had allowed her to get away with it. What would Darrell have done in that situation, she wondered? The answer to that was easy, for Darrell was such a frank, forthright person that she would have had no hesitation at all in putting June in her place. Well, if June continued to flout her, Felicity would have to find the strength of character to deal with her in the same way. After all, she was head-girl, and the third formers needed someone strong to lead them, and set an example, not someone who shrank from difficult or unpleasant tasks. Felicity made a promise to herself, there and then. It wouldn't be easy, and no doubt she would make mistakes along the way, but she *would* become a strong leader.

A dirty trick

June felt sore with Mam'zelle Dupont for some time after the 'aeroplane affair', as it became known. She had felt extremely humiliated at going to bed half an hour before the others, and, the next morning, had recited the French poem to the mistress in a sulky tone. Mam'zelle, who had begun to feel a little sorry that she had been so hard on the girl, noticed the tone, and June's petulant expression, and hardened her heart. Ah, she was a bad girl, this June, and a little punishment would be good for her.

Freddie, who admired June tremendously, also felt angry on her friend's behalf, and wished that she could think of some way of getting back at Mam'zelle Dupont.

Then June came up to Freddie one break-time and, taking her arm, said, 'I'm bored. Nothing ever happens around here! I think it's time we played the magic soap trick on Amy.'

'Super!' giggled Freddie. 'Shall we let the others in on it?'

June thought for a moment, then said, 'No, let's plan it out between ourselves – just the two of us! Then we can surprise the others.'

Freddie nodded happily and said, 'But how can we be

certain that Amy will use the right soap? If she doesn't it will simply ruin the whole trick.'

'I've thought of that,' said June with a grin. 'Amy has a bar of very expensive soap that her mother sent her, and it looks very like our special soap, so I'm simply going to switch the bars. She'll never notice the difference, and there's no fear of anyone else getting a dirty face, because dear Amy would *never* let anyone else use her precious soap!'

Freddie chuckled. 'Oh, June, it's going to be simply marvellous! And the whole of North Tower will be able to share in the fun, because Amy's face should start to turn muddy at breakfast-time. When are we going to do it?'

'Tomorrow,' answered June. 'I noticed this morning that Amy has almost used up all of her old bar of soap, which means that she will open the new one tomorrow.'

Freddie said nothing, for an idea had just come to her – an idea so breathtakingly bold and daring that June herself might have come up with it. But Freddie decided to say nothing to June, for she was going to give her friend a surprise. And she was going to give the whole of North Tower the biggest laugh it had ever had!

Felicity wondered what June and Freddie were up to as the third form dressed the following morning. The two of them whispered together excitedly, and there was a very mischievous twinkle in Freddie's eye! Freddie had asked June if she could switch the soap bars, and June had agreed. 'Be careful, though,' she had warned. 'Make sure that no one's around when you do it, and see that you put our special soap in exactly the same place as Amy's soap was. We don't want her smelling a rat!'

Now the two girls nudged one another and giggled as they watched Amy take the soap from the drawer of her cabinet and walk into the bathroom.

'What *are* you two up to?' asked Felicity, unable to contain her curiosity any longer.

'Why, nothing at all, Felicity,' answered June, making her expression as innocent as she possibly could. 'What makes you think that we're up to something?'

'You both seem very excited about something,' said Felicity, eyeing them suspiciously. 'Come on – come clean!'

Freddie gave a sudden snort of laughter, and June's lips twitched as she said, 'But there's nothing to come clean about, Felicity. Really there isn't. We're not trying to soft-soap you.'

This was too much for Freddie, who collapsed on to her bed in a fit of giggles and Felicity, realising that she wasn't going to get anything out of the pair, shook her head and went off to join Susan.

June gave Amy a sidelong glance as she came out of the bathroom, but the magic soap had not begun to do its work yet, and her complexion looked as clean and fresh as ever. But it wouldn't stay that way for long, thought June, smiling to herself. Just you wait, Amy!

But, as breakfast wore on, and Amy's face stayed the same, June grew impatient.

'Why is nothing happening?' she muttered under her

breath to Freddie. 'Don't say that Alicia has given me a dud bar of soap!'

'I'm sure she hasn't,' said Freddie confidently. 'In fact, I think that things are just about to happen!'

June lifted her head sharply, then realised that Freddie wasn't looking at Amy, but at the head of the table, where Mam'zelle Dupont sat. She followed Freddie's gaze – and gave a gasp! For Mam'zelle's skin was turning a muddy, dingy brown.

Pam and Susan, who sat either side of the French mistress, couldn't fail to notice the startling transformation as well, and they stared at Mam'zelle, who was quite unaware of her strange appearance, in mingled horror and astonishment. Each of them nudged the girl next to her, and soon the word was passed around the table, and the third form were all gazing at Mam'zelle, trying desperately to control their laughter. Most of the girls guessed, of course, that June had played a trick using the soap that Alicia had given her, but they simply couldn't imagine how she had got Mam'zelle to use it. How clever of her!

June couldn't imagine how Mam'zelle had got hold of the magic soap either, and turned to Freddie, but before she could ask for an explanation, a cry came from the head of the table. Mam'zelle had just looked down at her hands, and realised that they were covered in dirty, muddy streaks.

'*Mon dieu!*' she exclaimed. 'My hands, they are filthy. Yet I washed them this morning. What can have caused this?'

Carefully she examined her cup, her plate and even her

knife and fork, for dirty marks, and this was too much for Nora, who gave one of her sudden snorts of laughter. Most of the others were having difficulty in controlling their mirth as well, and people at the other tables began to notice.

'My word, just look at Mam'zelle Dupont!'

'What*ever* has happened to her?'

'Has she forgotten to have a wash this morning?'

'It must be a trick! I'll bet it was June!'

Mam'zelle became aware of the whispering and looked most uncomfortable, and Felicity took pity on her.

'Mam'zelle,' she said, when she could trust her voice enough to speak. 'I'm afraid it's not just your hands that are dirty, but your face as well.'

Amy, who always carried a little mirror around with her, fished it out of her pocket and handed it to the French mistress, who took one look at her reflection and gave a piercing shriek.

The dining-room was in uproar by this time and the other mistresses, who had now had a good look at Mam'zelle's dirty face, stared at one another in consternation. Miss Potts took charge, getting to her feet and raising her voice to demand silence.

'That will do!' she commanded. 'Mam'zelle Dupont, I don't understand how you appear to be covered in mud, since you looked quite clean when you first came in to breakfast, but I suggest that you go to one of the bathrooms and wash it off before your first class begins.'

So, summoning up what dignity she could, the little

French mistress tottered from the dining-room, and Miss Potts said sharply, 'June! I don't suppose you know anything about this, do you?'

'No, I don't, Miss Potts,' answered June quite truthfully, and Miss Potts stared at her hard, knowing that she could play the innocent very well when it suited her. But the girl looked just as bewildered as the others, though she didn't seem to find it as funny as they did – in fact, she looked rather angry.

'Well, it's a mystery to me how Mam'zelle Dupont could have entered the room looking as neat as a new pin, and left it looking as though she had been in a mud fight!' said Miss Potts. 'I don't know if I shall ever get to the bottom of it. Now, girls, please finish your breakfast quietly, then make your way to your first lesson.'

Miss Potts went back to the first-form table and, as soon as she was out of earshot, a babble of low-voiced chatter broke out among the third formers.

'June! It was you, wasn't it?'

'Of course it was. You used the magic soap on Mam'zelle, didn't you?'

'I must say, it was a splendid trick! Did you see poor old Mam'zelle's face?'

'Just like you not to own up.'

This last remark came from Amy, and June replied, 'I didn't own up because it wasn't me who played the trick, I tell you!'

'Then who was it?' asked Felicity, puzzled.

'It was me!' said Freddie gleefully, her eyes alight with

mischief. 'I did it to get back at Mam'zelle for being so hard on June the other day.'

Pam chuckled. 'Well, you certainly did that all right! So, do you mean to say that June wasn't in on the trick at all?'

'No,' said June rather shortly. 'I *thought* that I was, but it seems that Freddie decided to go it alone and use the soap on Mam'zelle, instead of the person we had chosen.'

'You'd better watch your step, June,' laughed Nora. 'Freddie will be taking over from you as the form joker if you aren't careful.'

June said nothing, and Freddie stared at her, rather puzzled at her coolness. Anyone would think that she wasn't happy about getting her revenge on Mam'zelle Dupont.

In fact, June was simply furious with Freddie for stealing her thunder. *She* was the leader in their friendship, and she wouldn't have it any other way. She was quite happy for Freddie to play second fiddle to her, and to act as her assistant in planning jokes and tricks, but she, June, was the joker of the form and no one was going to take that position away from her. Where another girl might have taken pleasure in getting top marks in class, or for her sporting achievements, all June cared about was getting praise for her jokes and tricks. And she didn't like to see Freddie getting a share of that praise now, feeling extremely jealous as the others congratulated her.

'Simply marvellous, Freddie,' said Susan, clapping her on the back. 'But however did you get Mam'zelle to use the soap?'

'Oh, it was easy, really,' answered Freddie. 'I just slipped into her bathroom when I knew that she was taking prep with the second form, and left the soap there.'

'Heavens, how daring!' said Bonnie, her eyes wide with admiration. 'What if someone had seen you?'

'Thank goodness no one did!' said Julie. 'That was the best laugh I've had in simply ages.'

June pushed her bowl of half-eaten porridge away, her appetite completely gone and her thoughts racing. Much as she liked the girl, Freddie was going to have to learn that there was only room for one joker in the third form. June would have to think of a way to turn Freddie's thoughts and energies in another direction. But how?

The answer came to June, quite by chance, one Saturday morning. She walked into the cloakroom to find Felicity and Susan putting on their hats and coats and said, 'Hallo – where are you two off to?'

'Oh, we thought we'd just go for a walk in the countryside,' answered Felicity. 'It's gloriously sunny out, although it's a little chilly.'

'Julie's ridden Jack over to Bill and Clarissa's,' put in Susan. 'And Nora and Pam have gone with her, so we thought we might make our way over there too.'

Bill and Clarissa were two old girls who had been in the same form as Darrell and Alicia, and they now ran a riding stables not far from the school. The Malory Towers girls were very fond of Bill and Clarissa, and often visited them, either to go riding or just for a chat. Miss Peters, who was also a great horse-woman and a close friend of the pair, was a regular visitor too.

'I say, do you mind if I tag along?' asked June. 'Poor old Freddie's been giving a basketful of mending to do by Matron and it's going to take her simply ages, so I'm at a bit of a loose end.'

So June put her hat and coat on, and soon the three girls were striding out of the gates of Malory Towers and along a pretty country lane, carpeted with russet autumn leaves.

'My word, this wind is pretty blustery,' said Susan, holding her hat on her head. 'Thank goodness we're not walking along the cliff, or we should have been blown over.'

Suddenly June stopped dead and lifted her finger, saying, 'Hush a minute! I think I heard something.'

The other two fell silent, then they heard the noise too – a plaintive little mew. This was followed by a woman's voice, saying, 'Oh dear, Sooty, don't say you've got stuck in that apple tree again! Now, how on earth am I to get you down?'

'It's coming from the garden of that little cottage over there,' said Felicity. 'I think that we should see if we can help.'

The cottage was surrounded by a wall, with a wooden gate in the middle, and the three girls let themselves in, to see an elderly lady standing in the middle of a neat little garden, looking up at an apple tree with an expression of dismay.

'Excuse me,' said Felicity. 'It sounds as if you're in some sort of trouble and we came to see if we could help.'

'Oh, how kind,' said the lady, her worried face creasing into a smile as she turned to face the three girls. 'Do you see what has happened? That silly cat of mine has been climbing the apple tree, and now he's got himself stuck and can't get down. Sooty doesn't seem to realise that I'm not as young as I used to be and can't go climbing up after him any more!'

The pitiful mew sounded again, this time from above their heads, and the girls looked up to see a little pointed black face with brilliant green eyes staring down at them.

'Don't worry,' said June, stepping towards the tree. 'I'll have Sooty down in a trice.'

Quickly and agilely she began to climb, while Felicity stood at the bottom of the tree ready to take the cat from her. Susan, meanwhile, chatted to the old lady, whose name was Mrs Dale.

'Do be careful, dear!' Mrs Dale called out, as June climbed ever higher. 'I'd never forgive myself if you were to fall and hurt yourself.'

But June had been climbing trees since she could walk, and this one presented no problem to her. Soon she reached the branch the frightened Sooty was on, and she grabbed him firmly, tucking him into the front of her coat to keep him secure, before shinning back down again. Sooty wasn't too pleased about being handed over to Felicity, and dug his claws firmly into June's coat, but the two girls managed to dislodge him and Felicity placed him safely on the ground.

'How can I ever thank you?' said Mrs Dale, stooping to stroke the little black cat.

'All in a day's work,' said June breezily. 'And now, I suppose, we'd best be on our way.'

'Oh no, you must come in and have some homemade cake and lemonade,' insisted Mrs Dale. 'It's the least I can do after you've rescued my Sooty. Besides, I don't get many visitors and I should enjoy your company.'

So, within minutes, the girls were seated round the table in Mrs Dale's cosy kitchen, enjoying big slices of the most delicious fruit cake, washed down with lemonade.

'This cake is first rate, Mrs Dale,' said Susan.

'Well, it's nice to see you girls enjoying it,' said the old lady, smiling. 'I suppose you all come from Malory Towers?'

'That's right,' said Felicity.

'Well, you're a credit to the school. Actually, my granddaughter goes there. I wonder if you know her? Her name is Amy Ryder-Cochrane.'

The three girls almost choked on their lemonade, for they would never have imagined that Mrs Dale was related to the snobbish Amy. Mrs Dale was just a nice, ordinary old lady, very like their own grandmothers, and there was nothing grand about her at all, while the little cottage she lived in was very modest indeed. The girls exchanged startled glances and Felicity said, 'Yes, we know Amy. She's in the same form as us.'

'But she never mentioned that she had a grandmother living nearby,' said June.

'Ah well, she wouldn't,' said Mrs Dale. 'Because she doesn't know I'm here.'

The old lady became pensive, looking at the girls as though deciding whether or not she could trust them. Eventually, it seemed, she decided that she could, for she went on, 'You see, my dears, Amy's father is a very wealthy, well-connected gentleman. And when he married my daughter, he didn't want all his fancy friends and relatives knowing that she came from quite a common background, so she wasn't allowed to see very much of me.'

The girls listened, appalled, and Felicity murmured to Susan, 'Now we can see where Amy gets her snobbishness from.'

'And when Amy was born, he didn't want her having anything to do with me either,' said Mrs Dale. 'My daughter brought her to see me when she was a baby, but I haven't seen her since. Jane – that's my daughter – visits now and again, but she never brings Amy because that husband of hers wouldn't approve.'

The girls didn't know quite what to say. Mrs Dale sounded quite matter-of-fact about the whole situation, but there was a hint of sadness in the faded blue eyes. It was left to the outspoken June to say what they were all thinking. 'But that's absolutely dreadful!' she burst out. 'Don't worry, Mrs Dale, we'll tell Amy that you're here and bring her along to visit you.'

'Oh no, my dear, you mustn't!' said the old lady, looking quite alarmed. 'You see, whatever my feelings are, it wouldn't be right to encourage her to disobey her father.

I admit that when I learned she was coming to school here, I hoped that I might get a glimpse of her now and then, for all I have of her is a photo that was taken when she was about five years old. But it would be very wrong of me to ask her to go behind her father's back, so I must ask you all not to betray my confidence.'

Rather reluctantly, the three girls promised Mrs Dale that they wouldn't divulge to Amy that she was living near the school, and the old lady seemed happy with this.

The girls, though, were far from happy, and they discussed the matter as they went on their way to the riding stables.

'Amy's father must be a dreadful man,' said Susan, giving a shudder.

'Well, her mother must be pretty awful too, for agreeing to turn her back on her own mother!' said June. 'My goodness, if *my* father tried to tell Mother that she couldn't take me to visit my granny she would soon tell him where to get off!'

'Yes, so would mine,' said Felicity. She gave a sigh. 'It's such a pity that we can't let on to Amy. Mrs Dale seems such a nice woman, and she's awfully lonely. I daresay a few visits from Amy would cheer her up no end.'

'Yes,' said June, looking thoughtful. 'Yes, I expect they would.'

Felicity, who mistrusted June when she wore that thoughtful expression, said sharply, 'Now listen, June! I don't know what's in your mind, but we gave our word to

Mrs Dale that we wouldn't say anything to Amy, and we must keep it.'

'My dear Felicity, I have no intention of saying anything to Amy,' said June.

'Good,' said Felicity. 'And we'd better not mention it to any of the others, either. We'll just keep it a secret between the three of us.'

Secrets and tricks

But June did tell someone else about Amy's grandmother – she told Freddie.

'You must promise not to say a word to any of the others, though,' June warned her solemnly. 'And don't let on that I've told you, or Felicity won't be very pleased.'

'I shan't say a word, June,' said Freddie, who had listened open-mouthed to June's tale. 'You can count on me. It's quite a sad story, isn't it? Poor Mrs Dale!'

'She's such a dear old lady,' said June, with a sigh. 'And I felt so sorry for her, for she seems awfully lonely. I did think of an idea to help her, but . . .'

June's voice tailed off and Freddie prompted eagerly, 'But what? Do tell, June.'

June sighed again and said, 'There's no point, for it wouldn't work. It needs someone really bold and daring to carry it off, and I just can't think of anyone who could do it.'

Freddie laughed. 'But there's no one bolder or more daring than you, June! Why can't *you* carry out this mysterious idea yourself?'

'Because Mrs Dale has already met me,' answered June. 'Besides, my colouring is too different from Amy's.'

Freddie's brow wrinkled in puzzlement. 'But what does your colouring have to do with anything? June, you simply must tell me what you have in mind, or I shall die of curiosity.'

'All right then,' said June. 'You see, Freddie, we can't break our word and tell Amy about her grandmother. So I thought it would be rather a splendid idea if we could get someone else to pretend to be Amy, and go and visit the old lady now and again, to cheer her up.'

Freddie gave a low whistle. 'We'd never get away with it! Mrs Dale would know at once that the impostor wasn't Amy.'

'No, she wouldn't,' said June. 'She hasn't seen Amy since she was a baby, and the only photograph she has of her is one that was taken when she was five. All we would need to do is choose someone fair – like you, or Nora.'

Freddie digested this for a moment, then said, 'Felicity would go mad if she found out.'

June gave a rather mocking little laugh. 'Oh, Felicity can be dreadfully pi at times. Not that there's any reason why she *should* find out.' She pretended to think for a moment, then went on, 'I wonder if Nora could be persuaded? It means letting someone else in on the secret, but that can't be helped. She might be a little scatter-brained, but she's good-hearted and I think she would want to help Mrs Dale. Nora's a good actress, and pretty daring, too – I don't think that *she* would be frightened of upsetting Felicity!'

June's tone was slightly scornful, and Freddie was

stung. She looked up to the other girl no end, and badly wanted to impress her. Lifting her chin, she said, 'There's no need to involve Nora, June. I'll do it!'

'Are you sure?' asked June, looking hard at her friend.

'Absolutely positive,' answered Freddie firmly. 'Look, there's half an hour until bedtime – let's slip away to the little music room near the dormy. No one ever uses it, so we shall be able to make some plans without being interrupted.'

So the girls made their plans, and, by the following Saturday afternoon, they were ready to put them into action. Freddie was full of bravado as she and June made their way along the lane to Mrs Dale's, keeping up a stream of light-hearted chatter. Inwardly, though, she felt extremely nervous and was even beginning to wish that she had never allowed June to talk her into this. But June – well aware of Freddie's nerves – kept going on about how happy the old lady would be, and how no one else but Freddie would be able to pull this off successfully, and looked at her with such admiration that it was impossible to back out. Within moments, it seemed to Freddie, they were knocking on Mrs Dale's door. The old lady opened it, giving a little start of surprise as she saw June. 'Why, it's the girl who rescued my cat!' she said. 'How nice to see you again, dear. And you've brought a friend! Do come in, both of you.'

She ushered the two girls into the kitchen, and June took Freddie – who was doing her utmost to remain in the background – by the arm, pulling her forward. 'I have a surprise for you, Mrs Dale,' she said, launching into the little speech that she had rehearsed. 'I know that you didn't want me and the others to tell Amy that you were here, and we kept our word. But I'm afraid that the three of us discussed the matter in the common-room later, and – unknown to us – Amy was outside, and she overheard us.'

Mrs Dale put her hand up to her mouth, an expression of dismay on her face. 'So she knows that I'm here?' she said. 'My Amy knows?'

Now it was Freddie's turn to speak, but her vocal chords seemed to have become paralysed. Unseen by Mrs Dale, June prodded her sharply in the back and, rather hoarsely, Freddie said, 'Yes, Gran. I know. And I insisted that June brought me to meet you.'

'Amy?' said Mrs Dale, her pale blue eyes opening wide. 'Amy, is it really you?'

Freddie nodded and June, smiling to herself in quiet satisfaction, said softly, 'I'm sure that the two of you must have a lot to talk about, so I'll go and leave you to it. Amy, I'll see you back at school in time for tea. Don't be late!'

Mrs Dale, still looking hard at Freddie, didn't seem to hear June, but Freddie did and stared at her in horror. This wasn't part of the plan! June had promised that she would stay and that she, Freddie, would not be left alone with Mrs Dale.

'June, wait!' she cried. But it was too late – June was already out of the door, and Mrs Dale was telling Freddie to sit herself down and she would make them both a nice cup of tea. Freddie had no choice but to do as she was told, though inwardly she was seething. Just wait until she caught up with June later!

June, for her part, was extremely pleased with herself and whistled jauntily as she made her way back to the school. Everything had gone just as she had hoped! Of course, Freddie would be simply furious with her, but June excelled at talking herself out of trouble and she would soon smooth things over.

But when the two girls met up outside the dining-room just before tea, Freddie seemed to have got over her ill temper. In fact, much to her own surprise, she had had an absolutely splendid time at Mrs Dale's! Freddie had no grandmother of her own, for both of hers had died when she was little, and she had often felt envious of other girls when they talked about their own devoted grandmothers, and how they spoiled them. So spending time with Mrs Dale had been a novel experience for the girl, and a very enjoyable one. Once Freddie had got over her nerves a little, the two of them had got along like a house on fire. Of course, Freddie hadn't been able to relax completely, for she had to guard her tongue so that she didn't give the game away. Even so, she had been delighted when Mrs Dale invited her to tea the following day.

'I know it's not what your father would like,' the old lady had said. 'I didn't set out to make you go against his wishes, but it's done now. We've met and there's nothing he can do about it. All the same, though, I don't think you should mention it to him just yet. Or your mother, for that matter.'

Freddie related all of this to June in a low voice as they had their tea, and June listened intently, pleased when the girl said that she was going to Mrs Dale's again tomorrow. The more the two saw of one another, the better, as far as June was concerned. Ah, Freddie might be enjoying herself now, but it wouldn't be long before her conscience began to prick her.

Meanwhile, June had a plan of her own to carry out – one that Freddie did not play a part in. Ever since Freddie had tricked Mam'zelle with the magic soap, June had been trying to think up a trick of her own – and this time she was determined that the glory would be hers and hers alone. And now she had come up with something which would put Freddie's effort in the shade. The victim, yet again, was to be poor, unsuspecting Mam'zelle Dupont, of course, and June smiled to herself as she pictured the reaction that her trick would get.

At the back of the third form's classroom, right behind June's seat, was a door into a small storage room. The room was home to old books, long-lost property and all kinds of odds and ends that nobody really wanted, and it was kept permanently locked. But June had discovered that the key hung on a nail in the handyman's little cubby-hole and, her ingenious brain getting to work, she had come up with a first-rate plan for baffling Mam'zelle.

That evening, as the third formers prepared for bed, Amy picked up a pot of cream from her cabinet and removed the lid. The girl was extremely vain about her complexion and possessed a marvellous array of lotions and potions. She was forever smearing something or other on to her face and the others often teased her about it.

'What do all these creams actually *do*, Amy?' asked Felicity, watching her in fascination.

'This one is a vanishing cream,' answered Amy, peering into the mirror.

'Well, it doesn't work,' called out June. 'We can still see you!'

'Oh, very funny, June,' said Amy. 'Actually, it's supposed to make spots and blemishes vanish. And now I've just used the last of it, so I'll have to ask Mummy to send me some more.'

She threw the empty pot into the wastepaper basket, and June gazed at it thoughtfully for a moment. Then she went and retrieved it from the basket, asking, 'Amy, is it all right if I have this?'

'If you really want an empty pot,' answered Amy, looking surprised. 'Though I can't imagine what use you have for it.'

'Oh, I have a use for it all right,' said June, grinning. 'Just you wait and see!'

June decided to play her trick on Monday morning, and took the others into her confidence the night before, when they were all gathered in the common-room. The third formers listened raptly as June explained what she intended to do, their eyes lighting up and broad grins on their faces. Even Veronica was looking forward to it, for she was no scholar, particularly when it came to French, and always felt in low spirits on Monday mornings, with the weekend over and a whole week of lessons ahead of her. Strangely enough, the only person who didn't seem thrilled at the idea was Freddie, who was unusually quiet and pre-occupied.

'Anything wrong, old girl?' Felicity asked in concern, noticing that the girl didn't seem her usual self.

'Mm? Oh, no, everything's fine, Felicity,' answered Freddie rather distractedly. 'I'm just a little tired, that's all.'

'Of course, you were out in the fresh air all afternoon, weren't you?' said Susan. 'Where did you get to?'

June quickly shot Freddie a warning glance, but it was quite unnecessary. She had no intention of saying anything that might alert the others to the fact that she had been to Mrs Dale's. Instead she replied vaguely, 'Oh, I just took a long walk along the coast road and the sea air has really made me feel sleepy.'

Felicity looked at her closely and frowned. Freddie didn't look tired – she looked as if she was worried about something. June was watching her friend too – but she knew exactly what was bothering her! Freddie had hardly touched a thing at teatime. Of course, that could have been because she had already eaten at Mrs Dale's earlier, but it didn't explain her rather subdued air. June had managed to snatch a few minutes alone with Freddie before prep and the girl said in a worried tone, 'June, I really didn't think this through properly when I agreed to pretend to be Amy. How am I going to get out of it? I can't go *on* pretending to be her all the time I'm at Malory Towers.'

'It's easy enough,' said June with a careless shrug. 'Just keep it up for a little while longer, then you can pretend that your parents – or rather *Amy's* parents – are sending you to a different school, far away from here.'

'I suppose I could do that,' sighed Freddie. 'But I feel so dreadful about deceiving her! She's such a dear old lady.'

'Yes, but you're deceiving her for the best of reasons,' said June persuasively. 'Mrs Dale was awfully lonely, and now she's not. She's happy because she's got your visits to look forward to. That's good, isn't it?'

Freddie agreed, but without much conviction, and June smiled to herself. Poor Freddie had so much on her mind that she was in no mood for jokes and tricks. Everything was working out just as she had hoped!

The third formers had a lot to look forward to, for as well as June's trick, the following weekend was half-term.

'Are your parents coming, Bonnie?' asked Amy.

'Oh, yes,' answered Bonnie, who was putting the finishing touches to a skirt she had made. 'Mummy's simply dying to see the school – and me, of course.'

As Amy watched Bonnie expertly finish a hem, her needle flying in and out, she said admiringly, 'How clever you are with your needle, Bonnie. I do wish that you would make something for me.'

Bonnie smiled angelically at the girl and said sweetly, 'I will. If you will do something for me in return.'

Amy, who was used to people agreeing to whatever she asked immediately, and was unaccustomed to bargaining, looked a little taken aback and asked, 'What is it you want me to do?'

Bonnie folded the skirt she had been working on neatly, and laid it to one side, before saying, 'Well, as you're no doubt aware, I'm not very good at French. It doesn't much matter when Mam'zelle Dupont takes us, because I can easily get round her. But Mam'zelle Rougier – well, I haven't worked out how to make her like me yet.'

'Mam'zelle Rougier always dislikes the girls who Mam'zelle Dupont likes,' said Amy. 'Veronica told me so. You'll *never* get her to like you.'

'Oh, I shall,' said Bonnie, with quiet certainty. 'I can always make adults like me. It's just that it takes longer to get round some than others. And in the meantime, Mam'zelle Rougier is being simply beastly to me. She returned all that work I did in prep the other night – pages and pages of it – and expects me to redo it all and hand it in to her at the end of the week. I simply can't do it.'

'So, you want me to help you with your French, and you'll make me a dress, is that it?' said Amy.

Bonnie nodded. 'If you will do that for me, we can pop into town one lunchtime and choose a pattern and some material.'

As Amy found French easy, she agreed to this readily and both girls were happy. Someone who was not happy with this arrangement, however, was Veronica. It seemed that Amy and Bonnie were growing closer, while she, Veronica, was being pushed out. She would have to put her thinking cap on, and try and find a way of getting rid of Bonnie. And she had something else on her mind, too. With half-term almost upon them, Veronica needed to come up with a plan to keep her parents away so that she might spend the day with Amy and her people. Veronica frowned. How could a term that had started so promisingly have gone so wrong?

Vanishing cream

There was a great deal of giggling and excited chatter as the third formers took their places in class the next morning and eagerly awaited the arrival of Mam'zelle Dupont.

'My word, this is going to be super!' chuckled Pam.

'Isn't it just!' said Felicity, with a grin. 'June, have you got everything ready?'

In answer, June held up the empty vanishing-cream pot Amy had given her, and the key to the little storage room. She had sneaked into the handyman's room earlier, while he was out, and taken it from the nail on the wall. With luck, she would have it back there before he even noticed it was missing!

But luck was against June that morning. For the mistress who swept into the room was not plump little Mam'zelle Dupont, but Mam'zelle Rougier! The girls looked at one another in dismay, and murmurs of disappointment rippled round the room.

'What a shame!' Susan whispered to June. 'You won't be able to play the trick now.'

June glanced at the stern face of Mam'zelle Rougier. She hated the idea of all her careful planning being in vain. What was more, if she went ahead now, she would have the distinction of being the only girl in the school ever to have the nerve to play a trick on Mam'zelle Rougier, and that thought appealed to her enormously! She would probably be punished for it, but it would be worth it. She winked at Susan and whispered back, 'Just watch me!'

The word went round, murmured from girl to girl.

'The trick is still on! June's going to play it on Mam'zelle Rougier!'

'You have to admire her nerve.'

'She's sure to be punished, but June won't care. I don't think she's afraid of anything!'

'June is the most daring girl in the school – even more daring than her cousin Alicia was. And her tricks are simply splendid!'

June overheard the whispered remarks and revelled in them. No other girl could hold a candle to her when it came to playing tricks – not even Freddie.

Mam'zelle Rougier also heard the whispers – though fortunately she didn't catch what was being said – and her lips tightened into a thin line as she rapped sharply on the desk with a ruler, making everyone jump.

'*Taisez-vous!*' she commanded, in her rather harsh voice. 'Now, Mam'zelle Dupont has been awake all night with the toothache, and has gone to the dentist. So I shall be taking your French class this morning.'

Her sharp eyes swept round the classroom. She looked tired and irritable, which indeed she was, for her bedroom was next to Mam'zelle Dupont's and the other French mistress had kept her awake most of the night with her moans and groans. Mam'zelle Rougier put a hand across her mouth to hide a yawn, then said, 'Bonnie!'

'Yes, Mam'zelle?' said Bonnie politely.

'Bring to me the prep which I gave you back,' said Mam'zelle Rougier. 'And let us hope that you have managed to get *some* of it correct this time! The rest of you, turn to page 21 in your French grammar books and begin reading, *s'il vous plait.*'

Bonnie picked up her French book, into which she had carefully copied Amy's work, and stood up. She glanced round briefly at June, who winked, then went up to the mistress's desk and stood in front of it, so that Mam'zelle Rougier's view of the class was obscured.

Then June slipped from her seat and into the little storage room, which she had unlocked earlier.

At last Mam'zelle Rougier finished checking Bonnie's work, remarking grudgingly, 'A much better effort, Bonnie. Please return to your seat.'

The little girl skipped back to her place and Mam'zelle Rougier got to her feet, saying, 'Now, let us –'

Then she stopped, frowning, and said sharply, 'Where is June?'

'I'm here, Mam'zelle Rougier,' came June's disembodied voice.

'*Tiens!*' cried the French mistress. 'June, are you hiding under your desk? I demand that you come out at once!'

'I'm not *under* my desk, Mam'zelle,' said June from the storage room. 'I'm *at* my desk. Can't you see me?'

Nora, who was very good at acting, raised her hand and

said in a scared voice, 'Mam'zelle Rougier, June seems to have become invisible!'

The French mistress gave a snort of disbelief and snapped, 'What nonsense is this? June, I command you to show yourself.'

'But Mam'zelle, I'm here!' said June rather plaintively.

Most of the girls were struggling not to laugh by this time and, had the victim of the prank been Mam'zelle Dupont, they would have been in fits of giggles. But it was decidedly dangerous to laugh at the bad-tempered Mam'zelle Rougier, who was growing angrier by the second, so they did their best to control themselves.

The French mistress stalked to the back of the class, a frown on her face, and passed her hand over June's chair, before bending over and peering under the desk. This was too much for Susan, who gave a choke of laughter, which she hastily turned into a cough. Then Mam'zelle spotted the empty pot of vanishing cream that June had left on her desk, and picked it up.

'*Tiens!* What is this?' she asked.

Freddie, who, in spite of her worries, was thoroughly enjoying the trick, said, 'It's June's vanishing cream, Mam'zelle Rougier. Oh, I say! What if she's used too much and vanished for good!'

'Vanishing cream? Pah, what nonsense!' said the French mistress. All the same, she did look rather alarmed when she took the lid from the pot and saw that it was empty.

'She's used it all!' said Nora, sounding horrified. 'Mam'zelle Rougier, what are we to do?'

'Yes, what if she doesn't come back and stays invisible forever?' put in Pam.

'I will not have girls vanishing into thin air in my lesson!' cried Mam'zelle Rougier. Several of the listening girls found this so funny that they had to stuff handkerchiefs into their mouths to stifle their laughter.

'I shall go and inform Miss Grayling at once that June has disappeared,' said Mam'zelle Rougier, turning sharply and walking towards the door. As soon as her back was turned, June quietly sneaked from her hiding-place and back into her seat.

'Mam'zelle Rougier!' cried Felicity. 'She's back! June is visible again! There's no need for you to go to Miss Grayling.'

The French mistress looked round and gave a start as she saw the wicked June, sitting at her desk as large as life.

'June!' she cried. 'How dare you leave the classroom in the middle of a lesson.'

'But Mam'zelle, I didn't leave,' protested June. 'I was here all the time.'

'That's true, Mam'zelle,' said Julie. 'We all heard her voice.'

'Yes, but I do not wish to hear *your* voice, *ma chère* Julie!' said Mam'zelle Rougier, who was working herself up into a fine rage. 'June, I am not so easy to fool as Mam'zelle Dupont! I know that a trick has been played, and when I find out how you have made yourself vanish and then reappear I shall punish you!'

With that, Mam'zelle Rougier stalked back to the

blackboard, her heels click-clacking on the floor. And June, as fast as lightning, darted from her seat and back into the storage room. Mam'zelle Rougier turned to face the class, and gave a shriek, pressing her hands to her cheeks. '*Mon Dieu!* The troublesome girl has vanished again!'

'Sorry, Mam'zelle.' Once more June's voice could be heard from thin air. 'But I really can't help it.'

Well, the girls were quite helpless with laughter by this time, and past caring about any punishment that Mam'zelle Rougier might dish out. This was such an excellent trick that it would be well worth it! Tears rolled down Felicity's cheeks, while Susan was doubled up. Even Veronica was laughing uproariously!

'Silence!' shouted Mam'zelle Rougier, stamping her foot so hard that a strand of hair came down from the bun she wore at the back of her head. 'I will not tolerate this behaviour, *méchantes filles!* You will all write me fifty lines tonight!'

This sobered the third formers a little and their laughter died away. But just then the door of the classroom opened, and Mam'zelle Dupont appeared in the doorway. The relief of having her aching tooth removed had put the little French mistress in an excellent mood, and she beamed round at the girls.

'*Bonjour, mes petites! Bonjour*, Mam'zelle Rougier! I must thank you for taking my class while I was away, for I know that you, too, had a restless night and must be tired. Ah, my tooth, how it ached! But now it is all gone.'

'That is not all that is gone, Mam'zelle Dupont!' said

Mam'zelle Rougier dramatically. 'You will step outside with me, please, for I have a strange tale to tell.'

As soon as the two French mistresses had left the room, June emerged from the little room once more, this time locking the door behind her and slipping the key into her pocket.

'My word, June, that was a super trick!' exclaimed Nora, as June sat down behind her desk. 'But Mam'zelle Rougier is simply furious!'

'Yes, I'm afraid that you're going to get into awful trouble, June,' said Felicity.

'No, I'm not,' said June, grinning wickedly. 'An idea came to me when I heard Mam'zelle Dupont say that Mam'zelle Rougier had suffered a restless night. I think I can get us all off doing lines as well. Freddie, take that empty pot and throw it out of the window into the bushes. Now, listen, everyone – this is what we're going to do . . .'

Moments later, the two French mistresses returned, and Mam'zelle Rougier was most astonished to see June, looking the picture of goodness, with her head bent over her book.

'Ah! See, Mam'zelle Dupont!' she cried, clutching at the other French mistress's arm with one hand, and pointing at June with the other.

'Yes, I see June, sitting at her desk and working hard at her French,' said Mam'zelle Dupont, eyeing Mam'zelle Rougier with concern. The tale that she had related had been quite astonishing, and Mam'zelle Dupont was rather worried about her countrywoman's state of mind. Girls did not vanish and re-appear at random – it was quite impossible!

The other third formers appeared to be concentrating hard on their work too, the dear, good girls, and surely this would not be so if something was amiss with one of their friends.

'June, you have come back!' cried Mam'zelle Rougier.

'Come back?' repeated June, with a puzzled frown. 'But, Mam'zelle, I haven't been away.'

'Ah, but yes, you vanished!' said Mam'zelle Rougier. 'You put the vanishing cream on and you disappeared. The other girls, they saw you turn invisible – is it not so, girls?'

The third formers looked at one another in bewilderment and Felicity said, 'Mam'zelle Rougier, June has been here all the time.'

'Vanishing cream?' said Julie with a puzzled frown. 'What vanishing cream, Mam'zelle?'

'Ah, you are bad girls, all of you!' cried Mam'zelle Rougier, marching over to June's desk. 'You are all trying to trick me. June, where is the vanishing cream? Open your desk at once.'

June obeyed, but there was nothing to be seen in the desk but books, pens and pencils.

'You have hidden it in your satchel, then!' said Mam'zelle Rougier, quite beside herself. 'I demand to search it!'

So June handed over her satchel but, of course, the pot of vanishing cream was not in there either. Poor Mam'zelle Rougier did not know what to think! Were the girls playing an elaborate joke on her, or was she going quite mad?

At last June said kindly, 'I think I know what has happened. You must have been dreaming, Mam'zelle.'

'June, please do not speak rubbish to me!' said the French mistress scornfully. 'How is it possible for me to dream when I am wide awake?'

Once more the girls looked at one another and Felicity said solemnly, 'You fell asleep at your desk, Mam'zelle Rougier. It was right after Bonnie brought her book to you.'

'Never have I fallen asleep in a class!' said Mam'zelle Rougier, looking mortified.

'But you did, Mam'zelle,' said Susan. 'We wouldn't have said anything about it if you hadn't started talking about June vanishing.'

'Ah, this is my fault!' cried Mam'zelle Dupont. 'For it was I who kept you awake last night, Mam'zelle Rougier. It is no wonder that you fall asleep at your desk! Now, you must go back to bed for the rest of the morning, and catch up on your sleep. I shall take your next class and all will be well.'

So Mam'zelle Rougier, now convinced that the whole episode had been a strange dream, went quietly from the room.

'And the best of it is that she thinks the lines she gave us were part of the dream too!' laughed Nora. 'Well done, June.'

'Yes, that was a splendid trick,' said Freddie, taking June's arm. 'It quite took me out of myself for a while. And no one else could have carried it off like you, June. I take my hat off to you!'

Somehow, word spread around the school that June had successfully tricked Mam'zelle Rougier. Even the sixth form got to hear about it, and Amanda Chartelow came up to June with a broad grin on her face. 'Don't forget you've got lacrosse practice this afternoon,' she said. 'We don't want you doing one of your vanishing acts!'

Bonnie also took advantage of June's trick to get on the right side of Mam'zelle Rougier. She picked a huge bunch of late-blooming flowers from the garden and took them to the French mistress later that day.

'Oh, Mam'zelle Rougier, I've been so worried about you!' she said in her soft voice. 'I often used to have trouble sleeping when I was ill, and I know how tired it makes you the next day.'

Surprised and rather touched, Mam'zelle Rougier took the flowers from Bonnie, saying, 'Thank you, *ma chère*. This is indeed most kind of you.'

Bonnie smiled her most charming smile at the mistress and went on her way. And from that day on, Mam'zelle Rougier remembered the girl's thoughtfulness and was much kinder to her in class.

'So there's only Miss Peters who you haven't managed to charm,' said Nora in the common-room one evening. 'And she's a really tough nut to crack. You'll never succeed with her, Bonnie.'

'I bet you a stick of toffee I will,' said Bonnie at once.

'You're on!' said Nora. 'If you haven't managed to wrap Miss Peters round your little finger by the end of term that's a stick of toffee you owe me!'

Half-term

Half-term arrived at last, and there was great excitement throughout the school. Even sleepyheads like Nora and Amy leaped out of bed early, looking forward to the day with eager anticipation. Felicity was simply dying to see her mother and father, while Bonnie couldn't wait to be spoiled by her doting parents once more. And Amy was looking forward to showing off her good-looking father and beautiful mother to the others. Only Veronica looked forward to the day with mixed feelings, for try as she might, she had been quite unable to think of a way to put her parents off coming for half-term. It wasn't that she didn't love her mother and father, for she did. But she didn't feel that they were quite good enough for her – and they certainly weren't good enough to meet Amy's people!

As it turned out, fate took a hand and, just as the first parents were arriving, Veronica was called to Miss Grayling's office.

'Veronica, I'm afraid I have some disappointing news for you,' said the Head, after she had greeted the girl. 'Your father telephoned me earlier, and I'm afraid that he and your mother won't be able to come today. You see, your mother has flu and, although they were hoping that she would feel well enough to travel today, she is still quite ill.'

'I see,' said Veronica, beginning to feel a little guilty. She had wanted something to happen to stop her parents coming, but she certainly hadn't wished for her mother to be ill! 'Mother will be all right, won't she?' she asked the Head a little anxiously.

'Of course, my dear,' said Miss Grayling kindly. 'She just needs plenty of rest at the moment, and I daresay she will be as right as rain in a few days. Now off you go and join the others – and try to enjoy half-term as best you can.'

Reassured that her mother wasn't seriously ill, Veronica made up her mind to do just that! Amy was sure to invite her to go along with her people, and Veronica would be at pains to impress them. Perhaps they might even invite her to stay with them during the holidays!

Bonnie was in for a disappointment too, for she received a message to say that her parents' car had broken down, and they had to wait for it to be fixed, so they wouldn't arrive at Malory Towers until tomorrow.

'Well, at least you'll have *one* day with them,' said Felicity, seeing the girl's unhappy face. 'That's better than nothing. Cheer up, Bonnie!'

'I do feel sorry for her,' Felicity confided to Susan, as the girl walked away. 'But at the same time, I hope Mother doesn't ask her to join us. Does that sound awfully selfish?'

'Of course not,' said Susan loyally. 'It's quite understandable that you want to have your parents to yourself at half-term. I know that I wouldn't want to share mine with Bonnie!'

'I say!' called out Pam, who was stationed at the dormitory window. 'There are some more cars coming up the drive. My word, just look at that Rolls Royce!'

'Why, that must belong to my people!' cried Amy, almost knocking Julie over in her eagerness to get to the window. 'Yes, it's them! I must go down and greet them.'

'Felicity, I think your parents are here too,' said Pam. 'And mine are right behind them – whoopee! Come on, let's go down.'

Soon the grounds were thronged with laughing, chattering girls and their families. As she chatted happily with her parents, Felicity saw Julie, with her mother and older brother, both of them red-haired and freckled, like Julie herself. Then she spotted Pam, walking arm-in-arm with her parents, and June, sharing a joke with one of her brothers. And over there, talking to Mam'zelle Rougier, was Amy, with her mother. Felicity couldn't help glancing at Mrs Ryder-Cochrane curiously. She was every bit as lovely as she appeared in her photograph, but the cat-like green eyes gave her rather a sly look, and Felicity decided that she didn't like her very much. Susan's big, jovial father was standing nearby, and Felicity saw, with a shock, that the man he was having a conversation with was Mr Ryder-Cochrane. And Amy's father didn't fit with the image that Felicity had built up in her mind at all! He was a most distinguished man, and at the moment he looked very relaxed and carefree, and was laughing heartily at something that Susan's father had said. Nothing could have been further from the cold, snobbish man that

Felicity had been imagining. Amy's father must be a very good actor indeed! Just then Mr Ryder-Cochrane caught her looking at him and grinned. But Felicity, thinking suddenly of Mrs Dale, and of how lonely and unhappy she was because of this man, could only manage a tight, polite little smile in return, before she turned away.

Freddie, too, had noticed Amy's parents, but she could barely bring herself to look at them, for she felt intensely angry with the couple. If it wasn't for Mr Ryder-Cochrane's stupid, stuck-up attitude and Mrs Ryder-Cochrane's weakness in not standing up to her husband, she wouldn't be in the uncomfortable situation she was in now!

At Mrs Dale's request, Freddie had visited her yesterday afternoon, and had left feeling guiltier than ever. The visit had been highly enjoyable to start with, and Freddie and Mrs Dale had chatted about all kinds of things. But then the old lady had begun recounting bits of family history, and had brought out some photographs of Amy's mother as a child, and Freddie had felt most uncomfortable – almost as if she was stealing a bit of Amy's life. Now, she was delighted to be with her own loving, sensible parents, and hugged them extra hard. She was determined not to let her guilt cast a shadow over the day, and to enjoy herself, but it was very difficult. How she wished that she could confide in her mother and father about Mrs Dale, but that was impossible of course. They would be so terribly disappointed in her!

As the day went on, Bonnie and Veronica, being the only two in the third form whose parents hadn't come, found themselves thrown together, which pleased neither of them! Big-hearted Mam'zelle Dupont, seeing them hovering on the edge of the crowd, bore down on them and said sympathetically, 'Ah, *les pauvres petites*! Do not be sad while all the others are out with their so-dear parents. We will have a splendid lunch in the school dining-room, and the two of you will sit with me, *n'est-ce pas*?'

Veronica nodded politely and Bonnie smiled her sweet smile, but both of them were hoping to be invited out to lunch. Bonnie had already dropped broad hints to Felicity and her parents, but Mr and Mrs Rivers, obedient to the silent message in Felicity's eyes, had steadfastly ignored them. So both girls' hopes now centred on Amy, who was coming towards them with her parents.

Amy introduced her parents to the two girls and, while Mrs Ryder-Cochrane greeted Bonnie, her husband turned to Veronica and attempted to make polite conversation. But alas for Veronica, Amy's father seemed so very grand that she became quite tongue-tied, unable to mutter anything but 'yes' or 'no' in answer to his questions. Bonnie, however, was determined to make a hit with the couple, and she looked at Amy's mother with undisguised admiration, complimenting her on her expensive dress and perfectly groomed hair. Mrs Ryder-Cochrane, who had been looking a little bored, thawed visibly and decided that Bonnie was rather a dear little thing.

'Bonnie is the girl I wrote to you about, Mummy,' said Amy. 'The one who makes such beautiful clothes.'

Veronica listened to this rather glumly. It seemed that

she hadn't been mentioned in Amy's letters home at all. And she didn't like the way that Mrs Ryder-Cochrane seemed to have taken to Bonnie. She tapped the smaller girl on the shoulder and said, 'It's almost lunchtime, Bonnie. We'd better go and get ready.'

'Of course,' said Bonnie, managing to make her smile both brave and pathetic. 'Oh, *how* I wish that *my* mother and father were here to take me out to a restaurant. Still, I'm quite sure that the school lunch will be delicious. Come along, Veronica.'

As the two girls walked off towards the school, Mrs Ryder-Cochrane said in a low voice to Amy, 'Why don't you ask little Bonnie to come out with us, darling? She seems such a sweet girl.'

'Oh, Mummy, can I?' said Amy, her eyes lighting up. She always enjoyed basking in her beautiful mother's reflected glory, and had been thrilled by how impressed with her Bonnie had seemed. 'I'll go and tell her now.'

'What about the other girl?' said Mr Ryder-Cochrane. 'It seems a bit mean to leave her behind. Amy, you had better invite her too.'

But Amy was already speeding off after Bonnie, and didn't hear what her father had said.

'Bonnie!' she cried, catching up with the two girls. 'Mummy says that you're to come out to lunch with us. You'd better let Miss Peters know, or she might think you've gone missing, but do hurry up.'

Then she dashed back to her parents, while Bonnie went off in search of Miss Peters. Veronica was left alone, looking very forlorn, and Felicity, who was in earshot, felt sorry for her. 'Really,' she thought indignantly. 'Amy might have asked Veronica along too!'

Something about the slump of the girl's shoulders as she turned away went straight to Felicity's heart and she made an impulsive decision. Without giving herself time to think about whether she would regret it later, Felicity ran over to Veronica and grabbed her arm, saying, 'Veronica, go and get ready – you're coming out with me and my people!'

For a moment Veronica thought that she had misheard Felicity, and she could only stand staring at her blankly. Felicity gave her a little shake and said, 'You do want to come, don't you? It's nothing grand, just a picnic lunch and a walk along the beach, but it's better than being here on your own.'

Veronica found her voice at last, stammering out her thanks, but Felicity cut her short, saying, 'Never mind that! Go and fetch your coat, while I run and let Miss Peters know what's happening. I'll meet you back here in five minutes!'

If Mr and Mrs Rivers were a little surprised to find that Felicity had invited a strange girl to share their picnic, they were far too well-mannered to betray it, and did their utmost to make Veronica feel welcome.

As they were getting into the car, Amy, her parents and Bonnie drove past, the two girls looking most surprised to see Felicity and Veronica together.

'How odd!' remarked Amy. 'I always thought that Veronica couldn't bear Felicity.'

'And I thought that Felicity couldn't bear Veronica,' said Bonnie, who felt quite jealous at seeing the two girls together. Why on earth had Felicity asked Veronica out instead of her, Bonnie? The girl brooded on it during the drive to the restaurant. Perhaps she had been spending too much time with Amy and neglecting Felicity. Although it had been Felicity's idea for her to make friends with Amy in the first place, so she ought to understand. But Bonnie had, in her own way, become quite fond of Amy as their friendship grew, and she certainly enjoyed her company. Maybe Felicity had sensed this, and had gone off with Veronica to get back at Bonnie. Yes, that was the only sensible explanation, for Felicity couldn't possibly *like* Veronica! Bonnie made up her mind that she would devote more time to Felicity when they got back to school, and show her that their friendship was still important to her.

Felicity, meanwhile, mercifully unaware of Bonnie's intentions, was having a simply marvellous time. And so, for a wonder, was Veronica. The girl had been a little stiff and shy with Mr and Mrs Rivers at first, but they were such a charming couple that this very soon wore off. She took a particular liking to Mrs Rivers, whose warm, friendly manner put her very much in mind of her own mother. As she walked along the beach beside Mrs Rivers, watching Felicity and Mr Rivers looking for shells a little way in front, a pang of conscience smote Veronica. How *could* she have been so stupid and wicked as to wish that her parents wouldn't be able to come today? Well, she had got her wish and now she had an overwhelming desire to see her mother, and speak to her. Her father too. She gave a sigh and Mrs Rivers asked kindly, 'Is anything wrong, dear?'

'I was just thinking about my parents,' said Veronica with a rather wobbly smile. 'And hoping that my mother isn't feeling too poorly.'

'Poor child,' said Felicity's mother, taking her hand. Then an idea occurred to her. 'Why don't you ask Miss Grayling if you can use her telephone to call them tonight? I'm sure that she wouldn't mind, under the circumstances. And you'll sleep better tonight after you've had a little chat with your parents, knowing that your mother is being looked after.'

Veronica brightened at once and said, 'Oh, that would be simply marvellous. Do you really think the Head would let me?'

'Well, if you like, Veronica, I will come along to Miss Grayling's office with you when we get back to Malory Towers,' offered Mrs Rivers. 'I am quite sure that she won't refuse.'

'Thank you, Mrs Rivers,' said Veronica simply. 'You have been so kind to me today.'

Veronica went up to Felicity in the dormitory that evening and thanked her too.

'It was jolly decent of you to invite me,' she said. 'I had a wonderful time – and I think you're very lucky to have such super parents.'

'I think I am too,' said Felicity with a smile, marvelling at the change in Veronica. Mrs Rivers had stuck to her word and asked Miss Grayling if the girl might telephone her parents. The Head had agreed at once, of course, and Veronica had felt much easier in her mind after talking to her father, and learning that her mother was feeling a little better. She had come into the common-room afterwards with a beaming smile on her face, and the third formers had looked at her in surprise.

'I've seen a different side to Veronica today,' Felicity had said to Susan. 'She seemed much – oh, I don't know – much softer and more humble somehow.'

June, sitting nearby, had given a scornful snort and said, 'Don't let her fool you, Felicity. You're too soft-hearted for your own good!'

'So you keep telling me!' said Felicity, nettled. 'But I think that only a *hard*-hearted person could have failed to feel sorry for Veronica today. It must have been dreadful for her being alone, when most of us had our people here.'

'She's putting on an act to gain sympathy,' scoffed June. 'Of course, what she *really* wanted was *Amy*'s sympathy – and lunch in a fancy restaurant. But that didn't work, so she had to fall back on you, Felicity. Veronica will be back to her old self again before long, you mark my words!'

'Perhaps the two of you should agree to disagree,' said the sensible, steady Susan, looking from Felicity's troubled little face to June's mocking one. 'Come on now – it's been a super day. Let's not spoil it with a silly argument.'

'Dear Susan!' said June with a laugh. 'Always pouring oil on troubled waters. No, don't glare at me like that, Felicity, for I have no intention of arguing with you. As Susan has so sensibly suggested, we'll agree to disagree.'

And the matter was left there, though Felicity still felt a little cross with June. The trouble was, she thought, June was always so sure of herself that she made those less confident – like Felicity – doubt their own opinions! So when Veronica came over in the dormitory and thanked her, Felicity felt heartened.

But the next day, Sunday, saw Veronica at Amy's side again. Bonnie's parents arrived to take her out, so Amy graciously invited Veronica to spend the day with her and her parents.

Felicity, unaware of this invitation, sought out Veronica and said generously, 'You know, Veronica, you're most welcome to come with me and my people again today.'

'That's awfully kind of you, Felicity,' said Veronica, blushing and looking a little awkward. 'But, you see, Amy has already invited me to spend the day with her and I've accepted.'

'Oh, well, that's up to you, of course,' said Felicity, with a careless shrug. Inwardly, though, she wondered how Veronica could have such little pride that she tagged along with Amy after the girl had so callously abandoned her yesterday.

Still, it was none of her business really, and it would be nice to have her parents all to herself. All the same, she hoped that June wasn't going to be proved right about Veronica. She was far too cocksure as it was!

Trouble in the third form

'Everything seems so flat after half-term,' complained Nora, as the third formers stood in the courtyard one break-time. 'I need cheering up! June, can't you play another trick?'

'No, you've had two this term already,' answered June. 'I don't want to spoil you. Besides, if we play too many tricks they just end up becoming commonplace and people don't appreciate them as they should.'

'Spoilsport!' said Nora, pulling a face. 'How about you then, Freddie? Can't you come up with something to give us all a laugh?'

But Freddie, who seemed to be in a world of her own, hadn't been listening to the conversation and didn't even realise that Nora was addressing her until June gave her a nudge.

'Sorry, Nora,' said Freddie, sounding distracted. 'What did you say?'

Nora repeated her request, but Freddie shook her head and said ruefully, 'I don't seem to be able to come up with any jokes or tricks at the moment, I'm afraid.'

Felicity frowned at this. Freddie's sense of fun certainly seemed to have deserted her lately. She said as much to

Susan, when the two of them were alone in the common-room later.

'She doesn't seem like her old, jolly self,' Susan agreed. 'Perhaps she's finding it a bit of a strain to keep up with June, who can do brilliantly at lessons *and* play the fool. But Freddie isn't quite as clever as June, and she needs to concentrate more in class to get good results.'

'Yes, you're probably right,' said Felicity, her brow clearing. 'Darrell used to say that Alicia was just the same. Let's hope that's all it is, anyway.'

'I saw you talking to Bonnie earlier,' said Susan, changing the subject. 'She seems to be hanging round you more and more since half-term.'

'Yes, I *had* noticed,' said Felicity wearily. 'She keeps trying to persuade me to make up a three with her and Amy, and no matter how often I refuse, she always comes back. I must say, for someone so dainty and fragile-looking, she's awfully thick-skinned!'

'Well, thank goodness we managed to get her to spend some time with Amy,' said Susan. 'Otherwise I should *never* have you to myself.'

'Yes, that little scheme worked a treat,' said Felicity. 'Though I don't suppose Bonnie would be too pleased if she knew that I had only suggested she try to split Amy and Veronica up because we didn't want her tagging along with us all the time! And Veronica would be simply furious too.'

'Well, thank goodness neither of them *will* find out,' said Susan complacently.

But she was quite wrong. For at that very moment, Veronica was standing on the other side of the common-room door! As usual, she hadn't *meant* to listen, and had only been on her way to the common-room to collect something. But on hearing voices, the urge to listen in had been too much. And now her feelings were very mixed. On the one hand, the knowledge that Bonnie had only befriended Amy as a favour to Felicity would be very useful indeed. But she also felt hurt and angry that Felicity had set Bonnie to work to break up her own friendship with Amy. Since half-term her feelings towards Felicity had softened a great deal, but now the old feelings of bitterness and resentment came flooding back. Just who did Felicity Rivers think she was? Well, she was in for a shock – and so was silly little Bonnie!

Bonnie grew quite exasperated with Veronica over the next couple of days. The girl kept giving her strange looks, and odd, triumphant little smiles that Bonnie was quite at a loss to understand. Veronica, typically, was enjoying savouring her new-found knowledge and keeping it to herself, until the moment was right to break the news to Amy. And the moment came after art lesson one afternoon.

Miss Linnie, the art mistress, was very good-natured and easy-going, and the girls were allowed to sit where they pleased in her class. Amy took a seat by the window, and both Veronica and Bonnie moved towards the empty seat beside her. Bonnie reached it first and sat down, much to Veronica's annoyance.

'I always sit next to Amy!' she protested.

'Well, it will be a pleasant change for her to have me beside her instead,' said Bonnie softly, looking up at Veronica with the innocent stare that always infuriated her. 'Off you go, Veronica.'

But Veronica wasn't giving up without a fight, and she said through gritted teeth, 'I'm not going anywhere, you little beast. Move at once!'

Amy, who loved to have people fighting over her favours, took no part in the quarrel, but stared rather smugly out of the window. It was left to Miss Linnie to intervene, saying calmly but firmly, 'That will do, girls! Veronica, there is a seat over there next to Julie. Please go and sit there.'

Veronica did not dare disobey the mistress, and reluctantly moved away to sit next to Julie, leaving Bonnie to enjoy her victory.

Miss Linnie's classes were always very free and easy, and the girls chattered away to one another as they worked. Veronica scowled as she watched Amy and Bonnie, their heads together as they talked and laughed. Well, Bonnie would be laughing on the other side of her face very soon!

After the art lesson finished, Veronica caught up with Amy and Bonnie outside.

'I do so love Miss Linnie's classes, don't you?' said Bonnie sweetly. 'Amy and I just talked and talked throughout the whole lesson.'

'Really?' said Veronica, a smile on her face and a

dangerous glint in her eyes. 'And did you talk about how you have only been sucking up to Amy because Felicity Rivers put you up to it?'

Bonnie turned pale, while Amy gasped and said, 'Bonnie, is this true?'

'It – it's true that Felicity asked me to try and make friends with you,' stammered Bonnie. Then she threw a spiteful look at Veronica and went on, 'She wanted me to try and get you away from dear Veronica's unpleasant influence. But I did genuinely like you from the first, Amy, and now that I know you better I like you even more. Please say that we can still be friends!'

Amy was quivering with indignation. She was used to people vying for her friendship, and to hear that Bonnie had only palled up with her because Felicity had put her up to it, was very hard for her to bear.

'I think I'll stick with Veronica,' she said, her tone icy. 'At least I know that *she* is a true friend. Come along, Veronica.'

'Just a moment,' said Veronica. 'Bonnie, there's something I need to tell you. You see, the main reason that Felicity asked you to befriend Amy was that she and Susan were sick to death of you following them round all the time and making a nuisance of yourself. Quite honestly, I can't say that I blame them.'

Stricken and longing to get back at Veronica, Bonnie snapped, 'And just how did you find all this out, Veronica? Through spying on people and listening at doors, I expect.' Veronica's guilty look told Bonnie at once that she had hit the nail on the head, and she said scornfully, 'I thought as much. You're despicable, Veronica!'

'Well I, for one, am extremely glad that Veronica *did* find all this out,' said Amy haughtily. 'Otherwise I should never have found out what a deceitful little creature you are, Bonnie.'

And with that, she took Veronica's arm and the two girls walked away, leaving Bonnie alone with her thoughts. Alas, they were not happy ones. She had lost Amy's friendship, and now it seemed that Felicity didn't want her either. Poor Bonnie gave a little sob. Was that what Felicity really thought of her – that she was nothing but a nuisance? And did she honestly prefer the company of that dull, boring Susan? Well, there was only one way to find out for sure – and that was to tackle Felicity.

The third-form common-room was very crowded and noisy that evening. Nora had put a gramophone record on, and she and Pam were doing an idiotic dance to the music, keeping the others in fits of laughter. As the music stopped, Bonnie raised her voice and said, 'Felicity! I need to speak to you. Is it true that you only encouraged me to be Amy's friend because you wanted me to leave you alone?'

Felicity bit her lip, seeing the hurt and anger in the other girl's eyes. But it was no use beating around the bush. The time had come to be straight with Bonnie.

'Yes,' she said. 'It's true. I'm sorry if you're upset, Bonnie, but I did try to let you down gently. You just wouldn't take the hint.'

The rest of the third form had gone quiet now, all of them listening intently as Felicity went on, 'Susan is my best friend, and you knew that from the start. And she always will be. No one can take her place with me.' Then, seeing that Bonnie looked as if she was about to burst into tears, she added more gently, 'You and I have very little in common, Bonnie, whereas you and Amy are interested in the same things. It's right that the two of you should be friends.'

'Excuse me, Felicity!' said Amy angrily, jumping to her feet. 'I prefer to choose my own friends, if you don't mind. And I most certainly do *not* want to be friends with a girl who has only been nice to me as a favour to you!'

And Amy flounced out of the room, slamming the door behind her.

Susan, who had been listening to all of this with a frown, said, 'Felicity and I never meant you to find out about this, Bonnie, and I'm sorry that you and Amy have fallen out because of it.'

'How *did* you find out?' asked Felicity, who had been puzzling over this.

'Veronica told me,' answered Bonnie, with a malicious glare in the direction of the culprit. 'I'll leave you to work out for yourself how she came by her information.'

Felicity rounded on Veronica at once, crying, 'So, you've been snooping again, Veronica! I did think, after I was nice to you at half-term, that you might have turned over a new leaf, but you're just as bad as ever.'

Several of the girls looked at Veronica in disgust and her

cheeks burned – until she remembered something else that she had overheard.

'It's just as well I did,' she retorted. 'For I found out that you egged Bonnie on to try and spoil my friendship with Amy. So don't dare act all high and mighty with me, Felicity Rivers!'

Then Veronica, too, stormed out of the room and June, who had been watching the dramatic scene avidly, laughed. 'Well done, Felicity!' she called out. 'That's two people you've managed to drive out of the room this evening.'

'Oh, shut up, June!' snapped Felicity, who was in no mood for June's malicious sense of humour tonight.

June said no more, but grinned as she lounged back in her chair, waiting for the entertainment to continue. Freddie looked hard at her friend, saw how she was thoroughly enjoying all the drama, and suddenly realised – with a little shock – that June thrived on trouble. And if life was going along too peacefully and smoothly, she would stir things up herself. For the first time a doubt crept into Freddie's mind. *Had* June been acting kindly and thinking of Mrs Dale's happiness when she suggested that she, Freddie, pose as Amy? Or had she used Freddie as a cat's-paw to play an outrageous prank that she had known would end in trouble? But there was no time to think about that now, for Bonnie had turned on Felicity again, her voice trembling as she cried, 'I hope you're satisfied, Felicity Rivers! *You* don't want to be my friend, and now – thanks to you – Amy doesn't either. I've got nobody! Nobody at all!'

Then she burst into noisy sobs and fled from the room, causing June to crow, 'A hat-trick! Nice work, Felicity!'

Seeing that the normally even-tempered Felicity looked ready to explode, Pam gave June a little shove and muttered, 'For heaven's sake, be quiet, June! Things are quite tense enough in here tonight as it is, without you stirring things up.'

'I shan't say another word, Pam,' said June, her eyes dancing mischievously. 'It looks as if our dear head-girl has quite enough on her plate at the moment, without me adding to her woes.'

Yes, and didn't June just relish the fact, thought Freddie, watching her through lowered eyelashes. If only she could make the laughing, carefree girl feel the weight of her conscience, just as she, Freddie, felt hers lying heavy on her shoulders. But did June even *have* a conscience? Freddie didn't know, but she intended to find out. And if it turned out that June *did* have one, Freddie was going to stir it into life!

Felicity felt very down in the dumps the following afternoon, as she and Susan got changed ready for lacrosse practice.

'I must be the only head-girl at Malory Towers ever to have been sent to Coventry by her own form,' she complained.

'What nonsense!' said Susan, laughing at her friend's gloomy expression. 'You haven't been sent to Coventry!'

'Well, Amy is barely speaking to me, while Bonnie and Veronica won't have anything to do with me at all,' Felicity sighed. 'And although I don't care for any of them very much, I can't altogether blame them. I really don't feel as if I've handled this very well.'

'Don't feel as if you've handled what very well?' asked Pam, coming into the changing-room in time to hear this.

Felicity told her, and finished by saying miserably, 'I don't think that I've been a great success as head-girl. Susan, you would have been a much better choice. Or you, Pam. You were absolutely fine last year.'

'Yes, but I was lucky,' said Pam, wrinkling her brow thoughtfully. 'Everything went really smoothly last year, and I didn't have people like Veronica, or Bonnie, or Amy to deal with. So you see, Felicity, I wasn't really tested.'

'Well, I've been tested all right,' groaned Felicity. 'And I've been found wanting.'

'There's still time to put things right,' said Pam bracingly. 'The term isn't over yet.'

'What Pam says is quite true,' said Susan. 'Everything will be sorted out in the end, Felicity, you'll see. Now come on, let's go and blow some of those cobwebs away on the lacrosse field. You know, Felicity, Amanda was telling me that you stand a jolly good chance of getting into the second team this year.'

'Did she really?' said Felicity, cheering up at once. 'Susan, you must practise hard too and let's see if we can both get on the team. Wouldn't that be simply marvellous?'

June had also been looking forward to lacrosse practice, but Freddie had other ideas.

'I told you, Mrs Dale has invited me to tea and she said

that I might bring a friend,' said Freddie. 'And the friend I'm bringing is you.'

'But Amanda's expecting me to turn up for lacrosse,' grumbled June, who didn't want to have tea with Mrs Dale at all. She had purposely distanced herself from the old lady and the situation she had created. But Freddie, seeing June through new eyes, was now aware of this and was determined that June wasn't going to keep her distance any longer.

'Amanda will understand,' she said firmly. 'It's Saturday, and the practice is optional, so you don't *have* to go. Besides, there's another one tomorrow afternoon if you're really that keen.'

June continued to protest, but for once Freddie was determined to have her way, and eventually the two set off together to Mrs Dale's. And, by the time they left, June's conscience was very much alive.

The girl started to feel a little guilty when Mrs Dale welcomed her warmly, as 'Amy's' friend, before sitting the two girls down to a simply sumptuous tea.

'Heavens, you must have been baking all morning!' exclaimed Freddie, her eyes staring at the table laden with homemade scones, cakes and apple pie.

'Well, it's nice having someone to cook for,' beamed the old lady. 'Now, tuck in, both of you.'

But, delicious as the food was, June found that her appetite had deserted her, and the food seemed to stick in her throat. This tea must have cost quite a lot of money, and it was obvious that Mrs Dale wasn't very well off. With a sinking heart, June remembered telling Freddie blithely what a sweet old lady Mrs Dale was. But June hadn't realised at the time *how* sweet and how kind she was. And what had seemed like a prank now began to feel like a very cruel deception. June also felt unnerved by the obvious, and very genuine, affection between Freddie and Mrs Dale, something that she hadn't bargained for. But worse was to come. As the girls were thinking about setting off back to Malory Towers, Mrs Dale suddenly exclaimed, 'Why, Amy, it's your birthday a week tomorrow, isn't it?'

Was it? thought Freddie, startled. Then she remembered hearing Amy mention something to Veronica about having a birthday coming up soon, and she nodded.

'Well, you must come over and I'll give you your present,' said Mrs Dale happily, as the two girls exchanged horrified glances.

'There's no need to give me a present, Gran,' said Freddie in a strangled tone. 'Please don't spend your money on me.'

'Well, what's the world coming to if I can't give my only granddaughter a present on her birthday!' tutted Mrs Dale. 'I've never heard the like!'

So the end of it was that Freddie had to promise to visit Mrs Dale on Amy's birthday, but she was deeply unhappy about it. And so was June. She was oddly silent on the walk back to Malory Towers, but inwardly she felt sick. She had meant to keep Freddie occupied, and had foreseen that the girl would begin to feel guilty about deceiving the old lady. But she – who prided herself so much on her careful planning – hadn't foreseen that the two would become so fond of one another, and she could have kicked herself. Not for the world would she willingly have hurt Mrs Dale – or Freddie either, for that matter. And the dreadful thing was, June couldn't see any way out of it without causing both of them a lot of pain. Nor could she fool herself into thinking that it was Freddie's problem and not hers. She was responsible for this whole, terrible mess, and somehow she had to think of a way to make everything right.

A shock for Amy

June felt very sorry for Freddie now that she understood some of what she had been going through, and knew how sickening it was to have something preying on your mind. It was really horrible, for even when you were laughing and joking with friends, it was always there, at the back of your mind, casting a dark shadow. But although she was kinder to Freddie, June's worries made her very short-tempered indeed with everyone else.

She went to Amanda's Sunday lacrosse practice, hoping for a respite from her cares, but unfortunately it only made things worse. The girl marking her, Fay, from South Tower, was an agile and most determined little player, and hardly allowed June near the ball at all. Frustrated, June lost her temper and tackled poor Fay most aggressively, knocking her to the ground and bringing Amanda's wrath down on her head.

'June!' cried Amanda, storming on to the field. 'Off! No, don't argue with me! Go and get changed at once.'

Angrily, June stomped off to the changing-room, but by the time she had got back into her uniform, her anger had deserted her and she felt deeply ashamed of herself. Amanda glared at her when she appeared among the spectators, but she was mollified when, at the end of the practice, June went up to Fay and apologised. She also said sorry to Amanda, and the big girl accepted her apology, saying, 'Very well, but you must learn to control your temper, June, for I can't possibly include you in a team until you do!'

But the next morning June was in hot water again, after cheeking Miss Peters in the Geography class.

'How dare you speak to me like that!' snapped the mistress, her rosy cheeks turning even redder, as they always did when she was angry. 'And stand up when I address you.'

Red-faced, June got sullenly to her feet and mumbled, 'I'm sorry, Miss Peters.'

'I beg your pardon, June?' said Miss Peters coldly, and June was forced to repeat her apology more clearly. Really, all she seemed to do lately was apologise to people!

'Come and see me after class,' said the mistress. 'When I shall have decided on a suitable punishment for you.'

And knowing Miss Peters, she wouldn't get off lightly, thought June, sitting down again.

As head of the form, Felicity took the girl to task for her behaviour, and June bore it as patiently as she could. Heavens, it wouldn't do if she fell out with Felicity as well! She really must try and concentrate on the problem that was causing her irritation, and not let her temper get the better of her.

Alas for such good intentions! June got in a rage again that very evening – this time with Amy.

Amy had been holding forth to a rapt Veronica in the common-room about her forthcoming birthday, and the others were getting heartily sick of her.

'As it's on a Sunday, Mummy and Daddy have got the Head's permission to come and take me out,' said Amy. 'We're going to that very grand hotel overlooking the beach for lunch, and they're sure to bring me a super present.'

Veronica exclaimed in admiration, and Amy went on, 'My aunt always sends me the most enormous cake, as well, so we can all share that at teatime. Did I ever tell you about the Christmas party they threw for my friends at home last year? My word, it was magnificent! We had –'

But at this point June, who had been trying to concentrate on the extra work Miss Peters had set her as punishment, threw down her book and leaped to her feet. 'Yes, Amy, you *did* tell Veronica about the marvellous party Mummy and Daddy threw for you!' she cried. 'And about the very expensive present they bought you, and about every birthday you've ever had since you were five years old! And I, for one, am sick and tired of hearing about it. You're nothing but a spoilt brat, Amy!'

Amy shrank back as though she had been slapped, while the others looked on in shocked silence. Amy *had* been annoying, but there was no need for June to be quite so vicious!

Felicity called her sharply to order and, had Amy not retaliated, the matter might have rested there.

But Amy, recovering from her shock, found her voice

and, looking down her long nose at June, she said, 'I suppose you're just jealous, June, because your parents aren't as wealthy as mine, and can't afford to throw splendid parties for you, or give you expensive presents.'

At once June fired up again and, without thinking, retorted, 'I'd rather have my parents than yours any day, Amy! Do you think I would want a father who is ashamed of my mother's family? Or a mother who is too weak to stand up to him? No, thank you!'

As soon as the words were out June regretted them and wished that she could take them back. But it was too late. Felicity and Susan were staring at her in horror. Freddie had turned pale, her hands tightly gripping the arms of her chair. And Amy was looking completely bewildered, as were the rest of the girls.

Contrite now, June said hastily, 'I'm sorry, Amy. Please forget that I said that. Honestly, I get into such a rage sometimes that I don't know *what* I'm saying half of the time!'

'I can't forget it,' said Amy, a queer look on her face. 'And I think that you knew exactly what you were saying, June. What did you mean?'

It was unlike June to be lost for words, but she was now and she looked at Felicity for help. And Felicity decided that it was no use trying to hide the truth from Amy any longer. She was absolutely furious with June for blurting it out like that, but she would deal with her later! As concisely as possible, she told Amy how she, Susan and June had met her grandmother, and how they had promised not to tell Amy that she was living near the school because she didn't want to go against Mr Ryder-Cochrane's wishes.

Amy listened intently, an incredulous expression on her face, and when Felicity had finished, she laughed and shook her head. 'You're mistaken, Felicity,' she said. 'My grandmother moved to Australia shortly before my parents married. And as for my father disapproving of her – why, that's nonsense! He promised me that we would go and visit her one day. In fact, we've been on the verge of going several times, but Mummy has always been taken ill, so it hasn't happened yet. I don't know who this woman is, but she certainly isn't my grandmother!'

The third formers didn't know what to think now, and exchanged puzzled looks. Then Pam, who had been looking very thoughtful, said, 'Amy, do you have a photograph of your grandmother?'

'Yes,' said Amy. 'It's one that she sent to Mummy from Australia '

'Go and fetch it then,' said Pam. 'And hurry up!'

Amy rushed from the room, and was back a few moments later, clutching a photograph, which she handed to Felicity.

'It's Mrs Dale!' said Felicity. 'Amy, I tell you this is definitely the woman that Susan, June and I met. Isn't that so, Susan?'

Susan, who was peering over Felicity's shoulder at the photograph, nodded solemnly, and Nora said, 'The plot thickens. I say, Amy, I don't suppose your grandmother has a twin sister?'

'Of course she hasn't!' said Amy, her thoughts in a whirl. 'It doesn't make any sense. If Grandmother has returned from Australia, why hasn't she been in touch with me, or with Mummy? I don't understand what's going on!'

'I think I do,' said June, who had been looking very pensive. 'But I don't think you will like what I have to say, Amy.'

'Well, that doesn't usually bother you!' said Amy harshly. 'Just spit it out, June.'

'Very well,' said June, looking rather grave. 'You see, Amy, it isn't your father who is ashamed of Mrs Dale – it's your mother!'

As Amy remained speechless, her mouth wide open, June went on, 'Mrs Dale isn't at all wealthy or grand. I think that your mother was afraid to let your father meet her, because she didn't want him to know that she came from a plain, ordinary family. So she pretended that her mother lived in Australia, and then fooled you and your father into thinking she was ill every time a trip to visit Mrs Dale was planned.'

'I don't believe it,' said poor Amy, her face ashen. 'How could Mummy do that? And how could she lie to Daddy and to me for all this time?'

Everyone felt very sorry for Amy, and Felicity put a hand on the girl's shoulder, saying kindly, 'All of this must have come as a dreadful shock to you, Amy. I think that you ought to sort things out with your parents when they come for your birthday.'

But Amy hardly seemed to hear what Felicity said, for there was one thought uppermost in her mind and she said firmly, 'I want to meet my grandmother.'

'Well, you can't go and meet her now!' said Susan, sounding alarmed. 'It's dark and it's almost bedtime.'

'Tomorrow, then,' said Amy determinedly. 'Felicity, you can come with me and show me where she lives.'

Suddenly, Freddie, who had remained silent and lost in thought throughout, stood up and said firmly, 'I'll come with you, Amy.'

Every head turned towards her in astonishment, and Felicity said, 'You, Freddie? But you don't know Mrs Dale!'

'I do,' said Freddie, looking extremely white and nervous. 'Amy, I know you've had a great shock tonight, but I'm afraid you haven't heard everything. You see, Mrs Dale thinks that I am you.'

'This gets stranger and stranger by the second!' said Julie, scratching her head. 'Freddie, how can Mrs Dale possibly think that you are Amy?'

Stammering, her voice cracking, Freddie explained.

'Well!' exclaimed Pam, as Freddie reached the end of her tale and hung her head. 'This is certainly a night for revelations! Does anyone else have anything extraordinary they would like to own up to?'

No one did, of course, and Freddie went over to Amy, taking both of the girl's hands in hers and saying earnestly, 'Please let me come with you tomorrow, Amy, so that I might explain things to Mrs Dale and apologise. I didn't mean to hurt her, truly I didn't. I just felt dreadfully sorry for her, and thought that I could cheer her up by visiting and pretending to be you. I should have thought it through more carefully. If I had I wouldn't have been so stupid, and would have said no to the whole crazy idea!'

Amy, whose mind was reeling, said nothing, but the others believed Freddie at once. She had acted rashly, foolishly and thoughtlessly, but her heart had been in the right place. It was different with June, though, who was now sitting alone in the corner, keeping unusually quiet and looking rather ashamed of herself. And well she might, thought Felicity, who felt quite disgusted with the girl. The whole idea had been June's, and Felicity knew that she hadn't acted from motives of kindness. No, June's twisted sense of mischief had been at work, and she had certainly meant to cause trouble for Freddie. Felicity wondered why, as she and Freddie were supposed to be friends. But then June had always had a rather odd sense of humour!

'Will you have to report this to Miss Grayling?' Freddie asked Felicity now, looking rather scared. June's heart sank as she heard this. It had never even occurred to her that the Head might become involved, and June knew that Miss Grayling would not go easy on her. She might even expel her, and June felt sick at heart at the thought.

'That's for Amy to decide,' answered Felicity, looking across at the girl.

'I don't know,' said Amy, on whose face the strain was beginning to show. 'I just can't think about that at the moment. All I want is to meet my grandmother and get to know her. Freddie, you can come with me tomorrow. And I can let her know that she has been wrong about my father, and that he would like to meet her as well.'

'No!' cried Felicity and Freddie together.

'Amy, you can't,' said Felicity. 'Your grandmother would be terribly hurt if she knew how your mother had behaved. And she's going to have quite enough shocks to deal with tomorrow as it is. I'm afraid that your poor father is going to have to remain the villain of the piece for the time being.'

'Of course,' said Amy, running a hand over her brow. 'I'm not thinking very clearly.'

'Well, I'm sure it's no wonder,' said Pam, getting up as the bell for bedtime sounded. 'You've had an awful lot to take in tonight. Now it's time for bed, and you'll feel much better after a good night's sleep.'

But the following morning, neither Amy nor June looked as if they had slept very well, both of them pale and heavy-eyed. Amy had had far too much going on in her mind to allow her to sleep properly, while June knew that she was going to be in disgrace with the rest of her form, and – even worse – perhaps with Miss Grayling as well. No one spoke to her as she dressed and ate her breakfast, not even Freddie, and the silence was very hard to bear. Felicity sought her out after breakfast, and led her to one of the little music-rooms.

'I suppose you're going to tell me off,' said June, folding her arms across her chest, defiant to the last, even though she knew that she richly deserved a scolding.

'Yes, I am,' said Felicity bluntly. 'June, what were you thinking of? How could you have been so stupid and so cruel?'

'I admit that it was stupid,' said June. 'But I didn't intend to cause Mrs Dale any hurt.'

'Perhaps not,' said Felicity. 'But you certainly meant to cause trouble for Freddie. Why, June, when she's your friend and has never shown you anything but kindness?'

June turned red, but stubbornly refused to answer, while Felicity wracked her brains for a clue that might explain the girl's extraordinary behaviour. Then, in a flash, it came to her.

'*I* know why!' exclaimed Felicity. 'You're jealous of Freddie, of how clever she is at jokes and tricks. Because you desperately want to be the third form's bad girl, the only who can play tricks and make people laugh. Well, June, you've certainly proved that you're a bad girl – but no one's laughing.'

June was now as white as she had been red, and she said harshly, 'Very clever of you, Felicity. Have you finished now?'

'Not quite,' said Felicity. 'We have yet to hear you offer an apology to Amy, or Mrs Dale, or Freddie for what you've done. And you must see that you owe them one, all three of them.'

'I know that!' said June, growing angry. 'And I *shall* apologise to them, in my own time and without any prompting from you, Felicity.'

'I'm glad to hear it,' said Felicity. 'And for your sake, June, I hope that Amy decides not to report the matter to Miss Grayling. I wouldn't want to be in your shoes if she does!'

June went away smarting. She always hated to be told off, and Felicity had made her feel very small indeed.

Freddie, meanwhile, wasn't looking forward to seeing Mrs Dale at all. She and Amy made their way to her cottage after afternoon school, and were silent on the short walk, each girl lost in her own thoughts. As the little cottage came into sight, Freddie's footsteps seemed to drag, as though she were trying to put off the dreadful moment when she would have to confess everything to the old lady. But then they were at the gate, and Freddie turned to Amy. 'We're here.'

Mrs Dale springs a surprise

'Why, I wasn't expecting to see you until Sunday!' exclaimed Mrs Dale, as she opened the door to the two girls. 'And you've brought someone else to visit me. Come along in, both of you.'

She led both girls into her tiny living-room, where they sat side by side on a small sofa. Mrs Dale's cat, Sooty, who had become firm friends with Freddie, jumped up on to her knee and rubbed his head against her arm, purring madly. Then he spotted Amy, and wondered if this stranger liked cats too. Sooty jumped from Freddie's lap to Amy's, and the girl gave a little start, for she wasn't used to pets and was rather nervous of them. But Sooty was prepared to overlook this, and curled up on her lap, purring his approval when Amy tentatively stroked his head.

'Well, Amy,' said Mrs Dale, now that Sooty had settled down to his satisfaction. 'This is an unexpected pleasure.'

'Yes,' began Freddie. 'You see, I had to come today, because –'

'Oh, I wasn't talking to you, my dear,' said Mrs Dale, with a strange little smile. 'I was talking to my grand-daughter, Amy.'

Then she looked directly at Amy, whose mouth had

fallen open in shock, and said, 'That is who you are, isn't it?'

'Yes, Grandmother,' answered Amy in a trembling voice. 'Oh, it's so lovely to meet you!' Then she got to her feet, dislodging the cat – who merely yawned and settled down on Freddie again – and hugged the old lady for all she was worth, while Freddie looked on in the utmost astonishment, questions crowding her brain.

At last Amy and Mrs Dale sat back down again, and Freddie said, in rather a high, nervous voice, 'How long have you known that I wasn't Amy?'

'I've known from the first,' answered the old lady quite serenely, her shrewd eyes twinkling. 'I might be old, but I still have all my wits about me! You see, a couple of days before you turned up on my doorstep claiming to be my granddaughter, I received a letter from Amy's mother. And in it was a recent photograph of Amy, in her new school uniform, taken just before she left for Malory Towers.'

'But – but why didn't you say anything?' asked the bewildered Freddie, absent-mindedly stroking the cat.

'Because I wanted to know what game you were playing,' Mrs Dale replied. 'I was at a loss at first, but I think I know what you were up to now. I realised the other day, when you brought June to tea. She was the one who put you up to it, wasn't she?'

Amy gave a scornful snort, while Freddie nodded and said, 'Yes, but you must believe that I didn't mean any harm, Mrs Dale. June said that you were lonely, and it seemed like a good idea at the time, but . . .'

Her voice trailed off miserably and Mrs Dale said, 'But your conscience started to trouble you.'

'Yes, it did,' said Freddie, looking the old lady straight in the eye. 'It troubled me a lot. And there was something else too. I grew very fond of you – and I hadn't expected that.'

'Well, I'm glad to hear it,' said Mrs Dale, her shrewd blue eyes twinkling. 'Because I grew very fond of you, too, and came to look forward to your visits, even though I knew you weren't really my granddaughter. Heavens!' She gave a little laugh. 'Do you realise that I don't even know what your real name is?'

'I'm Freddie,' the girl answered. 'And I'm so relieved that you aren't angry with me.'

'I could tell that you were a good girl at heart,' said Mrs Dale. 'And I knew that you would own up sooner or later. As for that June – well, I realised that she was a monkey the second I clapped eyes on her. That was the day she rescued my Sooty from the tree. My goodness, what a long time ago that seems now!'

'Monkey is putting it mildly!' said Freddie, with a grimace. 'I was an idiot to let her talk me into this in the first place.'

'Oh, we all act foolishly at times,' said Mrs Dale. 'I just hope June comes to see the error of her ways before she gets herself into real trouble. She reminds me very much of myself when I was that age, you know.'

Both girls looked astonished at this, quite unable to picture the old lady as a mischievous schoolgirl, and Mrs

Dale laughed at their wide-eyed expressions. 'Yes, I was young once myself,' she said. 'And now, Freddie, I'm going to ask you to leave Amy and me alone for a while. I'd like to get to know my granddaughter.'

'Of course,' said Freddie, getting up at once and putting Sooty, who didn't approve of all this activity, on the floor. 'May I come and visit you again, please, Mrs Dale?'

'I should like that very much,' said the old lady with a smile. 'Only next time come as Freddie, not as Amy. And send June to see me as well. I'd like a word with that young lady!'

Freddie felt as if the weight of the world had rolled off her shoulders as she made her way back to Malory Towers, and there was a spring in her step when she walked into the common-room. June was there alone, and she looked up as Freddie entered. It was a lovely, crisp, sunny day outside and the rest of the third form were making the most of it by getting some fresh air. But nobody had asked June if she wanted to go with them. Not that she cared tuppence, for she would much rather be on her own than with a group of girls whose disgust and disapproval of her was all too plain. There was a moment's awkward silence, then Freddie, who felt so happy that she could almost forgive June, cleared her throat and asked, 'Where is everyone?'

'They're all outside,' answered June, heartened by the fact that Freddie had broken the ice between them. There was another pause and then she asked, 'Er – how did it go at Mrs Dale's? Was she very angry with you?'

'No, surprisingly enough, she wasn't,' said Freddie and, unable to keep it to herself any longer, she launched into her tale. June was astonished, of course, and asked a great many questions, feeling quite as relieved as Freddie that everything was all right.

'Of course, Amy will still have to tackle her mother,' said Freddie, when she reached the end of her story. 'Can you believe that anyone would be so stuck-up and snobbish as to be ashamed of her own mother? Honestly, June, doesn't it make you feel grateful that we have ordinary, sensible parents?'

June agreed heartily with this, then, after a moment's silence, said in a rush, 'Freddie, I'm sorry. I placed you in a very uncomfortable situation, and one that could have got you into a lot of trouble. I hope that you'll accept my apology, and that the two of us can still be friends. Though if you don't want to, I won't blame you.'

'I *would* like us to carry on being friends, June,' answered Freddie, her expression quite serious. 'But first I must know *why* you put me up to impersonating Amy. Because I know that it wasn't concern for Mrs Dale that made you do it.'

'You're right,' said June, realising that she would have to be completely honest with Freddie if their friendship was ever to get back on its old footing. So she told Freddie the truth – how she had begun to feel jealous of her, and hadn't wanted Freddie sharing in the adulation and glory June received from the others for her tricks. And how petty and spiteful it sounded when she said it aloud! No wonder Freddie looked shocked, and June wouldn't blame the girl if she decided that she didn't want to be her friend after all. But Freddie said, 'Thank you for having the courage to be honest with me, June. And if we are to remain friends, you must go on being honest. Even if it means telling me things that I don't want to hear sometimes.'

June nodded solemnly. 'I will,' she said. 'And you must try to be a steadying influence on me, and try to talk me out of some of the crazy ideas I come up with.'

'I'll do my best,' said Freddie, with a grin. 'But I doubt if *anyone* could stop you once you've taken it into your head to carry out one of your madcap schemes!'

So, when the rest of the third form poured in, rosy-cheeked from their walk in the grounds, it was to find June and Freddie chatting together amicably. Some of them exchanged surprised glances but Felicity, who felt that there had been quite enough ill feeling in the third form recently, was pleased and, knowing that the others would follow her lead, said cheerily, 'Hallo, you two! I say, Freddie, where's Amy? Still at her grandmother's?'

And Freddie had to relate, once more, all that had happened at Mrs Dale's for the benefit of the rest of the third form.

'Well!' said Nora when she had finished. 'So the old lady knew all along that you weren't Amy. She tricked you far more successfully than you tricked her, Freddie.'

'Good for her!' laughed Julie.

'And you didn't have to go through the unpleasantness

of owning up after all,' said Susan. 'I'll bet that was a relief, Freddie.'

There was more good news when Amy came back, just in time for supper. Felicity had been a little afraid that Amy, once she got to know her grandmother, might not get on with her because she was not as grand as the rest of her family. But it was plain from the bright smile on the girl's face that she had had a very happy time with Mrs Dale, and was overjoyed to have met her at last. Amy also announced graciously that she was not going to report Freddie and June to Miss Grayling. Freddie, who guessed that she had Mrs Dale to thank for this, was extremely grateful, while June got up and said, 'Thank you, Amy. Freddie and I appreciate it. And I want you to know that I'm really very sorry for the part that I played in this business. It was completely my fault, and Freddie would never have thought of pretending to be you if I hadn't put the idea into her head.'

After only a slight hesitation, Amy took June's outstretched hand and shook it, while Felicity breathed a sigh of relief. June's frank, open apology had done much to lighten the mood of the third formers and they admired her for being brave enough to make it in front of them all. Perhaps, at last, things were beginning to settle down a bit.

But not everything was sorted out, of course. Bonnie and Veronica were still very cool towards Felicity, and towards one another, while Amy still flatly refused to make up with Bonnie. Felicity, who felt rather guilty about the rift between the two girls, tactfully broached the subject with Amy later that evening, suggesting that she and Bonnie clear the air between them, but she was brushed off.

'I know that you mean well, Felicity,' said Amy stiffly. 'But Bonnie deceived me. And, quite frankly, I've had enough of deceitful people to last me a lifetime!'

Felicity guessed, of course, that Amy was referring to her mother and said no more, deciding that it would be foolish to push the matter when the girl had so much on her mind.

And Bonnie herself went up to Amy in the dormitory, as the third formers got ready for bed. Bonnie had been deeply shocked at the way Amy had been kept apart from her grandmother, and the incident had made her think of her own doting grandparents, who had always played a large part in her life and whose spoiling she had rather taken for granted. She felt very sorry for Amy, who had missed out on her own grandmother's loving companionship for so many years. For probably the first time in her life, Bonnie genuinely wanted to be of help and comfort to someone else.

'Amy, I'm so pleased that your meeting with your grandmother went well today,' she said in her soft voice. 'Have you decided what you're going to say to your mother?'

But Amy merely looked at Bonnie coldly and said, 'Did Felicity tell you to come and speak to me?'

'Of course not!' said Bonnie, deeply offended. 'I'm just concerned for you, that's all.'

'Amy doesn't need your concern,' butted in Veronica, who had been hovering nearby, listening jealously. 'She knows that she can always rely on me in times of trouble.'

'I'm sure that Amy can speak for herself,' snapped Bonnie, giving Veronica a look of dislike. 'Amy, you might not be my friend any more, but I'm yours, whether you want me to be or not. And I shall be here if you need me.'

But Bonnie received no response other than a look of icy disdain so, rather despondently, she went off to her own bed, while Amy and Veronica each climbed into theirs.

'What *are* you going to do about your parents?' whispered Veronica to Amy. 'My word, your father's going to be simply furious with your mother when he finds out what has been going on all these years.'

'Yes, he is,' answered Amy in a low voice. 'But I'm afraid that can't be helped. Mummy has brought it all on herself. I've decided that I'm going to tackle her at the weekend, when she and Daddy come over for my birthday. Really, Veronica, I don't know how she can have imagined, even for a second, that Daddy would look down on Grandmother! He may be wealthy, but he's awfully kind-hearted, and would never disapprove of someone simply because they don't have very much money.'

'And what about you, Amy?' asked Veronica curiously. 'How do you feel about your gran?'

'Why, I love her, of course,' said Amy, sounding rather surprised at the question. 'I did from the moment I saw her. She is my grandmother, after all!'

'Of course,' said Veronica. 'But what I really meant was –'

She stopped suddenly, realising that the question she wanted to ask wasn't very tactful, and Amy gave a soft laugh, realising all at once what Veronica wanted to know.

'You mean do *I* look down on her because she isn't wealthy, don't you?' she said. 'Well, I don't, surprising as it may seem. I know that I'm stuck-up and snobbish, and all of the other things that people say about me – and I probably always will be. But somehow it's impossible to look down on someone you love.'

Veronica felt rather guilty on hearing this. Hadn't she looked down on her own parents and thought that they weren't good enough for her? Well, she had learned her lesson all right at half-term, and she understood exactly how Amy was feeling now. 'No,' she murmured. 'You're quite right, Amy. You can't look down on the people you love.'

Her voice was becoming drowsy and, beside her, Amy stifled a yawn.

'No more talking now, girls,' came Felicity's voice. 'It's time for lights-out.'

And, one by one, the third formers drifted off to sleep, each of them thinking that the last few days had been very strange indeed, and wondering what the remainder of the term had in store.

A bad time for Felicity

The following day started badly for Felicity, who was putting her shoes and socks on when the breakfast bell went, only to discover that one of her laces was missing.

'What *are* you doing, Felicity?' asked Nora, astonished to see the girl dive under the bed in search of her missing shoelace.

'One of my laces is missing,' came Felicity's muffled voice from under the bed. 'Blow! Where *can* it have gone? I know they were both here last night.'

'It must have fallen out,' said Julie.

'Laces don't just *fall* out,' said Felicity, who was now crawling round the floor. 'And they don't simply disappear into thin air either. I can't go down to breakfast without it, or I shan't be able to keep my shoe on.'

'I've got a spare pair of shoelaces,' said Susan, coming to the rescue. 'You can borrow one of them. Now do hurry up, Felicity, or you'll get into a row from Potty.'

Quickly Felicity threaded the new lace into her shoe and raced downstairs after the others, reaching the dining-room just in time to avoid a ticking off from Miss Potts.

'I can't think where my shoelace went,' said Felicity to Susan as she buttered a slice of toast.

'Well, I shouldn't worry about it too much,' said Susan. 'It's not as if you've lost something valuable, like jewellery or your purse. Perhaps someone removed it while you were asleep, for a prank. I daresay it'll turn up later.'

Felicity decided that Susan was probably right and thought no more about the matter – at first.

June's mind seemed to be somewhere else at breakfast. Indeed, she was so preoccupied that she would have put salt in her porridge instead of sugar, if Freddie hadn't been on hand to stop her.

'Whatever is the matter with you?' asked Freddie. 'You've been in an absolute dream since you got out of bed!'

'I've just been thinking,' answered June. 'I've apologised to you, and I've apologised to Amy. Now all I need to do is square things with Mrs Dale, and once I've done that I'll feel as if I can wipe the slate clean.'

'Yes, I think you should get it over with as soon as possible, then you'll feel much better,' agreed Freddie. 'She's a decent old soul, and I don't think she'll be too cross with you – especially as you remind her of herself when she was young.'

June laughed. 'I couldn't believe it when you told me that, and I still can't imagine dear, kindly Mrs Dale playing pranks on her teachers!' She sipped her tea and went on decisively, 'I'm going to slip across and see her in the lunch-break. If I run over there quickly as soon as I've eaten, I can be there and back again in time for English this afternoon.'

Freddie nodded in approval at this plan, while at the

other end of the table, Julie said, 'Felicity! Don't forget that you said you'd lend me your spare pen. Mine's broken and I shan't have time to go and buy a new one until the weekend.'

'Oh yes, I *had* forgotten!' exclaimed Felicity. 'It's in the common-room. I'll go and fetch it on the way to Maths.'

But when Felicity and her friends popped into the common-room a little later, her spare pen was nowhere to be seen.

'That's strange!' said Susan, looking baffled. 'I could have sworn that you put it in your locker last night.'

'Yes, so could I,' said Felicity, frowning. 'Half a minute, though! Nora, I lent it to you, remember, because you had left yours in your desk. You're so scatterbrained that you must have forgotten to give it back to me.'

'I *did* give it back to you, Felicity,' insisted Nora. 'I'm sure I did.'

'Yes, she did,' put in Pam. 'I remember seeing her hand it to you. But goodness knows where you put it. Really, Felicity, first you lose your shoelace then you misplace your pen! You're getting quite as scatterbrained as Nora.'

But Felicity wasn't at all scatterbrained, and had been brought up to take care of her things. It wasn't like her at all to lose something, or to forget where she had put it, and she began to feel a little worried.

'Well, we can't stay here all morning hunting for a pen,' said Susan briskly. 'I don't think that Miss Peters would think that an acceptable excuse for us being late.

Julie, you'll have to see if one of the others has a pen you can borrow.'

So the girls quickly made their way to the third-form classroom, where, fortunately for Julie, she was able to borrow a pen from one of the South Tower girls. Miss Peters did not look at all kindly on girls who turned up to her classes badly prepared and without the correct equipment!

Felicity, however, continued to puzzle over her missing belongings. It wasn't as if they were expensive possessions, or things that were particularly important to her, or items that couldn't be replaced. It was just so very *annoying*!

True to her word, June sped across to Mrs Dale's cottage after lunch, and Freddie was waiting for her by the school gates when she returned, relieved to see the happy smile on the girl's face.

'Mrs Dale is the nicest, most decent person I have ever met!' she declared. 'Of course, she gave me a bit of a ticking off, but that was only to be expected. Then she started telling me about some of the tricks she had played when she was at school, and I told her about the vanishing cream, and we got along like a house on fire! She's given me some simply super ideas for tricks as well.'

'Tell me about them later,' said Freddie, taking June's arm and walking briskly up the drive. 'If we're late for English we shall be in trouble with Miss Hibbert, and you don't want another ticking off.'

The two girls got to their classroom just before the English mistress and were spared a scolding, but alas for

Felicity, she very soon got into trouble with Miss Hibbert.

'We're going to carry on reading through the play that we started yesterday,' said the mistress, once the class was seated. 'Open your scripts at page three and . . . Felicity, please pay attention!'

Felicity, who had been rummaging around in her desk, hastily dropped the lid and said, 'I'm sorry, Miss Hibbert, but I can't seem to find my script.'

'Really, Felicity, as head of the form you're supposed to set an example to the others,' said Miss Hibbert, sounding exasperated. 'It's most unlike you to be so careless. Well, you will just have to share Susan's script for now.'

Her face flaming, Felicity moved her chair closer to Susan's, as her thoughts raced. She had put the script back in her desk after English yesterday, she was absolutely certain of that! To mislay one thing might be put down to carelessness or absent-mindedness, but this was the third thing that she had lost today. An unwelcome suspicion entered Felicity's head. Was someone playing a prank on her? If so, it wasn't a very funny one, for it had got her into hot water with Miss Hibbert. Her heart sank as it occurred to her that, perhaps, the culprit meant for her to get into trouble, and she glanced round at the other girls in her form, wondering which of them could be capable of such spite. She was certain that it *was* a third former, for nobody else could have sneaked into the classroom and the dormitory and the common-room without being spotted. But there was no time to think about that now, for Felicity had to give her full attention to Miss Hibbert and the reading of the play.

She voiced her suspicions to Susan later that afternoon, as the two of them sat on a wooden bench in the courtyard, and her friend looked very serious indeed.

'I must admit that thought occurred to me too,' said Susan. 'But who on earth could it be? Not Pam, or Nora or Julie, that much is certain.'

'No, we can certainly rule them out,' said Felicity. 'We've known them since we were first formers together and none of them would think of doing anything so beastly to me. I don't think it's the kind of thing Freddie would do either. There's no shortage of suspects, though. I've upset Bonnie, Amy and Veronica recently – though Amy does seem to have got over it, and I honestly think she has too much on her mind at the moment to bother about playing silly, spiteful little tricks on me.'

Susan agreed and said gravely, 'I hate to say this, Felicity, but there's someone else it could be.'

'Who?' asked Felicity in surprise.

'June,' answered Susan. 'Don't forget that you told her off over that business with Mrs Dale, and that won't have gone down well. If there's one thing that June hates it's being made to feel small. You can't deny that she has a malicious streak in her nature, and we all know that she can hold a grudge too!'

Everything that Susan said was true, but Felicity hated to think that June, who had also come up through the school with them, was capable of such spite against her, even though they hadn't always been the best of friends.

'No,' she said at last, shaking her head. 'I know that June was angry with me for giving her a scold, but she also knew that she deserved it. Besides, if she did have a grudge against me she would tell me so to my face – and probably in front of everyone too! No, this hole and corner stuff isn't like June at all.'

But Susan wasn't convinced. 'She has done this kind of thing before,' she said. 'Remember when we were in the first form and she sent those horrid anonymous notes to Moira?'

Felicity was silent. She had forgotten all about that! Moira had been a very unpopular and rather domineering fifth former who had got on the wrong side of June. And June had retaliated by sending the girl a series of unpleasant anonymous notes. But she had been found out, and it was only thanks to Moira's intervention that June hadn't been expelled.

'Yes, but she was only a first former then,' said Felicity at last, looking troubled. 'And almost being expelled really shook her up and taught her a lesson. Surely she wouldn't do anything like that again – would she?'

'I really don't know *what* to think,' said Susan, frowning. 'But perhaps we should tell Pam, Nora and Julie that we suspect someone is playing these mean tricks on you, then all of us can keep our eyes open and look out for anything suspicious.'

'Good idea,' said Felicity. 'Oh, Susan, I do hope that it isn't June! It's bad enough to think that there's someone in the third form who dislikes me enough to take my things and get me into trouble – but it's even worse to think that it could be someone that I've known for years!'

The two girls found Pam, Nora and Julie down at the stables, all of them fussing over Jack. To their astonishment, Bonnie was also there, feeding sugar to Miss Peters's big black horse, Midnight, and patting his sleek, dark neck. Felicity noticed that the girl looked a little nervous when Midnight whinnied, and she shied away from him when he tossed his big head.

'I didn't know that you liked horses, Bonnie!' said Susan, in surprise.

'There are a lot of things you don't know about me, Susan,' said Bonnie, rather loftily. Then she gave Midnight a final pat and whispered to him, 'I'll be back to see you tomorrow, boy,' before walking out of the stables, pointedly sticking her nose in the air as she passed Felicity.

'I'd love to know what she's playing at,' said Nora, staring suspiciously after her. 'Julie says that Bonnie has been to see Midnight every day this week, yet she's never shown any interest in him – or any of the horses – before.'

'She's a funny little thing,' remarked Pam. 'I don't quite know what to make of her!'

'Well, never mind that now,' said Felicity. 'Susan and I have something we want to tell you.'

And Pam, Nora and Julie listened open-mouthed as the two girls told them that they were certain someone was playing malicious tricks on Felicity.

'I believe you're right!' said Pam. 'It's not like you to be careless with your belongings, Felicity.'

'I'll bet it's Veronica!' Nora said. 'You know that she did something very similar to Katherine of the fourth form, of course?'

'No, I didn't know!' said Felicity, looking shocked. 'When was this?'

'It was when they were in the second form together,' said Nora. 'Apparently the two of them fell out over something – I can't remember what – and strange things started happening to Katherine, just as they have to you, Felicity. Her things went missing, and some of her work was deliberately spoilt, and eventually Katherine and some of her friends caught Veronica red-handed. That's why the fourth formers always disliked Veronica so much, and, if you ask me, it's why Miss Grayling decided to keep her down with us instead of going up into the fourth form this term. I think she wanted Veronica to have a fresh start with a new form.'

'And instead it looks as if she's been up to her old tricks again,' said Julie, looking quite disgusted. 'How jolly mean of her, especially as you were so kind to her at half-term, Felicity.'

'Let's find her and have it out with her!' cried Susan, indignant on her friend's behalf.

But Felicity said decisively, 'No, we can't. We don't have any proof that it's Veronica who is behind this, and it would be a dreadful thing if we accused her wrongly.'

'You're quite right, old thing,' said Pam. 'None of us

like Veronica, but just because she's done this kind of thing before doesn't mean that she is responsible this time.'

'Well, I'm going to be watching her,' said Susan. 'And if I catch her in the act she had better watch out!'

'Yes, but don't let her know that you're watching her,' warned Julie. 'If it is Veronica, we don't want to put her on her guard.'

There was quite a lot of spying going on in the third form over the next couple of days. Susan, of course, was watching Veronica. Felicity, meanwhile, kept an eye on June, for of all the girls she suspected, June was the one she desperately hoped was innocent. And Nora and Julie were watching Bonnie – not because they thought that she was the person playing tricks on Felicity, for both of them privately thought that Veronica was responsible – but they were extremely curious to know what was behind the girl's sudden interest in Midnight.

They found out on Saturday morning, when they were busy grooming Jack. Miss Peters came into the stables to saddle up Midnight, only to find Bonnie there petting him and feeding him a carrot. Midnight had grown very fond of Bonnie, and would whinny softly when she approached him, before nuzzling her shoulder. Bonnie, in turn, had quite lost her fear of the big horse and thought him rather sweet. He swallowed the last bit of carrot now and rested his black head on Bonnie's shoulder, while she threw her arms round his neck and said in her lisping voice, 'Dear Midnight, what a lovely horse you are! Miss Peters is so lucky to have you.'

'Why, Bonnie!' cried Miss Peters, coming up behind the girl. 'I had no idea that you and Midnight were such good friends.'

'Oh, Miss Peters, I didn't hear you come in!' said Bonnie, turning her big brown eyes on the mistress. 'Yes, I absolutely adore Midnight, though I must admit I was a little afraid of horses until I got to know him. But he's so sweet and gentle that now I can't believe what a silly I was!'

And, under the astonished eyes of Julie and Nora, Miss Peters – who loved Midnight more than anything or anyone else in the world – beamed at Bonnie and said kindly, 'I'm glad that he has helped you to overcome your fear. Perhaps you would like me to take you out on him one day, Bonnie? I can lead him while you sit on his back and just get used to being on a horse.'

'Oh, Miss Peters!' cried Bonnie ecstatically, her eyes shining. 'That would be simply marvellous.'

'Very well,' said the mistress, putting the saddle on to the horse's back. 'I can't take you out now, for I've arranged to meet Bill and Clarissa, but perhaps one day next week?'

Bonnie thanked Miss Peters again, and waved her off as she led Midnight out into the yard before nimbly mounting him and riding off. Then, as the clip-clop of the horse's hooves faded into the distance, she turned to the two third formers and said sweetly, 'Looks like you owe me a stick of toffee, Nora.'

And Nora had to laugh. Bonnie was quite a determined little character once she had made up her mind to do something, even overcoming her fear of horses because she knew that Miss Peters was sure to look kindly on anyone who liked her beloved Midnight. She really was the strangest girl!

Veronica in trouble

The following day, Sunday, was Amy's birthday and the girl had been looking forward to it with mixed feelings. The excitement she would normally have felt was dimmed, because she knew that she would have to tackle her mother about the lies she had told. All the same, it was pleasant to wake up to a chorus of 'Happy Birthday' from the third formers, and – as she knew that she wasn't the most popular girl in the form – Amy was both amazed and delighted to find that everyone had bought her a gift. They were only small things – a jar of bath salts from Veronica, chocolate from Felicity and a hair-slide from Pam, but Amy thanked everyone and smiled round pleasantly. She went into the bathroom to wash, and when she came back there was a large parcel on her bed, wrapped in silver paper with a bow on top. Curious, she ripped it open and gave a gasp. For there was the dress that Bonnie had promised her. The two girls had chosen the material together before they quarrelled, and Amy had assumed that Bonnie was no longer going to make the dress. But here it was, and what a super job Bonnie had done! Amy's eyes shone as she held the pale pink dress against her and Nora said, 'My word, Amy, that's simply beautiful! Is that Bonnie's work?'

'Yes, it is,' answered Amy, glancing across at Bonnie, who was sitting on her bed, bending over to tie her shoelaces, apparently unconcerned, but inwardly hoping that her generous gesture would mend the rift between herself and Amy. And it seemed that it had done the trick, for Amy walked across to Bonnie and, a little awkwardly, said, 'Thank you, Bonnie. That was very kind and thoughtful of you.'

Bonnie looked up and said, 'I'm glad you like it.'

'I like it very much,' said Amy. 'You must have worked like a Trojan to get it finished in time for my birthday. I shall wear it today.'

Immensely gratified, Bonnie smiled. Then she became serious again and said, 'Amy, please can we be friends again? I've missed you so much and I promise that I'll be a *true* friend to you from now on.'

And Amy, who was becoming a little tired of Veronica's company, and missed having someone to chat to about hair-dos and clothes, agreed. Of course, Veronica was not at all pleased that the two girls had made up their quarrel, for she had enjoyed having Amy to herself and now it seemed that she would have to vie with Bonnie for her attention again.

Amy's parents came to collect her at lunchtime and, as the girl got ready to go down and greet them, Felicity said to her, 'I do hope that all goes well for you, Amy, and that your father isn't too angry and upset with your mother. We shall be thinking of you.'

And the third formers did think of her, often, that day,

for although Amy hadn't done much to endear herself to them, they were good-hearted girls and wished her well.

But Felicity had problems of her own to think about, for her belongings were still going missing, and she and her friends were no nearer to finding out who the culprit was. Only yesterday, she had discovered her hairbrush had gone, and she had to borrow Susan's. Really, she thought, it was stealing, but the things the thief was taking were items that were of no value at all. What good was one shoelace, or a script for a play?

Only this morning she had said to Susan, 'I don't understand. Why doesn't she help herself to my purse, or the watch that my parents gave me for my birthday?'

'I think I understand,' said Susan, who had been giving the matter a lot of thought. 'Whoever it is doesn't want these things for herself, she's taking them to annoy you.'

'Well, she's certainly succeeding!' said Felicity. 'But she's going to have to stop soon or I shall have nothing left for her to take!'

Well, there was no point sitting around brooding about it, she decided now. Amanda was holding a lacrosse practice shortly, so she might as well go along to that. Susan had mentioned that she would like to go as well, so Felicity sped off to find her. Susan wasn't in the common-room, so Felicity went up to the dormitory to see if she was there. But as she approached, Felicity heard the sound of raised, angry voices coming from inside. Cautiously, she pushed open the door, and frowned as she realised that the two girls who were rowing were Susan and Veronica! Veronica looked upset and tearful, while Susan was obviously very angry indeed. And on the floor between them was the photograph of herself, Darrell and their parents that Felicity kept on her cabinet, its glass shattered.

'My photograph!' she gasped. 'What happened?'

'You had better ask dear Veronica,' said Susan in a hard voice. 'She can probably tell you where your missing things are as well.'

'No!' cried Veronica. 'I bumped into your cabinet, Felicity, and the photograph fell off and smashed. Susan came in and saw me bending over it, and jumped to conclusions.'

'But what were you doing near my cabinet anyway?' asked Felicity suspiciously. 'Your bed is at the other end of the room, so you had no reason to be over here at all.'

'I – I was looking out of the window,' stammered Veronica.

'What a lame excuse!' said Susan scornfully. 'We might be more inclined to believe you, Veronica, if we didn't know that you had done this kind of thing before.'

Veronica turned white and Susan went on, 'We know that you played mean tricks on Katherine, when both of you were in the second form. And now you're doing exactly the same to Felicity.'

'I admit that I was mean to Katherine,' said Veronica with a sob. 'And the rest of the form never forgave me, no matter how hard I tried to show that I was sorry. In the end I decided it wasn't worth being nice to them, and turned into the sly, sneaky creature they had already decided I was. But I *haven't* played tricks on Felicity!'

'I don't believe you,' said Susan, a disgusted expression on her face. 'You were caught out and now you're trying to talk your way out of it. Why can't you have the decency to own up and give Felicity her things back?'

'Because I don't have them!' yelled Veronica, tears running down her cheeks now. 'Felicity, you must believe me.'

'Veronica, I need to think about all this,' said Felicity, hardly able to look at the girl. She felt quite certain that Veronica was guilty, but at the same time she couldn't help feeling a little sorry for the girl.

'Come on, Susan,' she said at last. 'We'll be late for lacrosse practice if we don't hurry.'

Not that Felicity's mind was on lacrosse at all. She was quite unable to concentrate and didn't play up to her usual standard at all, which earned her a few sharp words from Amanda.

'Never mind, old thing,' said Susan, as they made their way to the changing-room afterwards.

'But I *do* mind!' said Felicity crossly. 'Blow Veronica! Not only has she been plaguing me with these spiteful tricks, but she's probably ruined my chances of getting into one of the teams this term as well!'

'Are you going to go to the Head about her?' asked Susan.

'I don't know,' sighed Felicity. 'As this is the second time she's done something like this, Miss Grayling will probably come down pretty hard on her. She might even expel her!'

'Well, it's quite her own fault,' said Susan unsympathetically. 'She simply can't go around behaving like that and expect to get away with it.'

'I'll sleep on it, and decide whether or not to report her to the Head tomorrow,' decided Felicity. 'And I suppose we'd better let the others know that we've solved the mystery.'

Veronica didn't put in an appearance at teatime, and Mam'zelle Dupont frowned when she saw the two empty places at the table.

'Who is missing?' she asked. 'Ah yes, Amy is out with her parents, is she not? But where is Veronica?'

'I don't think she was feeling very well, Mam'zelle,' said Felicity uncomfortably, feeling that someone ought to make an excuse for Veronica's absence in case the French mistress decided to make enquiries.

'Ah, *la pauvre*!' said Mam'zelle sympathetically. 'If she feels no better tomorrow, she must go to Matron and have some medicine.'

'I don't think Matron has any medicine that will cure a guilty conscience,' muttered Susan under her breath to Felicity. 'This proves that she's the one who was playing tricks on you, for she's afraid to come and face us.'

'What *are* you talking about?' asked Pam, who was on Susan's other side and had overheard some of this.

'We'll tell you later,' said Felicity in a low voice, leaning across. 'You, Nora and Julie come to the little music-room after tea. I don't want old Mam'zelle listening in.'

So, as soon as tea was over, the five girls rushed off to the music-room, and there was an outcry when Pam, Nora and Julie heard that it was Veronica who had been behind Felicity's troubles.

'The mean beast!'

'I *knew* it was her! A leopard never changes its spots.'

'And to think that she didn't even have the courage to own up when she was caught in the act!'

'My word, won't I tell her what I think of her when I see her!' said Julie angrily.

But Felicity said, 'Please don't say anything to her tonight, Julie. I need to think about whether I'm going to tell the Head or not. Besides, I should think that Amy has had quite a trying day, and I don't want her walking into a bad atmosphere when she comes back.'

'It's jolly decent of you to feel like that and to put Amy first,' said Pam warmly. 'But I suppose that's what makes you such a good head-girl.'

Felicity turned quite pink with pleasure and said, 'Do you *really* think that I'm a good head-girl?'

'I think you're first class,' said Pam firmly. 'You always consider other people's feelings, you're kind and helpful – and you're not domineering.'

'Hear, hear!' chorused the others.

'Thank you!' laughed Felicity, feeling very pleased indeed. 'Now we'd better go to the common-room, before the others send out a search party.'

'I wonder if Veronica will be there,' said Nora.

'Don't worry, Felicity, I shan't say anything to her, or to the others – yet.'

Veronica *was* in the common-room, looking very pale and red-eyed – and so was Amy. She was telling Bonnie and Veronica about her day, and the others gathered round to listen.

'Mummy didn't even attempt to make any excuses for herself, once she knew that I had met Grandmother,' Amy was saying. 'She said that she had intended to tell Daddy the truth once they were married, but that somehow the longer she put it off the harder it got.'

'Well, I can sort of understand that,' said Freddie. 'Was your father simply furious?'

'He was, rather,' said Amy, with a grimace. 'And terribly hurt that Mummy thought he wouldn't want to marry her simply because her parents hadn't been wealthy. He had come round a bit by the time I said goodbye to them though. He simply adores Mummy, you see, and he can never stay cross with her for very long. And meeting Grandmother helped. We went there after lunch, and she and Daddy are firm friends now.'

'That is good news!' said Felicity, happily. 'But how did you explain your father's rather sudden change of heart?'

'Well, we couldn't tell her the truth, of course, for it would have hurt her too much,' said Amy. 'So we just said that Mummy and I had talked him round and he realised how foolish and snobbish he had been. Poor Daddy had to apologise to Grandmother and, I must say, he did it very convincingly. I never realised that he was such a good actor! And the best thing of all is that Daddy is going to find Grandmother a little house near ours, so I shall be able to see her in the holidays.'

'That must have been the best birthday present of all!' cried Susan, marvelling at how happy Amy looked.

'Yes, it was,' agreed Amy. 'Oh, and Grandmother baked me the most *enormous* birthday cake, to bring back to school with me. We'll all share it at teatime tomorrow.'

The third formers rubbed their hands together at this, and there were cries of 'Jolly decent of you, Amy!'

Then Freddie, who had been looking rather wistful, sighed and said, 'I shall miss Mrs Dale awfully. I do think you're lucky to have her as a gran, Amy.'

'Well, she'll be here until the end of term,' said Amy. 'And I know that she'd like you to visit her again before she leaves, Freddie.'

That cheered Freddie up, and it was a happy bunch of third formers who trooped up to bed a little later. Apart from two of them. Felicity had been surreptitiously watching Veronica while they were in the common-room, and the girl had looked thoroughly miserable, lost in her own thoughts and hardly uttering a word. And Felicity herself, of course, was deeply troubled, as she knew that she would soon have to make a decision about whether or not to report Veronica to the Head. If only it was clear cut, but when the girl had been talking of her troubles with Katherine earlier, and of how her form had snubbed her efforts to make amends, Felicity had caught a glimpse of that humbler, softer Veronica that she had seen at half-term. The decision that Felicity made would affect Veronica's whole future, and the girl felt the responsibility weighing heavily on her slim shoulders.

At last Felicity fell asleep, and when she awoke her mind was clear. If Veronica went unpunished, and thought that she had got away with her mean tricks, it could lead her into far more serious trouble.

She signalled to Susan, Pam, Julie and Nora to stay behind in the dormitory as the others went down to breakfast, and told them of her decision.

'I really do think that you have made the right decision, Felicity,' said Susan. 'And I only hope that Veronica learns something from all this. When are you going to see Miss Grayling?'

'I'll go right after breakfast,' said Felicity. 'It's not going to be pleasant, and I'd rather get it over with as soon as possible.'

'I know that Veronica's behaviour has been despicable,' said Pam, with a frown. 'But I hope that Miss Grayling doesn't expel her.'

Suddenly a little squeal sounded from behind the group of girls and they all turned sharply, to see Bonnie standing there, a startled look on her face.

'Bonnie!' cried Felicity. 'I thought that you had gone to breakfast.'

'I was in the bathroom,' said Bonnie, an odd expression on her face. 'Pam, why should Miss Grayling expel Veronica?'

Pam exchanged a look with Felicity, who nodded and

said, 'There's no reason why you shouldn't tell Bonnie the truth. Everyone will know soon enough.'

'Well, Bonnie, we found out that Veronica was responsible for Felicity's things going missing,' Pam told the girl. 'Not only that, but she smashed her photograph.'

Bonnie said nothing, but just stood there looking absolutely stunned, and the girls, knowing that she was no friend of Veronica's, wondered why.

'I say, Bonnie, do you feel all right?' asked Julie.

'Yes, but I need to speak to Felicity privately,' said Bonnie, twisting her hands together agitatedly. 'Would the rest of you mind awfully leaving us alone?'

So, bursting with curiosity, the others went off to breakfast, while Felicity wondered what on earth Bonnie wanted. The girl hadn't spoken to her at all lately, unless she absolutely had to, so whatever she had to say must be extremely important.

Veronica gets a chance

'What is it, Bonnie?' asked Felicity, who was hungry and didn't want to get into trouble for being late in to breakfast.

Bonnie didn't answer. Instead, she went to the little cabinet beside her bed and pulled out a cardboard box, which she passed to Felicity.

'Take a look inside,' she said.

Felicity removed the lid – and gave a gasp. For there inside were her missing belongings. Her pen, the script of the play, a shoelace – and all the other things that she had mislaid recently.

'But I don't understand!' exclaimed Felicity, looking perplexed. 'How did they come to be in your cabinet, Bonnie? Did Veronica ask you to hide them for her?'

This seemed most unlikely, given that Bonnie and Veronica were hardly the best of friends, but Felicity could think of no other explanation.

'Of course not,' said Bonnie, gazing doe-eyed at Felicity. 'Veronica didn't take your things. It was me.'

'*You?*' said Felicity, sitting down plump upon her bed, so great was her astonishment. 'But – but why, Bonnie?'

'To pay you back for being mean to me, of course,' answered Bonnie simply, as though it was the most normal thing in the world for her to have played spiteful tricks on Felicity. 'You see, I thought you were my friend. And then, when I found out that you weren't, I was terribly angry. But, of course, I quite see that I couldn't let Veronica take the blame and possibly be expelled, much as I dislike her.'

Felicity was quite speechless for a moment, taken aback as much by Bonnie's matter-of-fact honesty as by the realisation that she was the person who had been playing pranks on her. At last she found her voice and said, 'Yes, it would have been very wrong of you to let Veronica take the blame. But, Bonnie, didn't it also occur to you that it was wrong to take my things in the first place? Why, it's stealing!'

'Of course it isn't!' said Bonnie. 'I never meant to keep your stuff. Why, what on earth would I want with an odd shoelace and a copy of a script that I already have? I always intended to give you your things back at the end of term. And I couldn't think of another way of getting back at you.'

Bonnie, thought Felicity, had a way of explaining the most extraordinary things so that they seemed quite ordinary! She tried once more to impress upon the girl that she had done wrong, saying, 'But you must have known that I was annoyed and upset about my things going missing?'

'Yes, I did,' said Bonnie, nodding her pretty head. 'But that was the whole point. I mean to say, what's the good of playing those kind of tricks on someone if it doesn't bother them?'

'Yes, but Bonnie, the thing is that you *shouldn't* have played those tricks on me at all,' said Felicity earnestly. 'I understand that you felt hurt, but that isn't the way that we deal with things at Malory Towers.'

'Really? Very well then, I shan't do it again,' said Bonnie blithely. 'Oh dear, Felicity, do look at the time! We shall get into a dreadful row if we go down to breakfast now. Not that I'm very hungry, are you?'

'Not any more,' answered Felicity, sighing. 'Bonnie, you do realise that I'm going to have to tell Susan and the others about this, don't you? Not to mention Veronica herself.'

'Must you?' said Bonnie, pouting a little. 'I was rather hoping that we could keep it just between the two of us.'

'Well, we can't,' said Felicity firmly. 'The others have a terrific down on Veronica because they think that she was behind all those tricks on me, and I must set them straight. And as for Veronica herself – my goodness, it must be simply dreadful to be wrongly accused of something when you know that you are innocent! I must tell her as soon as possible that her name has been cleared.'

'Yes, I suppose that you must do that,' agreed Bonnie, a little reluctantly. 'Though I suppose it means that everyone will turn against me now. How horrid!'

But somehow Felicity knew that Bonnie, who was a great deal tougher than she looked, would cope with the situation in her own way.

'The sly little beast!' cried Susan, when Felicity broke the news to her, Nora, Pam and Julie after morning school.

'That's the thing about Bonnie, though,' remarked Pam thoughtfully. 'Even when she's being sly, she's quite honest about it. I mean to say, she was going to own up to what she had done and give Felicity her things back all along. So really, she's *not* being sly.'

'She certainly has her own, unique way of looking at things,' said Nora, shaking her head. 'Although some of her ideas are quite wrong, of course.'

'I daresay some of our ways will rub off on her when she's been at Malory Towers for a while,' said Julie. 'That's the best of a splendid school like this – as well as learning things like Maths and English and all the rest of it, you learn other things that are equally important. Things like a sense of decency, fairness and responsibility.'

But Susan was less inclined to be lenient and, when the other three girls had departed, she said to Felicity, 'I hope that you are going to let Miss Grayling deal with Bonnie.'

'I hadn't really thought about it,' said Felicity, biting her lip. 'Do you think that I should, Susan?'

'Of course!' said Susan firmly. 'You were going to report Veronica to the Head, so I don't see what the difference is.'

'There *is* a difference,' said Felicity. 'Bonnie hasn't been to school before, and she doesn't fully understand –'

'Oh, Felicity, don't *you* start sticking up for her!' Susan interrupted impatiently. 'At her age she ought to know the difference between right and wrong. Not having been to school before can't be used as an excuse for simply *everything*, you know!'

Felicity knew that Susan was right. But she also knew

that Susan was angry at herself, as well as Bonnie, for she had been the first one to accuse Veronica directly of playing tricks on Felicity. So she slipped her arm through Susan's and said, 'Don't let's you and I fall out about this, old thing. That would be worse than anything! I'll think about reporting Bonnie, I promise. But before I do anything else, I must apologise to Veronica.'

Her anger cooling instantly, Susan gave Felicity's arm a squeeze and said ruefully, 'You're not the only one who owes Veronica an apology. I was very quick to accuse her, and didn't even bother listening to her explanation because I had made my mind up that she was guilty. This will certainly be a lesson to me not to judge people too hastily, I can tell you. Come along, let's go and find her now.'

Veronica was standing alone, glumly watching a group of second formers tossing a ball around, and both girls felt sorry for her. A thought occurred to Felicity and she said, 'I bet that Veronica's going to be pushed out, now that Amy and Bonnie have made up.'

Susan agreed and said, 'I never thought that Amy was very keen on Veronica anyway. The two of them have absolutely nothing in common. I can't say that I'm terribly fond of Veronica, but it must be simply dreadful having no one to talk to, or to share fun and secrets with. What a pity that we can't help her in some way.'

'But we can,' said Felicity, excitedly. 'You see, Susan, I think that there's another side to Veronica – a kind, decent side. I've seen it once or twice and I think that if we try hard – really hard – perhaps we can bring it out.'

Susan, eager to make up to Veronica for accusing her unjustly, said at once, 'What do you have in mind?'

'Well, I just think that we ought to give her a chance – you know, be nice to her and include her in things. Now that Amy isn't so eager for her company, I think she might take the chance that we are offering.'

'Yes, let's do that,' said Susan. 'Though I can think of one person who won't want any part of it – and that's June. She's never had any time for Veronica, and she's bound to pour cold water on the idea.'

'June can jolly well do as she's told and follow our lead for once,' retorted Felicity, a determined expression on her face. 'And if she dares to sneer at me I shall have a few words to say to her!'

And, looking at the glint in her friend's eye, Susan had no doubt that Felicity would do just that! But now they had another matter to deal with, and Felicity didn't beat around the bush, going across to Veronica and saying frankly, 'Veronica, I know now that it wasn't you who took my things and I'm sorry that I didn't believe you when you said that you were innocent. Please accept my apology.'

She held her hand out and Veronica, looking a little disbelieving at first, took it, and said, 'What's happened? Have you found out who really did it?'

'Yes,' said Felicity. 'It was Bonnie. She owned up when she found out that I suspected you.'

'And I'm sorry too, Veronica,' said Susan, coming forward. 'I saw you standing over the broken photograph and was ready to believe the worst of you. It was very wrong of me.'

Veronica, looking both surprised and pleased, turned red and said, 'No, it wasn't. It's quite my own fault if people think badly of me, I see that now. And I admit that I didn't like you very much at first, Felicity, but I could never do a mean act to someone who showed me the kindness that you and your parents did at half-term. No matter what happens between us in the future, that is something I shall never forget.'

Now it was Felicity's turn to go red, for she felt quite moved by Veronica's little speech – and there could be no doubting the girl's sincerity. Susan stepped into the breach, saying, 'Felicity and I were just off to lacrosse practice. Why don't you come along with us, Veronica?'

Amazed, and secretly delighted to be asked, Veronica said, 'There's no point in me coming. I'm not very good at lacrosse – or any games, for that matter.'

'Perhaps not, but you can still come along to watch, and shout a few words of encouragement to Susan and me,' said Felicity. 'Goodness knows we could do with them!'

So it came about that June and Freddie, who were already on the lacrosse field, were quite astonished to see Felicity, Susan and *Veronica*, of all people, coming towards them, all three girls chattering amicably together.

'Our dear Veronica seems to have made two new friends,' drawled June, once Veronica had taken her place on the sidelines and Felicity and Susan were on the field. 'Really, Felicity, I know that you always like to see the best in people, but surely even you must see that you're wasting your time with *her*.'

'You're wrong, June,' said Felicity, refusing to be ruffled by June's mocking tone. 'Susan and I have decided to give Veronica a chance to prove that she's not as bad as people think. And I would like the rest of the form, including *you*, June, to follow our lead.'

June laughed and said jeeringly, 'I'm not sucking up to that sly, spiteful beast. If you ask me –'

But June got no further, for Freddie piped up unexpectedly, giving June a push and saying sharply, 'No one did ask you, June! You ought to be the first to give Veronica a chance, considering the way you have behaved this term.'

'Freddie is quite right,' said Susan sternly. 'At least Veronica has learned something from her mistakes, but I don't think that you have, June.'

'Oh, June has nothing to learn,' said Felicity, giving the girl a hard look. 'She knows it all, don't you, June?'

Disconcerted by this sudden attack from all sides, June was lost for a suitable retort and Felicity went on, 'The trouble with you, June, is that nothing makes a lasting impression on you. I know that you regretted getting Freddie involved with Mrs Dale and were shaken by the upset you caused. And I'm willing to bet that you told Freddie – *and* yourself – that you had learned your lesson. But you haven't. Now that you've been forgiven by all concerned, you're back to your bold, bumptious, hard-hearted old self again.'

'Yes, and you promised me that you would do anything to make it up to me, if only I would forgive you,' said Freddie. 'Well, June, if you really mean that, I want you to back Felicity up and at least *try* to be nice to Veronica.'

June had to admit that there was a lot of truth in the others' words, and she certainly didn't want to fall out with Freddie again, so she said, 'I know that I can be hard, sometimes – it's just the way I am. My cousin Alicia was the same, though she softened a little as she got older, and perhaps I will too. As for being bumptious, Alicia used to say that I was like a rubber ball – no matter how hard anyone tried to squash me flat I always bounced back into shape again. Perhaps that will change one day, as well. And you're all absolutely right about one thing – I *have* behaved dreadfully this term and I *should* give Veronica a chance to prove that she has a good side. And that's exactly what I intend to do.'

That was good enough for Felicity. June had her faults – bad faults – but if she said she would do a thing she stuck to it.

Veronica was also doing her best, and surprised herself by becoming completely wrapped up in the practice game that took place, excitedly calling out her encouragement to the others.

'Play up, Susan!'

'Jolly good shot, Felicity!'

'Oh, well done, June!'

This last came as June took a particularly difficult shot at goal and managed to get the ball past the goalkeeper.

And Felicity was pleased when June heard Veronica's cry and turned to smile at her, giving her a cheery wave. With only one week to go to the end of term, perhaps things were finally sorting themselves out. Now, if only Felicity could decide what to do about Bonnie!

Felicity took a little time to herself after tea to walk alone in the grounds and consider the problem, but as dusk began to fall she was no nearer a solution. Bonnie certainly needed to be brought to a sense of her wrongdoing, and to learn that she couldn't take revenge every time someone upset her. She was spoilt, vain and quite unscrupulous when it came to getting her own way. But, Felicity had come to realise, the girl actually had quite a few good qualities too. She was single-minded and determined when she had a goal in sight, honest and not afraid to speak up for herself. And where better than Malory Towers for Bonnie to learn to cultivate these qualities and strive to make the good in her character cancel out the bad?

So lost in thought was she, that Felicity didn't realise she had walked as far as Miss Grayling's private garden, until the Head herself appeared in front of her.

'Why, it's you, Felicity!' she said in surprise. 'What are you doing over here, my dear?'

'I was thinking about something, Miss Grayling, and didn't realise that I had come so far,' said Felicity. 'I suppose that I had better make my way back to North Tower.'

Miss Grayling looked hard at the girl for a moment, then said, 'Actually, I'm glad you're here, for there's something I wanted to discuss with you. Come into my study.'

Felicity followed Miss Grayling across her neat little lawn, and through the French windows into her study, wondering what the Head wanted to talk to her about. Not more trouble, surely?

Miss Grayling took a seat behind her big desk and invited Felicity to sit opposite her, then she began, 'I wanted to speak to you about Veronica Sharpe. As you are probably aware, she wasn't very popular with her own form, which is why I decided to keep her back for a term, to see if a break from the girls who disliked her so much would do her good. As head-girl of the third form, I want to know what you think of her.'

'Well, we've had a few problems with Veronica,' said Felicity, feeling very honoured that the Head had asked her opinion and wanting to be as honest as possible. 'And she hasn't been awfully popular with our form either. But I think that, underneath it all, she's actually quite a decent person. We're all doing our best to give her a chance to prove herself, and she seems to be taking it.'

'That is good to hear,' said Miss Grayling. 'You see, Felicity, Veronica is really too old to stay down in the third form for more than a term. I have discussed the matter with Miss Peters and we both feel that Veronica ought to join the fourth formers next term. She will have had a long break from them, and they from her, so hopefully they will be able to start afresh.'

Felicity hoped so too. Perhaps she ought to have a talk with Katherine, who was now head-girl of the fourth, and see if she could persuade her to let bygones be bygones. If

Katherine was willing to hold out the hand of friendship to Veronica, the rest of the fourth formers were sure to do so as well. Then it occurred to Felicity that, if she was going to report Bonnie to the Head, now was as good a time as any. The trouble was, deep down inside, she *didn't* want to involve Miss Grayling, but would far rather keep what she had done a private third-form matter. Was it weakness on her part to feel like that? Felicity hoped not, for she so wanted to be a strong leader, like Darrell had been. As these thoughts flitted across the girl's mind, Miss Grayling's keen blue eyes watched her, seeing a lot more than Felicity realised. At last the Head asked, 'Is anything troubling you, Felicity?'

'Er – no, Miss Grayling, of course not,' she answered, nerves making her voice rather high.

'Are you sure?' asked Miss Grayling. 'You know that if you have any worries you can always bring them to me. That is what I am here for, after all.'

Felicity hesitated. Could she tell the Head what was on her mind without bringing Bonnie's name into it? She decided to try and began, 'Well, you see, Miss Grayling, I've had a problem with a girl in the third form. It's quite a trivial matter, and I think that I would rather deal with it myself than report it. But I can't be certain that I am doing the right thing, either for the form as a whole, or for the girl concerned. I keep asking myself what Darrell would have done in this situation, but –'

'My dear Felicity, what on earth does Darrell have to do with the matter?' the Head interrupted sharply.

'She was always so sure of herself,' said Felicity. 'And such a marvellous Head Girl. Somehow I feel that if I make the wrong decision, I will be letting her down as well as myself.'

'Darrell was an excellent Head Girl,' agreed Miss Grayling. 'But that isn't to say that she never made mistakes, particularly when she was lower down the school. Darrell wasn't perfect – nobody is. I recall that she had an extremely hot temper that caused her problems on a number of occasions!'

The Head smiled as she said this, and Felicity smiled shyly back, saying, 'She still *does* have a hot temper, though she has learned to control it a lot better now.'

'Exactly,' said Miss Grayling. 'She *learned* to control it. As you, Felicity, will learn to have faith in your own instincts and your own judgement. You see, Darrell isn't head of the third form – *you* are. And you are very different from Darrell, so you must stop wondering what she would do in this situation, or that situation. As for how you should deal with the matter you brought up – well, I think you have already answered that yourself. Do what *you* feel is right. It may turn out to be the wrong decision, but at least it will be *your* decision.'

And, as Felicity listened to Miss Grayling's words of wisdom, everything suddenly became crystal clear in her mind. She had worried too much about what other people thought of her, and about whether they were comparing her unfavourably to her older sister. Being a strong leader didn't always mean being outspoken, or forthright. It meant being true to yourself and your own character. And from now on, thought Felicity, as she said goodbye to the Head, that was exactly what she was going to be!

A happy end to the term

The last week of term simply flew by, and there was an air of great excitement throughout the school as the girls began to look forward to Christmas, pantomimes and parties.

'My first term as head of the form is almost over already,' said Felicity to Susan. 'And my word, what a term it's been!'

'It's certainly had its ups and downs,' agreed Susan. 'Thank goodness the last few days have been mostly ups!'

'Yes, Amy's been a lot happier since that business with her grandmother was settled,' said Felicity. 'And even Bonnie has been showing a bit of common sense since I gave her that talking to.'

Felicity, having decided that she wasn't going to report Bonnie for her bad behaviour, had taken the girl to one side to inform her of the fact. Bonnie, however, didn't seem to realise what a lucky escape she had had, merely smiling and saying off-handedly, 'Oh, thanks, Felicity,' before bending her head over the sewing she was working on. Felicity had stared down at the girl's curly head for a few moments, before coming to another decision. Bonnie might have been spared a dressing-down from Miss Grayling, but Felicity was jolly well going to tell her what standard of behaviour was expected of a Malory Towers girl.

Bonnie listened open-mouthed and, when Felicity finished her stern little speech, she managed to squeeze out a few tears. Felicity, though, was quite convinced that they weren't genuine and were just an attempt to gain sympathy, so she remained quite unmoved by them. And, over the next few days, she noticed that Bonnie did seem to be making an effort to behave more sensibly, which pleased Felicity immensely and made her feel that her words hadn't fallen on completely deaf ears.

Even Susan, who had thought that Felicity had made a mistake in choosing to deal with Bonnie herself, had to admit that she had been wrong.

'Bonnie certainly seems to have turned over a new leaf,' she said now. 'And as for Veronica – well, she's like a completely different person. That's thanks to you as well.'

Felicity brushed this off with her usual modesty, yet she couldn't help but feel a small stirring of satisfaction as she watched Veronica laughing and joking with Pam and Nora in a way that would have been quite unimaginable a couple of weeks ago. Felicity had kept the promise she had made to herself, and spoken to Katherine of the fourth form about Veronica.

Fortunately, Katherine was a good-hearted girl and she agreed to persuade the fourth formers to make Veronica feel welcome when she joined them the next term.

'I never thought I would say this, but I shall actually miss Veronica when she moves up into the fourth,' said

Felicity. 'Now that she's put her spiteful ways behind her, she's really a nice person.'

'And she's got quite a sense of humour too,' said Susan. 'My goodness, I thought she was going to burst with laughter when Freddie and June played that trick on Mam'zelle Dupont yesterday.'

Veronica hadn't been the only one who had nearly burst, for the trick had been very funny indeed!

Freddie had waited until Susan took her book up to Mam'zelle's desk to have her work marked, then let out a piercing scream, which caused the French mistress to start violently, sending a shower of small blots over Susan's book.

'*Mon dieu!*' Mam'zelle cried angrily. 'Freddie, you bad girl! See what you have made me do? I have ruined the poor Susan's work. What is it that makes you scream like that?

'A s-spider!' Freddie stammered, making her eyes big and scared. 'I'm sorry that I startled you, Mam'zelle, but I do so hate spiders.'

In fact, Freddie wasn't scared of spiders at all, but Mam'zelle was, and she turned quite pale. 'Where did it go?' she asked, her voice quavering a little.

'It scuttled across the floor towards your desk, Mam'zelle,' Freddie answered.

Poor Mam'zelle looked most alarmed at this, her beady eyes rapidly scanning the floor around her desk.

'I see no spider,' Mam'zelle said at last. 'Freddie, if this is a trick . . .'

'It's no trick, Mam'zelle,' Nora piped up, very seriously. 'I saw it too. It was huge – almost as big as a mouse!'

Mam'zelle gave a little shriek, but Felicity said soothingly, 'It's all right, Mam'zelle. I think it escaped under the door and went out into the corridor.'

'Ah, thank goodness,' Mam'zelle sighed in relief, adding unnecessarily, 'Me, I do not like spiders. Susan, *ma chère*, I am sorry that I have spoiled your so-excellent work. You may go and sit down now.'

Susan, who knew that she had made several mistakes, was not at all sorry and went back to her seat thankfully. For the next few minutes the lesson progressed smoothly, then, when Mam'zelle turned to write something on the blackboard, Bonnie let out a loud squeal. Once again, Mam'zelle jumped, the chalk that she was holding skidding across the blackboard before she whirled round to face the class.

'The spider, Mam'zelle!' Bonnie squeaked, before the French mistress could speak. 'It's back! I saw it run up the leg of your desk.'

Mam'zelle leaped backwards, swaying on her high heels and almost overbalancing, causing Nora to let out one of her terrific snorts. Fortunately Mam'zelle was too preoccupied to hear it and she called out, 'June! You are not afraid of spiders. You are not afraid of *anything*! Come out here and search for the creature.'

So June, managing to keep her face remarkably straight, went over to Mam'zelle's desk and walked slowly around it, her expression so ridiculously solemn that it was too much for some of the girls. Felicity shook with silent laughter, while Pam and Julie had tears pouring down their cheeks. As for Veronica, her shoulders heaved as she struggled to control her mirth!

At last June said, 'I can't see the spider now, Mam'zelle. Perhaps I had better check inside your desk, to make sure that it's not hiding in there.'

Mam'zelle agreed to this at once, so June lifted the lid of the desk and rummaged around inside very thoroughly, making a lot of quite unnecessary noise as she poked in all the corners with a ruler. But no spider emerged and, feeling that it was safe to do so, Mam'zelle sent June back to her seat.

Then she almost collapsed into her own chair, saying, 'Poof! My heart, it goes pitter-pat! I have the palpitations!'

And she reached into the large, black handbag that she carried everywhere with her, pulling out her handkerchief so that she could mop her brow. But something else fell out of Mam'zelle's bag as well – the most enormous spider she had ever seen in her life! The girls had seen June slip it into the French mistress's bag as she pretended to look for the spider, but Mam'zelle hadn't. Poor Mam'zelle was also completely unaware that the spider wasn't real, but was, in fact, the rubber one that Alicia had sent to her cousin. It landed on the desk in front of her with a plop and, for a second, the French mistress could only stare helplessly at the enormous beast, frozen in terror. Then she jumped to her feet so suddenly that her chair crashed to the ground, and she let out a scream far louder than either Freddie's or Bonnie's had been.

'June!' she cried in anguish. 'Rescue me from this monster at once!'

June obliged immediately, bustling to the front of the class and putting her hand over the spider. 'Heavens, it's a big one!' she exclaimed. 'Are you sure you don't want to keep it as a pet, Mam'zelle?'

Mam'zelle was quite sure, shouting, 'It is *abominable*! Remove it at once, June, I beg of you!'

And, to the delight of the class, June picked up the spider by one of its legs, shaking her hand so that it looked as if the creature was trying to escape. Mam'zelle gave a shudder of revulsion, while the third formers, quite unable to contain their mirth now, laughed helplessly.

Unfortunately for them, Miss Potts was taking the first form in the neighbouring classroom, and had wondered what on earth could be going on next door. Eventually the noise had become so intrusive that she had hardly been able to hear herself speak, the first formers looking at one another in bewilderment.

This is too bad! Miss Potts thought to herself crossly. Mam'zelle must have left the room for a moment, and the third formers are taking advantage of her absence to play the fool. They really are old enough to know better!

And the mistress swept from the room, rapping sharply on the door of the third-form's classroom. However, the class was in such an uproar that no one even heard the knocking, so Miss Potts pushed open the door, halting on the threshold as her keen eyes took in the scene before her. There was Mam'zelle, in a state of great agitation, the girls reduced to tears of helpless laughter, and June, in the thick of the action – as usual!

'Mam'zelle!' she said loudly. 'What is the meaning of this?'

The mistress's stern voice and expression effectively sobered the third formers, and their laughter died away, as Mam'zelle cried, 'Ah, Miss Potts! There is a spider! As big as a man's fist. But the dear June, she has captured it.'

'Has she, indeed?' said Miss Potts drily, turning her steely gaze on the suddenly sheepish June. And, at once, Miss Potts saw what Mam'zelle hadn't – that the spider was a trick one.

'How brave of you, June,' she said sarcastically, before turning back to the French mistress. 'Mam'zelle, I should take a closer look at that spider, if I were you.'

With that, Miss Potts went out, shutting the door none too gently behind her, while Mam'zelle stared after her, half-indignant and half-puzzled. Had Miss Potts gone mad? Why should she, Mam'zelle, want to take a closer look at the spider? She wanted to get as far away from the spider as possible! She turned back to face the class, and suddenly realised that all the girls were looking rather apprehensive. Especially June, still standing in front of her desk holding the spider. A very still spider, which wasn't wriggling or moving at all now. All at once, the truth dawned on Mam'zelle – she had been tricked!

'June!' she snapped. 'You are a bad girl – you are all

bad girls, for you have tricked your poor Mam'zelle. Go to your seat now, and I shall decide what punishment to give you.'

The third formers were extremely subdued for the rest of the lesson, though every so often one or other of them couldn't help smiling as she remembered Mam'zelle's reaction to the spider. It would be a shame if they were punished, of course, but at the same time – what a super trick it had been!

At the end of the lesson, Mam'zelle stood up and looked round the class with sombre dark eyes. At last, she said heavily, 'I have decided on your punishment. You will all of you write me an essay in the holidays on the habits of spiders – in French!'

There was a gasp of dismay at this, as the girls looked at one another, aghast. They had *far* more important things to do in the holidays than write a beastly French essay! Didn't Mam'zelle realise that it was Christmas?

The French mistress looked with satisfaction at the expressions of horror on the girls' faces. Then a slow smile spread over her face, and she began to laugh. 'Hah!' she cried. 'Now it is I, Mam'zelle, who have tricked you! There will be no essay for you to do in the holidays. But you are all wicked girls, and your punishment will be to work twice as hard for me next term!'

'We will, Mam'zelle! We promise!' everyone called out at once, both relieved and delighted.

'Good old Mam'zelle!' chuckled Felicity as the girls filed out of the classroom.

'Yes, she's a real sport,' said Susan.

'And that was a simply first-rate trick, June and Freddie,' said Pam, grinning. 'My word, I thought I should die of laughter when that spider dropped on to Mam'zelle's desk.'

'Super!' agreed everyone.

As she recalled the trick now, Felicity said, with a little sigh, 'Oh, what fun we've had. I'm so looking forward to going home, and Christmas, and seeing my parents and Darrell. But I know that in a couple of weeks I shall be simply dying to get back to Malory Towers again.'

'I wonder if you'll see much of dear Bonnie during the holidays,' said Susan, and Felicity gave a groan.

The only thing marring her anticipation of the Christmas holidays was the thought that Bonnie would still be living down the road. The two of them had been getting along a lot better now that the air had been cleared between them, though it was obvious that Bonnie was happy with Amy as her friend and no longer worshipped Felicity. But the lingering fear that, when she was separated from Amy, Bonnie would cling to her again, would not go away. After all, one could never be *quite* sure what was going on in Bonnie's head!

But there was one final piece of good news for Felicity. Two days before the end of term, Bonnie came up to her, a letter in her hand.

'Guess what, Felicity?' she said. 'I've had a letter from Mummy – and we're moving! Daddy has got a job in another part of the country, so we're going to live there.

We shall be leaving a few days after Christmas.'

Felicity hardly knew what to say, but at last she managed, 'Well, I'm – er – I'm very sorry to hear that, Bonnie. I – um – I shall miss you.'

Bonnie looked hard at Felicity, then went off into a peal of laughter. 'No, you won't! You'll be jolly glad to see the back of me – admit it!'

Bonnie didn't seem at all offended, so Felicity grinned and said, 'I wouldn't go quite *that* far. You know, Bonnie you're not so bad really. You've just got some rather strange ideas about things!'

'So you keep telling me,' laughed Bonnie. 'Well, I shall be coming back to Malory Towers after the holidays, so perhaps then I shall learn how to be a proper Malory Towers schoolgirl!'

'Well, let's hope so,' said Pam later, when Felicity repeated this conversation. 'She does seem to have gained a *little* common sense just lately.'

'Yes, but I just hope her parents don't go and undo the good work we've done,' said Felicity. 'They're bound to thoroughly spoil her over Christmas.'

'And there's someone else who will be completely spoilt when she goes home,' said Julie as Amy walked by. 'I wonder what fabulous gifts Amy's parents are planning to bestow on her this Christmas!'

'Mrs Dale will keep her feet on the ground all right,' said Freddie. 'Or at any rate, she'll do her best to.'

'Well, jolly good luck to her,' said Nora, who wasn't particularly interested in Amy or Bonnie, but was looking forward to spending time with her own family. 'My word, only two days to go, then we shall be home! Where has the term gone?'

No one could answer that, but the next day flew by even faster, and then it was the last day.

The big entrance hall was very crowded and noisy as girls and mistresses said their goodbyes, invitations to Christmas parties were exchanged and parents who had come to collect their daughters joined the melee.

'Goodbye, Miss Peters! Goodbye, Mam'zelle Dupont!'

'Don't eat too much Christmas pudding, will you, Pam?'

'I'll see you at the pantomime on Boxing Day, Susan.'

'Felicity, your parents are here! They're outside.'

And it was time for Felicity to leave. She ran outside to greet her mother and father, stopping when she got to the big front door to say, 'Goodbye, Malory Towers – see you next term. I shall miss you!'

And we shall miss you, Felicity. But we'll see you again very soon.

Malory Towers
Summer Term

Written by Pamela Cox

Contents

1 Off to Malory Towers 207

2 The new girls 219

3 A hard time for Esme 231

4 Settling in 241

5 A visit to Five Oaks 252

6 Secrets and surprises 263

7 The third form rallies round 275

8 A marvellous trick 284

9 Tricks and tennis 300

10 A super half-term 311

11 A family reunion 322

12 Mam'zelle is a sport 335

13 A shock for Julie 344

14 Detective work 354

15 A thrilling night 366

16 Heroines and villains 375

17 A surprise for June 385

18 A lovely end to the term 395

Off to Malory Towers

'Where *have* those two girls got to?' asked Mr Rivers impatiently, poking his head out of the car window.

'They will be here any minute,' said his wife calmly. 'Don't forget that they haven't seen each other for a few weeks, so I expect that they have a lot of news to catch up on.'

'Well, they'll have plenty of time to talk on the journey,' said Mr Rivers. 'If we don't leave soon, we shan't reach Malory Towers until after tea.'

Mr and Mrs Rivers were taking their daughter, Felicity, back to her boarding school, Malory Towers, after the holidays, and they had stopped to pick up her friend, Susan, on the way. Felicity had gone into the house to fetch her friend, and she seemed to have been in there for simply ages! At last the front door opened and two laughing, chattering girls emerged. The one with dark, bobbed hair and laughing brown eyes was Felicity, and the other, grey-eyed and snub-nosed, was Susan. Both of them wore the Malory Towers summer uniform, which was an orange and white checked dress, with short sleeves and a crisp white collar, and they looked very smart indeed as they walked arm-in-arm down the path. Behind them came Susan's parents, her mother carrying a night case and her father huffing and puffing as he carried his daughter's trunk to the car.

'My goodness, anyone would think you were going back to school for a whole year, not just a term,' he joked. 'I'm sure that you must have packed the kitchen sink in here.'

The two sets of parents greeted one another, and Mr Rivers got out of the car to help Mr Blake stow the trunk in the boot. Then Susan hugged her parents, the two girls settled themselves in the back seat of the car and they were off – back to Malory Towers.

The school was in Cornwall, and it was a very long drive, but Felicity and Susan had so much to talk about that the first couple of hours simply sped by.

'Won't it be marvellous to see all the others again?' said Susan. 'Good old Pam, and Nora and Julie – not forgetting Jack, of course.'

Jack was their friend Julie's horse, who lived in the stables at Malory Towers during term time, and all the girls were very fond of him indeed.

'I think the summer term is my favourite term of all,' said Felicity excitedly. 'There's so much to do. Picnics, swimming and horse-riding – and I mean to work really hard at my tennis. I'm determined to be picked for one of the teams this term.'

'Me too,' said Susan. 'My word, wouldn't it be super if we were both picked?'

'Super!' agreed Felicity. 'I wonder if there will be any new girls this term.'

'There are sure to be,' Susan said. 'I say, Felicity, I wonder what tricks June and Freddie will have brought back with them this term. Oh, I just can't wait to get back to Malory Towers.'

But, after a stop for lunch, the girls' conversation tailed off, as both of them began to feel a little drowsy from the long car journey. Susan had difficulty in keeping her eyes open, while Felicity actually dropped off to sleep for a little while. But both of them woke up completely when the car rounded a bend in the road and their beloved Malory Towers came into view.

'There it is!' cried Felicity, sitting bolt upright. 'Doesn't it look magnificent, with the sun right behind it?'

Susan was so excited that she couldn't speak, but she nodded her head vigorously, as Mr Rivers turned the car into the long driveway. In front of them was a very long, sleek, expensive-looking car and Felicity said, 'My goodness, just look at that! I wonder who it belongs to?'

'I wouldn't be surprised if it's Amy's,' said Susan. 'It would be just like her to turn up to school in a showy car like that.'

'That's an American car, girls,' Mr Rivers informed them. 'So I doubt very much that it belongs to your friend Amy's family.'

Just then the big car pulled in and a pretty, smartly dressed woman emerged. She opened the back door and a tall, willowy girl with beautifully arranged blonde curls climbed out. Felicity and Susan couldn't see her face, and were bursting with curiosity as she took the woman's arm and walked off gracefully with her.

'Heavens!' said Susan, as she stared after the girl. 'She looked awfully glamorous, didn't she? I wonder which form she'll be in?'

But there was no time to think about that, for, as Mr Rivers brought the car to a halt, Felicity spotted a group of third formers nearby and yelled, 'There are June and Freddie – and I do believe that's Nora!'

'Don't be in such a rush, Felicity,' protested her mother, as everyone got out of the car. 'You have plenty of time in which to chat to your friends, but Daddy and I shan't see you again until half-term.'

'Sorry, Mummy,' said Felicity contritely. 'I shall miss you both, you know. It's just that I get so excited about being back at school and seeing everyone again.'

'I know that you do, dear, and I quite understand,' said Mrs Rivers, smiling. 'Now, here's your night case – and yours, Susan. Have a good term, both of you, and write soon, won't you, Felicity?'

'Of course. Goodbye, Mother! Goodbye, Daddy!' And Felicity hugged each of her parents in turn, then she and Susan waved them off before running to join their friends, all of whom were greeting one another noisily.

'Hallo, June! Hope you've brought some good tricks with you.'

'My word, isn't it super to be back together again?'

'Pam, you're back! Had a good Easter?'

'And here are Felicity and Susan. Who's missing?'

'I haven't seen Amy and Bonnie yet. And I wonder

where Julie is?' said Nora, looking puzzled. 'She usually gets back early so that she can settle Jack in.'

'I bet she's still down at the stables,' said June. 'You know how she fusses over that horse of hers.'

'We'd better go and give our health certificates to Matron and unpack our night cases,' said Felicity. 'By the time we've done that, Julie will probably have satisfied herself that Jack isn't going to pine away if she leaves him for a few hours, and decided to join us.'

But by the time the girls had seen Matron and gone to their dormitory to unpack, there was still no sign of Julie, and even the placid Pam began to look worried, saying anxiously, 'I do hope that she hasn't been taken ill or something. Wouldn't it be dreadful if she missed the beginning of term?'

'I spoke to her on the telephone last week and she sounded perfectly fine then,' said Nora.

'Well, it's no use standing around worrying,' said Susan, sensibly. 'Let's take a walk down to the stables and see if she's there.'

So the group of third formers made their way to the stables, where they found several girls settling their horses in. But Julie and Jack were not among them.

'The stables are all full,' said Felicity. 'So even if Julie turns up with Jack now, there won't be room for him here.'

'How odd!' said Freddie. 'I say, you don't think that Miss Grayling has told Julie that she can't have Jack with her at school any more, do you?'

'The Head wouldn't do that,' said Nora. 'Why, Julie's

always brought him to Malory Towers with her!'

'But it is queer that there isn't a place left for him,' said Susan, frowning, as the girls walked back up to the school. Then a thought occurred to her and she gasped, 'Oh, my goodness! What if something has happened to Jack?'

The others turned pale at the thought and Pam gave a shudder. 'What a dreadful thought! Why, Julie would be simply heartbroken! That horse means the world to her. '

But just then, the girls heard themselves being hailed and they turned to see Julie herself coming towards them, dressed in her riding gear – and the broad smile on her freckled face was enough to tell them at once that Jack was safe and sound. There was another girl with her, who the others hadn't seen before, also dressed in riding clothes, and the third formers looked at her curiously.

'Hallo, everyone!' cried Julie. 'Sorry I'm late, but I've just been stabling Jack at Five Oaks.'

The girls looked a little puzzled at this, for Five Oaks was a riding school not far from Malory Towers, which was run by two old girls, Bill and Clarissa.

'We wondered where you were,' said Felicity. 'But why is Jack staying at Five Oaks, Julie? You always have him here with you.'

'Well, Miss Grayling telephoned me at home the other day and said that more girls than ever were bringing their horses to school with them this term. She said that there wouldn't be room for all of them in the school stables, and would I mind awfully taking Jack to Five Oaks instead. Well, I'm always glad of an excuse to visit Bill and Clarissa, and I know that they'll take jolly good care of Jack, so of course I said yes. Lucy is stabling her horse, Sandy, there as well.'

'Who is Lucy?' asked Nora.

'Oh, of course, I haven't introduced you yet!' exclaimed Julie, taking the new girl's arm. 'This is Lucy Carstairs and she's going to be in our form.'

Felicity, as head-girl of the third form, introduced the others to Lucy, who smiled happily round and said a cheery, 'Hallo, everyone!' She was a tall, slender girl, rather boyish in appearance, with a crop of short dark hair, brilliant blue eyes and a sprinkling of freckles across her nose. She and Julie seemed to have become firm friends, although they hadn't known one another for very long, and June said, 'I suppose we'll have to listen to the two of you gabbling away endlessly about gymkhanas and pony treks and what-not now! That's if we ever get to see you, for I daresay the pair of you will spend all of your spare time at Five Oaks this term.'

'That's the idea,' said Lucy, with a grin. 'I simply can't be away from Sandy for too long, or I'll just pine away.'

'Well, I've heard of horses pining for their owners, but never an owner pining for her horse!' said Felicity, with a chuckle. 'Anyway, welcome to Malory Towers, Lucy. I hope you'll settle in and be happy here.'

'I'm sure that I shall,' said Lucy, with her ready smile, and the others warmed to her at once.

'Well, it looks as if Julie has found a special friend of her own,' said Felicity to Susan, as the girls made their way down to the swimming-pool, which they were eager to show off to Lucy. 'Which is a very good thing. I know that she's always had Jack but, even though he's lovely, you can't really have a conversation with a horse.'

'Well, you can, but they tend to be pretty one-sided,' laughed Susan. 'I know what you mean, though. Julie gets along well with everyone, but it's so nice to have a special person to share jokes and secrets with. We're all paired up now, aren't we? There's June and Freddie, Pam and Nora, Amy and Bonnie, Julie and Lucy – oh, and not forgetting the two of us, of course!'

It was a glorious day, and the swimming-pool, of which Malory Towers was justly proud, was at its finest. The pool was hollowed out of rocks and filled naturally by the sea, and as she watched the sun glinting on the surface of the water, Felicity longed to plunge in. So did June, who said, 'It's so warm today. A dip in the pool would just cool me down nicely.'

'Jump in, then,' said Freddie, her eyes alight with mischief. 'I bet you daren't!'

Of course, it simply wasn't in June's nature to refuse a dare, and before the others realised what was happening, she had jumped into the pool fully clothed, making a terrific splash and sending a shower of water over Freddie, who was standing nearest.

'June!' cried Felicity, between shock and laughter. 'Come out of there at once! My goodness, you'll get into the most terrific row from Matron if she sees you in those wet clothes! Freddie, you're absolutely soaked too.'

Lucy was staring at June as if she couldn't believe her eyes and, seeing her expression, Nora laughed and said, 'June's a real dare-devil. You never know what she'll do next, but she certainly livens things up in the third form.'

'I'll just bet she does,' said Lucy, beginning to laugh as well. 'My goodness, I'm so glad that my parents decided to send me to Malory Towers. I've only been here a short while, but I know already that I'm going to love it.'

'Glad to hear it,' said Felicity. 'I've a feeling you're going to fit in here just fine, Lucy.' Then she gave a squeal, as June, who was still fooling around in the swimming-pool, sent a spray of water in her direction. Leaping back she yelled, 'That's quite enough, June. I don't want to get into trouble on my first day back, even if you do.'

'Yes, come on out now,' said Susan. 'It'll be time for tea soon, and you can't go into the dining-room looking like a drowned rat!'

Grinning, June climbed out of the pool, shaking herself to get rid of some of the water, and Pam said, 'You remind me of my dog, Monty! He shakes himself like that when he's had a bath.'

'Well, I feel as if I've had a shower!' complained Freddie, who had taken her socks off and was trying to wring the water out of them. 'You beast, June! Now I shall have to get changed too.'

'You two will have to get out of your riding gear as well,' said Felicity to Julie and Lucy. 'Let's be quick, for I don't want to be late for tea. I'm starving!'

'And let's hope we don't bump into Matron, or any

of the mistresses on the way back,' said Susan.

The girls didn't, but they did have the misfortune to meet a particularly unpleasant fifth former, Eleanor Banks, and she turned her nose up in disgust as she spotted the two dripping-wet girls. Eleanor had joined the fifth form last term, and had lost no time in making herself unpopular with the younger girls. She had a very cold, haughty manner and that, along with her pale colouring and silvery-blonde hair, had led June to nickname her the Ice Queen. Somehow this had got back to Eleanor, and there was no love lost between June and her at all!

'What on earth have you third formers been up to?' Eleanor asked now, her cold stare fixed on June.

'I've been up to my neck in water, Eleanor,' answered June cheekily, quite unabashed by the older girl's cool manner. 'And poor Freddie here caught the backlash.'

'June slipped and fell into the pool,' said Felicity hastily, seeing two spots of angry red appear on Eleanor's pale cheeks. 'She's just off to get changed now.'

Eleanor didn't believe that June had fallen into the pool by accident for a moment. The wretched girl was always acting the goat! But since she couldn't prove anything, she was unable to dish out a punishment, which made her feel extremely disappointed. Instead she had to content herself with a few sharp words. 'Well, hurry up about it,' she snapped. 'Or you'll be late for tea. And you two,' she turned to Julie and Lucy now. 'Change out of those riding clothes before you go into the dining-room. Come on, now – shake a leg!'

Then Eleanor squealed, for June suddenly shook her head violently, sending drops of water all over the fifth former.

'How dare you!' she gasped, pulling a handkerchief from her pocket and dabbing at her dress. 'Just look what you've done!'

'But you told me to shake my head,' said June, staring innocently at Eleanor, as the rest of the third formers struggled to hide their smiles.

'I said shake a *leg*,' said Eleanor, through gritted teeth. 'As you very well know!'

'Oh, did you?' said June. 'Sorry, Eleanor. I must have some water in my ears.'

Eleanor glared angrily at the girl, but at that moment someone called her name and she turned to see Bella Coombes, head of the fifth form, beckoning her over.

'Saved by the Bella!' quipped June, as Eleanor stalked away, and the others laughed.

'You'd better watch out for Eleanor, June,' warned Pam. 'She's always had it in for you, and she'll be even worse now.'

'Pooh!' said June scornfully. 'The Ice Queen will never get the better of me!'

'Was that the Head Girl?' Lucy asked Julie, as they made their way back to the school.

'No, Eleanor just *thinks* that she's Head Girl,' answered Julie drily. 'Mean beast! She came to Malory Towers last term because her parents went abroad. Her aunt and uncle live near Five Oaks, so she stays with them during the holidays.'

'If you ask me, Eleanor's parents went abroad to get away from her,' said June 'And I can't say that I blame them. Still, I daresay that her pitiful attempts to make trouble for me will provide us with some amusement this term.'

'I daresay they will,' said Felicity, grinning. What a super term this was going to be. Oh, it *was* good to be back at school!

The new girls

There was a surprise in store for the third formers as they poured noisily into their dormitory in the North Tower. Amy and Bonnie were there, unpacking, and with them was another new girl! She was talking to Bonnie when the girls entered, and had her back to the door, but Felicity and Susan recognised her at once as the willowy blonde girl who had been in the big American car.

Then she turned, and the third formers gasped in astonishment. For her face was almost identical to Lucy's! It was the same shape, had the same bright blue eyes and the same wide, generous mouth. But where Lucy looked boyish, this girl, with her blonde curls and sophisticated air, was very feminine indeed. And while Lucy strode briskly, the new girl was so graceful that she seemed almost to glide as she moved across to her bed.

The third formers greeted Amy and Bonnie, then Bonnie gestured towards the new girl and said in her soft voice, 'Have you met Esme yet?'

'No, we haven't,' said Felicity, smiling at the new girl. 'Welcome to the third form, Esme. Lucy, you never told us that you had a twin!'

But Lucy was looking every bit as startled as the others,

and not at all pleased. She said rather curtly now, 'She's not my twin. In fact, we aren't even sisters. Esme and I are cousins.'

'Golly!' exclaimed Freddie, looking from one to the other. 'The likeness is quite astonishing!'

'Our mothers are twins.' Esme spoke for the first time, and the others were surprised to hear her American accent. Most of the girls had never heard one before, except in films, and it was quite fascinating to listen to. She was rather fascinating to look at too, and seemed a lot more grown-up than the other girls. She was wearing lipstick, Felicity realised disapprovingly, and she had mascara on her eyelashes too. But how silly of her to want to wear make-up, when she was naturally so very pretty anyway.

Lucy was obviously very put out by her cousin's arrival and asked rather brusquely, 'What are you doing here, Esme?'

'Gee, it's nice to see you too, cousin,' drawled the girl, raising her eyebrows. 'I'm here for the same reason as you, I imagine. To get an education.'

'Surely they have schools in America,' said Lucy sharply, and the listening girls goggled, quite taken aback at her rudeness. Felicity looked at her hard and wondered if the first, favourable impression that Lucy had made on her had been false.

Esme, however, didn't seem at all upset, and merely replied calmly, 'Sure they do – very good ones. But Mother missed England, so we moved back here last month and we're going to be staying for a while.'

Lucy looked absolutely furious at this and snapped, 'Well, the school you went to in America can't have been *that* good, for you're a year older than me and should be in the fourth form, not the third.'

The third formers drank all this in avidly, casting sidelong glances at Esme to see how she was taking this. And they had to admire her composure when she refused to rise to Lucy's baiting and said matter-of-factly, 'Miss Grayling and Mother decided between them that it would be best to spend my first term in the third form, seeing as I've been studying different things from you girls. If all goes well, I'll go up into a higher form next term. So I guess you'll just have to get used to having me around for a while, Lucy.'

As though she didn't trust herself to speak, Lucy turned away from her cousin abruptly and began to get changed. The third formers were simply bursting with curiosity as to what could be behind the hostility between the cousins, but of course they were far too well-mannered to pry.

Lucy wasn't the only one who wasn't very impressed with the new girl, for Amy also looked down her rather long nose at her, Felicity noticed. She felt quite sorry for Esme, who seemed very easy-going and good-natured, and asked, 'How long have you lived in America?'

'About four years,' answered Esme. 'You see, my father's American and he met my mother when he was working over here. After the two of them married, they settled in England. They wanted to live here for good, but . . . well, things just didn't work out, so we all moved to

America. I loved it there, but Mother always felt homesick. She was so happy to come back home.'

'How is Aunt Maggie?' asked Lucy, unexpectedly, her expression softening a little.

'She's fine,' answered Esme. 'Just fine. And Aunt Janet?'

'She's very well, thank you,' said Lucy stiffly.

There was an awkward little silence, which was broken by the sound of a bell ringing, and Nora cried, 'Teatime! Thank goodness, I'm so hungry I could eat a horse.'

'Don't say that in front of Julie and Lucy,' laughed Pam. 'They'll have visions of you stalking Jack and Sandy with a knife and fork!'

'Gee, do you still have Sandy?' said Esme, turning to her cousin. 'He was little more than a foal when I left England.'

'Yes,' answered Lucy. 'He's stabled just along the road from here.'

'It'll be nice to see him again,' Esme said, as the third formers began to make their way down the stairs. 'I always had a soft spot for Sandy.'

Lucy didn't look thrilled at the idea of Esme getting too close to her beloved Sandy, and before she could dish out another rebuff to her cousin, Pam asked hastily, 'Do you ride, Esme?'

'Not very well,' answered the girl, with a rueful smile. 'I like horses, but I get a little nervous when I'm in the saddle. It always seems such an awfully long way from the ground!'

The others laughed at this, all except Lucy, who scowled fiercely at her cousin. Julie felt a little disappointed in her.

Lucy had seemed so happy and friendly at first, but since Esme's arrival she had gone all sulky and moody, making everyone else feel rather uncomfortable. And Julie couldn't see any reason for it. Because, although Esme was very different from the other girls, she seemed perfectly pleasant and friendly. As though sensing that Julie was unhappy, Lucy took her arm and pulled her aside from the others as they entered the dining-room.

'I'm sorry,' she said contritely. 'I didn't mean to cause an atmosphere, truly I didn't.'

There was an earnest expression in her blue eyes, and suddenly Lucy looked much more like the nice, fun-loving girl Julie had been introduced to at Five Oaks.

'But I don't understand why you're so hard on Esme,' said Julie. 'She is your cousin, after all.'

Lucy bit her lip and said, 'I don't want to say too much at the moment, but . . . well, there was a big falling out between our families a few years ago, and the two of us haven't seen one another, or spoken, since.'

Julie felt quite saddened by this, thinking what a lot of unhappiness was caused when families rowed. But the two cousins both seemed like good-hearted girls, and perhaps being at school together would give them the chance to patch up their differences. Lucy certainly seemed determined to brush her cares aside now, and, pinning a bright smile on her face, she clapped Julie on the shoulder and said, 'Don't take any notice of me! As Esme said, she's here for a while and I'll just have to get used to it. I certainly don't intend to let her spoil my time at

Malory Towers, or the fun that you and I are going to have together with Jack and Sandy.'

'That's more like it!' said Julie happily, returning the girl's smile. 'Now come on, let's go and get some tea before the others polish everything off.'

First-night suppers at Malory Towers were always marvellous, and tonight was no exception. There was cold chicken, potato salad and big juicy tomatoes, followed by the most delicious apple pie with cream. Jugs of ice-cold lemonade stood on the tables, and the girls helped themselves to big glasses as they ate.

'Gee, this food sure is good!' said Esme, tucking into her second slice of apple pie.

'Wizard!' said Susan, doing likewise.

'*Wizard?*' repeated Esme, looking puzzled. 'What does that mean?'

'It means super, smashing, first-rate, top-hole,' explained June, with a grin. 'Or, as you Americans would say, *wunnerful*!'

'Esme's not American,' protested Freddie, as the others laughed. 'She was born in England and spent most of her life here, so she's English.'

'Well, gee, she sure *sounds* American,' said Nora in a fine imitation of Esme's accent. Everyone laughed, and Esme said with a grin, 'That was just wizard, Nora.'

Then the third formers began to point out various girls and mistresses to the two cousins, Felicity saying, 'That's Kay Foster, the Head Girl, and the big girl next to her is Amanda Chartelow, the games captain. They're both good sorts, though Amanda has a bit of a temper at times.'

'Yes, but she's hot-tempered rather than bad-tempered,' said Susan. 'And she only gets really angry with people who are lazy, or don't make an effort when it comes to games.'

Esme looked rather dismayed at this and said, 'Do you play a lot of games here, then?'

'You bet,' said Pam. 'The tennis-courts are simply marvellous. If you like, I'll take you to see them after tea.'

'No, thanks, Pam,' said Esme, with a laugh. 'I'm afraid I'm not very interested in games or sports of any kind. I have better things to do!'

She sounded quite scornful and the others felt a little annoyed, June asking with deceptive sweetness, 'And just how do you spend your valuable time, Esme? Painting your nails? Dear me, I'd love to be a fly on the wall when you tell Amanda that you can't come to tennis practice because you're busy doing your hair! My goodness, she'll drag you out on to that tennis-court with your hair curlers in!'

Lucy and one or two others laughed rather unkindly, while Esme looked taken aback and turned red. 'I didn't mean to cause any offence,' she said. 'It's just that at my old school, in America, we didn't have to go in for games if we didn't want to.'

'Well, I'm afraid you'll have to at Malory Towers, Esme, whether you like it or not,' said Felicity. 'Everyone does.'

'Unless you can find a way of getting out of them,' put in Bonnie. She was a very small, rather doll-like girl, with big eyes and soft brown curls. But her appearance was deceptive, for Bonnie was a determined and resourceful character, who always found the most ingenious ways to get out of doing anything that she didn't want to do.

Esme liked Bonnie and her friend, Amy, and felt that she had a lot more in common with them than these other, rather hearty English girls. They were nice, feminine girls who took pride in their appearance and could think of more important things than chasing balls around, or plunging into an icy-cold swimming-pool! But although Bonnie seemed friendly enough, Amy was a bit stuck-up and rather cool towards her. Esme had caught the girl giving her one or two cold, haughty stares and wondered what she could possibly have done to offend Amy. But maybe that was the way she looked at everyone – after all, with a nose that long how could she *help* but look down it at people?

In fact, Amy had decided that Esme was rather vulgar and common, with that dreadful American drawl and that awful make-up. Didn't she realise how cheap she made herself look? She was surprised and displeased with Bonnie for paying the girl so much attention, and looked very unhappy now as Esme turned to Bonnie and began to talk about fashions. This was a subject close to Amy's heart, and normally she would have joined in, but her dislike of the new girl stopped her, and, instead, she sat there pushing the food around her plate, a scowl on her face.

'Just look at Amy,' whispered June to Freddie. 'She's

not at all pleased to see Bonnie making friends with Esme. I suppose she thinks that Esme is beneath her notice.'

'It hasn't taken Amy long to get back to her old, snobbish self again!' said Freddie. 'I did think, for a while, that she was going to forget her stuck-up ways and become one of us, but now that she has got over the shock of finding out that her mother's family isn't as grand as she believed, she is just as bad as she was before!'

Just then, plump little Mam'zelle Dupont, one of the school's two French mistresses bustled across. She had just arrived back from her holiday in France, and looked relaxed and happy as she sat down at the head of the table, crying, 'Ah, how good it is to see you all back again! Well rested and ready to work hard at your French.'

'Heavens, Mam'zelle, we shan't have any time for French this term,' said June, with a wicked grin. 'We shall be far too busy with other things. Swimming, for one.'

'And horse-riding,' put in Julie.

'And tennis,' said Felicity. 'Really, Mam'zelle, I don't know if we will have time to do any work at all!'

'Ah, you tease me, bad girls!' said Mam'zelle, smiling indulgently as she piled her plate with food. 'But I see we have two new girls – twins!'

'They aren't twins, Mam'zelle,' explained Pam. 'Lucy and Esme are cousins.'

'But they are so alike!' exclaimed Mam'zelle, scrutinising the two new girls so closely that they both became quite red with embarrassment. 'Yet, in some ways, not alike.' There was a slightly stern note in her tone, for she now saw that Esme was wearing make-up – and Mam'zelle did not approve of such things. But then the girl said something to Nora, and Mam'zelle, realising that she was American, softened towards her. American girls were different, thought the French mistress, philosophically. They seemed to grow up faster than English girls, and had different ideas. Once this Esme had been under the influence of Malory Towers and the dear third formers for a while, she would learn English ways and become a proper schoolgirl.

This was exactly what Felicity was hoping, too. A thought occurred to her and she said to Susan, 'Esme's arrival means that we aren't all neatly paired up any more, for she is the odd one out now.'

'Golly, yes, I hadn't thought of that,' said Susan. 'Well, she seems quite nice, although she's so different from the rest of us. We shall all have to do our best to see that she's not left out.' She looked across to where the new girl was chatting to Bonnie, and noticed that Lucy was watching too, a discontented frown on her face. 'I wonder why Lucy and Esme dislike one another so?' she said.

'Perhaps we'll find out one day,' said Felicity. 'I just hope that they manage to rub along together all right, and don't make everyone else feel uncomfortable.'

The two new girls managed to avoid one another in the common-room that evening. Lucy and Julie sat in a corner together, chattering nineteen-to-the-dozen about horses, while Esme joined the others.

'Gosh, I'm tired,' said Nora, with a yawn. 'I don't know

why the first day back at school is always so exhausting, for we don't do any work, but it always wears me out.'

'Well, the bell will be going for bedtime soon,' said Susan.

'But it's only eight o'clock,' said Esme, in surprise. 'That seems awfully early to go to bed.'

'We only go at eight on the first evening,' explained Pam. 'Because we're all supposed to be jolly tired after our long journeys. Normally we stay up until nine.'

'Gee, we went up much later than that at my school in America,' said Esme. 'I'll never be able to get to sleep at nine o'clock!'

'Oh yes you will!' Felicity told her, with a grin. 'Once you've played a few games out in the fresh air.'

'Yes, a few lengths of the swimming-pool tomorrow will tire you out,' said Susan. 'And if that doesn't do the trick, a few sets of tennis ought to help.'

Poor Esme looked horrified, and the others laughed at her.

'Don't worry, Esme,' said Freddie. 'Amanda will understand if you tell her that you haven't played much sport before, and she won't expect too much of you to begin with. In fact, she'll probably arrange some extra coaching sessions for you.'

Esme wasn't sure whether Freddie was joking or not – gee, she sure hoped that she was! Her mother had been so keen for her to come to Malory Towers, because she had said that Esme had begun to forget that she was half-English, and was becoming 'too American'. But if being English meant having to get hot, sweaty and untidy chasing a ball around, or getting her carefully set hair ruined in a pool, then Esme would rather be American any day! And then there was Lucy. Esme had got the shock of her life when she had realised that the cousin she hadn't seen for years was here too – and in the same form. She began to wonder if she would ever fit in at Malory Towers – certainly not if Lucy had anything to do with it!

A hard time for Esme

Felicity watched, torn between amusement and exasperation, as Esme got ready for breakfast the following morning. The girl had insisted on sleeping with curlers in her hair last night, even though the task of putting them in had had to be accomplished in darkness. Felicity was extremely strict about putting the lights out on time, and flatly refused to break the rule except in an emergency.

'But this *is* an emergency,' Esme had wailed. 'How am I going to make a good impression on our form mistress if my hair's a mess?'

'My dear Esme, I can assure you that Miss Peters won't give a fig for how your hair looks,' Felicity had informed the new girl, grinning to herself in the darkness at the thought of how the forthright, no-nonsense Miss Peters was likely to react to Esme. The mistress had no time at all for what she called 'frills and fancies', and Felicity could see trouble ahead for the girl.

Now Esme was standing in front of a big mirror, carefully removing the curlers and patting each blonde curl into place.

But Felicity's amused smile turned to a frown as Esme began applying lipstick, and she said to Susan, 'Now that's something that most definitely won't make a good impression on Miss Peters! And she's put that awful black stuff on her eyelashes as well.'

A couple of terms ago, Felicity would have been a little diffident about tackling Esme, for she had lacked confidence and been a little shy about expressing her opinions, always rather afraid of offending others. But two terms as head-girl of the third form had changed her. Felicity's belief in herself had grown, along with her confidence, and now she marched up to the new girl, saying forthrightly, 'Esme, you can't go downstairs with that stuff on your face! Wipe it off at once!'

'Why?' asked the girl, turning to face Felicity in surprise. 'What's wrong with it?'

'Well, for one thing, it looks simply awful,' said Felicity. 'I can't think why you want to go around looking as if you're about twenty, when you look perfectly fine just as you are. And, for another thing, Miss Peters will certainly send you out of the room to wash it off. The girls at Malory Towers don't wear make-up.'

'I can see that,' said Esme, a little stung by Felicity's words. 'You would all look so much more glamorous if you did.'

'We're not here to look glamorous,' Felicity told her sharply. 'We're here to learn, and play games and have fun. Perhaps you should try it, Esme.'

But Esme shook her head, saying in her lazy drawl, 'You and your friends are a nice bunch, Felicity, but I'm not like you. And – don't take offence – I don't *want* to be like you.

So I guess Malory Towers is going to have to take me as I am – and so is your Miss Peters.'

Felicity opened her mouth to argue, then changed her mind. What was the point? None of them could turn Esme into an English schoolgirl. Only Esme herself could do that – if she decided that she wanted to. And Felicity couldn't force the girl to wipe her make-up off, but Miss Peters could – and would! Esme was going to have to learn the hard way.

Immediately after breakfast, Esme, Lucy and the other new girls had to go and see Miss Grayling, the Head mistress. Esme felt very nervous, for she hadn't yet spoken to Miss Grayling. But she had seen her briefly in the dining-room, and had thought that she looked most distinguished and rather grand. So she was pleasantly surprised when, on entering the Head's study, Miss Grayling greeted the new girls with a warm smile. The words that she spoke made a great impression on Esme, and Lucy too. The Head began by welcoming each girl individually and asking her name and form. Then her expression became more serious as she addressed the whole group.

'I would like you all to listen carefully,' she said, her clear blue eyes moving from one girl to the next. 'For what I have to say is very important. One day you will leave this school and go out into the world as young women. You should take with you eager minds, kind hearts and a will to help. You should take with you a good understanding, a sense of responsibility, and show others that you are women to be loved, trusted and respected. These are all

qualities that you will be able to learn at Malory Towers –
if you *wish* to learn them.'

Miss Grayling paused, and every girl in the room felt
that the Head was speaking to her and her alone.

'I do not count as our successes those who have passed
exams and won scholarships, though they are great
achievements. I count as our successes those who are good-
hearted and kind, sensible and trustworthy. Responsible
women, on whom others can rely. Our failures are those
who do not learn those things during their years here.'

All of the new girls listened intently, every one of them
inspired by the Head's words and determined that they
were going to be one of Malory Towers' successes. Even
vain, silly Esme, who left Miss Grayling's study with her
pretty head in a whirl as, for the first time, she began
seriously to consider that perhaps there were more
important things in life than one's appearance. Goodness,
perhaps her transformation into an English schoolgirl was
beginning already!

But Esme still had a long way to go, and she soon fell
foul of Miss Peters. She and Lucy, along with three new
girls from other towers, hung back while the others chose
their seats. The coveted desks at the back of the class went
to the leaders of the form – Felicity, Susan and June.
Freddie slipped in next to June, while Pam, Nora and Julie
took the row in front of them. Soon only the new girls
were left standing. There was an empty seat next to Julie,
and Rita, a new South Tower girl, moved towards it,
only to receive a ferocious glare from Julie. So poor Rita

hastily backed away, and Julie beckoned Lucy across.

'Thanks,' said Lucy gratefully, slipping into the seat. 'I was awfully afraid that I wouldn't be able to sit next to you.'

Esme was left with a seat in the hated front row, right under Miss Peters's sharp eyes, but she took it without complaining, pretending not to notice the slightly pitying look that her cousin gave her. In fact, Esme didn't mind at all being in the front row, for it would be all the easier for her to make an impression on Miss Peters.

Alas for Esme! She certainly did make an impression on the mistress, but it wasn't a good one.

The third formers got to their feet as Miss Peters strode in. She was a rather mannish young woman, with short hair and a rosy complexion, and Esme couldn't help staring at her, for she had never seen anyone quite like her before. Miss Peters always looked rather uncomfortable in the smart blouse and skirt that she wore while teaching, and felt far more at home in her riding gear. She smiled round at her class now and said, 'Good morning, girls. Please sit down.'

The class sat obediently and the mistress said, 'I see that we have a few new girls, and I would like you all to stand up, one by one, and introduce yourselves to me and to the class.'

Rita, from South Tower, stood up first, her knees trembling, for it was quite nerve-wracking to stand up in front of all these girls. Her voice quavering a little, she introduced herself quickly, then sat down again, rather red in the face. It was Esme's turn next, and she was determined to make a better showing than Rita had. Eagerly she got to her feet and began confidently, 'Hallo, Miss Peters. Hallo, third formers. I'm Esme Walters and –'

'One moment!' Miss Peters interrupted her, looking hard at the girl. 'Esme, did you have jam for breakfast this morning?'

'Jam?' repeated the girl, puzzled. 'No, Miss Peters.'

'Then what is that red stuff all around your mouth?' asked the mistress.

Esme blushed a fiery red – as red as her lipstick – as muffled laughter ran round the classroom, and Miss Peters said firmly, 'Quiet, please! Esme, I am waiting for an answer.'

'It's lipstick, Miss Peters,' answered the girl.

'Lipstick!' repeated the mistress, sounding quite horrified. 'Go and wash it off at once, please. And is that mascara on your eyelashes? I thought so! Remove that as well. Quickly, now!'

Esme was every bit as horrified as Miss Peters, but one glance at the mistress's grimly determined face told her that it would be useless to protest, so she walked from the room, head down so that she didn't have to face the mocking glances of the rest of the girls.

She went into the nearest bathroom, where it took her a few minutes to remove her make-up. And how much younger and prettier she looked without it! Esme didn't see it like that at all, though, and thought that she looked very plain indeed. Almost as plain as these jolly English girls!

She felt rather humiliated too, certain that Lucy and a few of the others would crow over her. Gee, maybe she *should* have listened to Felicity after all!

The class was busy making out timetables when Esme returned, and everyone looked up as the door opened.

'Much better!' said Miss Peters approvingly. 'Sit down now, Esme, and begin copying the timetable from the blackboard.'

The girls thought that Esme looked much better too, and her resemblance to Lucy was much more striking now that the make-up had been removed. Felicity opened her mouth to say as much to Susan, but Miss Peters caught her eye and she hastily shut it again. The third-form mistress certainly didn't intend to stand any nonsense this term!

Nor did Miss Maxwell, the games mistress, and poor Esme found herself in hot water again during tennis practice that afternoon. Miss Maxwell partnered the girl with June, and the two of them played doubles against Felicity and Susan. The games mistress was pleased to see that Esme had a graceful style and a good eye – but unless the ball was placed where she could reach it easily, she made no effort to hit it, and refused to exert herself at all. This did not please June, who was a ferociously competitive player, chasing after every ball, even when it seemed impossible to reach.

'Esme!' she cried in exasperation, as one of Felicity's serves whizzed right past her. 'If only you'd run to the baseline you could have got that one back!'

'Gee, keep your hair on, June!' said Esme with a

comical expression. 'It's only a game!'

Unfortunately for Esme, this was the worst thing that she could have said, for June hated to be beaten at anything. Felicity and Susan were both very good players, while June was outstanding at tennis. Had June's partner been Freddie, who also played well, they would have stood a very good chance of winning. As it was, June felt that she was taking on her two opponents single-handed, and she soon grew hot, out of breath and irritable. Felicity took pity on her and sent a few easy shots Esme's way, which the girl managed to hit back. But June knew that Felicity was going easy on her, and that just made her even crosser.

Amanda Chartelow, who joined Miss Maxwell to watch the match, wasn't impressed with the new girl either.

'My word, June just gets better and better!' she said, a note of pride in her voice, for she had coached June herself. 'Did you see how powerful that serve was, Miss Maxwell? And just look at the way she's putting herself at full stretch to reach that return.'

'Felicity and Susan are coming along very well, too,' said the games mistress. 'There really are some very talented players in the third form this term.'

'And one extremely *un*talented one!' said Amanda, glaring in Esme's direction. 'Now there's a candidate for some extra coaching, if ever I saw one.'

'The pity is that she could be quite promising, if only she would make the effort,' said Miss Maxwell with a frown. 'She places the ball well, and her service is good.'

After watching Esme for a few moments, Amanda had

to agree, and said, 'But she's dreadfully lazy! She's leaving June to do all the hard work.'

And one thing Amanda had no patience with was laziness. She knew Esme's sort – she was the kind of girl who didn't like exerting herself in case it made her hair untidy, or her face red. Well, Amanda vowed, she was jolly well going to make the new girl skip around a bit and think about something other than her appearance!

So when the quartet of third formers came off the court, the games captain had a few words for each of them.

'Jolly well played, Felicity and Susan!' she said, in her loud voice. 'I must say, the two of you have improved no end. You must have been practising like anything in the hols.'

'We were,' said Felicity, thrilled at the bigger girl's words. 'I say, Amanda, do you think there's any chance of either of us playing for the team this term?'

'Well, I can't make any promises,' said Amanda, smiling at Felicity's eagerness. 'But you're both in with a chance, that much I will say!'

Then she turned to June and said, 'The same goes for you. You have it in you to do really well for the school if you put your mind to it.'

June grinned and thanked Amanda rather off-handedly, but inwardly she was very pleased indeed. She might appear don't-careish, but Malory Towers was beginning to have an effect on June, and she felt a sense of pride in it, and was starting to think that she might like to give something back.

'As for you,' began Amanda, looking rather sternly at Esme, 'I've never seen such a hopeless display in my life! What's your name?'

'Esme Walters,' answered Esme, looking rather afraid of this big, outspoken girl.

'Well, Esme, you're going to have to play up a bit if you want to get into one of the teams,' said Amanda crisply.

Esme didn't have the slightest interest in getting into one of the teams, but somehow she couldn't quite bring herself to say so to Amanda, who looked as if she breathed, slept and ate games! Amanda was quite unaware of Esme's complete absence of enthusiasm, for her imagination was not a lively one and it was quite unthinkable to her that anyone could fail to share her passion for games. So she said bracingly, 'I'm holding a coaching session on Monday afternoon. Come along and we'll see if we can get you up to scratch.'

With that she strode off, leaving Felicity and Susan struggling to contain their smiles at Esme's expression of dismay. June was not so restrained and said with an unkind laugh, 'Now do you see where your vanity has got you, Esme? If only you had made a bit more effort, Amanda wouldn't have singled you out like that. As it is, she's going to have her eye on you from now on. I hope for your sake that you make a better showing at swimming tomorrow, or you'll be down for extra coaching at the pool too!'

Poor Esme groaned inwardly, for she didn't like swimming any better than tennis. Oh dear, what a difficult term this was going to be!

Settling in

As the first week of term sped by, the two new girls settled down in their own ways. Lucy was moderately good at most of her lessons, and well behaved enough not to attract any unwelcome attention from the teachers, most of the time. However, when she became bored she had a habit of daydreaming about riding off across the fields on Sandy, and this earned her a ticking off from Miss Peters and the stern Mam'zelle Rougier on several occasions. On the whole, though, Lucy was very happy at Malory Towers and enjoyed life there. She and Julie got on very well indeed, and, as Five Oaks was only a few minutes walk from the school, the two of them managed to slip over there every day to check on their beloved horses and enjoy a ride together.

Life was not so easy for Esme, however. The girl wasn't stupid, by any means, but the lessons at Malory Towers were very different from what she had been used to in America and she sometimes struggled to keep up with the others. Rather surprisingly, the one thing she excelled at was English. Miss Hibbert took the third formers for this lesson, and although Esme's way of pronouncing certain words drove the mistress mad at times, she produced some very good written work.

'I find it very strange that the only girl who managed to get top marks for her essay this week is someone who has spent the last few years living in a different country,' Miss Hibbert had said at the beginning of one lesson. 'Very well done indeed, Esme.'

'Jolly good show, Esme,' Felicity had said after class, clapping the girl on the back, and Esme had turned red with pleasure.

She turned red during games as well – but from exertion, not from pleasure! Amanda Chartelow had kept her word and been most strict about ensuring that Esme attended her extra coaching. Amanda played a set against Esme herself, but instead of feeling honoured – as the others told her that she should – the girl just felt extremely nervous and made some silly mistakes. The games captain pointed these out to her in great detail, then proceeded to run her ragged! Poor Esme limped off the tennis-court at the end of the set with blistered feet, a red face and a very poor opinion of her ability! Nor did she fare much better at swimming. She wasn't afraid of the water – so long as she stayed in the shallow end – but complained that it ruined her hair. And when Felicity suggested that she wear a bathing cap, Esme didn't care for that idea either, as it would flatten her carefully set curls. The others found it very funny to watch Esme desperately trying to keep her head above the water as she swam around in the shallow end, and it soon became quite a sport among them to try to get the girl's hair wet.

Esme was quite popular with the third formers, but felt

that she had little in common with most of them. The two she felt most akin to were Amy and Bonnie, but although Bonnie seemed to like her, Amy showed all too plainly that she had no time for Esme. Which was a shame, for Esme felt that life at this no-nonsense English school would be much easier to bear if she had like-minded friends to talk to.

She spoke about it to Bonnie in the common-room one evening, saying with a sigh, 'Felicity and the others are really nice girls, but they're just not my type somehow.'

'Well, I don't mind if you want to tag along with Amy and me,' said Bonnie, who liked the good natured Esme and felt a little sorry for her.

'You might not mind, but I can't see Amy being too keen on the idea,' said Esme glumly.

'Oh, it's easy enough to get round Amy,' said Bonnie airily. 'All you have to do is flatter her, admire her and show her that you look up to her. She simply adores that sort of thing.'

'Really?' said Esme doubtfully, thinking that it sounded too simple to be true.

'Really,' said Bonnie firmly. 'Look, here she comes now. Try it and you'll see that I'm right.'

Amy walked over to the two girls, smiling at Bonnie, but ignoring Esme. The early evening sun shining through the common-room window glinted on her golden hair and Esme exclaimed admiringly, 'How lovely and shiny your hair is, Amy! I do wish that mine would gleam like that.'

Amy looked at the girl in surprise, then she gave a

faint, pleased smile and said, 'You should brush it a hundred times every night before you go to bed. That's what I do.'

Esme nodded, staring at the girl intently as though she were hanging off her every word, and said, 'I shall try that. You know, Amy, I think that you and Bonnie are far and away the prettiest girls in the form. And the nicest.'

Amy unbent still more, her smile widening as she said, 'Why, thank you, Esme.'

Bonnie's eyes danced as she picked up the sewing she was working on and she said to Amy, 'Esme was just saying that she doesn't really feel as if she fits in with the others.'

'Awfully hearty, aren't they?' said Amy, wrinkling her nose.

'Yes, that's exactly the word to describe them!' said Esme. 'But my mother wants me to be a proper English schoolgirl, just like them, and I don't think I can be.'

'Well, Amy and I are English schoolgirls and we are *nothing* like them,' said Bonnie.

'That's very true!' said Esme, looking thoughtful. 'You are just as English as they are, but in a different way – a *good* way. I wouldn't mind becoming more English if it meant that I could be like you two. If only you could teach me.'

'We *can* teach you!' said Amy, looking excited all of a sudden. 'We can teach you how to say "wonderful" instead of "wunnerful", and "twenty" instead of "twenny".'

'And how to look pretty in a natural way, without sleeping in curlers and putting that dreadful make-up on your face,' said Bonnie, staring hard at the girl. 'You've put that awful black stuff on your eyes again! Don't say that you haven't, for I can see it!'

'Well, I just put a little on,' admitted Esme sheepishly. 'I didn't think anyone would notice.'

Amy and Bonnie pursed their lips in disapproval and Amy said, 'Well, you must promise never to wear it again. And you must agree to do everything that we say.'

'Oh, I shall,' said Esme, nodding eagerly, feeling quite thrilled. She had made two friends, and she was going to please her mother by becoming more English. Perhaps things at Malory Towers weren't going to be so bad after all!

Julie and Lucy, meanwhile, were discussing their favourite subject – their horses.

'I can't wait until Saturday,' said Julie, her eyes shining. 'We can spend the whole day over at Five Oaks with Jack and Sandy.'

'I say, do you mind if Susan and I come along too?' asked Felicity, overhearing. 'I haven't seen Bill and Clarissa in simply ages.'

'The more the merrier!' said Julie, happily.

'In that case, I'll come as well,' said June. 'How about you, Freddie?'

Freddie nodded eagerly and Pam said, 'I say, why don't we all go and spend the day there? We could take a picnic along with us.'

'My word, what a super idea!' said Nora, clapping her hands together. Then she called out to Esme, Amy and Bonnie, 'I say, you three! We're all going to take a picnic to Five Oaks on Saturday. What about it?'

Amy, who was absolutely terrified of getting freckles if she spent too much time in the sun, shook her head and said, 'No, thank you. I don't want to ruin my complexion.'

'And I want to get on with the handkerchiefs I'm embroidering for Mother's birthday,' said Bonnie.

Esme hesitated. She wasn't afraid of going out in the sun, for her skin always turned an attractive golden brown. And she *so* wanted to see Sandy again! But she desperately wanted to keep in with Amy and Bonnie, and perhaps they wouldn't like it if she went off with the others. Amy solved her dilemma by murmuring in a low voice, 'Actually, it's a very good thing that they're all going out on Saturday. Bonnie and I can give you your first lesson in "Englishness", without *them* sticking their noses in and making fun of us.'

'Yes, we'll make an English rose of you yet, Esme!' said Bonnie.

'Gee, that's wunnerful!' cried Esme. 'I mean, gosh, how wizard!'

It was a happy group of third formers who went to bed that evening. Most of them were looking forward with great anticipation to their day out on Saturday, while Esme was delighted to have been accepted by Amy and Bonnie. Even Amy felt excited at the prospect of teaching Esme to become a lady, just like herself. She had never realised before just how much the girl looked up to her and wanted to be like her, and that kind of admiration was very pleasant to Amy. What a feather in her cap it would be if she could transform the American girl!

The following day, June had another encounter with Eleanor Banks. She, Freddie, Felicity and Susan were playing a game of doubles on the tennis-court. Amanda walked past with the Head Girl, Kay Foster, and, knowing that it was a free period for the third formers, she smiled and called out, 'My word, you girls are keen! That's just what I like to see. Keep it up, and I don't see how you can fail to get places on one of the teams!'

The four girls felt quite thrilled at Amanda's praise, and her words seemed to spur them on, all of them playing their hardest. Susan sent a particularly high ball across the net, placing it where June had no hope at all of returning it. But, being June, she had to try anyway, making a wild swipe at the ball and sending it soaring over the high mesh fence that surrounded the court. Unfortunately for June, Eleanor Banks happened to be walking by at that moment, and the ball bounced off the top of her head, causing her to squeal loudly.

'Gosh, sorry, Eleanor!' called out June.

But the fifth former was in no mood for apologies, although she had been more shocked than hurt, and she came over to the fence to scold June for her carelessness.

'It really was an accident, Eleanor,' said Felicity, hoping to placate the angry girl. But it was no use, for Eleanor disliked June intensely and was glad of any excuse to dish out a punishment. June, for her part, knew that it was useless to protest and kept her head down, hoping that if she put on a display of meekness, Eleanor would not give her too many lines to learn. And that's when she noticed that one of Eleanor's shoelaces had come undone. At once all thoughts of pretending to be meek vanished from June's head and, giving Freddie a nudge, she whispered, 'Distract her.'

'What? How?' Freddie hissed back, looking rather alarmed.

'I don't know! Think of something – quickly!' muttered June.

So Freddie did the only thing she could think of, and pointed rather wildly in the direction of a large tree, which stood just outside the tennis-court, crying dramatically, 'Look!'

Everyone but June turned their heads at once, Felicity saying, 'What is it, Freddie?'

'Can't you see it?' said Freddie. 'My word, I've never seen anything like it in my life!'

'But what *is* it?' demanded Eleanor, growing impatient. 'I can't see anything at all!'

'Nor can I, Freddie,' said Susan. 'What is it? A bird, or a squirrel or something?'

'Yes, that's it – a squirrel!' said Freddie. 'But it was no ordinary squirrel, for it was absolutely enormous.'

June, meanwhile, grinning to herself, had worked swiftly. The wicked girl had crouched down and pulled both ends of Eleanor's shoelace through the holes in the mesh, knotting them together very tightly, several times.

June straightened up as Eleanor snapped, 'Enough of this nonsense! I don't believe that there's anything in the tree at all.' Then she turned her head to glare at June and felt in her pocket for the little punishment book that all the fifth- and sixth-form girls carried with them. With a triumphant little smirk she pulled it out, at the same time going to take a step back from the fence. And that was when she discovered that she was quite unable to move her foot, for June had tied it securely to the fence! Felicity, Susan and Freddie noticed her predicament at once, the three of them gasping at June's audacity and struggling to hide their laughter as Eleanor roared, 'June! Untie my shoelace at once!'

But June pretended not to hear, and called to the others, 'Come on, you three! Let's carry on with our game.'

Freddie was at her side at once, but the more responsible Felicity and Susan hesitated. As head-girl of the form, she really ought to release the fifth former, Felicity thought, watching as Eleanor bent down, pushing her fingers through the mesh, and struggling to untie the knots in her shoelace. She wasn't having much success, though, for June had done her work well and the knots were very tight indeed.

Felicity and Susan exchanged a doubtful look, then an enraged squeal from Eleanor made them both burst into laughter.

'Felicity Rivers!' yelled the infuriated girl, red in the face with anger and humiliation. 'How dare you laugh at me? I shall report you to Miss Potts, all four of you!'

'The chances are that she'll report us whether we help her or not,' said Felicity with a chuckle. 'So we may as well have some fun!'

And with that, she and Susan picked up their rackets and took their places on the court.

'I say, Eleanor,' June called out. 'Throw us our ball back, will you? Oh no, you can't – you're a little tied up!'

The others roared with laughter, as the furious Eleanor, angry tears starting to her eyes now, beat at the fence with her fists, and Susan said, 'Not to worry, June, I have a spare ball in my pocket. Your service, I think!'

As the girls played on, Eleanor continued to work at the knots in her shoelace, and at last she managed to undo two of them. She gave a little cry of triumph, and began tugging at the third and final one. But this knot proved even more difficult and, in frustration, Eleanor screamed, causing June to drawl, 'My goodness, I don't think I've ever seen the Ice Queen get so hot and bothered. Careful, Eleanor, or you'll melt!'

In sheer frustration, the laughter of the third formers ringing in her ears, Eleanor kicked out at the fence with her free foot, and it was at this moment that Amanda returned to the court, with a small group of fifth formers, all dressed for tennis, in tow.

'Hey!' shouted Amanda, angrily. 'Eleanor Banks! What on *earth* do you think you're playing at?'

Horrified to be caught in such an embarrassing situation by members of her own form, Eleanor bent down and gave the knot a last, violent tug, and it came loose so suddenly that she toppled over backwards. Eleanor was not popular with her own form, and the laughter of the fifth formers joined with that of the third formers now, as

Amanda marched across to her and said wrathfully, 'How dare you distract the youngsters from their tennis practice with your fooling around? At your age, Eleanor, you really should know better!'

'But I wasn't fooling around, Amanda!' the girl protested. 'It was that beast of a June! She tied me to the fence when I wasn't looking, and –'

'What nonsense!' said Amanda scornfully. 'When I walked by this court, a short while ago, June was working hard at her tennis and she is *still* playing tennis now. It's a pity that you didn't have half of her dedication, Eleanor, then you could focus your energy on something worthwhile instead of disrupting everyone else. As you're a fifth former, I can't punish you as you deserve, but you had better jolly well stay out of my way, let me tell you!'

Eleanor, realising that it was pointless to argue with Amanda in this mood, murmured something which might have been an apology and slunk away.

June, meanwhile, looking the picture of goodness, shook her head sorrowfully at the departing girl, before finishing her game of tennis under the approving eye of Amanda.

'And the best of it is that Eleanor didn't even get round to giving me a punishment,' laughed June carelessly as the four girls walked off the court afterwards.

'My goodness, I haven't laughed so much in ages!' said Freddie, still chuckling to herself.

'It was very funny,' agreed Felicity. 'But the Ice Queen is going to be out for revenge, June – so watch out!'

A visit to Five Oaks

Saturday dawned bright and sunny, and the third formers leapt out of bed eagerly – apart from Nora, who always hated leaving her comfortable bed, even on a glorious morning like this.

'Just five more minutes,' she mumbled drowsily, as Pam tried to rouse her.

'I know you, my girl,' said Pam sternly. 'Your five minutes will stretch into ten, then fifteen, and you'll end up being late for breakfast.'

'I know what will get her up,' said June, coming over and winking at Pam. 'A nice cold, wet sponge! I'll just go and fetch one, shall I?'

Had the speaker been anyone but June, Nora would have dismissed this as an idle threat. But there was no limit to June's daring, and one never knew what she would do next, so Nora sat up abruptly, a scowl on her face, and Pam swiftly grabbed the girl's arm, hauling her out of bed before she could lie down again.

The girls got themselves ready in record time and, after breakfast, went to the kitchen to collect the picnic baskets that the cook had promised to leave ready for them.

'She's done us proud,' said Felicity, lifting the lid of one of the baskets. 'There are sandwiches of every kind, sponge cake, fruit – ooh, and two big bottles of lemonade! It makes me feel hungry already, although I've just finished breakfast!'

The third formers were in high spirits as they made their way to Five Oaks, carrying the picnic baskets between them, and Felicity said, 'I don't know how Amy, Bonnie and Esme can bear to be cooped up indoors on such a beautiful day. It would do the three of them the world of good to get out in the fresh air and think about something else besides their looks.'

'Well, if that's their idea of fun, I suppose it's up to them,' said Susan. 'I say, I'm looking forward to seeing old Jack again, aren't you?'

Felicity nodded. 'Malory Towers just isn't the same without him, somehow, although he's not very far away.'

And Jack was very pleased to see the girls, too, being on the friendliest of terms with all of them. Everyone made a great fuss of him, feeding him sugar lumps and patting his velvety muzzle, and Lucy's horse, Sandy, in the next stall, became very jealous indeed, whinnying for his share of attention. The third formers could see how Sandy had got his name, for he was the most beautiful pale, golden-brown colour.

'Just like the sand on the beach,' as Nora said, stroking his broad neck. 'He's adorable, Lucy.'

Julie turned to the young stable lad, who was busily cleaning some tack, and asked, 'Where are Bill and Clarissa, Jim?'

'Up at the house, miss,' he answered, and Felicity said, 'Well, let's pop in and say hallo.'

The girls walked across the stable-yard to the pretty little house that Bill and Clarissa shared, and Pam pushed at the door. To her surprise, it didn't budge, and she said, 'That's odd! I've never known Bill and Clarissa to lock their door before. Normally we just walk straight in.'

She rapped sharply on the door and, after a few moments, it opened slightly and a pale, thin face with bright green eyes and a worried expression appeared at the crack. Then the worried expression cleared, replaced by a smile, and the door was pulled wide open.

'Girls!' exclaimed Clarissa Carter. 'How lovely to see you all. Do come in!'

She stood aside, and the third formers filed past her into the big, cosy kitchen, where a young woman with short, dark hair and a tanned complexion sat at a large wooden table, looking rather pensive.

'Bill!' cried Felicity. 'I do hope you don't mind us all turning up like this.'

'Of course not!' said Bill, her face creasing into a smile. 'It's wonderful to see you all. I say, you've brought a picnic too – how marvellous!'

'Put your baskets over in the corner there, girls,' said Clarissa. 'It's in the shade, so everything will stay nice and cool.'

The girls did so, then Bill said, 'I'm afraid you'll have to take it in turns if you all want to ride, for we only have four horses free today.'

'I'm happy just to watch the others,' said Felicity, who was fond of horses, but wasn't a great rider.

'The same goes for me,' said Nora. 'I'm just here for a day out and a picnic!'

'I say, Clarissa, why was the door locked?' asked Pam. 'It's normally open house here.'

Bill and Clarissa exchanged worried glances and Felicity asked, 'Is anything wrong?'

'Well, yes, actually,' said Clarissa, gravely. 'I'm afraid a couple of things have gone wrong just lately.'

The third formers looked alarmed, and Bill said, 'Clarissa and I were giving riding lessons to some of the children from the village a couple of days ago, and while we were in the paddock, someone simply walked into the house and stole our cash-box.'

The girls were very fond of Bill and Clarissa, and knew how hard they had worked to make a success of the riding stables, so there was an immediate outcry at this.

'That's simply dreadful!'

'I wish I could get my hands on whoever did it – mean beasts!'

'Was there much money in the box?'

'Did you call the police?'

'Luckily there wasn't an awful lot of money in the box,' said Clarissa. 'But the thought that someone just walked in and helped himself – or herself – is most worrying, as you can imagine. That's why we have started to get into the habit of locking the door.'

'And we called the police,' added Bill. 'But the thief

didn't leave any clues at all, so they weren't able to be of much help. There's something else, too.'

Bill looked very serious indeed, and the third formers looked at her anxiously. Then she went on, 'Last night, while we were in bed, someone let Merrylegs out – and they left the gate open too. We got the horse back, but if he had got on to the road it could have ended very badly indeed.'

The girls exchanged horrified glances. Merrylegs was Clarissa's own horse, and the girls knew how dearly she loved him.

'I wish he had gone for my Thunder instead,' said Bill grimly, her eyes glinting. 'He's not as friendly with strangers as Merrylegs, and would certainly have given the intruder a rough time!'

'Are you sure that someone let Merrylegs out deliberately?' asked Freddie. 'I mean – isn't it possible that one of you didn't lock the stable door properly?'

Clarissa shook her head. 'Bill and I always go round and check everything thoroughly before we go to bed. And everything was just as it should be last night. Besides, I saw someone in the yard.'

The third formers gasped and Clarissa continued, 'I was asleep, and something woke me – some sort of noise from outside. I got up and went to the window, and saw someone in the yard.'

'Did you recognise them?' asked Susan, her eyes wide.

'No,' said Clarissa, with a sigh. 'It was too dark, and this person was dressed from head to toe in black. In fact, it was impossible even to tell whether they were male or female. But whoever it was looked up and saw me standing at the bedroom window, then made a run for it.'

'How about you, Bill?' asked Nora. 'Did you see or hear anything?'

'No, for my bedroom is at the other side of the house,' answered Bill. 'Of course, Clarissa woke me immediately and we ran down into the yard – and that's when we discovered that Merrylegs had been let out.'

The third formers looked at one another. It was all very mysterious – and very worrying, especially for Julie and Lucy, who had horses of their own at Five Oaks. Clarissa looked at the grave faces of the two girls and said, 'If you want to remove Jack and Sandy, we will quite understand. There are a couple of other riding stables in the area, but they are a few miles away from Malory Towers.'

But Julie said loyally, 'I wouldn't dream of taking Jack away. I know that you and Bill will do all you can to keep him safe.'

'And Sandy is staying too,' said Lucy. 'I shall teach him to kick out at anyone who is a stranger to him.'

Clarissa and Bill smiled, and Pam, who had been looking thoughtful, said, 'Do you think that the person who let Merrylegs out intended to steal him?'

'I don't know,' said Clarissa, with a sigh. 'He's not a particularly valuable horse, though he's priceless to me, of course. I would have thought that any horse thief would have gone to Mr Banks's along the road, for he keeps racehorses, and some of them are worth a lot of money.'

'That's a thought!' exclaimed Bill. 'I wonder if Mr Banks has had any unwanted night-time visitors at his stable-yard? I must remember to ask Eleanor when she pops over to ride Snowball later.'

'Is Eleanor keeping Snowball here?' asked June, looking puzzled. 'That seems odd, when her uncle has a perfectly good stable just a short distance away.'

'Yes, but it's full,' explained Clarissa. 'Mr Banks has bought several more horses recently, so there wasn't room for Eleanor to keep Snowball there. She usually visits him on Saturday mornings, so if there has been any funny business going on over there, Eleanor is sure to know. Anyway, I'm quite sure that you girls didn't come along here to listen to our woes, and we certainly don't want to spoil your day. Now, off you go outside and enjoy yourselves!'

And the third formers did just that! Julie and Lucy cantered round the big paddock on Jack and Sandy, with June and Freddie in hot pursuit on two of the riding-school ponies. Pam and Susan followed more sedately, while Felicity and Nora had a simply marvellous time watching the others, helping Jim with his chores and enjoying the sunshine. But as they ate their picnic in the paddock, the subject of Bill and Clarissa's troubles came to the fore again.

'It's strange that they should have had two strokes of bad luck in a matter of a few days,' mused Felicity, tucking into a sandwich.

'Very strange,' said June. 'In fact, it's almost as if

someone was out to cause trouble for them.'

'Surely not!' cried Susan, looking shocked. 'Why, dear old Bill and Clarissa don't have an enemy in the world!'

'Of course they don't!' said Julie. 'Everyone likes them.'

'Don't bite my head off!' said June. 'But it's quite clear that someone *doesn't* like them – the person who stole their money. And the person who let Merrylegs out. I wonder if they are one and the same?'

There was a brief silence as the third formers digested this, and at last Pam said, 'Well, at least Bill and Clarissa have been put on their guard now. If the troublemaker comes back and tries anything else, he might not find it so easy.'

When the girls had finished eating, and cleared away the remains of their picnic, they went into the stable-yard to find Bill talking to Eleanor Banks, who was mounted on a most beautiful pure white horse, with a snowy mane and tail, and the watching third formers stared.

'My word, what a super horse!' said Susan.

'He's certainly perfect for the Ice Queen,' said Felicity wryly.

'He's a great deal too good for her, if you ask me,' said Julie, with a frown. 'I don't believe that Eleanor cares for Snowball at all. She seems to see him as a possession, and doesn't love him as I love Jack, or as Lucy loves Sandy.'

Eleanor certainly cut an elegant figure in her smart riding gear, sitting up very straight in the saddle as she rode Snowball into the paddock. She gave June a cold glare as she passed the third formers, and the girl gave an exaggerated shiver. 'Brr, it suddenly seems to have turned chilly round here. Eleanor is so cold that I simply can't imagine her caring for anyone or anything!'

'I say, Bill!' called out Pam. 'Did you ask Eleanor if there had been any strange goings-on over at her uncle's stables?'

'Yes,' said Bill, coming over. 'But all has been quiet over there. She's going to warn Mr Banks to look out for anything suspicious, though.'

'Good,' said Julie. 'And now I suppose we had better get the horses back into the stables and make our way back to school.'

'I wonder what Amy, Bonnie and Esme have been doing while we've been enjoying our day at Five Oaks?' said Felicity, as the girls walked back to Malory Towers.

'Nothing very strenuous, I don't suppose,' said Susan with a grin. 'I bet they have been having a really lazy time of it!'

But in fact the three girls had, in their own way, been very busy indeed. First of all, Bonnie had insisted that Esme throw away every scrap of make-up, and had actually stood over her while she did it.

'Gee, this seems such a waste!' Esme had complained, reluctantly removing everything from her bedside cabinet and putting it into the bin. 'Can't I just keep *one* lipstick?'

'Absolutely not!' said Bonnie firmly. 'And don't say "gee"!'

Then, to Esme's horror, Amy had brushed out her carefully set curls, saying, 'I'm sure that you will sleep much better at night without those curlers in your hair.'

'I expect that I will,' said Esme rather doubtfully. 'Ow! Don't brush so hard, Amy – that hurt!'

'Well, sit still, then,' said Amy, unsympathetically. 'There, that looks much better! And when you've got into the habit of brushing it one hundred times every night it will soon start to shine, just as mine does.'

'I sure hope so,' said Esme, staring at herself rather glumly in the mirror. 'At the moment it just looks kinda strange.'

'Kind of, not "kinda",' said Bonnie, clicking her tongue. 'And it just looks strange because you're not used to it yet.' Then she looked down at Esme's hands and gave a little squeal. 'Take that nail polish off at once! If Miss Peters sees you wearing it she'll have a fit.'

'But it took me simply ages to paint them,' moaned Esme. 'Do I have to take it off?'

'Yes,' said the two girls, in unison, eyeing her severely, and, sighing heavily, Esme obeyed.

'Now you're really beginning to look like an English schoolgirl,' said Bonnie happily. 'Isn't she, Amy?'

Amy, looking Esme over critically, nodded and said, 'But we really need to set to work on your speech. Now, repeat after me – *wonderful*.'

'Wunnerful,' said Esme.

'Won*d*erful!' said Bonnie. 'It has a d in the middle, you know!'

Esme took a deep breath, a very determined look on her face, and said, 'Wunnerful.'

Amy and Bonnie shook their heads in despair, and Amy said, 'Oh dear. Perhaps you should just avoid saying wonderful altogether. Try "super" or "wizard" instead.'

But this wasn't good enough for Bonnie, who said firmly, 'No, that's just avoiding the problem, instead of solving it. Esme, try saying twenty.'

'Twenny,' said Esme, obligingly.

Bonnie frowned. 'Hmm. I don't know why you should find it difficult to pronounce words with t or d in the middle, but it's quite obvious that you do. Well, we can't do much about it now, for the others will be back soon, but I shall think of a way to overcome your problem.'

'Do you think you can?' said Esme, hopefully. 'If you could, it would be just wunner– I mean, just super!'

Secrets and surprises

Of course, it wasn't easy to keep a secret in the third form, and the girls soon found out that Amy and Bonnie were taking Esme 'in hand', as they called it. Everyone approved wholeheartedly of the change in Esme's appearance, and thought that she looked very nice indeed. And they were much amused by her attempts to imitate Amy's high, well-bred voice. It really did sound very funny, especially when the girl used English phrases that she had picked up from the others, then suddenly lapsed back into her American drawl.

'I say,' she said to June – in what the girls had come to call her 'Amy voice' – over breakfast one morning. 'Would you pass me the salt, old girl?'

June, her eyes narrowing with amusement, had passed her the salt cellar, and Esme went on, 'My word, these scrambled eggs are simply top-hole. Yessir, they sure are mighty fine.'

Then she looked completely bewildered when the girls burst into laughter, for poor Esme didn't seem to realise that she was switching from one way of speaking to the other.

'She's absolutely priceless,' chuckled Felicity, as she and Susan discussed it later that day.

'Well, they do say that imitation is the sincerest form of flattery,' said Susan, with a grin. 'But Amy didn't seem awfully flattered by Esme's attempt to mimic her accent!'

'I hope that she doesn't try to copy Amy and Bonnie *too* slavishly,' said Felicity, wrinkling her brow. 'That would be an awful shame!'

'Yes,' said Susan, thoughtfully. 'I know that none of us is perfect, but the two of them have more faults than most. Amy especially! It would have been much better if Esme had decided to model herself on someone down-to-earth and friendly and jolly, like you, or Pam, or Julie.'

'I think it would be best if Esme didn't copy anyone at all,' said Felicity thoughtfully. 'Her own personality is very pleasant and unique, and it would be a terrible pity if she lost her individuality through trying too hard to be something that she isn't.'

'You're quite right, of course, old girl,' said Susan. 'It must be awfully difficult for Esme, though, for I know that she wants to please her mother by learning English ways.'

'I expect that she will, after she's been here for a while,' said Felicity. 'But she must learn them in her own time and in her own way. It's no use trying to force things like that.'

But Bonnie, who could be extremely stubborn once she got an idea into her head, was determined that she was going to teach Esme to pronounce 'wonderful' correctly if it was the last thing she did! She spent ages coaching Esme, who soon grew heartily bored and began to wish that she hadn't asked the two girls for their help.

'Can't we do something else instead?' she complained, after failing in her pronunciation for about the tenth time. 'I'll never be able to say wonderful properly, so I might as well give up!'

Bonnie stared at the girl, hardly able to believe her ears. 'But you *did* say it!' she cried. 'You just said it then – wonderful!'

'Gee, did I?' asked Esme, looking stunned. 'Why, that's – wonderful!'

A delighted Bonnie clapped her hands together and squealed, 'Well done, Esme! Oh, how I wish that the others were here to listen to you.'

But the two of them were alone in the common-room. Amy had been called to Matron's room over the matter of some badly darned stockings, while the rest of the third form were outside enjoying the sunshine. Just then, Lucy came in to fetch her plimsolls from her locker, and Bonnie cried, 'I say, Lucy, isn't it marvellous? Your cousin has learned to say wonderful properly.'

'What an achievement,' sneered Lucy, looking at Esme with contempt. 'Honestly, Esme, I'm not surprised that Miss Grayling put you into the third form instead of the fourth. In fact, it's a wonder she didn't put you in with the first-form babies! But perhaps even they would have been too advanced for you, for they know how to speak English properly. As for you, Bonnie, I don't know how you can be bothered to waste your time on Esme – I really don't!'

And, before her cousin could retaliate, she snatched up her plimsolls and stalked out of the room, leaving Esme and Bonnie staring after her open-mouthed.

'Well!' exclaimed Bonnie, at last. 'How dreadfully rude of her.'

Esme shrugged, and managed a rueful smile as she said, 'That's Lucy for you. She never misses an opportunity to get in a dig at me.'

'But why?' asked Bonnie, frowning. 'It's none of my business, and I certainly don't mean to pry, but I just can't understand why she is so hostile towards you.'

Esme hesitated, then said, 'Well, it's all because of the family feud.'

'Family feud?' repeated Bonnie, her eyes wide.

Esme nodded solemnly, and began, 'This coldness between Lucy and me all started a few years ago. You see, our fathers became very good friends when they married sisters – my mother and Lucy's mother, of course. In fact the two of them used to joke that they were as close as brothers.' Esme sighed. 'It was such a good, happy life back in those days. We even lived next door to one another! Lucy and I were best friends then, too, and we were all just one big happy family.'

'So what went wrong?' asked Bonnie, astonished and quite unable to picture the two cousins as best friends.

'Well, Uncle Robert – Lucy's father – and my father are both interested in antiques,' said Esme. 'So they decided to buy a shop and run it together. It seemed like a splendid idea at the time, but that's when things started to go wrong. You see, my father and Uncle Robert are both very strong personalities, and each of them had quite different ideas about the way the shop should be run. Both of them wanted to take charge, and they began to argue quite dreadfully, for neither of them would consider the other's point of view, or agree to any kind of compromise.'

'Goodness!' said Bonnie, her eyes like saucers. 'That must have put a terrible strain on their friendship.'

'It did,' said Esme. 'For it was quite impossible for them to switch off their feelings of anger once they had finished work for the day. Soon Father and Uncle Robert were barely on speaking terms with one another. Of course, it started to affect our mothers, for mine felt that she had to take Father's side, while Aunt Janet took Uncle Robert's. It was horrible for them, because twins are so close and they had spent their whole lives together. I know that my mother was awfully upset about it, and I'm quite sure that Aunt Janet felt the same. To be fair, though, they did try to keep Lucy and me out of it, and never tried to stop the two of us from seeing one another. But we couldn't help overhearing things, and we soon figured out what was going on. And then, one day, we quarrelled as well. Lucy was trying to blame my father for things going wrong, and made some very hurtful remarks about him. Of course, I stuck up for him and said some pretty awful things about Uncle Robert.'

Esme shuddered at the memory and said, 'It was a dreadful row. Really horrible and vicious! Lucy said that she would never forgive me, but the things that she said about my father were just as cruel and nasty.'

'So your friendship with Lucy was spoiled too,' said

Bonnie, looking very grave. 'It just goes to show how family rows can get out of hand.'

'Well, this one certainly did,' said Esme, sighing. 'The next thing that happened was that Father announced that he couldn't work with Uncle Robert any longer. He told Mother and I that the shop was going up for sale, and that we were moving to America.'

'Heavens!' said Bonnie. 'That must have been a shock.'

'It was,' said Esme sadly. 'Mother didn't want to go, and nor did I, at first. We both hoped that Father and Uncle Robert might make up, but they never did. The shop was sold, and off we went.'

It was quite a sad story, thought Bonnie, and neither Esme's father, nor Lucy's, came out of it particularly well. Bonnie felt a sudden wave of anger. The two men had sacrificed the happiness of their wives and daughters, and split their big, happy family right down the middle. And all because they were both too stubborn to swallow their silly pride!

Suddenly the door of the common-room burst open and Amy stalked in, an angry scowl on her face. She was carrying a pile of stockings and she flung them down crossly, before flopping down in an armchair.

'Matron is a mean beast!' she declared. 'She's told me that I have to darn all these stockings again, because I haven't done them properly.'

'Well, I must say, Amy, she's quite right!' said Bonnie, picking up one of the stockings and examining it critically. 'I simply can't believe that someone who prides herself on her appearance, as you do, would use bright red wool for darning.'

'It was all I could find,' said Amy impatiently. 'Besides, I don't see why I should have to darn them at all. Why can't I just go out and buy new ones? It's not as if I can't afford them!'

'Because the rule is, that if you tear your things, you have to mend them,' said Bonnie, imitating Matron's crisp tone. 'I say, Amy, I don't mind darning these for you, if you do my French prep for me. What do you say?'

Amy looked thoughtful. This was a little arrangement that had worked well for the two girls until last term. Bonnie had done all of Amy's mending for her, while Amy had returned the favour by doing Bonnie's French prep. But Felicity had got wise to this scheme after a while, and put a stop to it.

'Bonnie, it's out and out cheating for Amy to do your French for you,' she had told the girl roundly. 'And as for you, Amy, I know you don't like mending. Nor do I, come to that! But, sadly, we all have to learn to do things that we don't like at times.'

Amy considered Bonnie's offer for a moment now, and reluctantly shook her head, saying, 'We shall only get into a beastly row from Felicity.'

'Ah, but Felicity isn't here,' pointed out Bonnie.

'No, but she could come back at any time,' said Amy, who was a little more in awe of Felicity than she cared to admit. The head-girl had a way of speaking to wrong-doers that made them feel very small indeed, and

Amy was in no mood for a scolding today.

'I suppose I shall just have to do it myself,' she sighed. 'You and Esme can chat to me whilst I work.'

But Esme had just glanced at her watch, and now she jumped to her feet, saying, 'Sorry, Amy, I must dash. It's almost time for my tennis practice and Amanda will be livid if I'm late.'

'It's a pity that you didn't come to me for advice before you let yourself in for all this extra coaching,' said Bonnie. 'I could have got you out of it.'

Esme, who was extremely impressed by Bonnie's talent for getting out of anything that she didn't wish to do, asked curiously, 'How come Amanda never picks on you, Bonnie?'

'Because she thinks that I try hard,' answered Bonnie. 'Whenever I see Amanda coming, I run and jump around the court for all I'm worth. But somehow I still never manage to hit a ball. So she's under the impression that – although I'm completely hopeless – it's the best I can do. And Amanda never wastes her time on anyone who she thinks is hopeless. Now, someone who has ability, but doesn't try, is a completely different matter!'

Amused, Esme laughed and said ruefully, 'If only I had known that earlier! But Amanda has got it into her head that she's going to make a good player out of me.'

Amanda had stuck to her word and was keeping Esme's nose to the grindstone as far as tennis was concerned. And, somewhat to her own surprise, the girl's game had improved dramatically.

As Esme walked down to meet Amanda, she could see Felicity and Susan having a fast and furious game on one of the courts, while on another, June was playing against Vanessa Tyler, a big East Tower girl. Esme couldn't help whistling softly to herself in admiration as June leapt high in the air to return Vanessa's serve, sending the ball whizzing past the bigger girl. Gee, thought Esme to herself, I wonder if I'll ever be half as good as that? Then she suddenly stopped in her tracks, horrified. Surely she wasn't turning into one of these jolly, sporting types of girl? Why, the thought was just too horrible to contemplate. Whatever would Amy and Bonnie say?

Amanda had spotted Esme and called out sharply, 'Come along, Esme! Don't dawdle. You're playing against Freddie today, and I want to see both of you doing your very best.'

But what Esme, Freddie and the others didn't realise was that Amanda was going to be watching them very closely indeed. For she had just arranged a very important tournament against a nearby school, and today the games captain was going to be making some decisions that could affect the outcome.

Freddie was a good player, but she had several weaknesses and Esme soon spotted these and learned how to turn them to her advantage. Esme, who hadn't been looking forward to the practice at all, soon lost herself in the game, and felt a peculiar thrill of pride when – to the astonishment of everyone watching – she narrowly beat her opponent.

'Jolly well played, Esme!' yelled Amanda, coming on to the court to clap the girl on the back, which she did so vigorously that Esme almost lost her balance!

Felicity also beat Susan, while June, in a very close-fought match indeed, triumphed over Vanessa. Amanda gathered all the players around her and said in her loud voice, 'I'm very pleased with all of you. You have all proved today that you are made of good stuff. Now, I want you to listen carefully. In a few weeks time, I will be taking a team of players to St Margaret's school, to compete against them in a tennis tournament. June and Vanessa, I want you both to represent Malory Towers in the lower-school singles matches. Felicity and Susan, you two will be taking part in the doubles.'

The four girls looked at one another, their eyes shining in wonder and delight. Hurrah! They had been picked for the team! Even June, whose manner was normally very offhand, and who rarely got excited about anything, couldn't keep the broad grin off her face. My word, she would play up all right! Amanda wouldn't regret her decision, June would make sure of that. Then the games captain was speaking again.

'Esme,' she said. 'You are to be a reserve, so if any of the four girls are unable to play on the day, you may have to take their place.'

'*Me?*' squeaked Esme, hardly able to believe her ears. 'Amanda, are you quite sure that you don't mean Freddie?'

'I'm quite sure,' said Amanda, laughing at the girl's expression of disbelief. 'You've worked very hard at your tennis, Esme, and come on in leaps and bounds. And this is your reward. Now, I want you to keep up your practice, and make sure that you get to know how Felicity and Susan play, for if one of them has to drop out you may have to partner the other.'

Esme listened to all this with her head in a whirl, and very mixed feelings. What *had* she let herself in for? Yes, she had worked hard at her tennis, but only to avoid getting into a row with Amanda. She had never even *thought* of getting on to the team.

Felicity guessed at her thoughts and, as they made their way back to school, clapped her on the shoulder and said, 'Don't look so worried, old girl. You're only reserve, after all, and the chances are you won't even have to play. I have no intention of getting ill, or breaking my leg, or anything silly like that. And nor has Susan.'

'And I shall be there all right, too,' said June, a determined look on her face. 'Come on, everyone, let's find the others and tell them the news. I say, where are Pam and Nora?'

The third formers couldn't find Pam and Nora, but they did spot Julie and Lucy, who had just returned from a ride at Five Oaks and were walking across the courtyard.

Susan hailed them, calling out, 'Hi, you two! My word, you'll never guess what has happened!'

'June, Susan and I have been picked for the tennis team!' yelled Felicity, rushing up to them. 'And Esme is reserve!'

Then she stopped, for Julie and Lucy didn't seem to be

listening to what she was saying at all. And now that she looked at them properly, the expressions on their faces were unusually grave. Heavens, *whatever* could have happened?

The third form rallies round

The others had noticed that the two girls looked unusually serious too, and glanced at one another apprehensively, as Felicity asked in alarm, 'I say, what's up? Don't tell me there has been more trouble over at Five Oaks?'

'I'm afraid that there has,' said Julie, her open, freckled face looking troubled. 'Someone has been hurt.'

'No!' gasped Susan. 'Who?'

'Let's go and sit under that tree,' said Julie, as a noisy group of first formers began playing with a ball nearby. 'And we'll tell you all about it.'

So the third formers sat in the shade of a large apple tree and Lucy said, 'Bill was riding Thunder, and showing a group of children how to take one of the practice jumps, when she fell off. We don't know how badly hurt she is yet, but it looks as if she's injured her arm.'

'Bill?' repeated June, incredulously. 'But Bill is a superb horsewoman! How could she possibly have had an accident taking one of those titchy little jumps?'

'That's just it,' said Julie, lowering her voice. 'It was no accident!'

'Whatever do you mean?' asked Freddie, looking puzzled.

'Well,' began Julie, 'when Bill fell off, everyone ran

across to help her, of course. Miss Peters was there – she's great friends with Bill and Clarissa, you know – and she said it looked as if the reins had snapped. But a little later, once all the fuss had died down, Lucy and I took a look at the reins, and it was quite clear that the reins hadn't snapped – they had been cut.'

'That's right,' said Lucy. 'It was a clean, straight cut, and there was no sign of wear, or fraying, as there would have been if they had simply snapped. Whoever did it only cut part of the way through, so that Bill wouldn't notice it immediately.'

'But why didn't Miss Peters notice that they had been cut?' asked Freddie, looking puzzled.

'She was more concerned with Bill than anything else,' said Julie. 'And she only glanced quickly at the reins.'

'So where is Bill now?' asked Felicity.

'At the hospital,' answered Lucy. 'Mr Banks took her there in his car and Miss Peters went with them.'

'Mr Banks? What on earth was he doing there?' asked Susan, astonished.

'Oh, he wasn't there, but Eleanor was,' said Julie. 'She saw at once that we needed someone with a car to take Bill to hospital, so she telephoned him from Five Oaks and he was there in a trice. I must say that he's quite different from what I expected.'

'Yes, he seemed awfully nice,' put in Lucy. 'And he was so concerned about Bill. He said that he would wait at the hospital for her and Miss Peters, and bring them both home again.'

'Quite different from Eleanor, then,' said June dryly. 'I say, Julie, who else was over at Five Oaks?'

Julie wrinkled her brow thoughtfully and said, 'A few youngsters from the village – oh, and Patsy and Rose from the second form. They have just started taking riding lessons. Then, of course, there was Jim, the stable boy.'

'Well, I can't imagine that any of *them* would have cut through Bill's reins!' said Felicity. 'We can certainly rule Miss Peters out. Patsy and Rose are fond of the odd joke, but they're good-hearted kids and wouldn't do anything so dangerous.'

'And it can't have been one of the village children, for they are hardly more than babies,' said Julie.

'What about Jim?' said Lucy, suddenly. 'I know that Bill and Clarissa are fond of him, but . . .'

Her voice tailed off as the others shook their heads, Felicity saying firmly, 'Jim has been working at Five Oaks since the girls opened the riding stables. It's quite unthinkable that he could have done such a thing.'

'That leaves Julie, Lucy and Eleanor who could have carried out the dark deed, then,' said June smoothly.

'I can assure you that Lucy and I are innocent,' said Julie stiffly, turning an angry red and glaring at June.

'Ass!' laughed June, giving her a push. 'Of course I know that you and Lucy are innocent! But I'm not so certain about Eleanor.'

'Surely she couldn't be responsible!' said Susan. 'I know that you don't like her, June – well, to be honest, none of us cares for her very much – but she always seems to have got along with Bill and Clarissa all right.'

'Yes, and soon as Bill fell she ran to telephone her uncle for help,' Lucy pointed out.

'Besides, it might not be anyone who was there today,' said Felicity, who had been thinking. 'Someone could have sneaked into the stables overnight and cut Thunder's reins then.'

'That's true,' said Julie. 'My goodness, I wish we could find out who was behind this beastly campaign! Wouldn't I like to tell them what I think of them!'

Miss Peters took the third formers for prep that evening, and her expression was unusually grim, thought Felicity, as if she was thinking very unpleasant thoughts. She seemed rather distracted too, and didn't even notice when June and Freddie whispered and giggled together, a crime that would normally have earned them a very severe punishment!

Felicity, Susan, Julie and Lucy stayed behind when prep was over, and went up to the mistress's desk.

'Miss Peters?' began Julie, rather hesitantly. 'We wondered if there was any news of Bill? Do you know how she is?'

Miss Peters looked into the anxious faces of the four girls, and her own stern expression relaxed a little, as she thought what kind, thoughtful girls they were.

'I'm afraid that Bill has broken her arm,' said Miss Peters. 'Fortunately it was a clean break, but it will be in plaster for a while, and it means that she won't be able to ride or be of much help in the stables for the next few weeks.'

The girls were very dismayed at this. Poor old Bill! And poor Clarissa. She and Jim were going to find it very hard work running the stables between the two of them, without Bill's assistance.

A thought occurred to Felicity and she said, 'Perhaps some of us could help! We could go over to Five Oaks before tea, or when we have a free period, and see if there's anything we can do.'

'That's a very kind idea, Felicity,' said Miss Peters, smiling. 'And I'm sure that Bill and Clarissa would appreciate it. Just as long as you don't let it interfere with your school work.'

The eager third formers assured Miss Peters that they wouldn't, then Julie said, rather seriously, 'Miss Peters, I think that there's something I ought to tell you. You see, after you and Bill went to the hospital with Mr Banks, Lucy and I had a look at those reins and –'

'I know, Julie,' Miss Peters broke in. 'They had been cut. I spotted it immediately.'

'Did you?' said Julie, surprised. 'But you didn't say anything at the time.'

'Well, I thought that there was quite enough drama going on,' said the mistress. 'And the immediate need was to get poor Bill to a hospital. However, I have informed Clarissa of my suspicions, though I've advised her to keep it from Bill for a few days. She will only fret over it, and that might hinder her recovery, you know.'

'Yes, of course,' said Felicity, a deep frown on her face. 'What with this and the other things that have happened, it really does look as if someone is out to make trouble for Bill and Clarissa. I just wish we knew why!'

'So you know about the other incidents?' said Miss Peters, looking sharply at Felicity, who nodded. 'Well, please don't spread it around the school,' said the mistress. 'It could be bad for the girls' business, and they have quite enough problems to deal with at the moment!'

The third formers nodded and Susan asked, 'Do you have any idea of who the troublemaker could be, Miss Peters?'

Miss Peters shook her head and said with a sigh, 'I only wish that I did, Susan! But I've wracked my brains and simply can't think of anyone who has a grudge against Bill and Clarissa.'

The third formers went to the common-room, to tell Pam and Nora – who hadn't heard about Bill's accident – the latest news. They were both very shocked, of course, and Nora said, 'I think it's a very good idea of yours, Felicity, for all of us to see if we can help out at Five Oaks. I certainly don't mind doing my bit.'

'You can count me in, as well,' said Pam.

Esme, who was sitting nearby with Amy and Bonnie, looked up, and wondered if she should volunteer as well. She didn't know this Bill and Clarissa that the girls were always talking about, and she certainly didn't relish the idea of getting her carefully manicured hands dirty, but it sure sounded like the two of them could do with all the help that they could get! Would Amy and Bonnie offer their services, she wondered, glancing at Amy. The girl was poring over a fashion magazine and didn't seem to have heard a word the others had said. No, helping out at the stables would be too much like hard work for Amy! Bonnie had also taken no part in the conversation, but she had been listening intently, and said now, 'Surely the most useful thing you can do for Bill and Clarissa is to catch the troublemaker.'

'Brilliant!' said June sarcastically. 'Why didn't we think of that? And just how do you suggest we go about it, Bonnie?'

'You set a trap,' replied Bonnie simply.

June opened her mouth to make a scathing retort, then shut it again abruptly. Actually, that wasn't a bad idea. In fact, it was a jolly good idea! The other third formers obviously thought so too, for they were looking at one another excitedly, and Nora said, 'Bonnie, you never cease to amaze me!'

Bonnie smiled, while Felicity said thoughtfully, 'We must plan it really carefully, if it's to work. Come on, girls, let's put our thinking caps on.'

There was silence in the common-room for a while, as the girls thought hard, but it seemed that it was all in vain. Even the ingenious June had to admit defeat, something she didn't like at all.

'I can't come up with a single idea,' she said, frowning.

'Nor can I,' sighed Pam. 'Perhaps we should sleep on it, and tomorrow we can get to work on it when our minds are fresh.'

'Good idea,' said Felicity. 'A few of us should pop over

to Five Oaks after tea as well, to see how Bill is, and offer our help. As long as we are back in time for prep it will be all right.'

'I shall come with you!' announced Bonnie rather grandly.

The third formers looked at one another in surprise. Felicity, amused at the way Bonnie sounded as if she was bestowing some great honour on them all, grinned, and even Amy looked up from her magazine, startled.

'Don't tell me that you're going to muck out a stable or groom a horse!' she said, wrinkling her nose in distaste.

'Of course not,' said Bonnie. 'But I'd like to have a look at the place. It might give me some ideas on how to set this trap of ours.'

'Well, goodness knows we could do with some!' said Susan. 'We'd better not all go, or we'll be tripping over one another. I think four of us should be enough.'

'All right,' said Felicity. 'So that's you, me, Bonnie – and who would like to be the fourth?'

'Me,' said June promptly, a very determined look on her face. June liked to be at the forefront of everything that went on in the third form. Not only that, but she prided herself on her ingenuity, and if anyone was going to come up with an idea to trap Bill and Clarissa's mystery troublemaker it was going to be her, and not Bonnie!

Esme, who felt that it was all right for her to volunteer her services if Bonnie was going, had been about to say that she would like to go, before June jumped in, and looked rather disgruntled. But she was mollified when Amy laid a hand on her arm and said, 'Thank goodness I shall have you here to keep me company tomorrow evening, Esme. I must say, I'm surprised at Bonnie choosing to spend her valuable free time in a smelly stable!'

A marvellous trick

There was a letter waiting for Lucy when she went down to breakfast the following morning. The girl read it as she ate, her expression growing rather serious, and Julie noticed that she seemed quiet afterwards.

'Anything wrong, old girl?' Julie asked her, when they went outside at break-time. 'I hope you haven't had bad news from home.'

'Oh no, nothing like that,' Lucy replied. 'The letter was from Mother, but it wasn't bad news. You see, I wrote to her at the end of my first week, and mentioned that Esme was at Malory Towers too. I thought that she would be quite as shocked as I was.'

'But she wasn't?' said Julie.

'No. Mother wrote that she hopes that Esme and I can be friends again, and that we won't let what has happened in the past spoil things,' said Lucy, looking troubled. 'I was most surprised to learn that she felt like that. And, to be honest, Julie, I don't know if it's possible for Esme and I *ever* to be friends again.'

'Lucy, what *did* happen in the past?' asked Julie, frowning. 'You can tell me to mind my own business if you want to, but sometimes it helps to confide in someone.'

Lucy looked at her friend's open, honest face and decided that perhaps it *would* help to tell someone the truth about why she and Esme were enemies. So, just as Esme had confided in Bonnie, Lucy poured out the whole story to Julie.

'Well,' said Julie, when the girl had finished, 'I can quite see why you and Esme find it difficult to be friends. But, really, what happened was nothing to do with either of you.'

'I suppose that's true,' sighed Lucy. 'But she's changed so much since living in America that I don't even know if the two of us have anything in common any more.'

'She's still the same Esme underneath,' said Julie wisely, taking her friend's arm. 'I think it would be a jolly good thing if you could make it up. But just don't go getting *too* friendly with her, that's all, or I shall be left out in the cold!'

'No chance of that!' laughed Lucy. 'Well, I can't see Esme and I becoming friends again overnight, but I shall try and be a little more civil to her.'

Immediately after tea, Felicity, Susan, June and Bonnie went over to Five Oaks. Bill was seated in a large, comfy armchair in the living-room, her feet up on a stool and a cup of tea at her elbow.

'Clarissa is taking very good care of me,' she told her visitors. 'And everyone has been very kind. So many people have called to see me, and Mr and Mrs Banks brought me that huge bouquet of flowers. Isn't it beautiful?'

It was indeed a beautiful bouquet, and so large that Clarissa had needed three vases to hold all the flowers.

'Mr Banks is awfully nice,' said Clarissa. 'Do you know, he even offered to lend us one of his stable boys for a few days to help out, but of course we wouldn't hear of it.'

'Goodness, that was kind of him!' said Felicity. 'But there's no need for you to worry about being short of help, because that's why we're here. A few of us third formers are going to come over and do what we can every day until Bill's arm is healed.'

The two girls thanked them heartily, and, after they had chatted to Bill for a little while, Clarissa took the third formers outside and set them to work.

Felicity and Susan helped Jim to muck out the stables, while June swept the yard. Bonnie, meanwhile, entertained everyone with her efforts to play detective.

'June!' she shrieked. 'There are hoof-prints over here by the gate! The intruder must have come on horseback.'

'My dear Bonnie,' sighed June. 'This is a riding stable. There are hoof-prints as far as the eye can see!'

'Oh, yes. I suppose there would be,' said Bonnie, rather crestfallen. But her spirits rose a little later when she discovered a scrap of green wool caught on one of the fences.

'Aha!' she cried. 'This could be a clue.'

Alas for Bonnie, her hopes were dashed again when Clarissa said, 'That's where I tore my green sweater the other day.'

Then, to the amusement of Felicity and Susan, Bonnie

subjected poor Jim to an intense grilling, before announcing her intention of going indoors to question Bill.

'No!' cried Felicity and Susan together.

'Bonnie, don't forget that Bill doesn't know yet that someone deliberately tried to harm her,' said Susan. 'And she doesn't need any more shocks at the moment.'

'Now what am I to do?' sighed Bonnie. 'I've explored every avenue, left no stone unturned . . .'

'You could always give us a hand,' suggested Felicity, without much hope.

But Bonnie suddenly decided that she had better look round the yard again, just in case there was anything she had missed!

June, her sharp eyes peeled for anything unusual, didn't fare any better. The one good thing about a routine chore like sweeping, she decided, was that it didn't need brains and gave one plenty of time to think. But all her thinking got her nowhere, and she was still unable to think up a scheme for trapping the mean beast who was making life so difficult for Bill and Clarissa.

'Well, that was a waste of time,' she said, rather glumly, on the way back to school.

'Nonsense,' said Felicity. 'We were able to be of help to the girls, so I don't think it was a waste of time at all.'

'But we're no nearer finding out who the culprit is,' said Bonnie.

'Cheer up!' said Susan, giving her a clap on the shoulder. 'One of us is bound to come up with an idea to trap him sooner or later.'

'Let's just hope it's sooner,' said June, impatiently.

An air of gloom seemed to hang over her and Bonnie after that, and when they got back to Malory Towers it seemed to pervade the whole form. In the common-room, after prep, everyone was rather quiet and listless and at last it all got too much for Freddie.

'For heaven's sake, cheer up!' she cried. 'I know it's disappointing that we're no nearer solving Bill and Clarissa's problems, but there's still plenty to celebrate. June, Felicity and Susan have all been picked for the tennis team, and Esme –'

She stopped suddenly, for Esme gave a cough and caught Freddie's eye. Freddie read the message she was conveying at once – Esme hadn't yet told Amy and Bonnie that she was to be reserve because she wasn't sure if they would approve! So Freddie went on smoothly, 'And Esme is becoming a proper English girl, thanks to Amy and Bonnie. I think that we should try to forget all of the bad things that are happening for a little while and plan some fun – a trick!'

This lifted everyone's spirits at once, and an excited murmur ran round the room.

'A trick! Marvellous!'

'What a super idea. Just what we need to take our minds off things.'

'June and Freddie's tricks are always so hilarious! I say, I wonder if they'll play it on Mam'zelle Dupont?'

'All right,' said June, a grin replacing her frown. 'I've got some things in the dorm that I ordered from one of my trick booklets. If we go up a few minutes before bedtime we can take a look.'

June had a simply enormous collection of trick booklets, and she was forever studying them, and sending away for sneezing powder, or invisible ink, or some other ingenious product which she could use to trick the hapless Mam'zelle. As Miss Potts, the stern head of North Tower, remarked, 'If June put half as much energy into her school work as she does into her jokes and tricks, she would probably be the most brilliant pupil Malory Towers has ever had!'

But June, with her quick brains and amazing memory, managed to do extremely well at her schoolwork with the minimum of effort. It was very galling, both to the mistresses, and to the other girls, who had to work far harder to obtain respectable marks. And, of course, it meant that June could reserve all of her energy for games, jokes and tricks, all of which she was superlative at.

The third formers trooped up to the dormitory ten minutes before the bell for bedtime went – which surprised Matron very much!

'Hmm,' she said suspiciously to Mam'zelle Dupont. 'It's most unlike the third formers to go to bed early! I hope that they aren't planning a midnight feast, or some other mischief! I shall check on them later.'

But when Matron quietly opened the door of the third-form dormitory shortly after midnight, all of the girls were fast asleep. For, of course, the mischief that they had been planning had nothing to do with a feast!

The girls had gathered round as June produced a bewildering array of jokes and tricks from her bedside cabinet.

'My word, June!' exclaimed Lucy. 'You must spend all of your pocket money on this stuff. Why, there's enough here to start your own shop!'

'Itching powder!' cried Nora, snatching up a small pot. 'Goodness, just imagine poor old Mam'zelle Dupont scratching away for all she's worth!'

'I have something better in mind than that,' said June, rummaging around in her cabinet. 'Ah, here it is!'

She stood up, a small box in her hand and Felicity peered over her shoulder, reading aloud, 'Disappearing chalk. I say, that sounds exciting! How does it work, June?'

Grinning, June took what appeared to be an ordinary stick of chalk from the box, and answered, 'Well, it works in a similar way to the invisible ink that I used on Julie in the second form. Remember that, Julie?'

'I remember all right!' said Julie darkly. 'Miss Parker gave me some lines to do, for talking in class,' she explained to the new girls. 'But dear June filled up my pen with her invisible ink, so that by the time I got to the end of the page, the lines that I had written at the top had disappeared!'

The others laughed as they recalled the trick and Pam said, 'It took you all evening to write those lines, until June finally confessed what she had done.'

'Yes, I was simply furious at the time, though I saw the funny side afterwards,' grinned Julie. 'But the ink wasn't completely invisible, was it, June? I seem to remember that if you looked at the writing in a dark room and shone a torch on it, you could see it.'

'That's right,' said June. 'Well, the chalk works in a similar way. When someone writes on a blackboard with this, it works just like normal chalk. But, after a few minutes, it disappears and the board appears blank again. Just watch!'

And, under the astonished gaze of the third formers, June scrawled a big, white zig-zag pattern on the door of her cabinet. Everyone stared at it, then Nora cried, 'It's beginning to fade! Look!'

So it was, and after a few minutes, there was no trace of the pattern at all.

Freddie, her lively mind seeing all sorts of possibilities, gave a laugh and said, 'We can trick Mam'zelle properly with this. Let's make some plans!'

So the third formers plotted and schemed, and Felicity even allowed the rule about no talking after lights-out to be broken, though she was normally very strict about sticking to it.

'Only for a few minutes, though – and for goodness' sake keep your voices down,' she warned. 'If any of the mistresses come along and hear us we shall be in hot water.'

By the time the girls were ready to settle down to sleep, their plans had been made, and it was arranged that the trick would be played on Mam'zelle Dupont in French class the following morning.

Just before Mam'zelle arrived to take the lesson, June

went up to the blackboard and removed the chalk that was on the ledge, replacing it with a stick of her own special chalk.

'Quickly!' hissed Freddie, who was keeping watch at the classroom door. 'Back to your seat, June. I can hear Mam'zelle coming.'

The little French mistress always wore high-heeled shoes, which made a tip-tapping sound as she walked, so that the girls could hear her approaching, which proved very useful on occasions such as this!

Swiftly, June slipped back to her seat, while Freddie remained by the door, holding it open for Mam'zelle to enter.

'*Merci*, Freddie,' said the French mistress, beaming round at the class. '*Bonjour, mes enfants*. Please sit down.'

Mam'zelle Dupont was in a very good mood. Yesterday, as the wicked June knew, she had been to the opticians to get some new spectacles, and she was very pleased with them indeed. The tortoiseshell frames were, thought Mam'zelle, *très chic*, and so much more attractive than her old black ones. Ah, and the dear girls, they had noticed the change in their old Mam'zelle's appearance too, for they were smiling at her in approval. Well, of course, the third formers were smiling in anticipation of the trick that was about to be played, but Mam'zelle had no idea of this and was happy. Especially when Bonnie, who was one of her favourites, said in her pretty, lisping voice, 'Oh, Mam'zelle, how lovely you look in your new glasses!'

Mam'zelle's smile grew even wider and she cried, 'Ah,

you flatter me, *ma chère*! Now, you will bring your books to me one at a time please, and I shall correct your prep. Nora, you first.'

'Heavens, I hope Mam'zelle isn't going to spend too long looking at everyone's prep,' whispered Freddie to June. 'Or we shan't have time to play the trick. Nora! Make sure that you don't keep her talking for too long!'

Nora was another of Mam'zelle's favourites, and the girl had a trick of engaging the French mistress in conversation whenever she took her book up for correction. Normally the third formers were happy to encourage this, as it wasted a great deal of the lesson, but today they wanted to get their prep marked as quickly as possible. So Nora was not as chatty as usual, and was back at her desk in no time at all. Soon Mam'zelle had looked at everyone's work, and she got to her feet. The French mistress usually began the class by setting a few questions, and she then went round the class asking for answers. She stuck to her routine today, saying, 'Now, I will test your French grammar by writing down some simple questions on the blackboard, in French. You will answer them orally, also in French, *n'est-ce pas*?'

Then Mam'zelle turned to the blackboard, picked up June's disappearing chalk and began writing. Nora wanted to laugh already, even though the trick hadn't begun yet, and she clamped a hand firmly across her mouth, while Julie and Lucy grinned at one another in anticipation. What a super trick this was going to be!

The girls were busily scribbling down the questions as

fast as Mam'zelle was writing them on the blackboard. They had to be sure to copy every word before the chalk disappeared, otherwise the trick would not work. By the time Mam'zelle finished writing the last question, the first one had already began to fade a little and, to distract the French mistress, Susan put up her hand and asked, 'Mam'zelle, are we to write down the answers to the questions, or do you want us to answer them orally?'

Mam'zelle looked at Susan in surprise and said, 'Why, you will speak your answers, of course, Susan. Have I not just said so?'

'Oh, did you, Mam'zelle?' said Susan meekly. 'Sorry, I wasn't concentrating.'

'This is not like you, Susan,' said Mam'zelle, a little sternly. 'Now, you shall answer the first question, and you will pay attention, *d'accord*?'

'*Oui*, Mam'zelle,' answered Susan seriously, glancing over the French mistress's shoulder and seeing that the blackboard was now quite blank.

'*Bien!*' said Mam'zelle, 'Now, the first question is . . .'

Mam'zelle turned to face the blackboard, giving such a start of surprise that her brand-new glasses slid down her nose. '*Tiens!*' she cried. 'My questions, they have vanished.'

'Whatever do you mean, Mam'zelle?' asked Susan, feigning a puzzled look.

'See for yourself!' exclaimed Mam'zelle, becoming agitated as she flung her arm out towards the blackboard. 'I wrote them carefully on the blackboard, and now they are gone!'

The rest of the third formers pretended to look very puzzled too, all except Nora, who could feel a terrific snort of laughter coming on and quickly lifted the lid of her desk so that she could hide behind it.

'Gone, Mam'zelle?' said June. 'Whatever do you mean? Why, the questions are there on the blackboard as plain as day. We can all see them, can't we, girls?'

The third formers all nodded and Mam'zelle cried, 'Ah, this is a treek! June, if the questions are there on the blackboard then read me the first one!'

June, who had memorised the first question so that she did not need to glance at her notebook, peered at the blackboard and read it out. Her expression was so grave and earnest that it proved too much for Nora, who gave one of her explosive snorts of laughter, which she hurriedly turned into a cough.

'You, Nora!' said Mam'zelle. 'You read me the second question.'

Nora, whose memory was not as good as June's, glanced quickly down at the paper on her desk where she had scribbled the questions, and repeated it rather hesitantly, mispronouncing a couple of words. Fortunately, she was poor at French anyway, so Mam'zelle did not notice anything out of the ordinary!

'It is a treek,' she muttered to herself. 'Either that, or my poor eyes are deceiving me!'

The French mistress asked Amy, Felicity and Susan to read out the next three questions, which they all did most convincingly, so that poor Mam'zelle was quite at a loss.

She walked up to the blackboard and ran her hand across it, then examined it from all angles, her expression of bewilderment so comical that several of the girls found it hard to contain their laughter.

'Perhaps it is something to do with your new spectacles, Mam'zelle,' suggested Pam.

The French mistress considered this, taking off her new glasses and looking at them closely. But that was no good at all, for without them Mam'zelle could hardly see a thing! She put them back on again, just in time to see June waving at someone through the open window – but there was no one there!

'June!' she called sharply. 'Who do you wave to?'

'Why, it's Amanda from the sixth form,' answered the wicked June. 'Look, there she is, over by the flower beds. Hi, Amanda!'

June leaned out of the window, waving frantically and Mam'zelle, fearing for her sanity now, cried, 'But there is no one there!'

'It's Amanda all right, as large as life,' said Freddie, also leaning out of the window. 'Coo-ee! Amanda!'

This was the signal for all the girls who were seated by the windows to begin waving furiously, all of them shouting to attract the attention of the non-existent Amanda, and soon the noise became quite deafening.

'Silence!' shouted Mam'zelle, covering her hands with her ears. 'Back to your seats at once!'

But, before the girls could sit down, the door opened and Miss Potts appeared. She had been taking the first formers in the classroom next door, and wondered what on earth was going on in Mam'zelle's class! The third formers were making so much noise that she could barely hear herself think!

The mistress pursed her lips as she took in the scene before her. Half of the third formers seemed to be hanging out of the windows yelling themselves hoarse, while the other half watched, with tears of laughter running down their cheeks. As for Mam'zelle herself, her attempts to restore order were having no effect at all!

Miss Potts raised her voice and said sharply, 'Mam'zelle Dupont! What is the meaning of all this noise?'

No one had heard Miss Potts enter, and Mam'zelle wheeled round sharply, the girls at the windows returning quickly to their seats, some of them looking a little scared.

'Ah, Miss Potts!' cried Mam'zelle. 'My eyes, they have gone wrong! The girls, they wave to that big Amanda, but I cannot see her!'

Miss Potts marched over to the nearest window and looked out. 'Mam'zelle, you can't see Amanda because she isn't there. June!'

June jumped at the sharpness of Miss Potts's tone and, turning slightly red, said, 'Yes, Miss Potts?'

'Was Amanda outside?'

'Well, I *thought* that I saw her,' said June, not wanting to tell an outright lie to the mistress. 'But I think that she's gone now.'

Before Miss Potts could reply to this, Mam'zelle claimed her attention again, crying, 'But that is not all, Miss Potts.

I cannot see the writing on the blackboard either. There is something wrong with my eyes, I tell you!'

Miss Potts looked at the blackboard and then at Mam'zelle Dupont, wondering if the French mistress was in her right mind that morning, and said crisply, 'Well, there is nothing wrong with *my* eyes, Mam'zelle, and I can see no writing on the blackboard either.'

Mam'zelle stared at Miss Potts and said, 'But this is impossible! The dear girls, they can see the writing.'

'Can they indeed?' said Miss Potts, sounding very sceptical indeed. 'I think, Mam'zelle, that the girls have been playing a trick on you. No doubt June or Freddie will be happy to explain it to you!'

And with that, Miss Potts stalked from the room, leaving the girls staring at one another apprehensively, while Mam'zelle stood in the middle of the floor, her mouth agape. At last she found her voice, and cried, 'So, June! And you, Freddie! Once again you have tricked your old Mam'zelle. You will please explain to me how it was done.'

So the two girls went to the front of the class, and while June explained to Mam'zelle how the disappearing chalk worked, Freddie demonstrated by writing her name on the blackboard.

Mam'zelle watched intently, and Felicity grinned to herself as she realised that Mam'zelle's anger was giving way to enjoyment, as the French mistress exclaimed over the ingenuity of the trick.

'*Oh là là!*' she exclaimed. 'See how the writing fades!

And now he has disappeared altogether. It is a most marvellous treek indeed!'

Then she made her expression very stern as she turned to face June and Freddie, saying, 'Of course, I must confiscate this chalk at once.'

'Yes, Mam'zelle,' chorused both girls meekly.

'I shall take it with me when I go to France in the holidays,' went on Mam'zelle, the stern look vanishing as she beamed. 'My sister teaches the *petits enfants* at the school in our village, you see, and I shall play a treek on her! How *les petits* will laugh when they see her writing vanish before their eyes!'

And how the girls laughed. What a sport old Mam'zelle was!

'Thank goodness that Mam'zelle Dupont has a sense of humour,' said Freddie to June later. 'If we had played that trick on any other mistress in the school we would be in real trouble. It was a jolly good trick, though, wasn't it?'

'I'll say!' said June, with a grin. 'And it has put me in the mood to play a few more!'

Tricks and tennis

Miss Potts, who knew Mam'zelle Dupont well, was not surprised to hear her squealing with laughter shortly after she had left the third form's classroom. And although Miss Potts couldn't help smiling to herself at Mam'zelle's little ways, she shook her head as well.

'I sincerely hope that you have punished those two girls, Mam'zelle,' she said to the French mistress later, in the mistresses' common-room.

'Of course,' said Mam'zelle, with great dignity. 'I confiscated the trick chalk that they used, and I scolded them most severely. The poor June was almost in tears.'

'Really?' said Miss Potts, disbelievingly, quite unable to picture Mam'zelle reducing anyone – let alone the brazen June – to tears.

Then the French mistress began to chuckle. 'Ah, it was a very funny treek they played on me, those wicked girls! That June, she is so clever.'

'Very clever and very naughty!' said Miss Potts, sternly. 'If you were a little firmer with her, Mam'zelle, she might not be encouraged to think that she can get away with anything!'

And, indeed, it seemed that June *did* think that she

could get away with anything, for she and Freddie went 'trick-mad', as Felicity called it, over the next few days. They made Bonnie squeal by putting insects in her pencil case, infuriated Amy by replacing her expensive talcum powder with itching powder, and ruined Felicity and Susan's tennis practice by substituting a trick ball for the real one.

June also managed to sneak a bottle of invisible ink into Eleanor Banks's satchel, laughing as she said to Freddie, 'I'd love to see Miss James's face when Eleanor hands her prep in, after she's used my special ink!'

But Felicity called the two to order after they put a frog in Esme's bed, and the girl screamed so loudly that both Matron and Miss Peters appeared on the scene. Neither of the grown-ups was amused at being dragged from their beds, but they accepted Esme's explanation that she had had a nightmare. And Esme went up in everyone's estimation for not sneaking on the two culprits, for she hated frogs and really had been very frightened indeed.

Lucy, with her mother's letter in mind, went up to her cousin the next morning and said, 'It was jolly decent of you not to split on June and Freddie.'

Esme, surprised and rather pleased at being spoken to in such a friendly way by Lucy, smiled and said, 'Well, I didn't want to get them into trouble. And they only meant it as a joke – I guess they weren't to know that I'm scared stiff of frogs!'

'I don't much like them either,' said Lucy, with a shudder. 'But of course, you know that already, don't you?

Do you remember that time when we were little and we found one by the pond in your garden?'

Bonnie and Julie, standing nearby, exchanged glances and Julie said in a low voice, 'Let's hope that this is the start of a better understanding between those two.'

Bonnie nodded and said, 'It must be difficult for both of them, after what's happened in the past.'

'Oh, so Esme told you about that, did she?' said Julie. 'Lucy confided in me as well.'

'Hmm,' said Bonnie, looking thoughtful. 'It's an awful shame. If only we could think of a way to get the family back together again. If you ask me –'

'Hush!' hissed Julie. 'They're coming over, and they won't be very pleased if they think that we have been gossiping about their private business.'

So Bonnie immediately changed the subject and began talking about the forthcoming half-term.

'I'm so looking forward to it,' said Julie, as Lucy and Esme joined them. 'My parents and brother are coming on horseback, and we're going for a picnic on the cliff-tops.'

'How super!' said Lucy enviously. 'My mother will be coming alone on the Saturday, as Father can't get away until Sunday. She doesn't care for horses, I'm afraid, so I won't be getting such a marvellous treat! I expect we'll be going to a restaurant instead.'

'Well, I think that's much nicer than a picnic, with the sun ruining your complexion, and insects buzzing around all the time,' said Bonnie. 'What about you, Esme? Are your parents coming?'

'I don't know yet,' said Esme. 'They're going on holiday the week before and they may not be back in time. I sure hope they can make it, though.'

All of the girls were looking forward to half-term enormously. Most of them had parents, or brothers and sisters, coming to take them out for the day, and to watch the tennis and swimming displays.

Felicity and Susan were both taking part in the diving, while June had been chosen to play against one of the fourth formers in an exhibition tennis match.

'It's a tremendous honour for the third, June,' Felicity told her, when they were in the courtyard one day. 'You're the only girl in the school who is playing against someone from a higher form. Has Amanda told you who you're going to be playing against yet?'

'Well, it was to have been Penelope Turner, but she sprained her wrist last week,' said June. 'So if she's not fully recovered, I shall be playing Hilda Fenwick instead.'

'Golly!' said Susan, coming up just in time to hear this. 'Penelope's a marvellous player, but Hilda is quite superb – and very aggressive! She came jolly close to beating Amanda herself once, and no one else has ever done that before. I hope for your sake, June, that Penelope is better in time.'

'Well, I'd rather play Hilda, thank you very much!' retorted June. 'And I'd rather lose against her than beat Penelope.'

'You must be mad!' said Susan roundly. 'Just think of the glory that you would bring to the third form if you beat Penelope.'

'To my mind, there's not much glory in beating someone who has just recovered from an injury,' said June. 'If I win against Penelope, people will say that she only lost because her wrist wasn't quite right. Now if I'm up against Hilda, I can really give it everything I've got. And, win or lose, no one will be able to say I didn't do my very best and put up a good fight.'

'Well!' said Susan, as June went off to find Freddie. 'Wonders will never cease! If anyone had told me a few terms ago that June would one day go all out to win a tennis match for the honour of her form, I would have said that they were quite mad.'

Felicity laughed, but said thoughtfully, 'Do you really think that she's doing it for the third form, Susan? Or for herself?'

'Whatever do you mean?' asked Susan.

'Well, June has certainly knuckled down to swimming and tennis since Amanda started taking an interest in her. But those are sports where one plays as an individual, and not as part of a team. And June still doesn't have any team spirit. Do you remember what happened when Amanda put her in the lacrosse team last term?'

'Yes,' said Susan. 'We drew, when we could so easily have won. Because June was determined to shoot a goal herself and hogged the ball. Elizabeth Jenkins from West Tower was in a perfect position to shoot in the last few minutes, and would probably have won the match for us. But June simply had to try and score herself, even though she was too far away.'

'Exactly!' said Felicity. 'June wanted to be the heroine of the hour, and that was more important to her than whether the team won or lost. Miss Maxwell was absolutely furious with her, and gave her a thorough ticking off afterwards.'

'I remember,' said Susan. 'But Amanda didn't scold her at all. I thought at the time that it was rather odd.'

'I overheard Amanda talking to Kay Foster about it afterwards,' Felicity said. 'She was frightfully disappointed that Malory Towers hadn't won the match, but she told Kay that she understood exactly how June felt. Amanda said that she had been just the same when she was training for the Olympics, and that she had always gone in for swimming and tennis because she didn't want anyone else sharing in her glory.'

'Golly!' exclaimed Susan. 'But old Amanda has plenty of team spirit now. Miss Grayling wouldn't have made her games captain otherwise.'

'Yes,' said Felicity. 'But she told Kay that she had only learned to play as part of a team since coming here. Which doesn't surprise me at all! If you have any team spirit in you at all, then good old Malory Towers is the place to bring it out.'

'Well, let's just hope that June has some team spirit in *her*!' said Susan. 'She still has a few years in which to find it.'

But, for now, June was concentrating solely on her tennis, determined to make a good showing at half-term and in the match against St Margaret's. She spent every spare moment on the tennis court, badgering Freddie, or Felicity, or Susan into going with her so that she had someone to practise against.

'My word, she's good!' said Penelope Turner to her friend Meg, as they watched June playing against Felicity one afternoon. 'I almost hope that my wrist doesn't get better in time for half-term! Imagine the humiliation of being beaten by one of those third-form kids!'

Someone else who was devoting a lot of time to tennis, much to the astonishment of the third form, was Esme. The girl had finally 'confessed', as she put it, to Amy and Bonnie that she was to be reserve for the tennis matches, and had been unsurprised at their reaction.

'Oh dear!' Amy had said, looking most dismayed. 'Please tell me that you aren't becoming one of these dreadful, sporting types, like Felicity, or that big, ungainly Amanda Chartelow.' Amy shuddered and went on, 'She's so loud and aggressive that I simply can't bear her. And she looks more like a boy than a girl.'

'I blame myself,' Bonnie had said sorrowfully. 'I should have thought of a way to get you out of tennis practice earlier. Perhaps it's not too late, Esme. Let me have a think and I'll see if I can come up with a plan.'

'Yes, but the thing is,' Esme had said, rather hesitantly, 'I – I don't actually *want* to get out of it. You see, until I came to Malory Towers, I didn't even *know* that I could play tennis. I've never really been good at anything before and – well, I actually feel quite proud of myself. Not only that, but I'm enjoying it as well.'

Amy looked quite horrified at this, but the more large-minded Bonnie said, 'It seems very queer to me, but I suppose if that's the way you feel there's nothing we can do about it. You must promise that you won't go all tomboyish on us, though. In fact, Esme, I think it's your duty to show Amanda and the rest of them that it's possible to play sport and still be feminine and pretty and graceful.'

'Yes, I'll do that,' Esme had agreed, relieved that Bonnie, at least, seemed to be taking the news quite well.

Amy, however, remained extremely disapproving and after Esme had left the common-room she said to Bonnie, 'I feel quite let down by Esme, when I think of all the help that we tried to give her. I don't know that I want to be friends with her any more.'

Amy sounded rather petulant, and Bonnie, picking up her sewing, smiled to herself. She knew that Amy had only befriended Esme because she thought that the American girl admired and looked up to her, and didn't have much genuine liking or affection for her at all. Attempting to turn Esme into a replica of herself had been more for her own gratification than the other girl's. And Amy's conceit made it difficult for her to accept that Esme was beginning to realise that she didn't *want* to be just like her.

Bonnie, for her part, genuinely liked Esme and, although she missed seeing so much of her, now that tennis was taking up a lot of her time, she was pleased that Esme had found an activity that she enjoyed. Unlike Amy,

Bonnie was interested in people, and her sympathy had been stirred by Esme's story of her family's quarrel. How she hoped that the two fathers would be able to put their differences behind them!

Esme, meanwhile, went off to her tennis practice. The good-hearted Freddie, overcoming her own disappointment at not being chosen as reserve, selflessly gave up her time so that the others could practise with her. Today, she and Esme were playing doubles against Felicity and Susan. The weather was extremely warm, and by the end of the first set all four girls felt uncomfortably hot.

'Phew!' said Freddie, flopping down on the grass and fanning herself with her racket. 'I'm worn out after just one set!'

'Me too,' said a red-faced Susan. 'I'm roasting! Perhaps we should stop now.'

Felicity frowned at this suggestion, but it was Esme who surprised everyone, saying bracingly, 'Nonsense! If we were playing in a tournament we wouldn't be able to stop after one set, simply because we felt hot and tired. I say that we should play on.'

'Hear, hear!' said Felicity. 'Come on, we'll have a drink of lemonade and then we'll all feel as right as rain.'

The girls had all brought bottles of lemonade with them, and they moved to the side of the court now, drinking thirstily. Felicity was right, and they all felt refreshed once their thirst had been quenched, playing on with new heart.

Felicity and Susan won the match, but it was a close

thing. As they walked off the court, Felicity said to Susan, 'I think Freddie was off her game a little today, otherwise we might have lost. Esme played superbly.'

'Didn't she just!' said Susan. 'Who would have thought, at the beginning of term, that she had it in her?'

'She really seems to be finding her feet at Malory Towers,' said Felicity, pleased. 'Doing well at tennis seems to have given her confidence in other ways. She doesn't copy Amy so much now, and she's trying much harder at her lessons. If she carries on like this, there's a chance that she might go up into the fifth form next term, while we go into the fourth.'

'Golly, that would be a shame,' said Susan, looking a little dismayed. 'A shame for us, I mean, though of course it would be a jolly good thing for Esme. I suppose that Lucy will be pleased to see the back of her too.'

'Perhaps, although the two of them do seem to be making an effort and getting on a little better now,' said Felicity. 'In fact, the only fly in the ointment at the moment seems to be this beastly business with Bill and Clarissa.'

'I shall be glad when Bill's arm is better,' said Susan. 'What with helping out at Five Oaks, tennis, swimming and lessons I feel absolutely exhausted!'

'Yes, it's been quite a busy term,' agreed Felicity. 'We shall all be jolly glad of a break when half-term comes.'

The girls were so busy that the last few days before half-term simply flew by. Then on Saturday morning, Felicity woke early. She knew that she was excited about something, but at first she couldn't think what it was. Then a little thrill of joy ran through her as she remembered, and she sat up in bed.

'Wake up, everyone!' she cried happily. 'It's half-term!'

A super half-term

The parents seemed to arrive slowly at first – in 'dribs and drabs', as Pam said. Then, as the morning wore on, more and more arrived, and soon the grounds were filled with groups of laughing, chattering girls and their families. Felicity was thrilled that her mother and father were among the first to arrive. She flew to meet them, hugging first her mother, then her father.

'Did you get my letter, Mother?' she asked eagerly. 'I'm taking part in the diving later, and so is Susan.'

'Yes, I got it, dear,' said Mrs Rivers, beaming happily at her excited daughter. 'Daddy and I were awfully proud to hear that you had been chosen. So was Darrell, of course. She telephoned me the other evening, and said to wish you luck.'

'How I wish that she could have come with you!' said Felicity.

'Well, she's working awfully hard at the moment,' said Mr Rivers. 'But the summer holidays aren't too far away, so you will see one another then.'

Nearby, Felicity could see Pam with her parents, and Nora with her mother and young sister. And in the distance she could see Susan, chattering nineteen-to-the-dozen with her big, jolly father, while Bonnie enjoyed being fussed over by her doting parents.

I wonder if Esme's parents are here too? thought Felicity. I do hope so.

Sadly for Esme, they weren't. She had received a message to say that her parents wouldn't be returning from their trip until late this afternoon, by which time it would be too late for them to travel to Malory Towers. But they meant to set off early the following morning, so that she would be able to spend tomorrow with them. All the same, the girl couldn't help feeling a little forlorn as she saw the happy time that the others were having. There was Julie, dressed in her riding gear, ready to go off with her parents and brother for their picnic. And there – looking so like her beloved mother that Esme gave a gasp – was Aunt Janet, with Lucy. Esme hadn't seen her aunt since the families fell out, and for a moment she stood rooted to the spot, hardly knowing what to do. But the problem was solved by her aunt, who spotted Esme and came over at once, a delighted smile on her face.

'Esme, my dear!' she said, kissing the girl on the cheek. 'How wonderful to see you again.'

'Hallo, Aunt Janet,' answered Esme, her voice a little shaky. 'I'm so pleased that you could come and see Lucy.'

Lucy, who had been hovering a little awkwardly in the background, said, 'I was just telling Mother that you weren't sure whether your people would be able to come, Esme.'

'No, they telephoned Miss Grayling this morning and

said that they wouldn't be able to get here today,' said Esme. 'But they are coming tomorrow.'

'Well, that's good,' said Mrs Carstairs. 'But you can't possibly stay here alone today, while everyone else is off enjoying themselves. I insist that you come out to lunch with Lucy and me.'

Esme glanced at her cousin, sure that she wouldn't be too happy about the invitation, but Lucy was smiling. So Esme smiled too, and said happily, 'Thank you, Aunt Janet. That *will* be a treat after I was expecting to stay here for school lunch.'

The restaurant that Mrs Carstairs took the girls to was a very good one, and they had a slap-up meal. But, even more than the delicious food, Esme enjoyed the company of her aunt and cousin. There were a few awkward moments when the girls mentioned their fathers, but on the whole they had a very pleasant time, recalling childhood incidents and telling Lucy's mother about life at Malory Towers. Mrs Carstairs teased Esme good-naturedly about her American accent and Lucy laughed, saying, 'You should have heard it when she first started at Malory Towers, Mother. It was much stronger then.'

'Was it really?' said Esme, looking surprised.

'Oh yes,' said Lucy. 'You seem to have lost some of it as the term has gone on. And you don't say "gee" half as much as you used to. Why, at times you sound quite English!'

'Heavens!' exclaimed Esme. 'Mother *will* be pleased.'

'How is your mother, Esme?' asked Mrs Carstairs, looking rather wistful. 'I do miss her terribly, you know.'

'Well, I know that she misses you as well,' said Esme. 'But you'll be able to see her tomorrow. Perhaps the two of you could talk, and –'

But Lucy's mother shook her head, regretfully. 'I only wish that we could, my dear. But your father will be there, and Lucy's father is hoping to come tomorrow as well, so that might make things a little awkward.'

Both girls looked uncomfortable now, so Mrs Carstairs hastily changed the subject, saying, 'Well, we've a little time to spare before the diving and swimming at Malory Towers, so what would you girls like to do now?'

They thought for a moment, then Esme said, 'Why don't we pop over to Five Oaks and see Sandy? I never did get to say hallo to him.'

Lucy, of course, was only too happy to agree to this, so her mother said, 'Very well. As long as you don't try to get me up on his back, Lucy! You know that I'm not a great one for horses.'

Julie and her people were also at Five Oaks, returning Jack to his stable after their picnic. There was a flurry of introductions, then, while Julie's mother chatted with Mrs Carstairs, Esme spotted Sandy, who had poked his head out of his stall to see what all the noise was about.

'Sandy!' she cried joyfully, going up to stroke the horse's nose. 'How marvellous to see you again, boy.'

Sandy whinnied softly and nudged Esme, who laughed and said, 'I really believe that he remembers me!'

'Perhaps he does,' said Lucy, with a smile.

Just then Bill and Clarissa appeared, and there were

yet more introductions, for neither Esme nor Mrs Carstairs had met the two girls before. Esme, who had heard so much about them that she felt as if she knew them very well indeed, looked at Bill and Clarissa with interest. Bill's arm was still in plaster, and she said, 'I have to go back to the hospital next week, and I'm hoping that the doctor will say that the plaster can come off. And won't I be glad when I can get up on old Thunder again! Not being able to ride has been simply dreadful for both of us!'

Soon it was time for the Malory Towers girls and their families to return to the school in time for the swimming and tennis, but before they left, Julie found an opportunity to take Clarissa aside.

'I don't seem to have had the chance to talk to you or Bill in private just lately,' she said. 'How are things? Have there been any more strange happenings?'

'No, thank heavens,' said Clarissa. 'Jim did catch a strange man prowling round here the other night, just before he went home for the evening. But he turned out to be one of Mr Banks's grooms. Mr Banks had sent him over to have a scout round and check that everything was all right.'

'That was thoughtful of him,' said Julie.

'Yes, he's been very good to us,' said Clarissa. 'Of course, Bill knows now that her "accident" was no accident. Now that she's feeling stronger, I thought it best to tell her so that she could be on her guard.'

'Good idea,' said Julie. 'Although it sounds as if

whoever was behind it may have decided to stop these rotten tricks.'

'I certainly hope so,' said Clarissa, with a sigh. 'It's been an awfully difficult time. Of course, we've tried to keep the whole business quiet, but somehow word has got out and some of the children from the village have stopped coming for riding lessons. Their parents are afraid that they may be hurt too, so they won't allow the children to come until they're certain that it's quite safe.'

'Oh, Clarissa!' cried Julie in dismay. 'I had no idea.'

'Well, I suppose one can't blame them,' said Clarissa, suddenly looking rather strained. 'But of course, it means that we don't have as much money coming in as we used to.'

Julie, guessing that Clarissa was a lot more worried than she was letting on, said stoutly, 'Well, you may be sure that all the Malory Towers girls will continue to come, Clarissa. We'll stand by you all right!'

But Julie wished that there was something else that she, and the others, could do to help Bill and Clarissa. She would bring it up after half-term, for she certainly didn't want to dampen everyone's spirits today, of all days.

And what a marvellous day it was!

All of the girls had been taken out to lunch by their parents, though those who were taking part in the sports that afternoon had been careful not to eat too much.

'I shall make up for it at tea-time,' Felicity had said to her mother, after refusing an ice-cream. 'Half-term teas are always absolutely super!'

Indeed they were, and the kitchen staff had worked very hard at producing scores of dainty sandwiches, cakes, scones and big bowls of fat, juicy strawberries with jugs of cream.

But first there were the tennis and swimming exhibitions. Chairs had been arranged around the tennis court, and June's parents sat proudly at the front.

June herself felt a little nervous – a most unusual thing for her – as she watched the upper-school matches and waited for her turn to come. Her opponent was to be Hilda Fenwick, after all, and – for a fleeting moment – June found herself wishing that the less aggressive Penelope was playing instead. Then she spotted Hilda, chatting with one of her friends. The fourth former saw June watching her, and gave her a scornful smirk before turning back and saying something that made her friend laugh. At once June's moment of self-doubt vanished, her fighting spirit coming to the surface again. So, Hilda thought that she was going to have a walk-over, did she? Well, she could jolly well think again!

Felicity and her parents were sitting with Susan and her people to watch the match, and, as June and Hilda walked on to the court, Felicity whispered to Susan, 'My word! Just look at June's face!'

June wore an expression of grim determination, and even Hilda looked a little taken aback as the two girls faced one another.

Miss Maxwell, who was acting as umpire, tossed to see who would serve first. June won, and the two girls took their places. Then Miss Maxwell shouted, 'Play!' and the match began.

As there were several exhibition matches to get through, each one consisted of only one set. This meant that the spectators did not become bored and restless, and the players didn't get too tired. June, her nerves completely gone now, played her first game superbly, getting a couple of aces past the bigger girl and winning comfortably. But Hilda fought back, taking the second and, for a while, the games went with service.

It was a very exciting match, both girls going all out to win and fighting fiercely for each point, while their supporters cheered loudly and yelled encouragement.

June, though, had quickly discovered that Hilda's backhand was her weak point, and as the match went on she exploited this ruthlessly. And, as the score stood at five games to four in June's favour, her persistence paid off. Hilda faulted on her first service, and her second was more cautious. *Too* cautious, for June slammed the ball back, placing it where the fourth former couldn't hope to reach it.

'Love, fifteen,' called out Miss Maxwell, while the third formers yelled themselves hoarse.

'Good shot, June!'

'Go it, June!'

'You can do it, June! Play up!'

And June played up for all she was worth, winning the next two points. There was a tense silence as Hilda served to stay in the match. But alas, her nerve seemed to have deserted her completely and she muffed the service, placing the ball almost at June's feet. The girl could almost taste victory, and she hit the ball back so that it just cleared the net. Hilda, still at the baseline, ran forward, but it was no use. June had won! The third formers clapped and cheered, while June's parents beamed with pride.

The two girls walked to the net and shook hands, June saying, 'Bad luck, Hilda.'

'It wasn't bad luck,' said Hilda ruefully, gracious in defeat. 'I was completely outplayed. Jolly well done, June.'

'June played marvellously, didn't she?' said Susan to Felicity, as the two of them changed into their bathing costumes ready for the diving. 'I only hope that we do half as well!'

In fact the two of them did very well indeed, their display of diving very graceful and thrilling to watch. Felicity's beautiful swallow dive from the top board brought 'oohs' and 'aahs' from the first formers, and gasps of admiration from the parents. And Susan received a round of applause for her daring somersault, which she had practised to perfection.

'Simply marvellous, darling!' cried Mrs Rivers, when Felicity joined her parents afterwards.

'Yes, I was proud of you,' said Mr Rivers, giving her a hug. 'And I managed to take some good photographs as well. I shall send some to Darrell once I've had them developed.'

Then it was time for tea and, all too soon, it seemed, the

girls were waving their parents off. Most of them were staying in nearby hotels so that they could come back tomorrow, while others, who lived nearer to Malory Towers, were going home for the night.

'Well, what a perfectly super day!' said Nora, as the third formers gathered in the common-room.

'First-rate!' agreed Pam. 'And June beating Hilda at tennis, and Susan and Felicity doing so splendidly in the diving was the icing on the cake!'

'And talking of cakes, wasn't that a simply wizard tea?' said Freddie. 'I've eaten so much today that I feel as if I never want to eat again!'

'I daresay you'll feel differently tomorrow,' laughed Felicity.

'Ooh yes, we've still got tomorrow to look forward to!' cried Bonnie, clapping her hands together excitedly. 'How lovely!'

Even Amy, who usually found something to complain about, was in a good mood, for she had enjoyed spending the day with her parents and grandmother.

'I've had a marvellous time,' she said. 'I really think that this has been the most perfect day.'

'I'll second that!' said Esme. 'Thank you for asking me along today, Lucy. I enjoyed myself so much.'

'Well, it was really Mother who asked you,' said Lucy. 'But I'm glad that you came too.'

'It was so nice to see Aunt Janet again,' Esme said, rather wistfully. 'And it's perfectly obvious that she and Mother are missing one another terribly. If only there was something we could do to bring them together. And Father and Uncle Robert, of course.'

'Well, there isn't,' said Lucy, with a sigh. 'Quite frankly, Esme, I don't see how this rift between our parents is ever going to be mended!'

A family reunion

But Esme couldn't get the idea of out her head. If only she and Lucy could make things right, and the two families could be as one again, it would be too marvellous for words! 'Lucy, we must try to think of something!' she said, urgently. 'Tomorrow our parents are going to be here. It will be the first time that the four of them have been together, in the same place, for years. We just *can't* let this opportunity slip by!'

Lucy looked at her cousin thoughtfully for a moment then, at last, she said, 'You're right. Look here, I can't concentrate with all this excited chatter going on. Let's slip away, and find somewhere quiet where we shall be able to hear ourselves think.'

So the two girls slipped quietly from the room and went off to one of the little music rooms. Esme perched on the piano stool, while Lucy sat cross-legged on the floor, their brows creased with concentration as they thought hard.

'I'm quite certain that Mother and Aunt Maggie would be only too glad of an excuse to make up,' said Lucy. 'Our fathers are the ones that we need to get to work on. They're both so dreadfully stubborn!'

'And proud,' said Esme, with a sigh. Then her face lit up. 'What we need is a situation where they have to forget about their silly pride, because something more important is at stake. I know! Suppose we were to push one of them into the swimming-pool, so that the other had to come to his rescue?'

'That would never work,' said Lucy scornfully. 'Both of them swim like fish, and wouldn't need rescuing. All that would happen is that you and I would get into a dreadful row.'

'Yes, I suppose you're right,' said Esme, rather glumly. 'Oh dear, how difficult it all is!'

But Lucy suddenly snapped her fingers and cried, 'Wait! Perhaps we could do it another way. We can't push Father or Uncle Philip in – but you could pretend to *fall* in!'

'*Me?*' said Esme, looking quite alarmed. 'But what good would that do?'

'Don't you see?' said Lucy. 'You'll have to make some excuse to get away from your parents, and come down to the swimming-pool, where I will be waiting with mine. Then you must throw yourself in the deep end, and pretend that you're in difficulties. Of course, my father will dive in and rescue you. And *your* father will be so grateful to him that it will be quite impossible for the pair of them to carry on being enemies.'

Esme looked simply horrified at this, and said, 'Why can't *you* pretend to fall in, and *my* father can rescue you?'

'Because I swim like a fish too,' answered Lucy. 'What's the matter, Esme? Are you afraid of spoiling your hair?'

'No, I'm afraid of drowning!' retorted Esme, nettled by the scorn in her cousin's voice. 'Lucy, you know that I'm not a very good swimmer, and I always stay in the shallow end.'

'Yes, and that's why it will be so much more convincing if *you* pretend to fall in, rather than me!' said Lucy. 'And there's not the slightest chance of you drowning. Even if my father doesn't come to the rescue – which he most definitely will – I shall be there to haul you out.'

Esme digested this in silence for a moment, then said, 'But suppose someone else rescues me? That would simply ruin everything! It's half-term, remember, and there will be lots of people about.'

'Well, we shall just have to choose our time carefully,' said Lucy, looking thoughtful. 'I know! We'll do it at two o'clock. There's a gymnastics display on then, so most of the parents will be watching that. The whole thing will only take a few moments. Now, once my father has pulled you out of the pool, you will have to pretend to be unconscious for a few minutes. Meanwhile, I'll dash off to fetch your parents and tell them that Father has saved you from drowning. We'll have to exaggerate a bit, of course, so that Uncle Philip feels properly grateful. And once your parents arrive at the pool, you can pretend to come round, and tell them that you owe your life to Father. If that doesn't get them talking, I don't know what will!'

Esme still looked rather doubtful and Lucy said earnestly, 'Esme, if you find the courage to go through with this, it will be the bravest and best thing that you have ever done. Our families will be reunited, and it will be all thanks to you.'

Esme was much struck by this, but a little voice piped up at the back of her mind: what if it doesn't work? What if something goes wrong?

Yes, but what if I let the chance of ending this stupid feud pass by? thought Esme. What if my parents, and Lucy's, never speak to one another again, because I didn't have the pluck to go through with our plan? That would be far worse than trying and failing.

She took a deep breath and said, 'I'll do it.'

'Good for you!' said Lucy, getting up and clapping her cousin on the back. 'I say, if it all works out, perhaps our parents will decide to move next door to each other again. Won't that be fun?'

'I'll say,' said Esme, her face breaking into a smile. 'Things will be just as they used to be.'

But they wouldn't be *quite* the same, thought Lucy, sobering suddenly, for Julie was her best friend now. And Lucy had no intention of throwing her off. She was getting on with Esme very much better now than she had at the beginning of term, and the old fondness they had felt for one another was starting to come back – but her cousin would never take Julie's place with her. She wondered how she could broach this subject without offending Esme, but, almost as if the girl had read her mind, Esme said, 'Of course, I realise that things have changed. *We* have both changed a great deal over the years. And I know that Julie is your friend now. I certainly wouldn't try to come between you – the two of you get on so well together that it simply wouldn't be right. But it will be nice for the two of us to have one another for company in the holidays.'

'Oh yes, that would be super,' agreed Lucy, relieved that Esme understood and accepted the situation. Grinning, she added, 'Perhaps I can teach you to ride.'

'And perhaps I can teach you how to dress properly, and do your hair so that you don't look like a boy!' laughed Esme.

Just then the bell rang for bedtime and Lucy said, 'Heavens, I had no idea it was so late! We'd better dash. You know what a stickler Felicity is for putting the lights out on time.'

So the two girls made their way to the dormitory, both of them feeling excited and a little apprehensive. If only their scheme worked, then this would turn out to be the best half-term ever!

The third formers gathered in the common-room to wait for their people after breakfast on Sunday morning.

'Your parents won't arrive any sooner because you're standing there watching, you know,' June called out to Freddie, who had stationed herself at the window.

'I know, but I get so impatient and restless when I'm waiting for people,' sighed Freddie. 'I just can't seem to settle to anything. Oh, here comes a car! Does it belong to anyone here?'

'No, those are Kay Foster's parents,' said Felicity, going across to join Freddie. 'But a few more cars are coming.

Bonnie, I do believe one of them belongs to your people!'

As Bonnie gave a squeal and ran from the room, Freddie said, 'Your parents are here, too, Lucy – or are they Esme's? Your mothers look so alike that I can't tell one from the other!'

The two cousins went across to the window, and Esme said in a rather hollow voice, 'They're mine.'

'Well, you don't sound very pleased to see them!' said Nora, surprised.

In fact, Esme's feelings were very mixed. Of course she was pleased to see her parents, but she was also feeling extremely nervous about the scheme that she and Lucy had come up with. She glanced at her cousin, who gave her a reassuring smile, then went off to greet her parents. She was doing this for the good of the family, Esme reminded herself firmly, and if the plan failed it wouldn't be because of a lack of courage on her part!

Susan's parents weren't able to come that day, so she was going out with Felicity and her people. The two girls ran outside together to greet Mr and Mrs Rivers as soon as their car drew up, almost knocking over Eleanor Banks, who was standing at the bottom of the steps, talking to her uncle.

'Watch where you're going, you third formers!' she said crossly.

'Sorry, Eleanor!' chorused Susan and Felicity, both of them glancing at Mr Banks rather curiously. He was a tall man – very pale, like Eleanor herself – with hooded eyes and thin lips, which seemed to be curved into a permanent smile.

'Is that Eleanor's uncle?' murmured Felicity to Susan. 'He looks rather sinister, don't you think? I never trust people who smile all the time!'

Susan laughed and said, 'You shouldn't judge a book by its cover. Mr Banks has been jolly good to Bill and Clarissa in their time of need.'

'Of course, I had forgotten about that!' said Felicity. 'Well, he must be quite decent after all – and I suppose he can't help the way that he looks.'

Esme and Lucy, meanwhile, were having a grand time with their respective parents, though there was a tricky moment when the two families came face to face in the courtyard. The two mothers greeted one another rather awkwardly, while Mr Walters and Mr Carstairs merely nodded unsmilingly, and rather stiffly, before walking on. Lucy, unseen by the grown-ups, gave her cousin a wink, and Esme grinned back. Her father wouldn't be so stiff and unfriendly once he thought that Uncle Robert had saved her life!

But, once the time came for Esme to carry out her part in this daring plan, she didn't feel like grinning at all! There were butterflies in the girl's stomach as she led her parents to a bench, under the shade of a tree, in the courtyard. The grounds had been thronged with people earlier, but now it was quieter, for the gymnastics display was due to start shortly, and many of the parents had gone to watch.

'How pleasant it is just to sit quietly for a few moments,' said Mrs Walters. 'We have had such a busy morning, with so much to see. I must say, dear, Malory Towers seems a splendid school.'

'And that games mistress of yours was telling me that you're beginning to shine at tennis,' said Mr Walters, looking proudly at his daughter. 'It sure looks like this English school is bringing out some hidden talents in you.'

Normally, Esme would have basked in her parents' praise, but now she was on tenterhooks, for it was time for her to go down to the swimming-pool.

'Are you quite all right, dear?' asked her mother, looking at her in concern. 'You look a little flushed.'

'I'm fine, Mother,' said Esme. 'It's just that I'm a little hot and thirsty. I might go to the kitchen, and see if Cook can spare us some lemonade.'

'Good idea,' said her father. 'Shall I come and help you carry it?'

'Oh no, I can manage, Father,' Esme assured him hastily. 'You sit here and relax with Mother.'

And Esme walked off towards the kitchen, changing direction as soon as she was out of sight of her parents, and running off to the swimming-pool.

Lucy and her parents were already there, Lucy feeling quite as nervous as her cousin, now that the time had come for them to put their plan into action. She glanced round as Esme approached, but Mr and Mrs Carstairs had their backs to the girl, and didn't spot her until she was on the ledge of rocks surrounding the pool.

'Hallo, Esme!' said her aunt, sounding surprised. 'What are you doing here?'

'Oh, I – er – I thought I saw Felicity here,' answered Esme, a little flustered. 'I just needed to ask her something. Hallo, Uncle Robert.'

'Hallo, my dear,' answered her uncle, a little gruffly.

Lucy gave her cousin a meaningful look, which Esme knew meant that she was supposed to fall into the pool. But *how* was she to do it in a convincing way? If she just threw herself in, it wouldn't look realistic at all. As it turned out, though, Esme's fall was very realistic indeed! The rocks around the pool were extremely slippery and, as the girl stepped forward, her feet suddenly slid from under her, and she tumbled headlong into the pool, her scream of fright quite genuine.

Lucy stood rooted to the spot, as Esme disappeared under the water, while Mrs Carstairs gave a little cry of horror. And Mr Carstairs sprang into action immediately, throwing off his jacket and plunging into the pool after Esme. For a moment he, too, vanished beneath the surface, then he came up, gasping for air, an unconscious Esme in his arms.

'I think she may have banged her head on the rocks!' he called to his wife. 'Help me to get her out. And Lucy, run as fast as you can and find Esme's parents – and you'd better fetch Matron, too!'

Scared now, Lucy ran like the wind towards the school. *Why* had she thought up this stupid idea? If Esme turned out to be badly injured, it would all be her fault, and she would never forgive herself! And where on earth was she supposed to start looking for her aunt and uncle, for she didn't have the faintest idea where Esme had left them! Perhaps she had better go and fetch Matron first, for there was no time to waste. But, as she reached the courtyard, Lucy spotted her aunt and uncle sitting on a bench, and raced up to them.

'Why, Lucy!' said Mrs Walters, alarmed at the girl's panic-stricken expression. 'What on earth is the matter?'

'It – it's Esme,' gasped Lucy, trying to catch her breath. 'There's been an accident. She's fallen into the swimming-pool and hit her head.'

Mrs Walters turned pale, while Mr Walters was on his feet immediately, a look of horror on his face.

'My father dived in and pulled her out,' Lucy said. 'And he sent me to fetch you both, and Matron.'

'We shall go there at once,' said Mr Walters, trying to speak calmly, as he helped his wife to her feet. 'Lucy, you carry on and find Matron, will you? Tell her to come to the pool immediately. Good girl!'

Lucy sped off into the school, and up the stairs to Matron's room. She burst in, without pausing to knock, giving Matron a terrific start.

'My goodness!' she cried, looking most displeased at the third former's lack of manners. But before she could begin to scold, Lucy's face crumpled and, between sobs, she cried, 'Matron, you must come quickly! There's been a dreadful accident, and Esme is hurt.'

Matron was on her feet at once, putting a comforting arm about Lucy's shoulders, and saying in her brisk but kindly manner, 'There now, Lucy. Do try to keep calm, my dear, or you won't be able to tell me what has happened. Take me to Esme, and you can explain what has happened on the way.'

But Matron and Lucy only got as far as the big hall when the door was suddenly opened and a very bedraggled Mr Carstairs appeared, followed by Mr Walters, who was carrying a pale, but conscious, Esme.

'Thank goodness!' breathed Lucy, while Matron took charge and said crisply, 'Bring her up to the San, Mr Walters. And Mr Carstairs, you had better get out of those wet things. Wait in my room, and I'll get someone to fetch you a blanket.'

With her usual efficiency, Matron soon had Esme undressed and in bed, where she examined her carefully. 'No bones broken, thank heavens,' she announced at last. 'But I'm afraid you're going to have a beautiful bruise on your forehead tomorrow, young lady!'

'I don't mind,' murmured Esme, a little smile on her lips. 'It was worth it.'

'Why, whatever do you mean?' asked Matron, astonished.

'I shouldn't be surprised if she was concussed,' said Lucy, hastily. 'I say, Matron, do you think I might have a word with Esme alone?'

Mr Walters frowned at this, and said, 'Gee, I don't know if that's a good idea, Lucy. Esme really needs some peace and quiet.'

But Esme said, 'It's all right, Father. I'd like to talk to Lucy. You and Mother will come and see me in a little while, won't you?'

'Just try to keep me away!' said her father.

'Don't keep Esme talking for too long, Lucy,' admonished Matron, as she ushered Mr Walters from the room. 'And now I'd better go and see how poor Mr Carstairs is doing.'

'I'll come with you, Matron,' the girls heard Esme's father say, as the door closed behind the two grown-ups. 'I've already shaken him by the hand once, but I need to do it again. He sure is a hero!'

'Did you hear that?' whispered Lucy gleefully. 'It worked! Esme, it worked!'

Esme smiled wanly and at once Lucy was contrite, saying, 'But I never meant you to get hurt, Esme. I wouldn't have had that happen for the world. I don't know about my father being a hero, but you're certainly a heroine.'

'No, I'm not,' said Esme, ruefully. 'I slipped and fell. So, you see, your father really *did* save my life!'

'But where are our mothers?' asked Lucy. 'I can't believe that they aren't here, at a time like this.'

'The last I saw of them, they were having a tearful reunion in the courtyard,' said Esme with a contented sigh. 'Though I daresay they will be here any minute. As soon as I came round, and Mother saw that I was going to be all right, she burst into tears. Of course, Aunt Janet comforted her, and before I knew what was happening, she was crying too, and the pair of them were hugging like nobody's business! As for my father, he simply couldn't thank Uncle Robert enough. Lucy, I do really think that everything will be all right now.'

So it seemed, for a moment later Matron bustled in, saying, 'I'm afraid I shall have to throw you out now, Lucy, for Esme's parents want to see her.'

'Darling, how are you feeling?' asked Mrs Walters, a very concerned look on her face as she entered the San.

'My head aches a bit, but I'll be all right,' answered Esme. 'I'm sorry to have given you both such a fright.'

'I'm just glad that your uncle was there,' said her father, gravely. 'I don't think I'll ever be able to thank him enough for saving you.'

'Does that mean that you're friends again now?' asked Esme hopefully.

'It sure does,' answered Mr Walters. 'I think what happened to you today made us realise how stubborn and foolish we had both been. But we won't let our pride get in the way of our friendship – or our families – again.'

'I'm so pleased to hear that,' said Esme contentedly. 'And I expect you are, too, aren't you, Mother?'

Mrs Walters nodded. 'I can't tell you how much I've missed my sister.'

'And Lucy and I are friends now, too,' said Esme. 'So everything has worked out perfectly. We're just one big, happy family again!'

Mam'zelle is a sport

The story of Esme's accident spread through the school like wildfire, and Lucy became quite embarrassed as one girl after another came up to her and congratulated her on her father's bravery.

'How lucky that he was there,' said Nora, in the common-room that evening.

'I'll say,' said Freddie, with a shudder. 'Just imagine what might have happened if no one had been around when Esme fell in.'

'You must be so proud of your father, Lucy,' said Felicity. 'I know I would be, if mine had done something so marvellous.'

'I saw your father and Esme's together at tea-time,' said Bonnie, staring hard at Lucy. 'The two of them were gabbling away nineteen-to-the-dozen. Just as if they were the best of friends.'

By now, the whole form knew the story of the feud between Lucy and Esme's family, and Susan said, 'Well, I should think it would be impossible for the two of them to remain enemies after what happened today. So at least something good has come out of it.'

Lucy turned red. Her father *had* been incredibly brave,

no doubt about it. But so had Esme, and it only seemed right and fair that the third formers should know it. So, taking a deep breath, she told the others the whole story of how she and Esme had planned the whole thing, to bring their families together.

'Well!' said Pam, looking quite astonished. 'Who would have thought that Esme would have the pluck to throw herself into the deep end.'

'As it turned out, she slipped and didn't need to throw herself in,' said Lucy. 'But she was quite ready to go through with it, so really, she was very brave as well.'

'Very brave and very foolish!' said Felicity, torn between admiration for Esme and horror at what could have happened. 'Heavens, she could have been seriously injured.'

'I know,' said Lucy, looking rather guilty. 'But thank goodness that she isn't. Matron says that she will be as right as rain in a day or two.'

To Esme's dismay, Matron insisted on keeping the girl in bed the following day.

'But I feel absolutely fine,' protested Esme. 'Really I do.'

After a dose of medicine and a good night's sleep, Esme's headache had completely vanished. As Matron had predicted, she had a simply enormous bruise on her forehead, and had been rather looking forward to going back to class and showing it off to the others!

But Matron was adamant, and said firmly, 'It won't do you any harm to have an extra day's rest, just to be on the safe side. As long as you don't have a relapse, you can join the others tomorrow.'

Esme had a steady stream of visitors throughout the day. Miss Grayling popped in, which made Esme feel very honoured indeed. And most of the third formers came to see her, as they thought that she had done a rather noble thing, and were secretly quite impressed.

Bonnie and Amy, armed with a large bottle of barley-sugar, visited after breakfast. Pam and Nora spent their lunch break gathering a huge bunch of the most beautiful wild flowers, which they presented to the invalid. And Felicity and Susan went along to the San after tea, taking a book for Esme to read, in case she was bored. Esme's ordeal had taken it out of her more than she realised and, despite her protestations that she felt well enough to return to class, she was beginning to feel a little tired. Felicity, who had intended to give the girl a scold for putting herself in danger, relented when she saw the large bruise on Esme's head, and noticed how pale she looked. Instead she said, 'Poor old thing! You have had a bad time of it, haven't you? Never mind, I daresay Matron will soon have you back to your old self.'

The two girls hadn't been there long when Matron herself bustled in, saying, 'It's time for Esme to have her nap now, girls. Please tell the others that she is to have no more visitors today.'

'What a tyrant you are, Matron!' complained Susan, as they were shooed out.

'I need to be a tyrant to keep you girls in order!' said Matron. But there was a smile on her face, and Felicity and Susan laughed as they went off to join the others.

They were all lazing about on the grass before prep, and Pam said, 'Isn't it a simply glorious day? I wish that we could do our prep out here.'

'If Miss Peters was taking us she might agree to it,' said Freddie. 'But it's Mam'zelle Dupont, and you know how she hates being outdoors for too long in the hot weather.'

'Yes, she's simply terrified of wasps,' laughed Felicity. 'And she can't bear all the flies buzzing around.'

'I bet I could get her to agree to it,' said June, who had been looking thoughtful. She jumped to her feet suddenly and said, 'Nora, come with me!'

'Why?' asked Nora, looking quite startled. She was stretched out on the grass with her hands behind her head, and looked very comfortable indeed. 'I'd just as soon stay here, if it's all the same to you.'

'Do you want to do your prep in a stuffy classroom, or would you rather do it out here?' demanded June.

Nora sighed, and sat up. 'I don't suppose I shall get any peace unless I agree to go with you. Where are we going, by the way?'

'To find Mam'zelle, of course,' said June, with a grin. 'Come on!'

The two girls walked off towards the school together, June talking rapidly to Nora as they went. They found Mam'zelle in the mistresses' common-room, where she was marking the fifth form's French essays. At least, that was what she was *supposed* to be doing, but it was so hot that she simply couldn't concentrate. She had taken off her high-heeled shoes and undone the collar of her blouse, and was fanning herself with one of the fifth formers' work.

Nora stifled a giggle as she peeped at the mistress through the open door, and June frowned at her, pulling her back along the corridor. Loudly she said, 'Mam'zelle Dupont would never agree to such a thing, Nora! Now, if it was Mam'zelle Rougier . . .'

'Nonsense!' replied Nora, just as loudly. 'Why, Mam'zelle Dupont is *far* more good-hearted than Mam'zelle Rougier – and a much better teacher. She knows that we can't possibly do our best work if we feel hot and uncomfortable.'

Mam'zelle stopped fanning herself abruptly as she heard the voices, recognising them at once. It was the bad June, and dear Nora – ah, what a good girl she was, to speak so kindly of her old Mam'zelle. The French mistress smiled to herself as she heard June say, 'I quite agree that Mam'zelle Dupont is an excellent teacher. In fact, I would go so far as to say that she is the best in the entire school. But I still say that she would never allow us to do our prep out in the open air.' June gave rather a scornful laugh, and added, 'She's far too scared of wasps and things.'

'What rubbish you do talk, June!' scoffed Nora. 'Mam'zelle might be scared of wasps, but she has pluck, and I know that she would brush her fear aside for the good of us girls.'

'Very well, then,' said June. 'If you're so convinced, you go and find Mam'zelle, and ask her if we can take our prep outside. I bet she's in our classroom right now, getting our work ready, for she always takes such care over our lessons.'

Nora sighed and said sorrowfully, 'I can't, June. You see, I wouldn't feel right taking advantage of Mam'zelle's good nature.'

'She is *very* good-natured, isn't she?' agreed June. 'If only some of the other mistresses were more like her! Though I still say that she would never consider letting us do our prep out of doors.' Then she sighed. 'Ah well, I suppose we shall just have to resign ourselves to a hot, uncomfortable hour in our stuffy old classroom.'

Then the two girls moved away, their voices fading into the distance as they walked down the corridor. Mam'zelle, meanwhile, sat completely still, feeling quite moved by all she had heard. Ah, the dear girls! They might play tricks on her sometimes, but they were fond of their old Mam'zelle. The best teacher in the school! Good-natured and good-hearted! Mam'zelle's heart felt warm as she remembered the girls' remarks. And Nora had said that she had the pluck. Mam'zelle knew what a great compliment that was, for English girls set great store by pluck! They were good girls, these third formers, and they deserved a treat. And she, Mam'zelle Dupont, would give them one. Ah yes, she would prove to them that everything they had said about her was true.

So, when the third formers trooped rather dispiritedly into their classroom for prep that afternoon, they were in for a surprise. Mam'zelle was already at her desk, and her little black eyes danced as she looked at the girls' weary, slumped shoulders and dragging feet.

'Freddie!' she cried, making her voice very stern. 'Stand up straight, and do not slouch so!'

'But Mam'zelle, it's so hot!' groaned Freddie.

'That is not an excuse for laziness,' snapped Mam'zelle. 'I expect you all to work hard at your prep tonight, no matter how hot you feel.'

'Yes, Mam'zelle,' everyone groaned.

'Good!' Then Mam'zelle's face broke into a broad grin and she said, 'Pick up your books, everyone, and follow me. For tonight, we do our prep outside!'

The girls looked at one another in amazement, then a resounding cheer broke out!

'Hurrah! What fun!'

'Yes, we'll work twice as hard out in the fresh air.'

'You're a real sport, Mam'zelle!'

As Mam'zelle beamed round, June nudged Nora and whispered, 'See! I told you it would work.'

Only Amy and Bonnie were not pleased at being allowed to do their prep outside, for neither of them were outdoor types. Also, both were terrified of getting freckles, and Bonnie pleaded with Mam'zelle.

'Can't Amy and I do our work in the classroom, Mam'zelle?' she asked in her soft voice, making her eyes as big as possible. 'We won't play the fool, I promise you.'

'I know that you will not, *ma chère*,' said Mam'zelle, patting the girl's cheek fondly. 'But, alas, it is the rule that you must be supervised whilst working at your prep. But do not worry, for you and Amy and I shall sit in the shade of one of the big trees, then none of us shall catch a freckle!'

So out they all went, and the third formers were true to their word, working most conscientiously. It was a pleasant late afternoon, for a cooling, gentle breeze sprang up, which was very refreshing, and Mam'zelle congratulated herself on making a good decision. Even when a caterpillar crawled on to the toe of her shoe, the French mistress was not unduly disturbed. She gave a little start when she first spotted it, but then she remembered Nora's remark earlier – she would prove that she had the pluck! But Mam'zelle could not bring herself to remove it, instead asking Bonnie, who was sitting beside her, to do it. Bonnie didn't care for what she called 'creepy-crawlies' any more than Mam'zelle did, so she picked up a twig and managed to dislodge it with that, earning the French mistress's undying gratitude. Nothing else occurred to mar the afternoon, and when the third formers gathered in the common-room after prep, they were in good spirits.

'Wasn't it fun having prep out of doors?' said Susan. 'A super end to the day.'

'It's been a funny sort of day, with poor old Esme laid up in the San,' said Nora.

'It's been a funny sort of *term*, if you ask me,' said Pam. 'What with Bill and Clarissa's troubles, and Lucy and Esme feuding.'

'Yes, but I believe that things are coming right,' said Felicity, who had been looking thoughtful. 'Lucy and Esme are friends again, and things seem to have gone quiet over at Five Oaks. It looks as if all our problems are behind us, and the second half of the term will be nice and peaceful.'

But Felicity had spoken too soon. For the third formers were in for a very big shock indeed!

A shock for Julie

The next morning, Felicity and Susan were making their way downstairs to breakfast, a little way ahead of the others, when they saw a boyish figure striding across the hall.

'I say, isn't that Bill?' said Susan.

'I believe it is,' said Felicity, calling out, 'Hi, Bill!'

But Bill was either in a great hurry or she simply didn't hear Felicity, for she carried on her way without so much as glancing up, and soon disappeared from view.

'Was that Bill I just spotted?' asked June, coming down the stairs behind the two girls. 'I wonder what she's doing at Malory Towers? And at such an early hour in the morning, too.'

'Perhaps she's come to visit Miss Peters,' suggested Susan.

'Before breakfast?' said Felicity. 'I doubt it. She seemed in an awful rush, wherever she was going.'

Miss Peters was already in the dining-room, having her breakfast, when the third formers entered, so it seemed that Bill had not come to Malory Towers to see her, after all. And someone else was already there, too – Esme! The third formers cheered when they saw her seated at their table and, in the excitement of greeting her, soon forgot about Bill.

'How are you feeling, Esme, old girl?'

'Good to have you back!'

'My word, that's a simply splendid bruise you have there!'

'You should part your hair on the side,' said Amy, looking at her critically. 'Then it will cover the bruise.'

'What a good idea!' exclaimed Esme. 'I think I shall wait until morning school has finished, though.' Lowering her voice, she added, 'Dear old Mam'zelle Dupont has been fussing over me like anything, thanks to my bruise. Perhaps it will work on Miss Peters too, and she will go a bit easy on me in class this morning.'

Esme did look much better today, though, thought Felicity. The colour had come back to her cheeks and, judging by the way she was tucking into her porridge, her appetite had returned too. Lucy, of course, was thrilled to have her cousin back. They might never be best friends again, but what had happened yesterday had created a bond between them. And Lucy sincerely hoped that that bond would never be broken.

Breakfast was nearly over when one of the school maids came into the dining-room and went across to Miss Peters. The maid said something to her in a low voice, and Miss Peters nodded, a slight frown on her heavy face, and got to her feet. Then she came over to the third formers and said, 'Julie! Miss Grayling wants me to take you to her study at once.'

Julie looked most alarmed, and began wracking her brains. But she couldn't think of a single reason why the Head would want to see her.

'Do you know what she wants, Miss Peters?' she asked, rather apprehensively.

Miss Peters shook her head, and said, 'I have no idea. But we had better not keep her waiting.'

'Heavens!' exclaimed Nora, her blue eyes wide, and her fluffy blonde hair looking almost as if it was standing on end. 'I do hope that Julie isn't in trouble. Has she been up to mischief, Lucy?'

Lucy, puzzled and a little worried, shook her head, while Pam said soberly, 'I say! I do hope that it isn't bad news from home.'

'Oh, don't say that, Pam!' pleaded Felicity. 'That would be just too awful.'

But Julie had still not returned by the time the girls made their way to their first lesson. And nor had Miss Peters, who was supposed to be taking the class.

Five minutes went by, then another five, and at last June said, 'Well, it doesn't look as if we're going to have our Geography lesson this morning at all!'

Normally the girls would have been delighted at this, but now they all felt rather uneasy. At the moment, each and every one of them would have given anything to see Miss Peters stride in, along with Julie.

'I wish we knew what was happening,' said Felicity fretfully.

'It must be something very serious for Miss Grayling to keep her so long,' said Susan, a grave expression on her face.

'But why is Miss Peters there too?' asked Lucy. 'I don't understand.'

No one understood, and just then Nora, who sat by the window, exclaimed, 'I say, who's this? Why, it's Clarissa!'

At once all the third formers dashed to the window, to see Clarissa walking up the drive. She looked awfully serious as she made her way to the big front door, and Susan said, 'Do you suppose that Clarissa is going to see Miss Grayling, too? And is that where Bill has disappeared to?'

'The plot thickens!' said June. 'I've a good mind to sneak along to the Head's study and put my ear to the door.'

'June, no!' said Felicity, firmly. 'If you were caught you would get into a fearful row, and the last thing we need is more trouble.'

June looked as if she was about to argue, but just then Bonnie squealed, 'Look! A police car!'

Everyone gasped, for now a police car was making its way up the drive, and the girls watched, open-mouthed, as a very serious-looking policeman got out.

The third formers looked at one another in consternation, and, with a rather nervous laugh, Freddie said, 'Heavens! Has Julie robbed a bank, or something?'

The girls watched and waited, and, at last, Bill and Clarissa emerged, so deep in conversation that they didn't even notice the third formers at the window.

'What a lot of coming and going!' said Freddie. 'But we are still no nearer to finding out what has happened.'

The time passed very slowly, as the girls waited for news. Then, at last, a few minutes before the lesson was due to end, Miss Potts came into the room, a very worried look on her face.

'Girls, Miss Peters will not be able to return to class before the end of the lesson,' she said, looking at the anxious faces before her. 'You may all go to break a few minutes earlier than usual.'

But even this news could not cheer up the third formers, and Lucy asked fearfully, 'Please, Miss Potts, do you know where Julie is? We're all terribly worried about her.'

'She has just gone along to the common-room,' answered Miss Potts heavily. 'Please be very kind to her when you see her, for I am afraid that she has had some extremely bad news.'

With that, Miss Potts left the room and, at once, a perfect babble broke out.

'Something has happened at home. I knew it!'

'It's Jack! Something has happened to Jack. Perhaps he's sick.'

'Oh yes, people always call the police when they have a sick horse on their hands!' said June sarcastically.

'I must go to her,' said Felicity, getting to her feet. 'She may be in need of comfort, or someone to talk to.'

'Felicity!' said Lucy, suddenly. 'May I go, instead of you? I know that you are head of the form, but I am Julie's best friend.'

Felicity thought for a moment, and then said decidedly, 'We shall all go! Then Julie will know that she has the whole form behind her, and that – whatever has happened – we shall all do what we can to help.'

So every one of the third formers, even spoilt, selfish

Amy, trooped to the common-room, where they found Julie sitting alone on a settee. She looked up as the door opened, her expression so bleak that the girls felt frightened. Her eyes were red, and it was obvious that she had been crying. But Julie *never* cried! At once, Felicity and Lucy rushed to sit either side of her, Felicity putting a comforting arm about her shoulders as she said gently, 'What is it, Julie, old girl?'

'It's Jack,' answered Julie, her voice sounding unnaturally high. 'He's gone. He's been stolen from Five Oaks.'

A horrified gasp went round the room. So *that* was why Bill and Clarissa had been here! And that was the reason the police had been called.

'Do the police have any clues?' asked June.

'Not really,' answered Julie, stifling a sob. 'There were faint tyre tracks in the lane leading to Five Oaks, so he may have been taken away in a horse box. But there is nothing to tell them who the thief is.'

'I can't believe that Bill and Clarissa would be so careless!' said Susan, shocked. 'After everything that has happened, I should have thought that they would be on their guard. But to let someone simply walk away with Jack, right under their noses –'

'Oh, but it wasn't their fault,' broke in Julie. 'Truly it wasn't. For a start, Jack wasn't stolen in broad daylight. It happened last night, but the girls didn't discover that he was gone until this morning. And the thief created a diversion.'

'A diversion? What do you mean, Julie?' asked Pam.

'You see, someone started a fire in the field behind the house, late last night,' explained Julie. 'It was right next to the small barn, where the girls store the hay for the horses. Bill said that it was only a small fire, but they were afraid that the barn would catch alight. So, of course, they had to dash out immediately and deal with it.'

'And, while they were putting the fire out, some wicked beast sneaked into the stable and took Jack,' finished Lucy, her eyes narrowed to slits. Angrily, she leapt up and began to pace the floor. 'My goodness, I hope that he's caught! I hope that the police lock him up and throw away the key! I hope –'

'Lucy, do calm down!' Felicity interrupted. 'And please stop pacing the floor like that, or you'll wear a hole in the carpet.'

'Sorry,' said Lucy, looking rather sheepish, as she stopped her pacing and sat down again. 'I just feel so terribly angry and upset!'

Lucy also felt a little guilty, too, because it could just as easily have been Sandy who was taken. But he was safe and well in his stall, while nobody knew where poor Jack was.

'Julie, have your people been told the news?' asked Nora.

'Yes, Miss Grayling telephoned them while I was in her study,' answered Julie. 'I was able to speak to them, too, and it was such a comfort. They both told me that they are certain Jack will come to no harm.'

'Of course he won't!' said Susan, bracingly. 'You may be sure that the police are doing everything possible to find him.'

'That's what Sergeant Dobbs told me,' said Julie. 'He's the policeman who came to see me this morning, and he was awfully nice. But I just feel so helpless! All I can do is wait, and wonder and worry!'

'Well, Julie, we will all be waiting, and wondering and worrying right beside you,' said Esme, who was quite as horrified as the others. What a welcome back this had turned out to be!

But the idea of sitting back and waiting for things to happen didn't appeal to June at all. She liked to be up and doing, and was turning over several ideas in her mind, which she prudently kept to herself, for Felicity most definitely would not approve.

Bonnie was also entertaining a pleasant daydream about unmasking the thief and reuniting Jack with his mistress. Why, if only she could pull it off she would be the heroine of the school!

The news of Jack's disappearance spread rapidly, of course, and everyone was shocked, for the little horse was a great character, and most of the girls loved him dearly. Several of the first formers were in tears, and had to be comforted by Matron and Mam'zelle Dupont. Not that tender-hearted Mam'zelle Dupont was much help, for she became so upset at the girls' distress that she had difficulty holding back her own tears!

Miss Peters, of course, understood better than any of the mistresses how Julie must be feeling, for she was a great horse lover. Her own beautiful horse, Midnight, meant more to her than anything, and she could only imagine how miserable she would feel if anything happened to him.

Even the stern Mam'zelle Rougier, who did not like horses at all, spoke kindly to Julie, and guarded her sharp tongue when the girl's thoughts wandered in class that afternoon.

Kay Foster, the Head Girl, came up to Julie, an earnest expression on her friendly, open face, as she said, 'What a dreadful thing to happen! Do let me know if there is any news, for everyone in the sixth form is terribly upset.'

Most surprisingly of all, Eleanor Banks sought Julie out and offered her sympathy. The third formers were in the courtyard when Eleanor – looking even paler than usual – approached them, and said to Julie, 'I'm so sorry to hear about what has happened. You must feel simply terrible.' Eleanor's voice shook a little as she went on, 'But I'm quite certain that you will have Jack back with you, safe and sound, in no time at all.'

Julie, rather taken aback at this, thanked Eleanor, but June, who had been watching the fifth former closely, raised her eyebrows and said, '*Why* are you so certain, Eleanor?'

But Eleanor immediately reverted to her usual, haughty manner, and said coldly, 'I was speaking to Julie, not to you, June.'

Then she stalked off, and Freddie said, 'Well! Wonders will never cease. Imagine the Ice Queen feeling sorry for someone!'

But Julie felt heartened by everyone's kindness and concern. That was one of the best things about a school like Malory Towers, she thought. When someone was in trouble, or things went wrong, everyone rallied round, ready to offer sympathy, and to help in any way they could. Even Eleanor Banks! Julie didn't much like the girl, but she desperately wanted to believe in her words. Jack would come back to her, safe and well. He *would*!

Detective work

June decided to pop over to Five Oaks and do a spot of investigating when afternoon lessons finished the following day and she was a little put out to discover that Bonnie had arrived a few minutes before her.

Each girl knew why the other was there, of course, and, after greeting one another, they went their separate ways.

June spoke to Clarissa, who looked very white and anxious.

'I feel absolutely terrible about Jack being stolen,' she told June. 'If the police don't find him, I don't know what I shall do.'

'It wasn't your fault, or Bill's,' said June. 'I don't see how either of you could have known that the fire was started to distract you.'

'Perhaps, but it doesn't stop us both from feeling guilty,' said Clarissa, sighing.

Just then, Bill came out of the house, and with her were two dark-haired, stocky young men.

'Who are they?' asked June curiously.

'Two of Bill's brothers,' said Clarissa. 'They are on leave from the army. Bill telephoned to tell them of our troubles. They said that they would come and stay for a while, to keep an eye on things.'

'Well, I should think that they will be more than capable of dealing with any intruders,' said June with a grin.

'Yes, and I must say that I do feel a great deal safer having Harry and John around,' said Clarissa. 'I just hope that it isn't too late to save Five Oaks.'

'Whatever do you mean?' asked June.

'Things aren't going well for us,' said Clarissa frankly. 'Of course, word has spread about Jack being stolen, and several people who had been stabling their horses with us have taken them away. And we aren't getting so many children coming for riding lessons as we used to. I suppose with Bill's accident, and then the fire, their parents feel that this isn't a very safe place.'

'But surely you're not thinking of selling Five Oaks?' said June, dismayed.

'We may have no choice,' said Clarissa, bleakly. 'You see, if we aren't making enough money, we simply can't afford to pay the bills or feed the horses. I know that Mr Banks would be happy to buy it from us, for he needs more room for his horses, and his land joins ours.'

'Is that so?' said June, narrowing her eyes thoughtfully. 'I say, Clarissa, would you mind if I have a scout round? I'd like to have a look at the place where the fire was started.'

'Be my guest,' said Clarissa. 'Though if you're looking for clues you won't find any, for the police have been over everything with a fine-tooth comb.'

Clarissa was right, for June found nothing that could be of any help at all.

Bonnie, however, *did* find something, though she was quite puzzled by it. The girl decided to take a look in the stable where Jack had been kept, in the hope that the thief might have been careless and dropped something. Eleanor Banks's beautiful white horse, Snowball, lived in the stall next-door-but-one to Jack's, and the fifth former was leading him out as Bonnie approached. Eleanor looked surprised and displeased to see Bonnie and said, 'What are you doing here?'

'I've come to see the horses,' answered Bonnie, coolly. 'Not that it's any business of yours, Eleanor.'

'Don't be cheeky!' said Eleanor, angrily. 'And if you have walked over here alone, it *is* my business. Girls from the lower forms are not allowed out on their own.'

This was true. The lower forms had to go out in twos or threes if they wanted to go into town, or take a walk along the cliffs. Normally everyone stuck to this rule very strictly – except when it came to visiting Bill and Clarissa. Because Five Oaks was only a few minutes' walk from Malory Towers, one or other of the girls would sometimes slip over alone. Most of the top formers turned a blind eye, but it was just like Eleanor to cause trouble! Thinking quickly, Bonnie said, 'Actually, June and I walked over together. She's here somewhere, and you can ask her if you don't believe me.'

She decided that she had better get hold of June later, and make sure that the two of them walked back to school together, just in case Eleanor was keeping an eye on them.

For now, though, the fifth former seemed satisfied, and

she walked away without another word, leaving Bonnie to pull a face behind her back.

Sandy, Lucy's pretty little horse, put his head over the door and whinnied a greeting. He was very pleased to see Bonnie, for he felt a little lonely now that his friend Jack was no longer living next door. Bonnie was a little nervous of some of the bigger horses, and was glad that they were all shut in, but Sandy was rather sweet, and very friendly. Bonnie patted his head and made a fuss of him, before going into the empty stable that had been Jack's, wrinkling her little nose up at the smell. Pooh! What on earth would Amy think if she could see her now?

Just then, something caught Bonnie's eye. A sheet of paper had been nailed to the wall.

Perhaps it's a ransom note, thought the girl excitedly, moving closer. But the sheet of paper was completely blank! How queer! Why on earth would someone nail a clean sheet of writing paper to the wall? Carefully removing it from the nail, Bonnie examined it closely. It couldn't have been there long, for it was clean and uncrumpled, with no signs of yellowing at all. Completely bewildered, the girl folded the paper up and put it in the pocket of her dress. It wasn't much of a clue, but it was all that she had!

Shortly afterwards, Bonnie went off to find June. She told the girl about her encounter with Eleanor and said, 'If she catches either of us walking back alone, I bet her punishment will be to confine us to the grounds, or something beastly like that.'

'Yes, that would be just like Eleanor,' said June scornfully. 'Well, I'm ready to go back to school, if you are.'

As the two girls walked along the lane to Malory Towers, Bonnie asked, 'Did you find anything useful?'

'Not a thing,' said June in disgust. 'You?'

'Well, I didn't find anything useful, but I did find something rather peculiar,' said Bonnie, and she pulled the piece of blank paper from her pocket. 'This was nailed to the wall of Jack's stable.'

'How odd!' said June, taking the paper and scrutinising it carefully, as Bonnie had done earlier. 'Why on earth would someone want to nail a perfectly plain piece of paper to the stable wall?'

'I simply can't imagine,' said Bonnie, folding the paper up again and putting it back in her pocket. 'I got quite excited when I spotted it, thinking that it might be a ransom note, but it turned out to be nothing of the sort.'

Then she sighed and said, 'I was talking to Bill earlier. Things are looking pretty black for her and Clarissa. They may have to sell Five Oaks.'

'Yes, Clarissa was telling me the same thing,' said June. She was silent and thoughtful for a moment, then she said in a rush, 'You know, Bonnie, I wanted to be the one to find Jack, and unmask the person who was behind all these beastly tricks simply for my own glory, and so that I could bask in everyone's admiration. I think that you had the same idea, didn't you?'

'Yes,' admitted Bonnie rather solemnly. 'But, since talking to Bill, I don't feel like that any more. It doesn't matter *who* solves the mystery. What is important is that *someone* solves it – and quickly! The girls' livelihood is at stake, and Julie needs to be reunited with Jack as quickly as possible.'

'That's exactly how I feel now,' said June. 'Perhaps we would get further if we worked as a team.'

'You and me?' said Bonnie, sounding very surprised.

'Yes, why not?' said June. 'Two heads are better than one, and all that.'

'All right, then,' agreed Bonnie. 'We'll pool our resources. Not that there's anything to pool at the moment!'

The other third formers had been very busy too. Felicity had come up with the idea of making some notices about the missing horse, and sticking them up around town.

'You know the kind of thing,' she said. 'We could write a description of Jack, and I'm sure that Miss Grayling won't mind if we put the telephone number of the school on them.'

'Yes, then we can stick them on lamp posts and trees, and ask some of the shopkeepers in town if they wouldn't mind putting them in their windows,' said Susan.

'That's a marvellous idea!' Julie said. 'It would make me feel as if I was actually doing something to help find Jack.'

'What a pity we can't offer a reward,' said Susan. 'I'm sure that would encourage people to go and look for him.'

'Perhaps we can,' said Julie. 'I'm sure that my father would put up some money, though it won't be an awful lot. And I would give up my pocket money for a year if it meant getting Jack back.'

'Let's get to work on the notices now,' said Pam. 'And then we can go out after lunch tomorrow and put them up.'

Miss Linnie, the art mistress, was happy to provide the girls with some paper, and allowed them to use the art-room to work on their notices.

'We can do the writing in bright colours, so that it will be really eye-catching,' said Felicity. 'And perhaps we can use some of Miss Linnie's special coloured paper for some of them.'

Pam, who was very good at art, did a beautiful and very life-like drawing of Jack on her notice, and coloured it in carefully.

'Pam, that's Jack to the life!' exclaimed Esme in admiration.

'Yes, you've even put in the little white patch that he has over one eye,' said Julie. 'We must put your notice in the sweet-shop, for that always seems to be busy, and lots of people will see it.'

Even Amy, who generally had little time to spare for anyone's worries but her own, made one of the 'missing' notices.

'It's good to know that she's willing to do her bit when someone is in trouble,' said Felicity to Susan as they went in to tea.

'Yes – though I expect she only joined us because Bonnie wasn't about, and she was at a bit of a loose end,' said Susan.

'Where *is* Bonnie?' asked Felicity. 'I haven't seen her

for simply ages. Or June either, for that matter.'

The two girls were at the tea table when the third formers went into the dining-room, hungrily tucking into bread and butter.

'We've been over to Five Oaks,' said June, and began to tell the others the news that Bill and Clarissa might have to sell up.

'They can't!' cried a horrified Nora. 'Why, Malory Towers just wouldn't be the same without Bill and Clarissa just along the road.'

'Isn't there *something* we can do to help?' asked Lucy.

'The only thing that will help is finding Jack, and the person who is trying to ruin the girls' business,' said Bonnie. 'And I'm afraid we seem to have come to a bit of a dead end there.'

But something was niggling away at the back of June's mind. Something concerning that piece of paper Bonnie had found. There was something significant about it, she was sure – if only she could think what!

The answer came to her in a flash, as she was in the common-room that evening. June suddenly sat bolt upright in her chair, and looked around for Bonnie. The girl was nowhere to be seen, and June called out, 'Amy! Where is Bonnie?'

'She's gone to fetch something from the dorm,' said Amy, and, in an instant, June was out of the door.

'Bonnie!' she cried, bursting into the dormitory. 'Where is that piece of paper that you found in Jack's stable? Oh, don't say that you've thrown it away!'

'Of course not,' said Bonnie, producing it from her pocket. 'What do you want with it, June?'

'I think that there might be something written on it after all,' June said. 'Do you remember, a few weeks ago, I slipped a bottle of invisible ink into Eleanor's bag?'

'Yes, I remember,' said Bonnie. 'Golly! Do you think that Eleanor might have written something on here, not realising that she was using invisible ink?'

'It's possible,' said June. 'It takes about ten minutes for the writing to disappear, so if Eleanor nailed the note up immediately after she had written it, she wouldn't know that no one would be able to read it.'

'Yes, but what reason could Eleanor possibly have for writing a note and putting it on the wall of Jack's stable?' said Bonnie, frowning. 'I say, June! You surely don't think that she could be behind Jack's disappearance, and all the horrible things that have happened to Bill and Clarissa?'

'I think that her uncle could,' answered June, gravely. 'And I think that Eleanor could be helping him. You see, Clarissa told me that Mr Banks would like to buy Five Oaks. So perhaps he is trying to drive the girls out.'

'I believe that you could be right!' said Bonnie excitedly. 'But what a pity that we can't read what was written on that paper.'

'We can,' said June, grinning. 'If we make the room dark, and shine a torch on the paper, we should be able to make out the writing. Draw the curtains, Bonnie!'

Swiftly, Bonnie darted to the big windows at the end of the dormitory and pulled the curtains across, while June fetched a torch from her locker. Then the two girls sat side by side on Bonnie's bed, and June shone the torch on the piece of paper.

The girls could hardly breathe as writing appeared, very faint, but readable.

'To Bill and Clarissa,' June read aloud. 'If you want Jack back, follow these instructions exactly. Both of you must come to the clearing in Bluebell Wood at midnight tonight. Don't tell the police, and don't inform anyone else of the contents of this note.'

The two girls stared at one another in consternation.

'Midnight tonight,' gasped Bonnie. 'June, what are we to do? Should we take the note to Miss Grayling? Someone must tell Bill and Clarissa! And Julie ought to be told, too.'

'Hush a minute,' said June, getting to her feet. 'I need to think!'

There was silence for a few moments, then at last June said, 'We can't take the note to Miss Grayling, for she is out. She and Miss Potts are going to the theatre tonight. And we can't tell Julie, in case this turns out to be a hoax, or something goes wrong. She would have her hopes raised, only for them to be dashed again.'

'Yes, that's true,' said Bonnie. 'June, do you think we should telephone the police?'

'Absolutely not!' said June, firmly. 'You saw what the note said, Bonnie. I think that we should sneak into the Head's study, and telephone Bill and Clarissa.'

'All right,' said Bonnie, standing up. 'Let's be quick then. You can telephone, and I'll keep watch.'

So the two girls sped downstairs and made their way to

Miss Grayling's study. Fortunately they didn't meet any mistresses on the way, but both of them felt very nervous as they opened the door to the Head's neat, comfortable study. June walked over to the desk and lifted the telephone receiver, while Bonnie stood at the door, looking up and down the corridor. At last, Bill answered the telephone and June poured out her story. The conversation seemed to take simply ages, for, of course, the astonished Bill had a great many questions to ask. But it was finally over and the two girls left Miss Grayling's study, shutting the door behind them.

'What did Bill say?' asked Bonnie. 'Are she and Clarissa going to the wood?'

'Yes,' answered June. 'But Bill's brothers are going to go there about half an hour before them, and lie in wait. What a jolly good thing that they turned up today!'

'Where is Bluebell Wood, anyway?' asked Bonnie.

'About a mile down the road from Five Oaks,' said June. 'We sometimes have picnics there. It's a beautiful spot during the day, but I should imagine that it's a little creepy at night.'

Bonnie gave a shudder. 'I wonder who will be there to meet Bill and Clarissa?' she said. 'Eleanor, or her uncle?'

'I shouldn't imagine that it will be either of them,' said June. 'Neither of them will want to come out into the open and admit that they are involved. It will probably be one of Mr Banks's grooms, or someone else that he has paid to do his dirty work for him!'

'Well, whoever he is, he's in for quite a shock when

he runs into Bill's brothers,' said Bonnie with grim satisfaction. 'They will make him talk, all right, then the game will be up for Mr Banks!'

'Yes,' said June, with a broad grin. 'And I intend to be there to see it!'

'June!' gasped Bonnie. 'You can't sneak out of the school at midnight!'

'Oh no,' said June blithely. 'I shall have to leave much earlier than that, if I'm to get a good seat. There's a nice big apple tree in the wood. I think I shall climb up there to watch. No one will be able to see me, but I shall have a splendid view!'

'You'll get into the most frightful row if you're caught!' said Bonnie, quite horrified.

'Well, I shan't be,' said June confidently. 'I shall slip out of the side door that leads into the garden, and leave it unlocked so that I can sneak back in again. And I'll borrow a bicycle from the shed, so that I can get there and back quickly. No one will be any the wiser – except you, of course, and I know that you won't say anything!'

'I shan't, of course, but I do wish that you would change your mind, June,' said Bonnie, looking rather unhappy. She couldn't think of anything more frightening than being alone in the wood at midnight, and simply couldn't understand why June was willing to risk a terrible punishment to be there.

'I won't change my mind,' said June. 'I wouldn't miss this for the world!'

A thrilling night

June didn't dare let herself fall asleep, in case she didn't wake up in time to join the fray at Bluebell Wood. She couldn't set her alarm clock, of course, in case the others heard it. Felicity would have a fit if she knew what June meant to do!

Bonnie was awake, too. Not from choice, but because she felt so uneasy about June's plan that she simply couldn't sleep.

The others, however, slept soundly, and when eleven o'clock struck, only Bonnie saw June slip from her bed and quietly get dressed. Then the girl put her bolster and pillow down the middle of the bed, pulling the covers over so that it looked as if someone was asleep there. If Miss Peters should happen to look in, that would fool her nicely!

June almost jumped out of her skin when Bonnie whispered her name as she walked past her bed.

'What is it?' June whispered back.

'Do be careful!' said Bonnie in a low voice. 'I shan't be able to sleep until I know that you're back safely.'

'Don't worry about me,' said June, smiling into the darkness. 'I shall have a fine night's entertainment and I'll be back before you know it!'

Miss Peters did look in, about ten minutes after June had left, but she didn't put the light on and went away again quickly, quite satisfied that nothing was amiss. After she had gone, Bonnie decided that it was pointless even trying to sleep, and sat up in bed, hugging her knees. Perhaps she should borrow June's torch, then she could read her book under the covers. But June had probably taken it with her. What a shame, for a diversion was just what Bonnie needed, to take her mind off things.

A diversion! The word seemed to trigger something in Bonnie's head, and suddenly she turned pale, as a thought occurred to her. A shocking, horrible thought! She sprang out of bed and went to Felicity, shaking her.

'Felicity!' she hissed in her ear. 'Felicity, do wake up!'

Startled, Felicity opened her eyes and sat up sharply.

'Bonnie!' she whispered, none too pleased. 'What on earth do you mean by waking me like this?'

'I need to talk to you,' murmured Bonnie urgently. 'Come into the bathroom, so that we don't wake the others.'

Tired, cross and bewildered, Felicity got out of bed, and reluctantly followed Bonnie into the bathroom at the end of the dormitory.

'What is it, Bonnie?' asked Felicity with a yawn, as she shut the bathroom door behind her.

As quickly as she could, Bonnie told Felicity of how she and June had discovered the note to Clarissa and Bill, of how they had alerted the two girls and, finally, of how June had gone off alone to Bluebell Wood, to watch the drama unfold. Wide awake now, Felicity listened open-mouthed. 'You and June have done very well,' she said at last. 'But what an idiot June is, to sneak off to the woods like that! It's bad enough being caught out of bed at night, but if she's caught outside the school she could be expelled! Just wait until I see her!'

'Yes, but do listen, Felicity!' said Bonnie, impatiently. 'On the night Jack was stolen, someone started a fire behind the house to create a diversion, remember?'

'Of course I remember,' said Felicity. 'But I really don't –'

'Don't you see?' cried Bonnie. 'Suppose that this note to Bill and Clarissa is a diversion too? To get them away from Five Oaks, so that Mr Banks – if he *is* the one who is behind all this – can do something else? Why, he might be planning on setting fire to the house, or stealing the rest of the horses, or – or anything!'

'My goodness!' gasped Felicity, pressing her hands to her cheeks. 'You could be right! And, if you *are* right, we must telephone the police at once. There's not a moment to lose!'

So, for the second time that evening, Bonnie found herself on the way to Miss Grayling's study to use the telephone.

She came to a halt outside the door and turned to Felicity, whispering, 'Suppose that the Head is in there? She must be back from the theatre by now.'

'Yes, but surely she will have gone to bed,' said Felicity. 'Besides, the chances are that we will have to wake her and tell her what has happened anyway! I shouldn't be at all surprised if the police turn up here, once they have finished at Five Oaks.'

So Bonnie tapped timidly at the door, but the Head's voice did not call out, so she pushed it open and went in. This time Felicity kept a look-out, while Bonnie called the police. Then she telephoned Five Oaks, to see if she could warn Bill and Clarissa of her suspicions, but there was no reply.

'They must have left for Bluebell Wood already,' said Bonnie. 'But the policeman that I spoke to said that he is going to send someone over to Five Oaks at once.'

'It's ten minutes to midnight,' said Felicity, coming further into the room and glancing at the clock on the wall. 'If Mr Banks is planning something, he won't act until midnight, when he knows that Bill and Clarissa will be out of the way.'

'Do you think that we ought to go and wake Miss Grayling, or Miss Peters?' asked Bonnie. 'I'd really rather not, but if you think that the police will turn up, perhaps we had better.'

And then the two girls got the shock of their lives, for a familiar voice spoke behind them.

'There is no need to wake me, girls,' it said. 'For I am already awake.'

Felicity and Bonnie had been standing with their backs to the door, and they turned sharply to see Miss Grayling standing there, in her dressing-gown.

'I thought that I heard a noise, and came to investigate,' she said, looking rather stern. 'I trust that the two of you have a good explanation for being in my study at this hour.'

'We do, Miss Grayling,' said Felicity, realising that there was nothing for it but to tell the Head everything now. Though she would try to keep the fact that June had sneaked away from the school out of it, of course!

Miss Grayling went and sat behind her desk, indicating that the two girls should sit opposite her. Bonnie had grown quite tired of recounting the events of the evening, so she let Felicity do the talking, interpolating a word here and there.

The Head was very shocked, of course, particularly when the name of Eleanor Banks was mentioned.

'If it is proved that Eleanor has been involved in this terrible business, her future at Malory Towers will be in serious doubt,' said Miss Grayling very gravely.

'Well, if it hadn't been for that note, written in invisible ink, we wouldn't have suspected that she, and her uncle, were involved at all,' said Bonnie.

Miss Grayling smiled, and said, 'You and June are to be congratulated, Bonnie. That was a very neat piece of detective work. Where *is* June, by the way?'

Felicity hesitated for a moment, not quite liking to lie to the Head. Bonnie, however, had no such scruples, and said at once, 'Why, asleep in bed, of course, Miss Grayling.'

'It's not like June to be asleep when there's excitement afoot,' said Miss Grayling, raising her eyebrows. 'Didn't you think to wake her, Bonnie, when you realised that the note might have been a ruse to get Bill and Clarissa out of the way?'

'No, for she seemed so tired earlier,' said Bonnie, glibly. 'And I thought that Felicity was the proper person to consult, as she is head of the form.'

'Well, you both acted very sensibly in calling the police,' said the Head. 'Of course, you should have come to me first, or to Miss Potts, but I realise that time was of the essence.'

Then she noticed that Felicity was shivering slightly. Both girls had come downstairs without their dressing-gowns on, and although the days were hot, the nights were a little chilly.

'Let me go and find Matron,' said Miss Grayling, getting to her feet. 'I'll ask her to make us all some nice, hot cocoa.'

'Phew, that was close!' said Felicity, as the door closed behind the Head. 'For a moment, I was afraid that Miss Grayling was going to suggest that we wake June.'

'So was I,' said Bonnie, with a nervous giggle. 'I do hope that she comes back soon, and manages to get in without being seen!'

Soon Miss Grayling was back, followed by Matron, bearing a tray with three mugs of steaming cocoa on it.

'Well!' said Matron, putting the tray on the desk. 'Miss Grayling tells me that you girls have had quite an adventure this evening. Now, you drink this cocoa and it will warm you up. I don't know what you're thinking of, wandering around without your dressing-gowns on.'

The two girls hoped fervently that Matron wouldn't

take it into her head to go up to the dormitory and fetch their dressing-gowns herself. Her sharp eyes would soon spot that June's bed was empty if she did that!

Luckily, though, it seemed that Matron was far too busy, for she said, 'I must dash, for I have young Jenny from the second form in bed with a stomach upset, and I don't want to leave her for too long.'

Heaving a sigh of relief, Felicity and Bonnie sipped their cocoa, and hoped that June would not be long. Both girls were beginning to feel most peculiar. They felt very tired, but at the same time very excited. And there was more excitement to come, for as the girls drank the last of their cocoa, they heard the sound of cars outside. Miss Grayling went to the window and pulled aside the curtain.

'The police are here,' she said, turning back to the girls. 'Now, perhaps, we shall find out if this mysterious note really was a ruse, after all. And no doubt they will want to interview you, Bonnie, and June.'

Felicity and Bonnie exchanged glances of horror, and the Head said, 'I hate to disturb June, but I really think that you had better go and fetch her, Bonnie.'

June, meanwhile, was not enjoying herself at all. She had borrowed a bicycle from the shed and ridden to Blueberry Wood, hiding it in a hedge before shinning up the big apple tree. Then she had settled herself as comfortably as possible on a large branch, her back against the trunk, and waited for events to unfold. Bill's brothers had arrived a few moments later, and June watched as the two of them hid in the bushes, snatches of their conversation floating up to her on the still night air.

'I hope this fellow isn't going to keep us waiting for too long,' said John, in a menacing tone. 'I've a thing or two that I want to say to him!'

'Yes, he might be a little more careful about who he picks on next, when we've finished with him,' growled Harry.

'We'd better keep quiet now,' said John. 'If we frighten him off before the girls turn up, the whole thing will have been a waste of time.'

Then, a little later, Bill and Clarissa themselves turned up on horseback, both of them looking pale and nervous.

The two girls caught a glimpse of John and Harry in their hiding place, but ignored them, in case anyone else was watching.

However, the only person watching was June, and she soon grew heartily bored. There was no sign of anyoneelse, no sound of footsteps, no snapping of twigs. She was also becoming very uncomfortable, perched on her branch, with the trunk of the tree digging into her back. The minutes ticked by, and the people in the wood heard the sound of a car in the distance. Everyone waited with bated breath, but the sound died away, and all was silent again.

'Well!' said Bill, at last. 'It doesn't look as if anyone is coming, does it?'

'No,' agreed Clarissa, sounding rather crestfallen. 'Blow! I really did hope that we would have some good news for Julie tomorrow.'

The two boys came out from the bushes and dusted themselves down.

'Might as well go home,' June heard Harry saying. 'Either that note that the girls found was a hoax, or the writer has got cold feet.'

And with that, the four of them departed, and a very disgruntled June climbed down from the tree. What a waste of a perfectly good night! To think that she could have been tucked up in her cosy bed, instead of sitting up a tree! And, worst of all, Jack was still missing. Thank goodness that they hadn't let Julie in on the secret, and built her hopes up, for her disappointment would have been hard to bear.

The thought of her bed was a very welcome one indeed, and June yawned as she mounted her bicycle. Soon she was cycling along the lane towards Malory Towers, but, alas, with the school in sight, she came to grief. A rabbit darted across the lane in front of her, and June swerved to avoid it, falling off the bicycle and landing in an undignified heap. June was more shocked than hurt – or so she thought, until she tried to stand up and discovered that she had painfully twisted her ankle. With a little groan of pain, she righted the bicycle and gingerly climbed back on. But it was far more painful to pedal than to walk, so, clinging to the handlebars for support, the girl hobbled the last few yards to the school, and through the gates. And then what a shock she got! Two police cars were parked on the drive, and lights were blazing all over the school. What *was* going on?

Heroines and villains

June looked at the scene before her open-mouthed. Well, really! She had spent the last hour or so waiting for something to happen, and it seemed that all the excitement had been taking place at Malory Towers! Now, if only she could get back in without being spotted.

Her ankle was growing more painful now, and June limped slowly across to the shed, where she replaced the bicycle. Then, keeping close to the bushes, she made her way to the little side door, which she had left unlocked. As she was about to turn the handle, the door was suddenly pulled open, and June almost fell inside, very relieved to see that the person standing there wasn't Miss Grayling, or Miss Potts – but Bonnie! And the girl was holding June's pyjamas and dressing-gown.

'Thank heavens,' said Bonnie, thrusting the clothes at June. 'Get changed, quickly! Miss Grayling has sent me to fetch you.'

'Miss Grayling wants to see me? Why? Bonnie, do tell me what's happened!' begged June. 'There are police cars in the drive, and lights on all over the place, and –'

'Never mind that now!' said Bonnie, impatiently. 'Get into your pyjamas, for I've been gone simply ages, and the

Head will send someone to look for me if I don't take you to her soon. I'll explain everything to you on the way.'

So June scrambled into her pyjamas, and Bonnie threw her day clothes into a nearby cupboard, saying, 'We can collect these later. Now, make your hair look tousled, as if you've just got out of bed – yes, that's it.'

Then she grabbed June's hand and began pulling her along the corridor.

'Ow!' groaned June, stumbling, as her ankle began to hurt once more. 'Careful, Bonnie! I've twisted my ankle.'

'Golly!' said Bonnie. 'How did you do that?'

'Fell off my bicycle,' said June, glumly. 'And it was all a waste of time, for no one turned up. But never mind that! I want to know what has been going on here.'

Bonnie told her as they walked, and June came to a halt suddenly.

'So, *you* solved the mystery after all,' she said in rather a small voice.

'No, I didn't!' said Bonnie. '*You* were the one who worked out that our blank piece of paper wasn't blank, after all. Without knowing that, we wouldn't have got anywhere. I simply guessed that it was a ruse to get Bill and Clarissa out of the way. So, you see, June, we *both* played a part. It was teamwork!'

'So it was!' said June, looking brighter. 'Well, I'm beginning to think that there's rather a lot to be said for teamwork!'

'I'm glad to hear it,' said Bonnie, with a smile. 'Now, do come along, or the Head will start thinking that we have run away! Oh, and you will have to try and hide your limp. Miss Grayling will never believe that you twisted your ankle lying in bed.'

'I'll do my best,' said June, wincing. They were outside Miss Grayling's door now, and she said to Bonnie, 'Is there anything else I should know, before we go in?'

'Oh yes,' said Bonnie, tapping at the door. 'The police are inside and they want to interview both of us.'

It was the early hours of the morning by the time Felicity, June and Bonnie got to bed. By that time, the whole dormitory was awake, for Bonnie had accidentally bumped into Esme's bed when she slipped in to fetch June's night-clothes. Bonnie had disappeared by the time Esme was fully awake, and the girl had lain there for a moment, wondering what had disturbed her. Then she sat up and, as her eyes became accustomed to the darkness, she spotted the three empty beds, and gave an involuntary cry of alarm. This roused the others, of course, and they stared at the empty beds in astonishment, quite unable to imagine what could have happened to the three absentees.

'Surely they haven't all gone off somewhere together!' said Amy, rather put out that she hadn't been taken into Bonnie's confidence.

'Well, if they haven't, it's a bit of a coincidence,' said Susan, who was also feeling rather hurt that Felicity had gone off somewhere without her.

'I know some of the South Tower girls were talking about a midnight feast,' said Freddie. 'Do you suppose they have been invited to that?' But if that was so, why hadn't June invited her along too, she thought, feeling rather left out.

Pam shook her head decidedly, and said, 'You know that there is a strict rule about girls leaving their tower to go to another, after lights-out. June and Freddie might break it, but Felicity *never* would.'

'No, she wouldn't,' said Susan, her brow clearing a little.

'Perhaps they're hiding somewhere, and playing a trick on us!' suggested Nora.

'Yes, that's it!' cried Freddie. 'I'll bet they are all in the bathroom, listening like anything, and laughing their heads off at us!'

And Freddie had leapt out of bed and run to the bathroom, pulling open the door. But, of course, it was empty.

'Where *can* they be?' asked Freddie, scratching her head.

There was a good deal of speculation, until the three girls themselves walked in. First Felicity, then Bonnie, and then June, who was limping quite badly now. They were immediately pounced on by the others. And what a tale they had to tell!

The note *had* been intended as a diversion. When the police – alerted by Bonnie – arrived at Five Oaks, they had caught Mr Banks and several of his grooms in the act of letting the horses out.

'And then they planned to set fire to the stable block!' said Bonnie. 'Did you ever hear of anything so wicked?'

'The police got there in the nick of time,' explained Felicity. 'Of course, Mr Banks and his accomplices were arrested, and they admitted being behind all the unpleasant happenings at Five Oaks.'

'Yes, it seems that Eleanor's uncle wanted to buy Five Oaks for himself,' said June. 'But he knew that the girls would never sell willingly, and set about trying to put them out of business, so that they would have no choice in the matter.'

'Mr Banks! Who would have thought it?'

'And we all thought that he was being so kind to Bill and Clarissa, when all the time it was an act!'

'You said that he looked sinister, Felicity,' said Susan. 'And you were right!'

Julie had sat pale and silent as the tale unfolded, for, exciting as it was, there was only one thought in her head. With a flicker of hope in her eyes, she looked at the three girls now, and said, 'What about Jack?'

'That's the best news of all!' said June happily. 'Jack is safe and well! The police found him stabled at Mr Banks's. He has been well looked after, and not ill-treated in any way. They took him straight back to Five Oaks, so you can go over and visit him tomorrow.'

There was silence for a moment, then a rousing cheer went up. Suddenly everyone went mad, jumping up and down on the beds, and clapping one another on the back. Lucy hugged Julie so hard that the two of them almost over-balanced, while Nora did a little tap dance in the middle of the floor!

'June and Bonnie, I simply can't thank you enough!' said a grateful Julie, her face shining with happiness. 'I just wish there was some way I could repay you! If there's ever anything I can do for either of you, anything at all, you have only to say the word!'

'You're a real pair of heroines,' said Lucy. 'Three cheers for June and Bonnie!'

And, once again, the third formers cheered for all they were worth, while June and Bonnie turned red and beamed with pride.

'Oh, how I wish I could go and see my darling Jack right this very minute!' said Julie longingly.

'Well, you're just going to have to be patient!' laughed Felicity. 'I've had quite enough excitement for one night, thank you.'

'Sandy will keep an eye on Jack for you tonight, old girl,' said Lucy, clapping her friend on the shoulder. 'He will be so glad to have his old friend back!'

Julie's expression grew serious suddenly, and she said bitterly, 'Eleanor must have known where Jack was all along. And she pretended to feel sorry for me. The beast!'

'Yes, what part *did* dear Eleanor play in all this?' asked Amy.

'Well, she was in on the plan to drive Bill and Clarissa out, of course,' said Bonnie, taking up the story. 'It was she who stole Bill and Clarissa's cash-box, on her uncle's orders.'

'I always knew that Eleanor was mean, but I didn't think that even she would stoop so low,' said Pam in disgust.

'Apparently, Mr Banks told the police that Eleanor tried to talk him out of stealing Jack,' said Felicity. 'But he had made his mind up. And she had no idea that he had planned to burn the stables down tonight. It was Eleanor who wrote the note that Bonnie found in Jack's stable, but she really believed that her uncle was going to hand Jack over to Bill and Clarissa tonight.'

'We saw her, briefly, after the police had spoken to her,' said June, sounding very serious, for once. 'They must have been quite hard on her, for she looked simply dreadful, and very shaken indeed.'

'I'd jolly well like to shake her, all right!' said Lucy, harshly, 'Perhaps she didn't know all of her uncle's plans, but she *did* know that he was up to no good – and she went along with it.'

'Of course, Miss Grayling isn't going to keep her here,' said Felicity. 'She is to leave tomorrow, and go to live with her aunt until her parents are back in the country.'

'So she'll still be nearby,' said Nora in disgust.

'Not for long, I don't suppose,' said June. 'I should think that Mrs Banks will want to sell up and move away, for the shame will be too much to bear once word gets around that her husband is an out-and-out villain!'

'Bill and Clarissa must be awfully bucked,' said Pam. 'They won't have to sell Five Oaks after all.'

'Yes, they arrived home just as Mr Banks was being arrested,' said Bonnie. 'Of course, Bill's brothers were all for dealing with him themselves, Sergeant Dobbs said, but the police wouldn't allow it.'

'Pity,' said Nora, with a sigh. 'I daresay they would have taught him a lesson he wouldn't forget in a hurry.'

'And Sergeant Dobbs also said that Mr Banks will have to pay the girls compensation, for all the damage he has done to their property and their reputation,' Felicity said happily. 'So that's jolly good as well.'

June and Bonnie's interview with the police had been a much more pleasant experience than Eleanor's. Sergeant Dobbs and his colleagues had been most impressed with their detective work, and had praised the two girls quite extravagantly.

'Well, it's no more than you deserve,' said Julie, when the girls recounted this.

'I'll say!' agreed Esme. 'My goodness, what a night it's been!'

'Yes, it's just a pity that we missed most of the excitement,' said Nora.

'Well, I missed most of it too, as it turned out,' said June, with a comical expression. 'For I spent most of the night sitting up a tree, and ended up falling off a bicycle!'

The others roared with laughter at this, and at last Felicity said, 'I was going to tick you off properly for sneaking out, June. But everything has turned out so well, and I feel so happy, that I just can't be angry with you any more.'

'I should jolly well think not!' said June, putting on an enormous air of self-importance. 'After all, I *am* a heroine! Besides, I've punished myself already, for my ankle is going to be black and blue tomorrow.'

'Golly, yes, your poor ankle!' said Freddie. 'We shall have to think up a story to account for that.'

'Perhaps you can pretend to slip on your way downstairs tomorrow,' said Susan, with a yawn.

'Tomorrow? You mean today,' said Pam, looking at her alarm clock. 'It's almost three o'clock!'

'Heavens!' said Felicity. 'We have to be up in a few hours, and I suddenly feel worn out. I shall never be able to do it.'

Just then they heard the sound of footsteps outside the dormitory, and then the door opened and Miss Grayling herself stood there. It was a most unusual occurrence for the Head to visit one of the dormitories, and the girls stopped talking at once, all of them looking rather sheepish. Gracious, they must have been making a frightful din to have brought Miss Grayling on the scene! But the headmistress's blue eyes twinkled, and she said, 'It's all right, girls, I haven't come to tell you off, for I realise that this has been no ordinary night. In fact, it has been quite *extra*ordinary!'

The girls smiled at this, and the Head went on, 'I know that you have all had a lot to talk about, and no doubt feel thoroughly overexcited, but I really must insist that you get to sleep now.'

'But, Miss Grayling, if I drop off now I shall never wake up in time for breakfast,' protested June. 'Can't we go to bed early tonight, instead?'

'No, June,' said the Head firmly. 'Once you close your eyes, I think you will find that you are a lot more tired than you realise. All of you, into bed at once, please.'

The third formers obeyed immediately, for most of

them really did feel very tired and were secretly quite glad to be ordered into bed.

'Now, I don't want another sound from this dormitory until the dressing-bell rings,' said the Head, turning off the light. Then she stood quite still for a moment, silhouetted in the doorway. 'There is just one more thing that I need to say to you, June, and to Bonnie,' she said softly. 'I am very, very proud of both of you.'

And with that, Miss Grayling closed the door gently, and the third formers heard her footsteps fading away into the distance.

'Well!' whispered Freddie. 'Fancy the Grayling saying *that*! I bet that you're as pleased as punch, aren't you, June? June?'

But there was no answer, for Miss Grayling had been quite right. June was fast asleep.

A surprise for June

Felicity, June, Bonnie and Nora all found it quite impossible to get out of bed the following morning.

'Though I don't know why *Nora* should be so tired,' said Esme, looking down at the sleeping girl. 'She didn't have an adventure last night, like the other three did.'

'Nora can *never* get out of bed in the morning,' laughed Pam, bending down to give her friend a shake. 'Come on, sleeping beauty! Wakey wakey!'

Nora opened her eyes a fraction, mumbled something that no one could understand, then turned over and promptly went back to sleep again.

'There's only one thing for it,' said Pam. 'We shall have to pull the covers off her.'

And Pam and Esme did just that, causing Nora to sit up angrily and shake her fist at them.

But no one quite liked to dish out the same treatment to the other three who were still asleep. If anyone had earned a lie-in, they had!

Just then, though, Felicity opened her eyes, lying quite still for a few seconds as the events of the previous night came back to her. For a moment she thought that it had all been a strange dream, but then she saw Julie, chattering happily to Lucy, a beaming smile on her face, and she knew that it had really happened. Julie would not look so happy if her beloved Jack were still missing.

Bonnie began to stir too, then June, and just as the three girls were thinking about getting out of bed, Matron bustled in.

'Come along, you third formers!' she chivvied them. 'There will be no breakfast left for you, if you don't get a move on.'

'I say, Matron,' said Pam. 'We shan't have to face Eleanor in the dining-room, shall we?'

'Indeed you shan't!' said Matron grimly. 'Her aunt will be along to fetch her very shortly, and until she arrives, Eleanor will stay in her dormitory, out of the way.'

Privately, Matron thought that it would have done Eleanor the world of good to have to face the scorn and hard stares of the others, but the girl was far too weak to do that. She would never be able to look at any of the Malory Towers girls again!

Felicity swung her legs over the edge of the bed, and Matron said, 'Not you, Felicity! Or June, or Bonnie. Miss Grayling has given orders that you are to have breakfast in bed today.'

The three girls looked at one another in delight, and Nora called out hopefully, 'Can I have breakfast in bed too, Matron?'

'No, you jolly well can't!' cried Matron, trying her best to look stern, though her eyes twinkled. 'In fact, if you don't finish getting dressed this minute,

Nora, you'll be on bread and water.'

Muttering darkly, Nora quickly dressed, and followed the rest of her form downstairs, leaving the other three alone.

'Breakfast in bed!' sighed June contentedly, propping her pillow up behind her and snuggling into it. 'What a treat!'

And soon the girls were tucking into big bowls of creamy porridge, followed by fluffy, scrambled eggs and buttered toast, all washed down with big mugs of tea.

'Yummy!' said Felicity, spreading marmalade on a piece of toast. 'But my goodness, how these crumbs do get into the bedclothes!'

'The secret is to hold the plate right under your chin,' said Bonnie, demonstrating. 'Gosh, this marmalade is simply delicious! I don't know why breakfast always tastes so much nicer when it's eaten in bed, but there's no doubt that it does!'

The girls ate in silence for a few moments, then June said, 'Everything is going to feel a bit flat now, after all the excitement yesterday.'

'Oh, I don't know,' said Felicity. 'There is still the tennis tournament with St Margarets to look forward to.'

'So there is!' said June, sounding more cheerful. 'With everything that has happened lately, I had almost forgotten about that.'

Then her face fell and she cried, 'Oh, my goodness! There's something else I'd forgotten about – my ankle! Suppose it's not healed in time for me to play?'

'Have you looked at it this morning?' asked Bonnie. 'Perhaps it will be better now.'

June put her breakfast tray aside and gingerly pulled back the covers – then all three girls gasped. Far from being better, June's ankle had swollen up dreadfully, and was quite horribly bruised.

'Oh, June!' said Felicity, in dismay. 'That looks awfully painful.'

'Well, I can't feel it at all while I'm just lying here,' said June. 'But I expect it will be painful when I try to stand.'

'You had better arrange to have a little accident before Matron sees it,' said Bonnie. 'She'll be back to take our breakfast trays away soon.'

'I know!' cried Felicity. 'Go into the bathroom, and you can pretend that you've slipped on the soap. Hurry, for I think I can hear Matron coming!'

Trying not to put any weight on her ankle, June carefully got out of bed and hopped into the bathroom. She shut the door behind her just as Matron came into the dormitory.

'All finished?' she asked. 'Good! I'm pleased to see that last night's little adventure hasn't affected your appetites. But where is June?'

Before either of the girls could answer, there came the sound of a crash from the bathroom, followed by a squeal.

'Ow!' yelled June. 'Do help me, someone! I've hurt myself.'

Felicity and Bonnie were out of their beds in a flash, but Matron reached the bathroom before them.

'Goodness me!' she exclaimed, throwing open the door. 'What on earth have you done to yourself, June?'

'Someone dropped a bar of soap on the floor, Matron, and I slipped on it,' said June, who was half-sitting, half-lying on the floor, her face screwed up in pain most convincingly. 'I seem to have twisted my ankle.'

Matron crouched down beside the injured girl and rolled up her pyjama leg a little way.

'You certainly *have* twisted it!' she said. 'Quite badly, by the look of it. Normally the swelling and bruising don't come out for a good few hours,' she added, looking hard at June.

She stood up and helped June to her feet, saying, 'You'd better come along to the San with me, my girl, and get it bandaged up.'

Then Matron turned to Felicity and Bonnie, who were hovering by the bathroom door, saying briskly, 'Get dressed, please, girls, and go to your first lesson. Explain to Miss Peters what has happened, and tell her that I will send June along as soon as I have finished with her.'

'Yes, Matron,' chorused the two girls, trying not to laugh as June winked at them behind Matron's back.

Matron helped June to get dressed, then insisted that the girl lean on her on the way to the San. Their progress was impeded, as they ran into several girls on the way, all of whom wanted to congratulate June for the part she had played in reuniting Jack with his mistress, putting things right for Bill and Clarissa, and bringing Mr Banks to justice.

'Jolly good show, June!'

'You deserve a medal.'

'Yes, a lot of people have reason to be grateful to you and Bonnie, June.'

Matron, knowing that June deserved their congratulations, bore with this patiently. But her patience was at an end when Mam'zelle Dupont suddenly appeared and, spotting June, tottered over on her high heels.

'Ah, this brave and clever June!' she cried. 'Matron, this girl is to be applauded! If it was not for her, and the dear Bonnie, the evil Mr Banks might have got away with his so-wicked plan.'

'I am well aware of that, Mam'zelle,' said Matron crisply. 'But I really must get June to the San, for she has injured her ankle.'

'*Mon dieu!*' exclaimed Mam'zelle, looking shocked. 'How did this happen? June, were you injured performing some act of bravery, or bringing some desperate villain to justice?'

'No, Mam'zelle,' said Matron impatiently. 'She slipped on the soap.'

And, leaving Mam'zelle to gaze after them in astonishment, she bore June off to the San. There she bandaged her ankle up very tightly, and very efficiently.

'You are to rest it completely,' she instructed, in a tone that invited no argument. 'Keep the foot up as much as possible and, with a bit of luck, you should be as right as rain in a few weeks.'

A few weeks! The tennis tournament took place in three weeks, and June was absolutely determined that her ankle would be healed by then and she would be able to play.

There was another surprise for June and Bonnie when Bill and Clarissa arrived at Malory Towers halfway through the morning. Miss Peters, most surprisingly, allowed them to interrupt her lesson so that they could thank June and Bonnie in front of the whole form.

'But for you two, we might have had to sell Five Oaks,' said Bill gratefully. 'We simply can't thank you enough.'

'We can't afford to give you a reward,' said Clarissa. 'But the two of you can have free horse rides whenever you want.'

Bonnie, who was no horsewoman, didn't look awfully thrilled at this, though she appreciated the spirit in which the offer was made. June, though, was quite delighted, and cried, 'I shall take you up on that – once my beastly ankle is all right!'

Alas for June, she was not a good invalid! It chafed her to watch the others splashing around in the swimming-pool, or playing tennis, while she could only sit and watch. It drove her mad when Freddie and Nora had a pillow fight in the dormitory one night and, instead of taking part, she was a mere spectator. And the hardest thing of all to bear was when the third formers decided to have a picnic at the foot of Langley Hill.

Langley Hill was a popular beauty spot, and the girls were thrilled when Miss Peters suggested that they have a picnic tea there one day.

'Super!' said Felicity. 'Cook is going to make us some sandwiches and sausage rolls to take with us. Susan and I are going to provide the ginger beer.'

'And I have a tin of biscuits in my locker that Mother sent,' said Pam. 'I'll bring those.'

All of the girls agreed to bring something along to the picnic, except for June, who remained oddly glum and silent.

'Anything up, old girl?' asked Freddie, concerned. 'Aren't you looking forward to the picnic?'

'I shan't be coming to the picnic,' said June in a tight little voice. 'Langley Hill is a good half hour's walk away, and my ankle will never stand it.'

'Oh, June!' cried Freddie in dismay. 'I never thought of that! Well, I shan't go to the picnic either, then. The two of us will stay at Malory Towers and do something together.'

But June would not hear of this. 'No, I don't want to spoil your fun,' she said, trying to sound like her usual, carefree self.

But Freddie wasn't fooled for a minute. And nor was Julie, who overheard this. An idea came to her suddenly. She was very much in June's debt, and she was going to repay that debt by making sure that June joined in the picnic.

Julie, of course, was absolutely thrilled to have Jack back, and had spent every spare moment over at Five Oaks.

'Almost as if she's afraid to let him out of her sight!' as Pam said to Nora.

Julie wasn't afraid, for now that Mr Banks was out of the way, she knew that Jack was not in any danger. But she had missed him quite dreadfully, and wanted to make up for lost time. But she wasn't so wrapped up in Jack that she couldn't spare a thought for anyone else – especially June, to whom she owed so much.

She took the others into her confidence and, on

Saturday afternoon, when they were in the common-room, Felicity said to June, 'Do hurry up! We're going to leave for Langley Hill in a few minutes.'

'I told you, I'm not coming to Langley Hill,' said June rather crossly. 'How can I?'

Felicity exchanged a glance with Freddie, who nodded. Then the two girls each grabbed one of June's arms, hauling her up out of her chair.

'Hey!' cried June, bewildered. 'What do you think you're doing?'

'We're taking you on a picnic,' laughed Freddie.

Between them, the two girls managed to get June outside. And there, waiting for her, was Julie, leading Jack.

'I've organised some transport for you, June,' said Julie, with a grin. 'All you have to do is sit on Jack's back, and he will carry you to Langley Hill. I'll hold his reins, so that he doesn't take it into his head to gallop off with you, or anything.'

June was speechless for a moment – a most unusual thing for her. Then her face broke into a broad smile, and she cried, 'My word, what a picnic this is going to be!'

And indeed it was. The girls feasted on sandwiches, sausage rolls, cake, biscuits – and all kinds of goodies. Then they lazed around drinking ginger beer, chatting and telling jokes. It was a very happy day. But, all too soon, it was time to clear up and make their way back to school.

'Thank you, Julie,' said June, as the girl helped her up into the saddle. Then she leaned forward and patted

Jack's neck. 'And thank you, Jack. I've had a simply marvellous time!'

'It really has been a nice day,' said Felicity to Susan, when the girls arrived back at Malory Towers. 'No quarrels, no unpleasant shocks, no excitement – just a lovely, peaceful time. Just what we all needed after everything that has happened lately.'

The girls were in the common-room that evening when a second former put her head round the door and called out, 'I say! Miss Grayling wants to see Esme Walters in her study.'

'Goodness, not more trouble!' said Susan. 'What does Miss Grayling want with you, Esme?'

But Esme didn't have the slightest idea, and went off to the Head's study feeling mystified and a little worried. Whatever could the Head want to see her about?

A lovely end to the term

'Come in!' called out Miss Grayling, as Esme knocked timidly on her door. Looking rather scared, Esme went in, but the Head was smiling as she invited Esme to sit down.

'Esme,' she began, 'I have been speaking to Miss Peters, and she tells me that your work has improved a great deal as the term has gone on. Miss Hibbert and both the Mam'zelles are very pleased with you too. Now that you have settled down and learned to work hard, you are far ahead of most of the third formers in many subjects.'

Esme turned quite red with pleasure and said, 'Well, I really have been trying my hardest, Miss Grayling.'

'That is quite obvious,' said the Head. 'And your hard work has paid off. You see, Esme, you are quite a bit older than the rest of your form. Starting off in the third form was only ever meant to be temporary, until we saw what you could do. And Miss Peters agrees with me that, next term, when the others go up into the fourth form, you should go up into the fifth.'

Esme was so astonished that she couldn't utter a word! Her feelings were rather mixed. On the one hand, it was a great honour to go up into the fifth form next term, and her parents would be absolutely delighted with her. But she would miss the others quite dreadfully – Lucy, Bonnie, Amy, Felicity and the rest.

Almost as if she could read the girl's thoughts, Miss Grayling said, 'Of course, I understand that you will miss your cousin, and the friends that you have made. But, although you won't be in the same form any longer, you will still be able to see them.'

'Yes,' said Esme. 'But friendships aren't quite the same if you are in different forms.'

'True,' said Miss Grayling. 'But there will be new girls for you to meet, and new friendships to make.'

That sounded exciting, and Esme felt a little cheered as she returned to the common-room to tell the others her news.

The third formers, too, had mixed feelings, for although they were thrilled for Esme, they would have liked her to stay with them. She really had changed a lot as the term went on, and since she had stopped trying to copy Amy, her own natural, very likeable personality had shone through.

Felicity and Susan's shouts of, 'Good for you, Esme!' mingled with Bonnie's plaintive, 'Oh, I shall miss you so much, Esme!'

'And I will miss all of you,' said Esme. 'Though I feel terribly pleased that Miss Grayling thinks that I'm good enough to go up into the fifth.'

'I don't suppose you will want anything to do with us next term,' said Freddie, with a laugh. 'You'll go all high-and-mighty on us, I expect!'

'Never!' said Esme. Then she turned to Lucy and said, 'Well, cousin, just as we've made friends again, it looks as if we're about to be split up.'

'Of course we aren't, silly!' said Lucy. 'We shall still be able to have the holidays together – and I shall expect my fifth-form cousin to look after me next term!'

'I'll jolly well take you under my wing, all right!' said Esme, and the others laughed.

'You sounded quite English for a moment, there, Esme,' said June. 'Another term, and I think your American accent will be gone completely.'

'Well, I don't know if I will ever lose it completely,' said Esme. 'I quite enjoy being a bit of a mixture, to be honest. But I have come to see that there are a lot of good things about being an English schoolgirl. Why, I'm even looking forward to learning how to play lacrosse next term!'

This was going too far for Amy, who uttered a faint murmur of protest, but Felicity clapped Esme on the back and said, 'Well, if you do as well at lacrosse as you have done at tennis, you'll be just fine!'

'Speaking of tennis,' said Pam, 'do you think that you will be able to play in the tournament, June?'

'Yes, of course,' said June, with more confidence than she felt. 'Matron says that I should be able to take the bandage off next week, and as long as I take things slowly for a few days, everything should be all right.'

When the time came for the bandage to be removed, it was difficult to read Matron's expression. She prodded June's ankle gently, 'hmm-ing' and 'aah-ing' a good deal.

Poor June grew quite nervous. Surely she couldn't have done any serious damage – could she?

But, at last, Matron said, 'It's healing very nicely. The bruise has almost disappeared, and the swelling has gone down quite a bit. All the same, I don't want you doing anything too strenuous for a while, June, or you'll set yourself back.'

'Yes, Matron,' said June in a meek voice that didn't fool Matron at all!

Then she went off to the tennis court, to find Amanda Chartelow. The sixth former was playing a practice game against one of her friends and, as she watched, June marvelled again that someone who was normally so ungainly could be so graceful and lovely to watch when she played tennis.

Amanda spotted June as she came off the court, and went across to her.

'Ah, you've had your bandage off!' she said, looking pleased. 'Did Matron say that you will be fit to play against St Margarets?'

'As long as I take things easy in the meantime,' said June. 'Which is exactly what I intend to do, for I badly want to play in the match.'

This was just what Amanda liked to hear, and she clapped June on the back, saying, 'That's the spirit! All the same, June, if there's the slightest doubt in your mind about whether you are fit to play, I would rather you told me. I'm going all out to win this tournament.'

And, although she was quite fed up with watching the

others all have the fun, June stuck to her word and didn't do anything that might strain her ankle for the next week or so.

Two days before the tournament, she said to Amanda, 'I really think it would be as well if I practised a little today. It seems like absolutely ages since I last played tennis.'

'Yes, I suppose that would be an idea,' said Amanda. 'And it will be a good way of testing if your ankle really is up to the strain. Go and have a game with Freddie.'

So June found the ever-willing Freddie, and the two of them took their places on the court. She and Freddie played pat-ball at first, just to get June used to swinging her racket again. But June soon grew impatient with this, and said, 'That's enough! Let's play properly, Freddie – and no going easy on me!'

Freddie took June at her word, and a couple of fiercely fought games ensued. Then June ran forward to return one of Freddie's serves, and suddenly her ankle just seemed to give way. She stumbled, but didn't fall. And, although June managed to stop herself crying out in pain, she winced.

'What's up?' called Freddie, walking up to the net. 'Oh! Don't say that your ankle's given out.'

'No such thing!' said June, determined to play on. 'I just tripped, that's all. Serve again, Freddie!'

Freddie did, and no one would have been able to tell from June's manner that she was in pain. True, her game was a little off, but Freddie put that down to the fact that she was out of practice. June even managed to laugh and joke with Freddie as the two of them walked off to the changing-rooms, but how relieved she was to be able to sit down on one of the benches in there and take the weight off her ankle. Blow! she thought. If only she had listened to Bonnie and not gone to Bluebell Wood that fateful night, she would never have fallen off that beastly bike. Now what was she to do?

It didn't take June long to decide. She *would* play in the tournament! And she would jolly well do her best to win. Why, when people learned afterwards that she had played with a badly hurt ankle, they would simply praise her to the skies!

So it came about that, when the Malory Towers team gathered on the drive to wait for the coach that was to take them to St Margarets, June was among them.

As usual, Amanda gave the team a little pep talk while they were waiting.

'I want you all to do your best, for the honour of Malory Towers,' she said. 'No one can ask more of you than that. If you play as well as you possibly can, and lose, I shall still be proud of you. But woe betide anyone who doesn't try her very hardest!'

The girls stood straight and proud, all of them looking very smart in their white tennis dresses and cardigans, as they listened to their captain. Each and every one of them felt determined not to let their school down. But June looked rather pensive. Amanda's words had given her food for thought. How could she possibly play her best, and try her hardest, when she simply wasn't up to it? She was letting Malory Towers down just by taking her place on the team – a place that should be taken by someone who really *could* give of her best. Taking a deep breath, June went up to the games captain and said, 'Amanda! There's something I need to tell you. You see, my ankle isn't really better at all. I thought that it was, and when I realised it wasn't I kept quiet, because I so badly wanted to play in the tournament. I see now, though, that the best thing I can do for Malory Towers is to stand aside and let someone else play.'

Amanda stared hard at June for a moment. She looked very stern, and June waited for the storm to break over her head. Then Amanda's face broke into a smile and she said gruffly, 'Good kid! I know it must have cost you a great deal to give up your place on the team, but you have done the right thing. I really believe that you are beginning to learn about team spirit.'

And Amanda was quite right, June suddenly realised. There were times when one had to put one's own desire for personal glory aside, for the good of others. She had first discovered that when she and Bonnie had worked side by side to find Jack, and to get Bill and Clarissa out of trouble. And it had been a lesson well learned, for when Amanda called Esme over and informed the surprised girl that she would be playing after all, June felt no bitterness or jealousy. Instead she patted Esme on the back and said heartily, 'Good luck, Esme! Make sure that you play up.'

Just then, the big coach drew up and, as June began to walk towards the school, Amanda called out, 'And just where do you think you're going, June?'

'I thought I'd go and sit in the common-room for a bit,' answered June, surprised.

'Well, think again!' said Amanda, taking her arm and steering the girl towards the coach. 'There are a couple of spare seats, so you can come with us and be our mascot. Just make sure you cheer us on, good and loud!'

'Oh, I will, Amanda,' said June happily. 'Yes, I'll do that, all right.'

And June yelled herself hoarse! Amanda won her match easily, the St Margarets girls gasping at the brilliance of her play. Poor Vanessa Tyler wasn't so lucky and, although she played her heart out, was narrowly beaten by her opponent. Then came the doubles match, and Felicity and Susan walked out on to the court, both of them feeling very proud and very nervous.

'Come on, Felicity!' shouted June. 'Come on, Susan!'

And, to the delight of June and Amanda, the two girls played superbly. Their opponents were very good too, and did their best, but they were no match for the Malory Towers pair.

'Jolly well played, kids!' shouted Amanda. 'Two–one to Malory Towers! Emily, from the fourth form, is playing next. I should think that she's certain to win.'

But alas, this was Emily's first match in front of a crowd, and her nerves overcame her completely. She made some bad mistakes, with the result that the St Margarets girl won.

'It all depends on Esme now,' said Amanda, looking

very tense. 'Her match will decide whether we go back to Malory Towers as winners or losers.'

June cheered her head off as Esme came out, a tall, graceful figure. The girl she was playing against was much more heavily built, and had a powerful serve, but a calm determination had settled on Esme, and she fought back well. The play was very even, until the last couple of games, when the Malory Towers girl really settled down and, to the delight of her team-mates, took the lead. Then it was the final game of the set, and Esme was serving for the match.

At the side of the court, June and Amanda were silent now, both of them holding their breath. Esme served beautifully, the ball whizzing across the net and sending up a little puff of chalk as it bounced off the line.

'The St Margarets girl will never reach that!' said June, clutching excitedly at Amanda's arm.

And she didn't! Game, set, match and tournament to Malory Towers!

While the girls from the other school clapped sportingly, the Malory Towers team – and June, of course – went quite mad with joy. They shouted, cheered, hugged one another and leapt up and down.

'Congratulations,' said the St Margarets captain, coming over to shake hands with Amanda. 'That's quite a team you have there!'

'Yes,' said Amanda, beaming round proudly at the girls. 'The best team ever!'

Of course, the girls got a heroes' welcome when they

returned to school, Felicity and Esme clutching the big silver cup that was the team prize between them.

'What a super end to the term!' said Pam.

'Absolutely marvellous!' agreed Freddie.

'But it's not *quite* the end of term,' said Nora. 'There are still a few days to go.'

And those few days simply sped by, and then it really *was* the end of term. The girls were plunged into the usual last-minute frenzy of packing and, in the dormitory, chaos reigned.

'Has anyone seen my slippers?'

'I say, where *has* my hairbrush got to?'

'Nora, do get your big feet off my music case!'

'Felicity! Felicity! What do you mean by going off with my pyjamas?'

'Oh, are those yours, Lucy? Sorry, they look exactly like mine.'

Matron, popping her head round the door to see how the third formers were getting on, winced as a wave of noise hit her, and clapped her hands over her ears, before quickly withdrawing again.

At last, everyone was packed and they made their way down to the big hall, where girls from all of the towers were waiting for the coaches to take them to the station, or for their parents to collect them by car. Mam'zelle Dupont was fussing round everyone, as she always did, saying fond goodbyes, and the girls smiled to see her.

'Dear old Mam'zelle,' said Susan. 'I shall miss her funny ways during the holidays.'

'I shall miss everything about Malory Towers,' said Felicity with a sigh. 'My last term as head of the form is over now. And what an eventful term it has been!'

'Yes, it's certainly had its ups and downs,' agreed Susan. 'Luckily, in the end, the ups seemed to outweigh the downs!'

'I wonder what will be in store for us next term?' said Felicity.

'Who knows?' said Susan. 'We'll just have to wait and see.'

And that's what we will have to do as well – wait and see.

Malory Towers

Winter Term

Written by Pamela Cox

Contents

1	On the train	411
2	The first evening	423
3	Exciting news	436
4	The new mistress	446
5	Olive is annoying	460
6	A very successful trick	471
7	Miss Tallant interferes	482
8	Bonnie in trouble	495
9	A shock for the fourth form	507
10	Miss Tallant strikes again	518
11	An interesting half-term	530
12	Exciting plans	541
13	A trap is set	554
14	The ghost of Malory Towers	566
15	Miss Tallant's niece	578
16	Where is Olive?	588
17	Bonnie puts things right	604
18	The Christmas concert	613

On the train

'Mother, there's Susan!' cried Felicity Rivers, as she and her mother made their way along the station platform. 'Susan! Hi, Susan!'

'Felicity, don't run!' called Mrs Rivers. 'It's far too crowded and you will bump into someone!'

But it was too late. Felicity was determined to reach her friend Susan and she ran along the platform, dodging the groups of people that stood here and there. Many of them were girls in the Malory Towers uniform, waiting for the train that would take them back to school for the winter term.

But Mrs Rivers was right, and it wasn't long before Felicity *did* bump into someone – a tall, red-haired girl with a serious expression and grey eyes.

'Felicity Rivers!' said the girl, looking rather cross. 'Do watch where you are going! And what do you mean by running around like a mad thing?'

'Sorry, Fenella,' said Felicity meekly, turning red. Of all the people she could have bumped into, why did she have to pick Fenella Thornton, the new Head Girl?

Fenella glared at her for a moment. Then, suddenly, her face broke into a wide smile, making her look quite different.

'Go on, push off!' she said with a chuckle. 'And this time, walk! Remember, you're a fourth former now, Felicity, not a silly little third former any more.'

Golly, so I am! thought Felicity, walking over to join Susan and her mother. Fancy *me* being a fourth former!

She and Susan greeted one another noisily, for they had to tell one another *everything* that had happened in the holidays. Then Mrs Rivers came up and chatted to Susan's mother, and at last it was time for the two girls to board the train.

Each of them hugged her mother, and Mrs Rivers said, 'Do write, won't you, darling? And I know that Darrell would love to hear from you, too.'

'I'll see you at half-term, dear,' said Susan's mother. 'Have a marvellous time!'

Felicity and Susan waved their mothers off, then grinned at one another as they walked down the train to find their carriage.

'The beginning of a new term,' said Susan. 'And now we are fourth formers!'

'Yes, we are, so why are you going towards the third-form carriage?' laughed Felicity, pulling her friend back. 'We don't want to sit with *those* babies!'

'Of course not,' said Susan loftily. 'Babies!'

Just then, the guard outside blew his whistle and, with a lurch, the train began to move forward slowly – on its way to Malory Towers!

'I say, isn't it exciting to be getting the train all on our own?' said Felicity.

'Much better than being in a stuffy old car,' agreed Susan.

The girls usually came to school by car, but Felicity's father had needed to drive to an urgent appointment, so she was getting the train for the first time. And, as she and Susan were quite inseparable, Susan's parents had agreed that she could catch the train with Felicity, too.

A sudden shout of laughter came from one of the carriages further along the train, and Felicity said, 'I'd know that laugh anywhere!'

'So would I,' grinned Susan. 'It's June!'

Quickly, Felicity and Susan made their way to the carriage that the laughter had come from, and slid open the door. And there, all chuckling their heads off, sat three of their fellow fourth formers – June, Freddie and Nora. There was another girl sitting in the corner of the carriage too, one that the girls hadn't seen before, but she wasn't laughing. In fact, her expression was very sullen indeed.

Heavens, she doesn't look very friendly, thought Felicity. I do hope that she isn't in North Tower with us.

The new girl, who was rather plain, with straight, mousey-brown hair, which fell to her shoulders, looked up as Felicity and Susan took their seats. Then she looked away again almost immediately, without so much as smiling at the newcomers. The two girls looked at one another and grimaced, but there was no time to worry about the new girl now, for their friends were welcoming them noisily.

'Hallo there, you two! Had good hols?'

'Isn't it grand to be going back to good old Malory Towers?'

'And this time we shall be in the fourth form! My goodness, we *are* going up in the world!'

'I don't know that I want to be a fourth former,' said Nora, frowning a little. 'We shall have to settle down a little and be more responsible now that we are in the upper school. It won't be nearly as much fun!'

The sullen-looking girl, who had been huddled miserably in the corner, looking out of the window, turned her head again at this, and threw Nora a scornful look. Fortunately, Nora didn't see it, but Felicity did, and felt quite shocked. Whatever had Nora done to deserve *that*?

'I have no intention at all of settling down,' said June. 'I don't see why we can't have a little fun, just because we are fourth formers.'

'Quite right!' said her friend, Freddie. 'We can still play the odd trick . . .'

'And have the occasional joke,' put in June.

'And, perhaps, we might even arrange a midnight feast!' said Freddie, her blue eyes lighting up.

The eyes of Felicity, Susan and Nora lit up too. A midnight feast would be simply too marvellous for words! They hadn't had one for absolutely ages. On the other hand, though, what Nora had said was quite true. The girls *were* expected to settle down a little once they were in the fourth form. But then Felicity remembered that when her sister Darrell had been in the upper fourth, they had held a feast. And if it was good enough for Darrell, it was good enough for Felicity!

'Perhaps we *could* have a feast,' she said, grinning. 'It's not as if we would be doing any harm. And as long as we keep it to ourselves, we can't be accused of setting a bad example to the lower forms.'

'My sentiments exactly!' cried June, clapping her on the back. 'My word, we're in for some fun this term.'

June's wicked, dark eyes were shining. She and Freddie were the jokers of the form, and fun was never far away when they were around!

'There's a very mischievous look about you this term, June,' said Susan, watching the girl.

'June *always* looks mischievous,' laughed Nora.

'Yes, but she looks even more mischievous than usual,' said Susan. 'And so do you, Freddie! Secretly planning lots of tricks, I expect!'

'Us?' said June, making her eyes very wide and innocent. 'Of course not!'

'As if we would!' said Freddie, also looking very innocent.

But the others knew that Freddie had spent the last few days of the holidays at June's. And June's brothers, who were also great jokers, had been there too. No doubt the two girls had come back with all kinds of jokes and tricks up their sleeves!

The new girl, who had sat in silence while the chatter went on around her, gave a sniff, and Felicity and Susan looked at the others enquiringly.

'Oh yes,' said June, as though she had only just

remembered that the girl was there. 'I haven't introduced you to our new member of the form, have I? This is Olive Witherspoon.'

Felicity and Susan said hallo, and the girl returned their greeting unsmilingly, in a tight little voice.

'Have you been to boarding school before, Olive?' asked Felicity, pleasantly.

'Yes,' said Olive shortly.

'Well, that's good,' said Susan, brightly. 'As you're used to it, I don't suppose you will feel too homesick, will you?'

'No,' came Olive's curt reply, and June muttered under her breath, 'Don't waste your time. She won't volunteer any information, and all you will get out of her are one-word answers. I gave up after about five minutes.'

'Yes, cheerful little soul, isn't she?' murmured Freddie.

Nora pulled a face and said in a low voice, 'Never mind about her! We've tried to be friendly, but she obviously doesn't want our company. Let's talk about something else instead. I say, did you know that Fenella Thornton has been made Head Girl, now that Kay Foster has left?'

'Yes, and old Amanda's gone, too,' said June. 'Ruth Grainger is taking her place as games captain.'

'I like Ruth,' said Freddie. 'And Fenella's not a bad sort, although she has a bit of a temper.'

'Yes, Fenella can be hot-tempered at times,' laughed Felicity. 'I bumped into her on the platform, quite literally! She was cross with me at first, but she soon got over it.'

'I wonder who will be head of the form?' said Susan.

'Well, it won't be me,' said Felicity. 'I had my turn in

the third form. I must say, I'm quite looking forward to taking a back seat this year.'

'And it certainly won't be me,' said June comfortably. 'I'm far too irresponsible.'

'And it won't be me, either,' laughed Freddie. 'For the same reason.'

'I'm much too scatterbrained,' said Nora. 'Potty and Miss Williams would never choose me.'

'Perhaps it will be Pam,' suggested Susan. 'She's so steady and good-tempered. And she was head girl when we were in the second form.'

'Pam was a super head-girl,' said Felicity. 'But I think that Miss Williams should give someone else a chance this term. It might be you, Susan!'

'No!' said June at once, with a horrified expression. 'Why, Susan would be no good at all as head-girl.'

'She would be marvellous!' retorted the normally even-tempered Felicity, firing up in defence of her friend. She had turned rather red, and June gave her a push, saying, 'Ass! I was only joking. Of course I know that Susan would be a splendid head-girl. I say, just imagine if Miss Williams made Bonnie head of the form? Or Amy?'

'I don't know which of them would be worse,' said Susan, with a shudder. 'It would certainly be an entertaining term if one of those two were chosen, but somehow I can't quite picture it happening!'

The chatter continued as the train went on its way, but still Olive took no part. Felicity, who thought that perhaps the girl was just very shy, felt a little sorry for her. Every now and then she tried to draw Olive into conversation, but, as before, the girl responded with terse answers, and asked no questions of her own.

She really was rather odd, decided Felicity, giving up. She remembered how excited she had felt about starting at Malory Towers, and how she had bombarded her older sister, Darrell, with questions. Yet Olive wasn't at all excited, and she didn't seem remotely curious about her new school either. It was very strange!

At last the train drew up at the little station near Malory Towers and, dragging their trunks and carrying their night cases, the girls alighted. Several big coaches were waiting to take the girls to the school, and Felicity and her friends boarded the first one, Olive following. Felicity and Susan sat together, of course, and so did June and Freddie. Which left Nora to sit next to the new girl, something which neither of them looked very pleased about.

Felicity and Susan felt sorry for Nora, for they would not have liked to sit next to the surly Olive either. They sat behind the two girls, and did their best to include Nora in their conversation, for which she was very grateful.

The coach journey was only a short one, and the girls grew very excited as the coach rounded a bend in the road, and their beloved Malory Towers came into view.

Felicity always loved this first glimpse of her school, thinking how magnificent it looked – almost like a castle, with its four towers, one at each corner.

In excitement, she cried out, 'Olive, look! There is Malory Towers, up on the cliff. Isn't it just the most beautiful building you have ever seen?'

Olive looked, but she made no comment. And Nora, stealing a sideways glance at the new girl, thought that her frown seemed to deepen.

There was great excitement as the coaches pulled up in the driveway, those girls who had arrived earlier by car gathering round to greet their friends.

'Felicity! I wondered where you were!'

'And there's Susan! Had good hols, Susan?'

'Hallo, June! And Freddie! My, isn't it good to be back?'

'Nora, old girl! Hurry up, and let's take our night cases to Matron.'

This was Nora's friend, the placid, even-tempered Pam. She looked with interest at Olive, who was coming down the steps behind Nora, and said in her friendly way, 'Hallo there! Welcome to Malory Towers. Are you going to be in the fourth form with us?'

'Yes,' answered Olive, in her funny, stiff little voice.

'Got your night case? Good, you can come along to Matron with the rest of us. I say, where did Felicity and Susan get to?'

Felicity and Susan had been swallowed up by a group of fourth formers. There was pretty little Bonnie, the haughty Amy, and freckle-faced Julie, with her friend, Lucy.

Julie and Lucy had brought their horses to school with them, and all of the girls were eager to go down to the stables and greet them.

'Thank goodness that there was room in the stables this term for Jack and Sandy,' said Felicity.

'Yes, it's wonderful to have him with me again,' said Julie. 'I don't blame Bill and Clarissa one little bit for what happened last term, of course, and I know that it won't happen again. But I just feel happier knowing that Jack is here, at Malory Towers.'

Last term there had been no room in the school stables for Jack and Sandy, so Julie and Lucy had stabled their horses at Five Oaks, a nearby riding school, which was run by two old girls. But there had been great consternation when Jack had gone missing. Fortunately, he had been found, and the culprit arrested, so everything had ended happily.

Now, though, Julie was even more reluctant to let Jack out of her sight than usual.

'Come along, everyone!' came Pam's voice from behind the little group. 'Let's take our health certificates to Matron and unpack our things. I'm simply dying to see our new dormitory and common-room.'

So the girls picked up their night cases and trooped inside North Tower to the big hall. A small group of first formers stood there, all of them looking nervous and a little lost.

'Poor little dears,' said Susan to Felicity. 'Shall we offer to take them upstairs to Matron?'

Felicity nodded, but before they had time to approach the first formers, a large, fair girl with a round face and very rosy cheeks strode up to them.

'Come on, kids!' she commanded, in a loud, very hearty voice. 'Follow me, and I'll take you to Matron's room. No lagging behind now!'

'Heavens, who's that?' asked Susan.

'Must be a new girl,' said June. 'Probably a fifth or sixth former by the look of her. I say, she looks like a mother duck, with all her little ducklings following behind her, doesn't she?'

The fourth formers burst out laughing, for that was exactly what the big girl did look like! Susan, however, was a little put out. It simply wasn't done for a new girl to be so bossy, and take charge of the young ones like that – even if she was a top former!

Just then, someone called out, 'Hallo, you kids! No loitering in the hall now, or I shall dish out a punishment.'

The girls turned to see a tall, graceful girl standing there, a wide smile on her face.

'Esme!' they cried. 'How marvellous to see you!'

Lucy, who was Esme's cousin, punched the girl gently on the shoulder, and said, 'I'm surprised that you even bother with us small fry now that you're a fifth former.'

'It's only because there's no one else around,' said Esme with a perfectly straight face. 'Of course, if I should happen to pass you when I'm with any of my form I shall simply walk past with my nose in the air.'

Then she laughed, and the others laughed with her, for they knew that Esme – who had been in their form last term – would never go all high-and-mighty on them, no matter what.

When the girls arrived at Matron's room, the big, fair-haired girl was there, still fussing over the first formers. Matron herself was looking rather irritated, but her stern face relaxed into a smile when she saw the fourth formers. 'All got your health certificates?' she said, in her brisk tone. 'Good. Now, I want no illnesses, and no broken bones this term. Is that clear?'

'Yes, Matron,' chorused the girls, all except Olive, who hung back and looked at Matron suspiciously. The others knew that Matron was only joking, and there was no one they would rather have look after them if they fell ill. But, to Olive, she seemed a most unsympathetic person. Matron noticed the girl watching her, and, looking at the list in her hand, said with a smile, 'You must be Olive Witherspoon. And I have another new girl here for the fourth form, too. Sylvia, come and meet the rest of your form.'

The girls followed Matron's gaze and realised, with surprise, that she was talking to the rather bossy girl who had borne the first formers off. Heavens, was she going to be in the fourth form too?

The first evening

The girl turned at once, and strode across to the others, a broad smile on her round face. 'How lovely to meet you all!' she boomed, in her hearty voice. 'I'm Sylvia Chalmers, and I'm so happy to be at Malory Towers. I was at St Hilda's until the end of last term, you know, but our Head was taken ill and it had to be closed down. So sad! It was a simply super school, but I'm sure that Malory Towers will be every bit as nice.'

Sylvia paused to take a breath, and Matron seized the chance to say, 'Well, Sylvia, the girls will show you and Olive to your dormitory, then you can all unpack.'

'Oh, I know where the dormitory is, Matron,' said Sylvia. 'I arrived early this morning, you know. And my things are already unpacked. I was just going to show the youngsters to their dormitory, because I always like to help out if I can.' She beamed round at the others, who were all staring at her open-mouthed. Heavens, what a chatterbox!

Bonnie put a hand to her forehead, and murmured to Amy, 'I'm beginning to get a headache.'

'Oh, poor you!' said Sylvia, whose sharp ears had caught this. 'My mother suffers dreadfully from headaches, so I know just what you should do! You need to take –'

But Bonnie never found out what she needed to take, for Matron, quite affronted, cut in, to say crisply, 'Thank you, Sylvia, but *I* am Matron of North Tower, and if Bonnie has a headache she can come to me for a remedy.'

Then she reached up and took a large bottle of green medicine down from one of her shelves, shaking it in Bonnie's direction. 'A dose of this will cure your headache, Bonnie,' she said.

But, miraculously, Bonnie found that her headache had suddenly disappeared!

'I thought it might,' said Matron drily, putting the bottle back on her shelf. 'Now, off you go, all of you, for the first day of term is a very busy one for me, and you are all in my way.'

The fourth formers went out, but Sylvia lingered, saying, 'Matron, I was hoping that I might show the first formers where their dormitory is, and help them to settle in.'

Matron, who was growing a little tired of Sylvia and her pushy manner, said firmly, 'The first formers can learn to find their own way around, Sylvia. They certainly don't need you chivvying them round. Now do, please, go and join the others.'

'Well, what a know-it-all!' said Nora, as the rest of the fourth form made their way along the corridor.

'Isn't she just?' said Susan. 'And she acts as if she has been at Malory Towers for years, not just a few hours.'

'I can see that she's going to be jolly trying,' said Felicity. 'I wonder how she knows her way around so well?'

'You can ask her,' said June. 'Here she comes!'

And, when Sylvia caught up with them, Felicity *did* ask her.

'Oh, whenever I go anywhere new, I always make a point of exploring, so that I can find my way around,' explained Sylvia in her loud voice. 'I do so hate having to ask where I'm supposed to be going all the time, don't you?'

Felicity opened her mouth to answer, but Sylvia swept on, 'It can be quite uncomfortable being the new girl, among so many others who have been here for a long time, especially when you have been used to being *somebody* at your old school.'

'*Somebody?*' repeated Julie, with rather a dazed expression.

'Oh yes, I was head-girl in several forms at my old school,' said Sylvia airily. 'I'm afraid I do have rather a tendency to rule the roost.'

'Really?' said June in a smooth little voice. 'I would never have guessed.'

The others giggled, and before Sylvia could hold forth again, Susan said, 'Well, let's get along to our dormitory, or we shan't have time to see anything before tea.' Then, in a lower tone, she murmured to Felicity, 'My word, if Sylvia tries to rule the roost in the fourth form she'll be in for a shock!'

Indeed she would, thought Felicity, smiling to herself. There were several very strong characters in the fourth, and they would have no hesitation in putting Sylvia in her place if she became too bossy!

The fourth-form dormitory was a very pleasant room, large and airy, with cream-painted walls. Each bed had a brightly coloured bedspread on it, and a locker beside it, so that the girls had somewhere to keep their personal belongings.

Sylvia, of course, had already unpacked and arranged several things on top of her locker, and she hovered round the others now, saying brightly, 'If anyone wants a hand with their unpacking, they only have to say the word.'

'If they can get one in edgeways,' muttered June darkly, making the others laugh.

Olive, in complete contrast to Sylvia, had remained very much in the background and, as the fourth formers entered their dormitory, Felicity turned to the girl.

'Settling in all right?' she asked, with a smile.

Olive merely nodded, and Felicity, determined to draw her out, tried again, asking, 'Which school did you go to before you came here?'

'Chartley Manor,' answered Olive.

'What made you leave and come to Malory Towers?' asked Susan, coming over to help Felicity in her efforts.

And, quite suddenly, Olive's face lost its sullen, uninterested expression, becoming angry and red, as she hissed at Susan, 'Mind your own business!'

Then she turned away, flung her night case on to the nearest bed and began furiously pulling things out.

'Well!' said Susan, annoyed and rather shaken. 'What on earth brought that outburst on? Of all the nerve! Olive can remain in her shell now, for all I care! I certainly won't bother trying to make conversation with her again.'

Felicity, angry on her friend's behalf, glared at Olive. But the girl kept her head down as she concentrated on her unpacking, and didn't even notice.

'I've a jolly good mind to go and tell her what I think of her!' said Felicity, her cheeks glowing red.

But Susan said, 'Don't let's bother about her, Felicity. I'm certainly not going to let her spoil our first day back at school. Besides, at least I managed to get *four* words out of her, instead of just one!'

Felicity laughed at this, but she still felt sore with the new girl, sitting as far away from her as possible at the tea table later.

The girls rubbed their hands together happily as they went into the dining-room, Nora sniffing the air appreciatively. 'Sausages and mash, with gravy, unless I'm much mistaken,' she said. 'And treacle sponge for pudding. Yummy!'

Mam'zelle Dupont, the plump little French mistress, was already at the head of the fourth-form table when the girls seated themselves, and she smiled round, delighted to see everyone again, crying, '*Bonjour, mes enfants!*'

The fourth formers were very fond of Mam'zelle, and smiled back. But they didn't have a chance to return her greeting, for, once again, Sylvia pushed herself forward, saying brightly, '*Bonjour*, Mam'zelle! I'm Sylvia Chalmers, and we met earlier.'

'Ah yes,' began Mam'zelle. 'I remember. Miss Potts –'

'Miss Potts introduced us,' interrupted Sylvia. 'And you

and I had a lovely, long chat about France, for I spent my summer holiday there, and I was telling you all about it.'

Mam'zelle's smile began to slide a little, and she murmured, '*Oui* – it was a very, *very* long chat indeed.'

'I simply must show you the photographs I took, Mam'zelle,' Sylvia chattered on. Then she looked round the table, and said, 'I'm sure that you would all find them most interesting, girls. You see, we stayed in the most beautiful chateau, and . . .'

Then, to Sylvia's astonishment, the fourth formers all began to talk to one another, very loudly and very pointedly. Even Mam'zelle turned away and began to talk rapidly to Nora, taking care not to meet Sylvia's eye again.

As for Sylvia herself, she began to eat her sausages and mashed potato, feeling puzzled and a little hurt. She wanted *so* badly to fit in here, and really had gone out of her way to be friendly. Poor Sylvia! She simply couldn't see that she was trying just a little *too* hard.

It was a strange meal, thought Felicity. Normally the fourth formers would have pointed out all the mistresses to the new girls, telling them which ones to beware of, and which ones were easy to get round, or good to play tricks on. But Olive didn't seem in the slightest bit interested, while Sylvia seemed to know all there was to know already!

Just then, June glanced towards the first-form table, and noticed that there was a new mistress sitting there, beside Miss Potts, the head of North Tower.

'I wonder who that is, with Miss Potts?' she said, and

the others turned to look. The mistress looked very young, and had tightly curled blonde hair, which looked very striking with her dark brows and brown eyes.

'Do you know who she is, Sylvia?' asked June.

'Of course not,' said Sylvia, rather defensively. 'Why should I?'

'Well, you seem to know everything else,' said June.

'She looks awfully young,' said Nora. 'I wonder what she is going to teach?'

'Ah, I know who this new mistress must be!' cried Mam'zelle, who had been listening, and surveying the new teacher with great interest. 'Perhaps you do not know, *mes filles*, but our good Miss Hibbert was taken ill during the holidays, and has been ordered to stay at home and rest.'

The fourth formers were sorry to hear this, for Miss Hibbert, who taught English and Drama, was an excellent teacher, with a knack of making her lessons very interesting indeed.

'That's bad news!' said Felicity, looking very grave. 'I do hope that there is nothing seriously wrong with Miss Hibbert, Mam'zelle?'

'*Non*, but she must not return to Malory Towers until she has fully recovered,' said the French mistress. 'That is why Miss Grayling has engaged someone else to take her place this term. Her name, I think, is Miss Tallant.'

'She's very pretty,' said Bonnie, surveying the mistress critically.

'In a rather common sort of way,' said Amy with a sniff. 'I bet her hair is dyed.'

'She looks as if she might be good fun,' said Lucy. 'The younger mistresses often are.'

'I think she looks rather hard,' said June to Freddie, in a low voice that could not be overheard by Mam'zelle. 'Mark my words, our Miss Tallant is going to be trouble, and not fun at all!'

Olive, meanwhile, sat silently and ate very little, merely pushing the food around her plate. She wasn't interested in the new mistress. She didn't like Malory Towers. And she didn't like the girls! Not that nosy Susan, nor snobbish Amy, and certainly not the bossy Sylvia. As for Nora and Bonnie, they were both the kind of girls that Olive disliked most, with their big eyes, pretty faces and sweet, innocent expressions. Olive knew all about girls like them. She knew how they used their sweetness and prettiness to get their own way, and to make themselves the centre of attention. While plainer girls, like Olive herself, had to find other ways to make themselves noticed, or be ignored altogether.

Certainly the new girl had not made any impression on Mam'zelle, who had barely noticed that she was there. Felicity suddenly realised, with a pang of guilt, that no one had bothered to introduce Olive to the French mistress. Really, she thought, it was quite Olive's own fault if she was left out of things, for she had made no effort at all to respond to the others' attempts at making friends. All the same, someone ought to make the introduction, and as Felicity had been head of the form last year, she decided that it was up to her.

'Mam'zelle,' she said. 'I don't think that you've met our other new girl, Olive Witherspoon.'

'Ah, you are so quiet, *ma petite*, that I did not notice you!' said Mam'zelle, smiling at the girl. 'Well, these fourth formers will make you welcome, for they are good girls, and soon you will be just like them.'

Just then, Bonnie let out a squeal that made everyone jump, and leapt up from her chair, wailing, 'Oh no, I've spilled my tea all over my skirt!'

'You are scalded, *ma chère*!' cried Mam'zelle dramatically, getting to her feet. 'I shall take you to Matron at once!'

'I'm not scalded, Mam'zelle, for the tea was almost cold,' said Bonnie, dabbing rather ineffectually at the damp patch on her skirt with a handkerchief. 'It was just such a shock, that's all. Thank heavens I have another skirt in my trunk. Amy, be a dear and pour me another cup of tea, would you?'

How typical, thought Olive, watching the little by-play with a sour expression. Bonnie was quite obviously one of Mam'zelle's favourites, and the girl simply couldn't bear to see the French mistress paying attention to someone else. So she had purposely spilled her tea in her lap and then made a big – and quite unnecessary – fuss about it. Olive's lip curled scornfully and, seeing this, Felicity nudged Susan, murmuring, 'Just look at Olive's face! It's enough to turn the milk sour!'

In fact, Olive was being extremely unjust, for Bonnie had been deep in conversation with Amy, and hadn't even realised that Mam'zelle was speaking to Olive. Nor had she spilled the tea on purpose, for it really *had* been an accident.

But the new girl had taken a completely irrational dislike to both Bonnie and Nora, and it came to the fore again when the girls were relaxing in the common-room that evening.

'I must say, this is a jolly nice common-room,' said Sylvia, whose hurt silence at the tea-table had lasted all of five minutes. She liked the sound of her own voice far too much to be quiet for any longer! 'Very cosy! I'm sure we shall have some wonderful times in here, all chattering away together!'

'What Sylvia means is that *she* will chatter, while *we* are forced to listen to her,' muttered Amy under her breath, scowling at the new girl. 'I think it's dreadfully vulgar, the way that she pushes herself to the fore all the time!'

'Of course, when I was head of the form at St Hilda's, we used to have all kinds of fun and games in the common-room,' the new girl went on. 'I organised most of them myself, for if there is one thing I pride myself on it's being a good organiser. And, if I do say so myself, I'm jolly good at thinking up games to play. I could show you some of them, if you like, and . . .'

'Thanks. If we ever feel that we need someone to organise us, or tell us what to do in our free time, we'll let you know,' said June, with heavy sarcasm.

But Sylvia was too thick-skinned to recognise sarcasm, and she continued to talk and talk and talk! At last it became too much for Nora, who jumped up and put a gramophone record on.

'Good show, Nora!' called out Freddie.

Then, to the amusement of the fourth formers, Nora began to do a little tap dance in the middle of the floor.

'You're full of beans tonight!' said Pam, in surprise. 'Usually it's all you can do to keep your eyes open after the journey back to Malory Towers.'

'Ah yes, but I have been staying at my aunt's, and she doesn't live many miles from here, so it was only a short drive back,' explained Nora, stopping in mid-dance. 'So I feel quite wide awake, for once!'

'You're not a bad dancer, Nora,' said Sylvia – rather patronisingly, the others thought. In fact, Nora, who was naturally graceful, was a very good dancer and had been taking lessons in the holidays. She opened her mouth to tell the others this, but Sylvia got in first, saying, 'I simply love dancing, and, if I do say so myself, I have quite a talent for it.'

'My gosh, can you imagine it?' muttered Lucy, under her breath. 'It would be like watching a baby elephant!'

This was a little unkind, but Julie couldn't help laughing, and Sylvia, quite oblivious, went on, 'I coached some of the youngsters in dancing, for their part in the school concert last year, and it all went swimmingly. The parents thought that it was marvellous, and I do think that I have a knack for teaching people things, even if –'

'Even if you do say so yourself,' interrupted June smoothly, as muffled laughter ran round the room.

Sylvia looked a little puzzled at this, and while she was temporarily lost for words, Nora cried, 'Let me show you all a dance I learned in the holidays. Turn the music up, Felicity.'

Felicity obeyed, and the others moved back to make room for Nora. Then they watched, entranced, as she danced for them, her movements very graceful and balletic. Nora was a complete scatterbrain, and a bit of a duffer at most of her lessons, so it was very nice to see her excel at something, thought Felicity.

As Nora curtseyed daintily, the fourth formers clapped and cheered. All except Olive, who sat with her arms folded, her mouth set in a thin line and an expression of scorn on her face.

Susan, who still felt angry with the girl because of her earlier outburst, nudged Olive rather sharply and said, 'What's the matter with you? You could at least join us in clapping Nora.'

'Why should I?' said Olive sullenly. 'Nora is a show-off, and I don't like show-offs!'

The others gasped and muttered angrily, Pam saying hotly, 'How dare you, Olive! You take that back at once!'

'I shan't,' said Olive obstinately. 'She *is* a show-off, and so is Bonnie! Both of them have to be the centre of attention, all the time.'

Poor little Bonnie looked quite stunned, for she couldn't think what she had done to make the new girl dislike her so. Why, she had barely exchanged more than a few words with her.

'I see what it is!' said Amy, suddenly. 'You're jealous. Bonnie and Nora are both pretty, and dainty, while as for you ...' The girl paused as she looked Olive up and down, rather scornfully. 'Well, no one could call *you* pretty!'

Olive turned pale, and shrank back as though Amy had struck her. Everyone else was quiet, for – although Nora and Bonnie felt grateful to Amy for sticking up for them – most of the girls felt that she had gone a little too far. Olive *was* very plain, but it had been rather cruel to point it out in front of everyone like that.

'That's enough!' said Felicity sharply. 'There are only five minutes until bedtime, so let's not waste them in arguing.'

'Well done,' said Susan, grinning at Felicity, as everyone dispersed. 'Once a head-girl, always a head-girl!'

Felicity laughed and said, 'Well, *someone* had to take charge, before things got out of hand. I must say, though, that I think we've been rather unlucky in our new girls this term.'

'Haven't we just!' agreed Susan. 'Olive is a real misery, and I'm afraid it looks as if she's going to be rather spiteful, too. And Sylvia is simply too pushy for words! She'll try and take over everything if we aren't careful.'

Felicity nodded, and said, 'I've a feeling that this is going to be quite a difficult term!'

Exciting news

After breakfast the following day, all of the new girls had to go and see Miss Grayling, the Head mistress. Fenella Thornton, the Head Girl, rounded them all up from the four towers and took them along to the Head's study.

There were six girls altogether, from various forms, most of them looking a little nervous as Fenella lead them to Miss Grayling's room. Olive, wearing her habitual sulky expression, walked a little way behind the rest, dragging her feet. She hadn't wanted to come to this stupid school in the first place, and she couldn't think that anything the Head mistress had to say would be of the slightest interest to her. Sylvia, on the other hand, was very eager to meet Miss Grayling, and felt quite certain that she would make a good impression on her.

She strode along confidently beside Fenella, and said brightly, 'I've heard that Miss Grayling is a wonderful person.'

'She is,' said Fenella. 'There is no one I would rather go to if I was in any kind of trouble, and –'

'Our headmistress at St Hilda's was just the same,' cut in Sylvia. 'So wise and kind.' Fenella, who was not accustomed to being interrupted when she spoke to a lower-form girl, looked rather taken aback. A sharp retort sprang to her lips, then she reminded herself that Sylvia was new and rather over-enthusiastic, so she held her tongue.

But even Sylvia was silent in the presence of Miss Grayling. The Head was a calm, dignified woman, with a rather serious face, which could, at times, break into the most beautiful smile. She could also be very stern indeed, when the need arose, and although Miss Grayling looked perfectly serene now, each of the new girls hoped fervently that they would never be called before her for misbehaviour!

Fenella left the room, and the Head spoke to each girl individually, asking her name and form. Even Olive found that she did not dare address Miss Grayling in her usual, surly manner, and answered politely. But she still looked rather miserable, and the Head stared at her hard. She knew far more about Olive Witherspoon than that young lady realised! Sylvia, for once, was quite subdued, and confined herself to answering the questions that Miss Grayling asked her, rather than chattering endlessly about herself.

Then the Head addressed the group as a whole, saying gravely, 'One day you will leave school, and go out into the world as young women. You should take with you a good understanding of many things, along with a willingness to accept responsibility and help others. I do not count as our successes those who have won scholarships and passed exams, though these are worthy achievements. I count as our successes those who learn to be good-hearted and kind, sensible and trustworthy – good, sound women the world can lean on.'

The six girls before Miss Grayling listened intently, her words making a great impression on them. Sylvia felt quite determined to become one of Malory Towers' successes.

Olive was quite certain that *she* would not be one. But Miss Grayling's words were so inspiring that, just for a moment, she wished that she could be.

By the time that the new girls joined the others, in the fourth-form class-room, all of the seats had been taken, apart from three, side-by-side, in the front row. Another new girl called Sarah, who was in East Tower, quickly slipped into the one nearest the window, leaving the two North Tower girls to take the others.

'I think that Sylvia and Olive are going to be thrown together quite a lot,' said Susan to Felicity, as the new girls slipped into the empty seats. 'They are the only two who don't have a special friend to pair up with.'

'Well, perhaps they will be good for one another,' said Felicity. 'In spite of her faults, Sylvia seems jolly and good-hearted, so perhaps some of that will rub off on to Olive.'

'Let's hope so,' said Susan. 'And, with a bit of luck, Olive might quieten Sylvia down a little.'

'Shh!' hissed Freddie, who was standing by the door. 'Miss Williams is coming!'

At once everyone stopped talking and stood up very

straight, while Freddie politely held the door open for the fourth-form mistress.

Miss Williams thanked her, and walked to the big desk at the front of the class. She was a scholarly woman, with a rather prim appearance and a gentle manner. But she also had a quiet air of authority, and certainly knew how to keep her class in order.

'Good morning, girls,' she said, smiling round.

'Good morning, Miss Williams,' chorused the girls.

'Please sit down. Now, before we get on with the business of making out timetables and handing out books, there are one or two things that I have to say to you.'

'I bet that she's going to announce who will be head of the form!' whispered Nora to Pam.

'Quiet please, Nora,' said Miss Williams, without raising her voice.

Heavens, thought Felicity, she must have awfully sharp ears, for Nora sat near the back of the class.

'First of all,' began the mistress, 'I am sure that you are all eager to know who is to be head-girl of the fourth form.'

Everyone sat up straight in their seats, and Miss Williams went on, 'I consulted Miss Potts and Miss Peters before making a decision, and, in the end, we all agreed that we would like to try Susan Blake.'

A cheer went up, and those nearest to Susan patted her on the back, while Felicity cried, 'Well done, old girl! You'll be first-rate, I just know it.'

Susan, who had turned quite pink with pleasure, could

hardly speak for a moment, then, at last, she said, 'Thank you, Miss Williams. You won't regret your decision, I promise you. I shall do my very best.'

'I am quite sure that you will,' said the mistress, smiling at the girl. 'And now, I have something else to tell you all. At the end of the term, the three top forms will be putting on a Christmas concert, which the parents will be coming to watch. The concert will last for approximately an hour and a half, so each form will have to fill half an hour. It is entirely up to you what you choose to do – sing carols, recite, or perform a short play. But I want every member of the form involved in some way, either as a performer, or behind the scenes.'

The fourth formers looked at one another, absolutely thrilled, as an excited murmur ran round the class. My word, what fun this was going to be! Each of the girls was absolutely determined that their contribution to the concert, whatever it was, would far outshine the fifth and sixth formers.

Miss Williams smiled at the girls' enthusiasm and went on, 'Susan, as head-girl, you will be in charge of the whole project, of course. And I am quite sure that you will have no shortage of willing helpers.'

There was no doubt about that! Half a dozen voices cried, 'We'll help you all right, Susan!'

Sylvia was just as excited and interested as the others. Why, at her old school she had produced a play and it had been a roaring success. If only Susan would hand over the reins and let her, Sylvia, produce the fourth's contribution to the Christmas concert, she would really be able to show the others what she could do!

Miss Williams rapped on the desk with a ruler and said, 'Well, I'm very pleased that you are all so eager. But we really must settle down and get on with more mundane matters. However, before we do so, I should just mention that we have a new English and Drama teacher this term. Her name is Miss Tallant, and she will be replacing Miss Hibbert for a little while. Miss Tallant will, of course, be happy to give you – and the other forms – any help that you require with your contribution to the concert.'

'Thank you, Miss Williams,' said Susan, whose head was in a perfect whirl. 'It's nice to know that there is someone we can call on if we need advice.'

The fourth formers crowded round Susan at break-time.

'I say, what a marvellous term this is going to be!'

'I simply can't wait to get started on our piece for the concert.'

'Yes, we'll show the fifth and sixth formers how it should be done, all right!'

'Well, we'd better have a meeting in the common-room, after prep this evening,' said Susan. 'Bring plenty of ideas with you, everyone, for we shall need them.'

'We'd better find out what the fifth and sixth formers intend to do as well,' said Felicity. 'I mean to say, it will be no use if all three forms decide to sing carols, or something. That will be terribly boring for the audience.'

'Yes, you're right,' said Susan. 'Well, I'll have to have a word with Fenella, and Katie Ellis, who is head of the fifth, then we can all make sure that we are doing different things.'

So, when the fourth formers gathered for their meeting that evening, Susan was armed with the necessary information.

The girls sat on the chairs and sofas, while Susan perched on the edge of a table, a notebook and pen in her hand. There was a good deal of excited chatter going on, and Susan clapped her hands together for silence.

'Well,' she began. 'I've found out that the fifth form are going to sing carols, and the sixth are planning to do a selection of Christmas readings.'

'Sounds a bit dry,' said Freddie, pulling a face.

'That's exactly what I thought,' said Susan, with a grin. 'Though, of course, I didn't say that to Katie and Fenella!'

'So, it looks as if it's up to us fourth formers to add a little fun to the proceedings,' said June, looking thoughtful.

'I say!' said Julie. 'Remember that splendid pantomime that Darrell, Alicia and the others put on when they were in the fifth? Wouldn't it be marvellous if we could do something like that?'

'We could never squeeze a whole pantomime into half an hour,' said Felicity.

'No, it would be impossible,' said Pam. 'Besides, super though their pantomime was, I don't think that any of us really want to copy Darrell and the others. It would be much better if we came up with a completely original idea.'

There were murmurs of agreement, and Nora piped up,

'How about a display of dancing? We could all dress up as fairies, and angels, and what-not, and . . .'

'And you could take centre-stage,' said Olive, with a sneer.

Nora turned bright red, stung by the injustice of this. She had made the suggestion because of her love of dancing, but she certainly wasn't the kind of person who wanted to steal the limelight all the time! Fortunately, the others knew her well enough to realise this, and Susan said coolly, 'Do you have any ideas about what we could do as our contribution to the concert, Olive?'

'No,' muttered Olive, sulkily.

'I thought as much. Well, if you don't have anything useful to say, kindly keep quiet.'

Then Susan turned to Nora and said, 'Thanks for the suggestion, but most of us can't dance as well as you can, so I really don't think it would work. We need something that we can all be involved in.'

'What about putting on a short play?' said Felicity. 'There are lots of scripts for plays in the library, so we could try and find one with a Christmassy theme.'

This sounded more like it, and the girls looked at one another excitedly.

'Marvellous idea!' cried June. 'And if we can find something that has a bit of humour in it, so much the better.'

Sylvia, who had been unusually silent, perked up at this and said, 'That sounds super! We put a play on at St Hilda's once, and it brought the house down. Of course, I produced it, and –'

'And I expect you wrote it yourself, too, didn't you?' said Freddie.

'Oh no, though I did add a few lines of my own,' said Sylvia, looking pleased at Freddie's apparent interest. 'You see –'

'I bet you designed all the costumes,' put in Bonnie.

'And painted the scenery yourself,' said Lucy.

'And probably took the leading role, too,' said Nora.

'Oh no, that would have been far too much work for just one person!' said the thick-skinned Sylvia, still completely unaware that the others were making fun of her. 'Naturally I supervised everything, for I think it's so important to have someone in charge who can organise things, and see that they go smoothly. And everything really did go like clockwork, if I do say so myself.'

'If she says that once more, I shall go mad,' muttered Amy savagely, while Susan went on smoothly, 'I do so agree with you, Sylvia. It's *very* important to have someone who can organise things at the helm. And, as Miss Williams has put me in charge, *I* am that someone. But that doesn't mean to say that I intend to go all bossy on you, and take over everything. This is going to be *our* play, and I will welcome any sensible suggestions, and listen to them.'

That was the right way to run things, thought Felicity. Susan was firm, yet not the slightest bit domineering, and she was determined that this was going to be a form effort.

'We really need to decide on a play as quickly as possible,' said Pam. 'We can't start casting parts, or deciding who is going to do what, until that has been sorted out.'

'Right,' said Susan. 'So, what I suggest is that as many of us as possible go along to the library over the next few days, and read through some of the scripts that are stored there. If anyone finds anything that they think might be suitable, please bring it to me. Then we'll hold another meeting in here on Saturday, and make a decision.'

'Good show!' someone called out, and Susan grinned.

'That's just what I hope it will be,' she said. 'A good show. The best show that Malory Towers has ever seen!'

The new mistress

Soon the old girls felt as if they had been back at school for weeks, not just days. Sylvia, too, settled down in her own way, though she often irritated the others with her never-ending chatter, and the way she always tried to take the lead.

This was particularly galling to Felicity, Susan and June, who had always been the leaders of their form, and the three of them often found it necessary to put Sylvia in her place.

'I thought that June was going to explode yesterday, when Sylvia took it upon herself to show her the best way to hold her lacrosse stick,' said Felicity, smiling, as she remembered.

Susan grinned too, and said, 'She *will* explode, one day, if Sylvia keeps it up. And I can't honestly say that I blame her! Sylvia is such an expert on everything – even things she's not very good at, like lacrosse.'

'It's difficult to dislike her wholeheartedly, though,' said Felicity, looking thoughtful. 'She's annoying, but she doesn't have any mean, petty faults.'

'Unlike dear Olive,' said Susan, with a sigh. 'Who has so many mean, petty faults that it is quite impossible to like her!'

'I really don't think I've ever met anyone so unfriendly in my life,' Felicity said. 'I tried to start a friendly conversation with her in the dorm yesterday morning, just to see if I could get through to her, and almost got my head bitten off!'

Felicity had seen the girl putting a photograph on her bedside cabinet, and went over to take a look. It was a picture of Olive, with a man and woman, whom Felicity took to be her parents. Her mother and father were smiling happily, but Olive's mouth was set in its usual, sullen droop.

'Are these your parents?' asked Felicity, pleasantly.

'That's my father,' Olive answered flatly. 'And my stepmother.'

As Felicity leaned forward to take a closer look, she noticed something odd about the photograph. Mr Witherspoon had his right arm out at an odd angle, as if he had it around someone's shoulders. But there was no one on his right side at all. In fact, the edge of the photograph was jagged, as if a piece had been torn off.

'There's someone missing,' said Felicity, mildly curious. And Olive's temper had flared up at once.

'No, there isn't!' she had cried. 'I tore part of the photograph off so that I could fit it into the frame, that's all. Not that it has anything to do with you – interfering little busybody!' With that, Olive had snatched up the photograph and flung it into her bedside cabinet, slamming the door shut.

'I wish I had never been sent to this beastly school!' she

raged, angry tears starting to her eyes. 'I knew exactly how it would be, with everyone poking their noses into my private business!'

Felicity was quite flabbergasted, of course. She hadn't meant to pry at all, and had only been making polite conversation. Just as she was on the verge of giving the new girl a thorough dressing-down for her rudeness, Felicity received some unexpected support.

'Pooh!' said a small, lisping voice. 'Who on earth is interested in *your* business, Olive?'

It was Bonnie, of course, her little nose wrinkled in disdain, as she went on, 'I think that you are quite the rudest girl I have ever met.'

Olive had turned on Bonnie, saying scornfully, 'Do you think I care what people like *you* think of me? Why, you're nothing but a silly, babyish little doll!'

'*Doll?*' Bonnie had squeaked. '*Doll?* How dare you! Do you know, Olive, I'm beginning to think that Amy was right, and you are jealous! I can't think of any other reason why you dislike me so much.'

And Bonnie had flounced off, while Felicity said to Olive, 'I'd be careful, if I were you. Bonnie is nowhere near as silly as you seem to imagine, and she can be a dangerous enemy. Watch out, Olive!'

But Olive had merely shrugged, so Felicity had left her to it, thinking that it was just impossible to help some people.

'Yes, she's a strange one, all right,' said Susan now. 'And I, for one, am quite tired of her and her unpleasant ways.'

'Let's not waste any more time talking about her, then,' said Felicity, slipping her arm through Susan's. 'We have our first Drama lesson with the new mistress shortly. That should be interesting.'

As it turned out, it was a *very* interesting lesson indeed!

Bonnie held the door open for Miss Tallant, as she entered the class-room, and gave the mistress one of her sweet smiles. Miss Tallant smiled back, and went to the front of the class, her dark, dramatic eyes sweeping round.

The girls eyed her just as keenly, for they had never seen a teacher quite like Miss Tallant before. Most of the mistresses at Malory Towers dressed neatly and sensibly, in quite plain clothes. The new mistress, though, was wearing a flowing, brightly patterned skirt and a very fussy blouse, with lots of frills. She also wore big, dangling earrings, which swung to and fro every time she moved her head, and Pam murmured to Nora, 'Heavens! She looks as if she has a couple of dinner gongs hanging from her ears!'

Nora gave one of her explosive snorts of laughter, and Miss Tallant turned her head.

'Do you find something amusing?' she asked softly, a smile on her face.

'N-no, Miss Tallant,' stammered Nora, looking rather apprehensive now. 'I'm sorry, I didn't mean –'

'Stand up when you address me,' said the mistress, still in the same calm voice, and still smiling.

Very red now, Nora got to her feet, and Miss Tallant asked, 'What is your name?'

'Nora Woods, Miss Tallant,' answered poor Nora.

The mistress's smile grew wider, and she said, 'Well, Nora Woods, it might interest you to know that I don't stand for any nonsense in my classes. Come and see me after the lesson, and I will think of a suitable punishment for you. Sit down.'

A gasp ran round the class as Miss Tallant turned to face the blackboard, and a great many sympathetic glances were sent in Nora's direction. But nobody dared to speak to the girl, for fear that they would be punished too.

The mistress turned to Bonnie, her ridiculously large earrings swinging, and she asked, 'What is your name, my dear?'

'Bonnie Meadows, Miss Tallant,' lisped Bonnie, her wide gaze fixed admiringly on the mistress.

'Bonnie, please hand these round to everyone,' said Miss Tallant, indicating a pile of books on her desk. 'As quickly as you can, there's a good girl.'

Nimbly, Bonnie skipped round the room, handing a book to each girl, before returning to her seat.

'Thank you,' said Miss Tallant, smiling at her with approval. 'Now, girls, we are going to begin reading a play. You will all take it in turns to read, until I tell you to stop. I really want to see you get into character as you read each part, so that I know what you can do. Bonnie, dear, you go first.'

The play was an extremely dramatic historical one, and normally the fourth formers would have enjoyed reading it enormously. But they could not forgive the new mistress for her harsh treatment of Nora, who was an extremely popular member of the form, and – with the exception of Bonnie, who seemed determined to impress Miss Tallant – they read their parts as sullenly as they dared. After a particularly poor show from Pam, who had read her part in an expressionless monotone, Miss Tallant shook her head, and sighed. 'Dear me! Bonnie seems to be the only member of the form with any dramatic flair at all. It is your turn next.' The mistress pointed at June. 'And for goodness' sake, do try and put a little *expression* into it.'

The corners of June's mouth twitched humorously. So, Miss Tallant wanted her to be expressive, did she? Well, she would give the drama teacher just what she had asked for.

'Do you mind if I stand up, Miss Tallant?' the girl asked politely. 'I feel that I will be able to throw myself into the part more.'

'Very well,' said the mistress. 'But do hurry up, for there are only ten minutes of the lesson left.'

Winking at Freddie, June got to her feet – then what a surprise the class, and Miss Tallant, had. For June really *did* throw herself into the part of the dashing young hero! Putting on a deep, booming voice, she read the lines loudly – so loudly that Mam'zelle Rougier, who was taking a class in the room next door, wondered who on earth could be speaking. The only male teacher in the school was Mr Young, the music master, and that, most certainly, wasn't his voice!

Enjoying herself hugely, June began to add some actions to her performance – clutching at her brow, throwing her arms out, and even, during one particularly moving moment in her speech, falling to her knees.

Miss Tallant stared at her in astonishment, wondering if the girl really meant to be taken seriously, or if she was playing the fool. The fourth formers, of course, were in no doubt at all, feeling laughter bubble up inside them, though they did their best to hide it. It was fortunate for Nora that June's voice completely drowned out her sudden snort of laughter, or she would probably have been given a second punishment!

'June . . .' began Miss Tallant, in her low, calm voice. But it was no use, for June pretended not to hear, and simply carried on with her impassioned speech.

'June!' said the mistress, speaking a little more loudly. 'I really think . . .'

But, to the amusement of the others, the girl ignored Miss Tallant, almost smacking poor Freddie in the face as she flung her arm back, in a dramatic gesture.

'Here, watch out, June!' cried a startled Freddie, moving her chair back a little, while the others were now quite unable to control their mirth.

Felicity and Susan were holding their sides, while tears slid down Pam's cheeks. Nora had stuffed a hanky into her mouth to stifle her giggles, and even the miserable Olive had a smile on her face. Only Sylvia, who did not have much of a sense of humour, did not seem to understand that June was fooling, and looked puzzled rather than amused.

Miss Tallant, however, noticed none of this, for her attention was all on June. Really, the girl was quite dreadful! And it seemed as if she would go on and on, right through the morning break and into the next lesson! Miss Tallant pursed her lips. She hated to raise her voice, or appear that she was losing control in front of her class, but it seemed as if she would have to!

'JUNE!' shouted the mistress and, at last, June stopped, looking round the class as if she had just woken from a dream.

'So sorry, Miss Tallant,' she said. 'I tend to get rather carried away when I'm acting a part. Perhaps next time I can show you how I would tackle a humorous role.'

'Thank you, June,' said the mistress rather frostily. 'I think that you have now given us a quite adequate display of your – er – talents.'

Just then the bell sounded to signal the end of the lesson, and the girls waited expectantly for Miss Tallant to tell them that they could leave. The mistress looked round the class, her eyes going from one girl to another. At last, she said, 'Well, if this form is an example of the standard at Malory Towers, I can see that I am going to have my work cut out. What Miss Hibbert taught you, I simply don't know.'

Of course, this little speech did nothing at all to endear the new teacher to the girls. Not only had she insulted their beloved Malory Towers, but she had found fault with Miss Hibbert. The fourth formers felt what little respect they had for Miss Tallant waning, for they knew that there was a strict rule among the staff that they did not speak against one another in front of the girls.

'Dreadful woman,' said Pam, as the fourth form went

to the cloakroom to fetch their coats. 'I wonder what she has in store for poor old Nora?'

Nora was not with the others, for, of course, she had had to stay behind to learn what her punishment would be. Sylvia was not there either, for she had gone to speak to Matron about something.

'Well, perhaps it will be a lesson to Nora,' said Olive, rather smugly. 'It will do her good to learn that there is one of the mistresses who won't let her get away with anything!'

'Don't tell me that you're a fan of our spiteful Miss Tallant, Olive?' said Susan, looking at the girl rather hard.

'Of course not,' said Olive hastily, turning a little red. 'I'm just pleased that she can see through Nora, that's all.'

'You keep that nasty tongue of yours still,' said Pam, angrily, giving the girl a little push. It was most unusual for the placid, good-natured Pam to lose her temper, but Nora was her best friend and the girl already felt annoyed with Miss Tallant for picking on her, without this spiteful new girl saying beastly things about her as well.

Seeing that Pam was really upset, Felicity gave her arm a squeeze, saying, 'We'll all back Nora up against Miss Tallant, Pam, you know that. And against anyone else who is mean to her as well.'

This last remark was obviously meant for Olive, who scowled at Felicity, before putting on her coat and going outside.

'Mean beast!' said Bonnie, pulling a face, as the door shut behind the new girl. 'What a lot of spite we are going to have to deal with this term, what with Olive *and* that horrid Miss Tallant.'

'Well, you're a fine one to talk!' said June, quite astonished. 'You were sucking up to Miss Tallant no end.'

'Of course I was,' replied Bonnie, calmly. 'Someone has to.'

'Whatever do you mean, Bonnie?' asked Susan.

'People like Miss Tallant always have to have a favourite,' explained Bonnie. And everyone listened intently. Bonnie might be silly in some ways, but she was surprisingly shrewd, and very good at sizing people up.

'She is the kind of person who needs to have someone who thinks that she is wonderful, and will stick up for her. So, I thought that it might as well be me. It might be useful to us, if she thinks that she has someone on her side.'

'Sort of like a spy in the enemy camp, you mean?' said Felicity.

'Exactly!' said Bonnie.

'I think that's a very good idea,' said Freddie, who had been listening thoughtfully. 'I really do. And Bonnie is certainly the right person to carry it off.'

The others murmured their agreement. With her charming manner, innocent air and sweet smile, Bonnie found it quite easy to get people to confide in her. Often far more than they intended to!

'We had better keep this a secret from Olive,' said Felicity. 'I don't trust her, and she might go running to Miss Tallant and tell her the plan, just to stir up trouble for Bonnie.'

'Perhaps we had better not let Sylvia in on it either,' Julie said. 'She *seems* decent enough, but we don't really know her very well.'

'We know that she can't keep her mouth shut!' said Amy, with a haughty toss of her head. 'I don't know which of the two new girls I dislike more – Olive, or that awful Sylvia.'

'Oh, come off your high horse, Amy,' said Lucy. 'Sylvia might be annoying in a lot of ways, but I don't think she's a bad sort.'

'Neither do I, but perhaps we had better not tell her any secrets just yet, just to be on the safe side,' said Susan. 'She's such a chatterbox that she might let something slip out without meaning to.'

The others agreed, and just then the door opened. Nora came into the cloakroom, a very woebegone expression on her face.

'Fifty lines!' she groaned, sinking down on to one of the wooden benches. 'Just for laughing! Honestly, girls, I'm beginning to think that I'm jinxed this term! First Olive takes a dislike to me, and now Miss Tallant. Am I really so horrible?'

The fourth formers crowded round Nora at once, anxious to reassure her.

'It certainly isn't you who is at fault!' cried Julie. 'Miss Tallant is quite the most unpleasant grown-up that I have ever met, while Olive seems to dislike *everyone*! Though, I must say, you and Bonnie do seem to get under her skin more than the rest of us. I can't think why!'

'I told you – it's because she's jealous,' put in Amy. 'She's so unattractive herself that anyone who is pretty simply makes her *green* with envy.'

June gave a crow of laughter. 'Olive-green!' she cried. 'That's a jolly good nickname for her. Next time she makes one of her spiteful remarks about Nora, or Bonnie, or anyone else for that matter, that's what we'll call her!'

The others approved wholeheartedly of this, and even Nora managed a smile. She cheered up even more when the girls told her about Bonnie's plan to suck up to the new mistress.

'I just hope that it pays off,' she said.

'Well, one thing I am absolutely determined about is that we shan't be asking Miss Tallant to help us with our play, or give us any advice at all,' said Susan firmly. 'I don't want her taking any of the credit for our hard work – we shall do it all by ourselves, and we shan't tell her anything about it at all!'

'Hear, hear!' cried the others, and Lucy asked, 'When are we going to have our next meeting, Susan? We're all simply dying to get started.'

'Well, I've looked at a few scripts, and there is one in particular that I think might be just right for us,' said Susan. 'Let's meet in the common-room on Saturday afternoon, and we can make a decision.'

'Good idea,' said Felicity. 'Now, come along, every-one, let's go out and get some fresh air, or our break will be over.'

'I'm looking forward to starting rehearsals for our play,

aren't you?' said June to Freddie, as the two of them followed the others outside.

'Yes, and that's not all I'm looking forward to,' said June, a wicked expression on her face.

Freddie knew that expression well, and, with a grin, she asked, 'What mischief are you plotting now?'

'Well, Freddie, I was just thinking that this is the last term where we will really be able to let ourselves go and have fun at Malory Towers,' answered June. 'Next term we will all have to knuckle down and study for School Cert. And, once we go up into the fifth form, things like tricks and midnight feasts will be out of the question. We shall have to go all serious and dignified, and set a good example to the lower forms.'

'Golly, so we shall!' said Freddie, much struck.

'And that is why I intend to have as much fun as possible *this* term,' said June. 'Are you with me, Freddie?'

'I should say!' said Freddie, her eyes alight with laughter. 'June, it's your birthday in November, isn't it? Wouldn't it be marvellous to celebrate it with a midnight feast?' Then she frowned. 'As long as Susan agrees to it, of course.'

'She will,' said June, confidently. 'Susan might be a bit goody-goody at times, but she's a sport.'

'And just think of the tricks that we can play on Mam'zelle Dupont!' breathed Freddie, looking quite ecstatic.

June laughed, and said, 'Oh, I have quite a few tricks up my sleeve. And Mam'zelle isn't the only one who is going to be on the receiving end! I think that both of our new girls need taking down a peg or two. And as for that beastly Miss Tallant – well, she had better be jolly careful. We're going to have to think up something very special for her.'

'We will,' vowed Freddie. 'She's going to be really sorry that she was so mean to Nora. The Malory Towers mischief makers are out for revenge!'

Olive is annoying

Of course, it wasn't long before Miss Tallant discovered that June's dramatic performance in her class had been a joke – and she felt extremely angry about it. It was Miss Potts, the stern head of North Tower, who set the new mistress straight. The two were in the mistresses' common-room together when Mam'zelle Rougier walked in and cried, 'Miss Tallant! Was there a man in your class this morning?'

'A man?' repeated Miss Tallant, puzzled. 'Of course not, Mam'zelle Rougier. I was taking the fourth form for drama this morning, and there was certainly no man present.'

'But yes, I heard him,' said Mam'zelle Rougier. 'His voice, it was deep and booming, and he talked, and talked, and . . .'

'Ah, that was June,' said Miss Tallant, her brow clearing. 'She was reading the part of the hero, in the play that we are learning. She gave a most extraordinary performance, flinging herself around all over the place and over-acting like nobody's business! It's quite obvious that she considers herself a very talented actress, but I am afraid that she is nothing of the kind! Why, even her friends were laughing at her! June didn't seem to notice, though, and just kept on going. She didn't strike me as terribly bright, I must say!'

Miss Potts looked up sharply from the work she was marking, and said drily, 'I am afraid that you have been taken in. June is very bright indeed, but unfortunately she chooses to use her good brains to amuse the others, rather than on her work. Watch out for her, Miss Tallant, for now that June has succeeded in duping you once, she will certainly try to do so again.'

'Ah yes, she is a bad girl, that June,' said Mam'zelle Rougier, shaking her head. 'A *very* bad girl. When I think of the tricks that she has played on poor, foolish Mam'zelle Dupont! Of course, *I* am not so easy to fool, and June knows that she would be punished most harshly if she tried any of her tricks on me! But you, Miss Tallant, you are young, and not so experienced in the ways of girls as Miss Potts and myself. Be on your guard, for if June thinks that you are weak, she will certainly take advantage of you, and try to make you look stupid – just as she does with Mam'zelle Dupont!'

The new mistress turned scarlet with humiliation. So, that wretched June had duped her! Well, she would very soon come to regret it! As for Mam'zelle Rougier – how dare she couple her, Miss Tallant, with the weak and silly Mam'zelle Dupont?

'I can assure you that June won't find it so easy to take me in again,' said the mistress rather stiffly. 'Nor will any of the others. I fully intend to nip such silliness in the bud.'

Fortunately, the fourth formers were quite unaware of

Miss Tallant's plans as they gathered in the common-room on Saturday to discuss their contribution to the Christmas concert. Once again, Susan was in charge of the meeting, and she sat at the table in the common-room, with a small pile of scripts in front of her.

The fourth formers from the other towers were there too, as it was to be a joint effort, and the common-room seemed very crowded indeed, with girls perched on top of cabinets and on the arms of chairs. Susan began, 'There are several good plays here, but this is the one that I think would be the best, for it is very short and gives us plenty of scope to add a few touches of our own. Felicity has read it as well, and she agrees with me. The play is called *The Christmas Tree Fairy*, and I'd like to read it out to you all now, and see what you think.'

And, in her low, clear voice, Susan began to read the play. The story was quite a simple one, about a fairy doll who has been abandoned in a dusty attic, along with lots of other old toys, and is rescued by a lonely little girl.

'I like it,' said Pam decidedly, as Susan finished her reading. 'It really captures the spirit of Christmas somehow.'

'And I love it when the toys come to life, when there's no one around!' squeaked Bonnie excitedly.

'We won't have to worry about shifting scenery either,' said Felicity. 'For the whole thing takes place in the attic.'

'Yes, but it's far too short,' complained Mary from South Tower. 'It certainly won't fill half an hour.'

'It will by the time we've finished with it,' said Susan.

'We can add a few jokes, and perhaps a song and dance routine. I think it'll be super.'

'Good idea,' said Mary. 'But who is going to write the song?'

'How about you, Mary?' suggested Felicity. 'You're excellent at music.'

'Good idea!' said Susan. 'That's settled, Mary. You are our official songwriter.'

'Oh, my word!' cried Mary, a comical expression of dismay on her face. 'What *have* I let myself in for?'

The others laughed, and Mary's friend Doreen clapped her on the shoulder, crying, 'Don't make a song and dance about it, old girl! I'll help you out.'

'June and Freddie, I have a job for you two as well,' said Susan.

'Us?' chorused the two girls, looking very surprised. 'What do you want us to do, Susan?'

'I want you to take the script away and add a few jokes here and there,' said Susan. 'It's quite a sentimental play, and I think it needs a touch of humour. And who better than the two form jokers to add one!'

Everyone cheered at this, and June and Freddie grinned, both of them absolutely delighted with the task they had been given.

'I'm going to produce the play, with Felicity as my assistant,' said Susan. 'And, of course we will –'

But Susan got no further, for Sylvia called out, 'Susan! If you need anyone else to help produce the play, I am only too keen to help. As you know, I've done this kind of thing before, and you know what they say about many hands making light work.'

'Yes, and I know what they say about too many cooks spoiling the broth,' muttered Susan under her breath to Felicity.

But Felicity was rather touched by the earnest, eager-to-please expression on Sylvia's round, rosy face and she said in a low voice, 'It seems a shame to discourage her when she's so willing. And, who knows, she might prove very useful indeed. Perhaps we should give Sylvia a chance to show what she can do.'

Susan didn't look entirely convinced, but she said, 'Perhaps you're right. But if she becomes too bossy I simply won't stand for it!' Then she raised her voice and said, 'Thank you, Sylvia. A third producer might come in very handy. Now, everyone, I'm going to ask if we can use the big hall for our next meeting, for it really is dreadfully cramped in here. Then we will cast the parts, and decide who is going to help backstage and so on. Any questions?'

There were no questions, but, after the girls from the other three towers had left, there was a good deal of excited chatter. Nora was hoping that she would be considered for the role of the fairy, and said to Pam, 'I do hope that Susan will let me try out for it.'

'Of course she will,' said the loyal Pam, at once. 'You're a marvellous actress, and you can dance beautifully. In fact, I can't think of anyone who could play the fairy as well as you could.'

But someone else was quite certain that *she* was destined to play the role of the fairy – and that someone was Bonnie. 'I have a fairy costume at home that I wore to a fancy-dress party once,' she told Amy, breathlessly. 'I must ask Mother to send it to me.'

'You would certainly make a lovely fairy,' said Amy, looking the pretty, dainty girl over with approval. 'I don't think any other girl in the form would fit the role as perfectly as you.'

Bonnie beamed with pleasure and said, 'Will you be trying out for any of the parts, Amy?'

'No, I don't want to push myself forward,' answered Amy rather piously. 'Let the others have a chance.'

The truth was that Amy wasn't particularly good at drama, dancing or singing, and she was well aware that she didn't stand a chance of getting one of the lead parts. And as she wasn't going to be centre stage, the girl would have preferred not to be involved in the project at all. But this was a vain hope, for Susan wanted everyone to play a part in the success of the form's play, however small.

'Though I can't imagine what we are going to find for Olive to do,' she said to Felicity, as the fourth formers got ready for bed that evening. 'The only talent she seems to have is for rubbing people up the wrong way!'

Felicity laughed and said, 'Well, if all she's going to do is stir things up and cause ill feeling, perhaps it would be best just to leave her out altogether.'

But Susan wouldn't hear of this, and she said stubbornly, 'No, Olive is a member of our form, whether she likes it or not. And she is jolly well going to take part in our play!'

'I wonder why she is so bad-tempered and angry all the time?' said Felicity, with a frown. 'I do hope that she settles down and cheers up a bit, for the sight of her miserable, scowling face puts a damper on everything!'

But, as Pam remarked a few days later, Olive only seemed happy if someone else was getting into trouble.

'She's so spiteful and mean-spirited,' said Pam, with distaste, as the fourth formers got changed after lacrosse practice. 'Did you see the smirk on her face when Miss Maxwell ticked Amy off for not trying hard enough?'

'And she nearly laughed herself sick when June got Mam'zelle Dupont to use that trick pencil in French this morning,' said Nora.

'Well, we *all* laughed at that,' pointed out Julie. 'That was the whole idea, after all!'

'Yes, but Olive wasn't laughing at the joke,' said Nora. 'She was gloating over the tremendous scolding that June got from Mam'zelle afterwards.'

'Good!' said Bonnie, with satisfaction. Then, as the others turned to look at her in surprise, she went on, 'Because June will have it in for Olive, and will get her own back on her. And I, for one, am looking forward to it!'

As Bonnie flounced off with Amy, Susan gave a sigh and said, 'I do so hate all this spite and bad feeling that seems to be brewing.'

'Horrible, isn't it?' agreed Felicity. 'Though I must say, Olive has rather brought it on herself. Petty spite is one of the hardest faults to forgive, and it always stirs up more spite in return.'

'Yes, you're quite right,' said Susan. 'And I think that Bonnie was right, too, when she said that June will try to get her own back on Olive. I say, where *is* June?'

'She and Freddie got changed in a trice, and dashed off somewhere,' said Lucy. 'I wouldn't be a bit surprised if they're plotting revenge on Olive right this very minute.'

'You know, Susan, as head of the form, I really think that it's your duty to speak to Olive about her behaviour,' said Sylvia, an earnest expression on her face.

Susan was rather taken aback, and not at all pleased at this unwanted piece of advice from the new girl. Felicity, too, felt annoyed, and she said, 'Really, Sylvia, I don't think that it's your place –'

But Sylvia didn't even realise that Felicity was speaking, and went on, in her rather loud voice, 'We had a girl just like Olive at my old school. Of course, as head-girl, I had to reprimand her pretty severely. It did the trick, though, if I do say so myself.' She smiled at Susan and said sympathetically, 'There is such a lot to learn when one first becomes head-girl, isn't there? Especially if one has never held a position of responsibility before. But I am always on hand to give help and advice, Susan.'

And, leaving the fourth formers staring after her, open-mouthed, Sylvia put on her coat and went out of the changing room.

Felicity made an explosive little sound of irritation as the door closed behind the new girl, while Susan scoffed,

'As if I would ask Sylvia for advice about anything! If I needed anyone to help me, I would ask you, Felicity, or Pam. You have both had a turn as head-girl, and I'll bet you both made a better job of it than Say-So Sylvia!'

A shout of laughter went up at this, and Nora cried, 'What a marvellous nickname – Say-So Sylvia!'

'I suppose it *is* rather a good nickname,' said Susan, with a pleased grin, and the others chorused, 'IF YOU DO SAY SO YOURSELF!'

June and Freddie, meanwhile, were indeed plotting revenge on Olive. They were up in the dormitory, looking through June's box of tricks, the pair of them chuckling as they recalled jokes that they had played in the past.

'Do you remember the time that Mam'zelle used that soap, which made her face look as if it was streaked with dirt?' laughed Freddie. 'I say! I don't suppose you have any more of it, do you June? That would be a super trick to play on Olive.'

'No, I lent it to my brother, Peter, in the holidays,' answered June, before lapsing into a thoughtful silence. Olive's unpleasant habit of gloating over those who got into trouble rankled with her. Perhaps the girl would think twice about doing it again if *she* was on the receiving end of a scold from one of the mistresses!

June said as much to Freddie, who agreed heartily. 'It would certainly serve her right,' she said. 'I say, can't we think of something to do in Miss Tallant's class tomorrow?

There must be a way that we can get her to lose her temper with Olive.'

June clicked her fingers suddenly. 'I think that there is,' she said, grinning. 'Have you noticed how frightened Olive is of the mice in the biology room?'

'I know that she always sits as far away from their cage as possible,' said Freddie. 'And she jumps every time one of them moves. What have you got in mind, June?'

'Well,' said June, her eyes glinting wickedly. 'Just suppose that one of those mice found its way into Olive's desk. My word, wouldn't she squeal!'

'June!' gasped Freddie. 'It would be a marvellous trick to play, but dare we?'

June, who was bold enough for anything, said at once, 'Of course we dare. Miss Tallant's lesson is right after break, so we can slip along to the biology room at break-time, get one of the mice out and put it into Olive's desk.'

'Poor little mouse,' giggled Freddie. 'Fancy having to face the wrath of Olive! I say, June, he will be able to breathe inside the desk, won't he?'

'Of course,' answered June. 'He won't be in there for long, and I shall return him to his cage as soon as I can.'

'Shall we tell the others?' asked Freddie.

'Yes, let's,' said June. 'But we had better do it when Sylvia is not about. I don't think that they went in much for jokes and tricks at her old school, for, in spite of her jolly, hearty attitude, she doesn't have much of a sense of humour. And we certainly don't want her warning Olive of what's in store for her!'

Freddie nodded and said, 'You're absolutely right about Sylvia. I told her one of my best jokes the other day, and when I had finished she simply looked puzzled. It was quite obvious that she didn't understand it at all. A waste of a perfectly good joke, I thought!'

'Well, when Sylvia has been in the fourth form for a while, perhaps her sense of humour will come to the fore,' said June.

'I don't see how it can fail to,' said Freddie. 'Not once Sylvia realises what fun it is to play tricks and share jokes. That's one of the good things about laughter – it's infectious!'

'Well, one person certainly won't be laughing tomorrow,' said June, with a touch of malice. 'And that will be dear Olive!'

A very successful trick

The fourth formers were in a great state of excitement as they went into Miss Tallant's class the next morning. Everyone but Sylvia – and Olive herself, of course – knew about the trick, and Olive looked puzzled as a few sly glances came her way.

All the mice in the biology room were quite tame, and the one that June had picked up didn't seem to mind being handled at all. He liked it in Olive's desk as well, for there was plenty of room to run around, and lots of interesting things for him to sniff at. 'Quiet, everyone!' hissed Felicity, who was standing by the door. 'Miss Tallant is coming.'

The girls stood up politely as the mistress swept into the room. As usual, she was wearing one of the fussy, frilly blouses that she was so fond of, and a pair of earrings with enormous pink stones in them hung from her ears.

Bonnie, playing up to Miss Tallant for all she was worth, said admiringly, 'Oh, what a lovely blouse, Miss Tallant! You do look so pretty.'

'Why, thank you, Bonnie,' said the mistress, preening a little, while the fourth formers grinned at one another. 'Good morning, girls. Sit down, and we will continue with the play that we began reading the other day. Get your books out, please.'

The fourth formers watched with bated breath as Olive lifted the lid of her desk. But the little white mouse was hiding behind her pencil case, and the girl closed the lid again, without even realising that he was there.

'Never mind,' whispered June to Freddie, Felicity and Susan. 'Olive will have to open her desk again later to put the book away. She's certain to spot the mouse then.'

But the mouse had ideas of his own, and had no intention of waiting until the end of the lesson to make his appearance!

After about ten minutes, he grew rather bored with his new surroundings, and, feeling lonely, decided that he would like to go back to his friends. But how was he to get out? The mouse scuttled into a corner, the sound he made startling Olive very much indeed. What on earth could it be, she wondered? It seemed to be coming from underneath her ink-well. Cautiously, Olive removed the ink-well from its hole in the lid of the desk and the mouse, seeing daylight, stuck his head up through the hole.

Olive's expression of terror was quite comical. For a second she could only sit there, frozen in horror, then she let out a blood-curdling scream, jumping up so hastily that she knocked her chair over.

Miss Tallant, who had been listening intently as Lucy read out part of the play, jumped violently and cried, 'Olive! How dare you disturb the class in this way? Whatever is the matter with you?'

Her eyes wide with horror and her hand trembling, Olive pointed at her desk and stammered, 'A m-mouse! In my d-desk!'

The little mouse had been quite as frightened of Olive as she had been of him, particularly when she screamed so loudly, and he had swiftly retreated back through the hole, into the safety of the desk. He moved so quickly that even Sylvia, who sat next to Olive and turned her head sharply as the girl screamed, hadn't spotted him.

As for Miss Tallant, she didn't quite know what to think. On the one hand, she sincerely hoped that there wasn't a mouse in the desk, for she didn't like them any better than Olive did. But if, on the other hand, there was no mouse, that would mean that Olive was playing a trick, for no other purpose than to disrupt the class.

June, seeing the uncertainty on the mistress's face, was quick to take advantage of it.

'I'll take a look, if you like, Miss Tallant,' she offered, standing up. 'I'm not afraid of mice, and if there is one in Olive's desk I shall be able to remove it.'

The mistress had made up her mind that she didn't like June at all, after learning that her peculiar performance in class the other day had been a joke, but she felt extremely grateful to her now, and said in a relieved tone, 'Thank you, June. Please do so at once.'

June strode up to Olive's desk, saying, 'Better stand aside, Olive, just in case he makes a dash for it. You don't want him running up your leg.'

Olive certainly didn't want that, and she hastily stepped

into the aisle, moving towards the back of the room. June opened the desk, and immediately spotted the poor little mouse, cowering in a corner. Standing with her back to Olive, so that the girl couldn't see what she was doing, she swiftly picked up the tiny creature, slipping it into the deep pocket of her skirt. If only he didn't poke his head out and give the game away! But the mouse, quite worn out by his adventure, rather liked the warmth and softness of June's pocket and decided to settle down there for a nap!

Some of the others had seen what June had done, though, and were now struggling to contain their laughter! This became extremely difficult for them when the wicked June began rummaging violently in Olive's desk for the mouse, scattering books, pencils and all kinds of belongings over the floor. At last she straightened up and, facing Miss Tallant, said solemnly, 'There is most definitely no mouse in Olive's desk.'

'There is!' cried Olive. 'I saw it, I tell you.'

Miss Tallant, feeling bolder now that June had assured her there was no mouse, moved towards Olive's desk and peered in. Of course, there was nothing to be seen, and Miss Tallant pursed her lips, turning to Olive.

'Pick up your belongings from the floor at once,' she said coldly. 'And put them back in your desk.'

The mistress looked and sounded so angry that Olive didn't dare to argue. But as the girl turned away, her eye caught June's and she saw the glint of malice there. Suddenly she realised the truth. June was responsible for the mouse being in her desk. And June must have removed it. But where was the creature now? Olive's eyes fell on the suspicious-looking bulge in June's pocket, and she thought that she saw a slight movement. So that was it, she thought, her eyes narrowing. June had somehow managed to slip the mouse into her pocket. Olive opened her mouth to tell Miss Tallant what had happened, but June hissed, under her breath, 'If you sneak it will be the worse for you.'

She sounded so menacing that Olive felt quite alarmed. Sneaks were not looked upon favourably at any school, she knew that. And there was no point in making her life at Malory Towers any more difficult than it already was. So Olive shut her mouth, said nothing and turned to the task of putting her things back in her desk.

June, meanwhile, went back to her place, winking at the others, who grinned back at her. 'Olive!' snapped Miss Tallant. 'Come and see me when you have finished your lunch.'

'Yes, Miss Tallant,' said Olive bleakly. What a beastly school this was!

'That was simply marvellous, June,' laughed Felicity, as the fourth formers made their way down the corridor after the lesson.

'Yes, and now I had better get this little fellow back to his home,' said June, taking the mouse from her pocket and stroking him with one finger. 'Unless, of course, you want to do it, Olive?'

Olive scowled, then, as June held the mouse out towards her, gave a squeal and ran off down the corridor, the laughter of the fourth formers following her.

'Serves her jolly well right!' said Nora. 'Let's hope that she will think twice before laughing when one of us gets scolded now!'

Sylvia, who had watched in amazement as June produced the mouse from her pocket, said now, 'So there was a mouse, after all! But why did June pretend that she couldn't find it? I don't understand.'

'It was a trick, Sylvia,' explained Pam patiently. 'To pay Olive back for all the times she has crowed over other people when they have got into trouble.'

'Oh,' said Sylvia rather blankly. 'I do hope that June is going to own up to Miss Tallant.'

'Of course she's not, idiot,' said Freddie scornfully. 'The whole idea was to teach Olive a lesson. And that is exactly what we have done!'

'It seems rather mean to me,' said Sylvia, with a frown. 'I really think . . .'

'Sylvia, if you're thinking of sneaking to Miss Tallant, don't!' Susan warned her. 'Because we don't take kindly to sneaks at Malory Towers, and if you aren't careful you might find that *you* become just as unpopular as Olive!'

'I wouldn't dream of sneaking,' said Sylvia stiffly, her rosy complexion turning even redder. 'I just think that June ought to be persuaded to own up. If I were head-girl –'

'Well, you're not,' Felicity interrupted rudely. 'Susan is, and she agrees that Olive needed to be taught a lesson.'

'We *all* agreed,' said Susan, glaring at Sylvia. 'Of course, if you want to go against the whole form, that is quite up to you, Sylvia.'

But Sylvia didn't want to do anything of the sort. She so badly wanted to fit in at Malory Towers and make friends. At once she said, 'Naturally, I shall go along with what the rest of the form decides. I don't like Olive any more than you do, you know, but I think that I would have chosen a different way of dealing with her. I'm not awfully fond of jokes and tricks, you see.'

'How odd!' exclaimed Bonnie. 'That's rather a shame, because we play quite a lot of them in our form. Well, June and Freddie do. Really super ones, too!'

Unsurprisingly, Sylvia didn't look terribly thrilled by this, but as the fourth formers had reached the dining-room by this time, she said no more.

The girl was unusually silent during the meal, lost in her own thoughts. Olive, too, was quiet and sullen, but then she usually was, so the others didn't take much notice of this. As soon as she had finished her meal, Olive left the table and went to find Miss Tallant, to discover what her punishment would be.

'Well, if Miss Tallant gave me fifty lines just for laughing, she's certain to come down much harder on Olive,' said Nora, quite unable to keep the note of glee from her voice.

'After all, she did disrupt the whole class.'

'I think that what Olive did is worth two hundred lines at least,' said Bonnie, happily.

'That ought to keep her busy while we are in the

common-room this evening, so she won't have time to make any of her spiteful remarks!'

But when the fourth formers gathered in the common-room that evening, it seemed that Miss Tallant had not punished Olive at all, for the girl sat down in an armchair and began reading a book.

Felicity nudged Susan and whispered, 'I say, look at Olive. You don't think that she's going to be so silly as to ignore Miss Tallant's punishment, do you?'

Susan frowned at this and, raising her voice, called out, 'Olive! Why aren't you doing the lines that Miss Tallant gave you as a punishment?'

'She didn't give me any lines,' said the girl, sullenly.

'Don't tell me that she let you off scot-free!' exclaimed Pam.

'Olive, you had better not have sneaked on me,' said June sternly. 'I warned you what would happen if you did.'

'I haven't sneaked on you,' retorted Olive, glaring at June. 'But Miss Tallant has given me another punishment, instead of lines.'

'What is it?' asked Felicity. 'Are you to go to bed early?'

'No, I'm to do extra prep with Miss Tallant on Saturday morning,' said Olive gloomily. 'Not that it's any of your business!'

This really was a horrid punishment, for the girls enjoyed having their weekends all to themselves. They were happy, jolly times where everyone could do as they pleased, whether they chose to play games, go horse-riding or simply sit around laughing and joking in the common-room. And next Saturday would be even more fun than usual, for the casting of the Christmas play was to take place that afternoon. But nobody felt in the slightest bit sorry for Olive, for all of the fourth formers thought that she had well and truly earned her punishment.

The girl ignored the grins of the fourth formers and went back to her book, though Felicity, who stole several glances at her, noticed that she didn't turn the pages at all. She's only pretending to be engrossed in her book, thought Felicity. I wonder what is going on in Olive's head? What a odd girl she is!

Most of the fourth formers were looking forward to the meeting on Saturday afternoon, and the rest of the week seemed to pass by very slowly indeed!

But, at last, it was Saturday, and June, looking out of the common-room window after breakfast, said, 'It looks quite sunny for the time of year. Freddie, shall we take a walk along the cliffs in a little while?'

'That would be super,' answered Freddie. 'Would anyone else like to come?'

Amy and Bonnie, neither of whom cared for exercise and fresh air, both shook their heads, but several of the others agreed eagerly to the suggestion.

'Lucy and I will join you,' said Julie. 'But, of course, we will be on horseback.'

'What about you, Olive?' asked June, in a deceptively sweet tone. 'Would you like to come with us? Oh no, half a minute! I completely forgot – you have to do extra prep for Miss Tallant, don't you?'

Everyone laughed, and Olive scowled, before stalking angrily to the door and flouncing out. As the door slammed behind her, Felicity said, 'Miss Tallant will keep her nose to the grindstone, all right, while we are all out enjoying the fresh air.'

'It seems a jolly odd punishment to me, though,' said Bonnie, who had been looking thoughtful. 'I know that Miss Tallant is not on duty this weekend, for she told me so herself. Yet she has chosen to give up part of her Saturday too, so that she can sit in the classroom with Olive.'

This seemed very strange indeed, for the girls knew how hard the mistresses worked, and how they treasured their free time.

'I never thought of that!' exclaimed Lucy. 'Fancy wanting to give up part of a weekend off to spend time with a sourpuss like Olive.'

'Perhaps Miss Tallant has nothing better to do,' said June. 'The mistresses sometimes go home to visit their family or friends when they have a weekend off. Miss Tallant might not have a family. And I'm quite sure that she can't have any friends. I don't think she's awfully popular with the mistresses here either.'

'She's not,' piped up Bonnie. 'I stayed behind to help her tidy the classroom the other day, and she told me that Mam'zelle Dupont dislikes her. So does Miss Potts.'

'She really shouldn't say such things to you, Bonnie,' said Susan disapprovingly. 'I'm quite sure that none of the other mistresses would!'

'I think it's a jolly good thing that she did,' said June

warmly. 'After all, the whole point of Bonnie sucking up to Miss Tallant was so that she could get to know things about her. Well done, Bonnie!'

Of course, this was the first that Sylvia had heard about Bonnie's plan to become Miss Tallant's favourite, and she looked extremely startled.

Seeing her expression, Freddie said, 'I suppose you don't approve, Sylvia?'

'You're wrong,' said Sylvia, to everyone's surprise. 'I don't like Miss Tallant. She's sly, and if Bonnie can find out what she's up to that will be a very good thing.'

Bonnie smiled, and said, 'Actually, it's rather lucky for us that she doesn't seem to have any friends, for that means that I am the only person she has to talk to.'

'I don't think it's lucky at all,' said Nora, dismayed. 'If Miss Tallant is going to start dishing out Saturday morning preps as punishment simply because she has nothing better to occupy her time, we shall all have to watch our step!'

'Golly, yes,' said Julie, horrified. 'I always spend Saturdays with Jack, and Lucy with Sandy. And I'm not very good at English or Drama, so I'm certain to get a row from Miss Tallant sooner or later.'

'Well, perhaps we had better give our dear Miss Tallant something to do,' said June thoughtfully.

'Do you have anything in mind?' asked Felicity.

'Not yet,' said June. 'But I'll think of something, you may be sure. Now, let's go and get our hats and coats on and enjoy the sunshine.'

Miss Tallant interferes

The fourth formers enjoyed their lunch, for their walk in the fresh air had made them very hungry indeed. Only Olive seemed to have no appetite, pushing the food around her plate with a fork, but eating very little. She looked even more miserable than usual, thought Felicity. Miss Tallant had probably given her a really bad time. Despite her dislike of Olive, Felicity couldn't help feeling a little sorry for her, and said kindly, 'You must feel glad that your punishment is over, Olive. Did Miss Tallant give you a lot of extra work to do?'

'Quite a lot,' answered Olive, who was surprised to discover that she felt a little cheered by Felicity's interest. Then Bonnie, who was sitting nearby, said, 'Well, I walked by the classroom earlier, and you certainly didn't seem to be working very hard then. You were standing by Miss Tallant's desk, and the two of you were talking about something.'

'She was explaining the work to me,' snapped Olive, giving Bonnie a look of dislike. 'And how dare you spy on me?'

'I wasn't spying,' said Bonnie, with a disdainful little laugh. 'I just happened to be passing. As if I would want to spy on *you*.'

Olive flushed angrily, and lapsed into her usual morose silence. When the meal was over and the girls left the dining-room, Olive turned to go towards the common-room. Susan called her name, and said, 'Where do you think you're going? Have you forgotten that we are holding auditions for our play in the hall?'

Olive hadn't forgotten, for the girls had talked of little else for days. But she had been hoping to slip away unnoticed, and avoid having anything to do with the stupid play.

'Do I have to come?' she asked Susan now, her mouth set in a discontented droop.

'Yes, you jolly well do,' answered Susan sternly. 'Just for once, Olive, show a bit of team spirit, and do something to help the form.'

So, reluctantly, Olive followed the others over to the big hall. There was a stage at one end of the room, with several rows of chairs set out in front of it. Felicity, Susan and Sylvia, as producers, took three chairs in the front row, while the rest of the fourth form filed into the seats behind. There was a great deal of scraping of chairs and shuffling of feet, but once the noise died down, Susan stood up and addressed everyone. 'Well, girls, you all know why we are here,' she said in her clear voice. 'So let's begin casting the parts, and not waste any time. Of course, the two most important roles in the play are those of the fairy doll, and Amelia, the little girl who finds her. Now, who is interested in auditioning for the part of the fairy?'

Three girls put their hands up at once. One was Jenny,

a tall, dark, West Tower girl, who had a beautiful singing voice. The second was Nora. And the third, of course, was Bonnie.

'Very well, we shall try all three of you out in the part,' said Susan. 'As you know, whoever plays the fairy has to sing and dance, as well as act, so we really need someone who is a good all-rounder. Jenny, if you would like to take the stage first, please, we can –'

Just then the big door at the back of the hall opened, and Susan stared in surprise as Miss Tallant entered. The rest of the girls turned to see who had come in, getting politely to their feet when they realised that it was one of the mistresses. But whatever was she doing here?

They soon found out! Miss Tallant strode briskly to the front of the hall and said, 'Sit down, please, Susan.'

Astonished, and none too pleased, Susan did as she was told, and Miss Tallant faced the fourth formers.

'I understand that you have decided to perform a play called *The Christmas Tree Fairy*,' she said. 'Quite a good little play, though rather short.'

The fourth formers looked at one another in consternation. This was *their* play. What business of Miss Tallant's was it? Susan spoke up. 'We are going to make it longer by adding a few touches of our own, Miss Tallant.'

'I see,' said the mistress. 'What do you have in mind?'

'Well, we are going to add a song and dance, and June and Freddie are going to write a few jokes,' explained Susan.

Miss Tallant gave a cold little smile and said, 'Indeed?

Well, I shall have to approve them first. Now, I suggest that we begin casting the parts.'

The girls began to mutter among themselves, quite horrified now. Miss Tallant was trying to take over their play!

Susan, however, had other ideas. As head of the form, it was up to her to take the lead and she stood up and faced the mistress. This was really very brave of Susan, for she knew that Miss Tallant could be spiteful and vindictive, and her knees shook a little. But her voice was steady as she said firmly, 'Excuse me, Miss Tallant. I don't mean to be rude, but Felicity, Sylvia and I are going to produce the play, and the three of us would like to decide who to cast in the different parts.'

Miss Tallant stared at Susan as if she was something extremely nasty, and said coldly, 'And just what do you girls know about producing a play?'

June, whose temper had been rising as she listened to the mistress, got to her feet and said, 'Nothing at all, Miss Tallant. And we won't have the chance to learn anything if we aren't left alone to make our own mistakes.'

Miss Tallant turned quite white with anger and hissed, 'How dare you cheek me like that, June? I should watch your step, if I were you, or I might feel compelled to enquire a little more closely into that affair of the mouse in Olive's desk.'

June blinked, quite lost for words, for once. How on earth had Miss Tallant come to suspect that she, June, was behind that? Suddenly, yet another interruption occurred.

Miss Williams, the fourth-form mistress, had seen Miss

Tallant go into the hall, and had frowned to herself. She knew very well that her form was holding a meeting about the play, and wondered what Miss Tallant was doing there. Only that morning, Miss Williams had spoken to Susan about the play, and the girl had said politely, but very decidedly, that the fourth formers wanted to do everything themselves, without asking for any assistance from Miss Tallant. Miss Williams had been pleased to hear this, for it would be a very good thing for the girls to take responsibility for their play, and learn how to organise themselves. Moreover, the fourth-form mistress did not like Miss Tallant, and she felt that the new mistress might well be more of a hindrance than a help to the girls. Miss Williams went across to the door of the big hall and pushed it open a crack, so she heard what Miss Tallant said to Susan. She had been about to intervene herself when she heard the way that Susan coolly stood up to the mistress, and she smiled to herself. Then June spoke, and Miss Williams, opening the door a little wider, saw the angry, spiteful look on Miss Tallant's face. The trouble with June was that she was likely to get carried away, and perhaps go too far in her rebellion against Miss Tallant. And then the girl would only end up getting herself into trouble.

So Miss Williams strode briskly into the room and said, 'I am sorry to interrupt your meeting, but . . . Why, Miss Tallant, what are you doing here? Susan, I distinctly remember you telling me that you intended to produce the play yourself, with assistance from Felicity and Sylvia.

And I must say that I was very pleased to hear it. Don't tell me that you have changed your minds?'

'No, Miss Williams,' said Susan, noticing a glint in Miss Williams's eye and realising that the mistress was well aware of what had been happening. 'Miss Tallant very kindly offered her services, but I was just telling her that there was no need for her to trouble herself over us.'

'Most commendable!' said Miss Williams warmly. 'It's always nice to see you girls using your initiative and doing things for yourselves. Miss Tallant and I shan't hold you up any longer.' Then she turned to the other mistress, and said brightly, 'Come along, Miss Tallant. The girls are very busy, so let's leave them to it.'

Miss Tallant had no choice but to follow Miss Williams from the hall. And once the door had closed behind the two mistresses, a perfect hubbub broke out.

'Of all the nerve!'

'Who does Miss Tallant think she is? How dare she try to order us about like that?'

'Thank heavens that Miss Williams turned up when she did.'

'Yes, she has sized Miss Tallant up, all right,' said Susan. 'And now that they have both gone, let's get down to business!'

So, one by one, Jennifer, Bonnie and Nora took to the stage, as the rest of the fourth form watched with interest.

Jennifer's singing was so lovely that the fourth formers cheered when she came to the end of her song. She read a few lines from the play, too, and Felicity murmured to

Susan and Sylvia, 'She's not a bad actress. A little stiff, perhaps, but I daresay that's because she feels nervous.'

Then Mary sat down at the piano and played a lively tune, while Jennifer danced. Alas, her dancing was nowhere near as good as her singing or her acting, and Sylvia said, 'Well, I suppose it would be too much to expect her to be good at everything.'

'That's just it, though,' said Susan. 'The girl who takes this part *has* to be good at everything.' Then she raised her voice and said, 'Thank you, Jennifer, you may sit down now. Bonnie! Your turn next.'

There was no doubt that little Bonnie certainly looked the part of the fairy to perfection. She seemed even smaller and daintier than usual as she stood alone on the big stage. She danced gracefully and, when it came to reading the lines, the girl really threw herself into the part. Alas, Bonnie floundered when it came to the song, for not only was she out of tune, her voice was so high pitched that some of the listening girls covered their ears. Grimacing, Susan said, 'Simply awful! A pity, because she acts and dances well.'

Then it was Nora's turn. Nora's singing voice was not as pure as Jennifer's, but it was very pleasant, and the fourth formers clapped eagerly when she finished her song. And she was by far the best dancer of the three girls. Nora proved, too, that she was a fine little actress, and Felicity said, 'Nora is very humorous, too, and I feel quite sure that she will be excellent at doing the jokes and the funny lines that June and Freddie are going to write.'

Susan and Sylvia agreed with this at once, and Susan said happily, 'Well, it looks as if we have found our fairy! I shan't tell Nora yet, though. We shall audition for the other parts first, and let everyone know what we have decided at the end.'

'Bonnie isn't going to be too pleased,' said Felicity. 'I just hope that she doesn't throw a tantrum. You know how difficult she can be if things don't go her way.'

'Don't you worry about Bonnie, Felicity,' said Susan firmly. 'I shall deal with her when the time comes.'

Felicity felt a little apprehensive. Susan had a blunt way of speaking at times, and didn't always see that it was sometimes necessary to handle things with a little tact.

The auditions went very smoothly indeed, and both Felicity and Susan found themselves warming to Sylvia. The girl hadn't tried to push herself forward at all, and had worked amicably alongside Felicity and Susan. Soon all of the parts had been cast, and it was time to let the fourth formers in on the decisions that had been reached.

Susan stood up to face the girls, and said, 'Thank you to all of you who auditioned. Everyone did very well indeed. And now it's time to tell you who is going to play each part.'

The listening girls sat in expectant silence, those who had auditioned feeling both nervous and excited. At last Susan said, 'We have decided that the lead role of the fairy doll will be given to . . . Nora!'

A great cheer went up at this, while Nora looked as if she simply couldn't believe her ears. Those closest to the girl clapped her on the back, and Pam cried, 'Splendid choice! You'll be marvellous, Nora, old girl.'

Jennifer managed to hide her disappointment, and congratulated Nora, but Bonnie was quite unable to hide hers. Her bottom lip jutted out, and she scowled fiercely at Susan.

'Horrid beast!' she lisped to Amy. 'Susan has never liked me, because I used to be friends with Felicity, and this is her way of getting back at me. I don't like Miss Tallant, but perhaps it would have been a good thing if she had stayed after all, for I'm sure that *she* would have chosen me for the part.'

Once the noise and excitement had died down, Susan announced, 'Amelia, the little girl, is to be played by Molly.'

Molly, a very small girl from East Tower, with rather a serious expression, suddenly found herself beaming from ear to ear, as a rousing 'hurrah!' went up from the East Tower girls.

Quickly Susan gave out the other parts. Pam was to play Amelia's aunt, Julie was going to be a toy soldier, and Lucy laughed out loud when she learned that she was to dress up in a big, furry costume and play a teddy bear!

'There will be something for everyone to do,' said Susan. 'Mary is writing a song for us, of course, while June and Freddie are adding some humorous touches to the script. And we're going to need plenty of people to help paint scenery and do hair and make-up, and so on.'

'I've a good mind not to do anything at all to help,' muttered a disgruntled Bonnie to Amy.

But Susan hadn't finished. 'There is one more thing,' she said. 'There is one person I haven't mentioned, who is going to be very important to our little play. In fact, I would go so far as to say that she is vital.'

The fourth formers looked at one another in surprise. Who on earth could Susan be talking about?

'That person is our wardrobe mistress,' said Susan, looking very serious indeed.

'Because there are so many costumes, we really need someone who is an expert at needlework. Someone who has flair and taste, and a good eye for detail. Someone who, once she sets her mind to a task, works tirelessly to complete it. There is only one person in the form – in the whole *school*, in fact – who fits that description. And that person is Bonnie Meadows.'

Bonnie gave a gasp, her big brown eyes growing even bigger. Instantly, her disappointment at not being cast as the fairy was forgotten. And Susan was no longer a mean beast. On the contrary, she was very shrewd and perceptive indeed. Bonnie couldn't imagine how she had ever thought that she didn't like her!

Felicity grinned to herself. Good old Susan! She was learning that, with some people, a little tact worked wonders. Now she had turned Bonnie's sulks to smiles, and made sure that the fourth formers had an excellent wardrobe mistress, in the neatest possible way! Most of the others guessed what Susan was up to as well, and played along by cheering Bonnie, and praising her extravagantly.

'Simply marvellous! I can't think of anyone who would do a better job!'

'Yes, we can be sure of having just the right costumes now, with old Bonnie in charge.'

'I should say! Good for you, Bonnie!'

Bonnie beamed round and thanked everyone prettily. 'I shan't let you down,' she said. 'And I shall be glad of some help from anyone who is good with a needle, for there will be a lot of work to do.'

Several girls from other towers immediately volunteered their services, and Bonnie said, 'Perhaps tomorrow afternoon we can all go and look in that little room behind the stage, where all the old costumes from past Malory Towers plays are stored. We are sure to find some things that will be useful to us in there.'

'My word, you're eager, Bonnie,' called out Julie.

'If a job's worth doing, it's worth doing well,' said Bonnie, briskly. 'I intend to take my responsibility as wardrobe mistress very seriously indeed. Now, if you'll excuse me, the library has a fine book on play costumes, so I think I shall pop along there and borrow it.' Then she called out to the girls who had offered to help her, 'Two o'clock sharp, tomorrow afternoon, you girls.'

And with that, she walked purposefully from the room, as Felicity chuckled, 'Bonnie really *does* go all out when she takes on a task. I feel quite sorry for the girls who have offered to help her, for I think that she may turn out to be quite a slave-driver!'

Susan laughed at that, and said, 'Well, I call that a

highly successful meeting – in spite of Miss Tallant's attempts to sabotage it! Mary told me that she has almost finished writing the song, and June and Freddie have already written a few jokes into the script – and very funny they are, too. At this rate, it won't be long before we are able to hold our first rehearsal. Shall we go back to the common-room before tea?'

Felicity agreed to this at once, and as the two girls were walking along the corridor, June and Freddie caught them up. June's expression was unusually serious, and Felicity asked, 'Anything up, old girl?'

'Yes, there is, actually,' said June. 'It has just occurred to me that Miss Tallant knew the name of the play we are doing. But how *could* she know, for we haven't told anyone outside the form. And we agreed that we weren't going to tell Miss Tallant anything.'

'Perhaps someone let something slip out by accident,' suggested Susan.

'Who would do *that*?' asked Freddie rather scornfully. 'It's not as if any of us are in the habit of having cosy chats with Miss Tallant, for none of us can bear her.'

June's brow cleared suddenly, and she snapped her fingers. 'Bonnie!' she cried. 'She's always hanging round Miss Tallant, offering to help tidy the classroom and what-not.'

'Yes, but only as part of her plan to suck up to her,' Felicity reminded June. 'She certainly doesn't do it because she has any real liking for Miss Tallant.'

'I know that,' said June. 'But she could easily have

given something away by accident. And there's something else, too. Miss Tallant mentioned that business with the mouse, and it was pretty clear that she suspected I was involved. I don't see how she can have reached that conclusion unless someone told her.'

'Yes, we all heard her say that,' said Susan, looking grave. 'I didn't think anything of it at the time, but you're quite right, of course. We certainly don't want our dear Miss Tallant poking her nose into fourth-form business.'

The others were in wholehearted agreement with this, and June said, 'Bonnie said that she was going to the library, didn't she? Well, let's find her and tackle her about it. She has to learn that it simply isn't on to give away fourth-form secrets!'

Bonnie in trouble

June stormed off down the corridor, the other three in hot pursuit. Susan caught up with her as they reached the library, and grabbed her arm.

'Now look here, June,' she began. 'Don't go rushing in and accusing Bonnie of things, when, for all we know, she may be quite innocent.'

'Susan is quite right,' said Felicity. 'I know that Bonnie can be devious in some ways, but I really don't think . . .'

Her voice tailed off suddenly, for through the glass pane in the library door, Felicity had spotted Bonnie sitting at a table with a book. And bending over to speak to her, her blonde head very close to Bonnie's darker one, was Miss Tallant. Both of them were smiling, and Miss Tallant patted Bonnie's shoulder, before reaching into her bag and pulling out a bar of chocolate. She handed this to Bonnie, then walked towards the door. Swiftly, the four girls outside retreated along the corridor before they were spotted, and went into one of the empty music-rooms.

'Well!' said Freddie, looking astonished. 'Did you see that?'

The other three nodded, and June said grimly, 'Well, that seems to point to Bonnie being the culprit. And from the look of things, the information she passed to Miss Tallant certainly didn't slip out by accident.'

June felt just as shocked and dismayed as the others, for although she had suspected Bonnie, she had never, for one second, imagined that the girl's actions had been deliberate.

'It certainly looks that way,' said Susan, frowning deeply. 'Why would Miss Tallant have given Bonnie chocolate, unless it was in return for a favour?'

No one could imagine, and Felicity said thoughtfully, 'This puts a different complexion on things. If Bonnie *is* sneaking fourth-form secrets to Miss Tallant, it might be best not to tackle her just yet, for it will put her on her guard.'

'Quite right,' said June. 'Until we can think of a way of catching Bonnie out, we must carry on as usual, and all behave in a perfectly normal way towards her.'

'What do you think, Susan?' asked Freddie. 'You are head of the form, after all.'

'Yes, I agree with Felicity and June,' said Susan, who was looking very upset indeed. 'I must say that I am terribly disappointed in Bonnie. I know that she and I have had our differences, but I really didn't think that she would stoop this low.'

'Shall we tell the others?' asked Felicity.

Susan thought for a moment, then said, 'No. Obviously we can't say anything in front of Amy, for she is Bonnie's friend. We can't rely on Sylvia to keep her mouth shut either, and as for Olive – well, I certainly don't trust *her*!'

All the same, the four girls found it very difficult to stick to their word and behave normally with Bonnie. They had very strict ideas of honour, and anyone who sneaked, or gave away secrets, was beneath contempt, as far as they were concerned. It was June who came up with an idea to trap Bonnie, a few days later. She and Freddie got into a huddle with Felicity and Susan in the courtyard one break-time.

'We will pretend that we are planning to play a trick on Miss Tallant, and make sure that Bonnie overhears us,' explained June. 'Then Bonnie will run off and tell her tales, and Miss Tallant will try to foil our trick.'

'And that will prove that Bonnie is working against the fourth form,' said Felicity with a sigh. 'What do you have in mind, June?'

'Well, I thought we could pretend that we are going to do something similar to the mouse trick that we played on Olive,' answered June. 'We could say that we are going to put a big spider in the drawer of Miss Tallant's desk, perhaps.'

'Good idea,' said Freddie. 'Miss Tallant is very like Mam'zelle Dupont in that she doesn't care for spiders, or mice or anything like that.'

'Exactly!' said June. 'We will make sure that Bonnie is nearby when we are plotting, and we shall be able to judge from Miss Tallant's reaction when she goes to her desk whether Bonnie has sneaked.'

'Very well,' said Susan. 'The sooner we get definite proof that Bonnie is the one giving things away to Miss Tallant, the better, I suppose.'

So when the four girls went into the common-room that evening, they made a point of sitting close to Bonnie. The girl had her head bent over her needlework, as usual, and was chattering away to Amy as she sewed. Pam, Sylvia and Olive were there as well, while the others had gone off to see a slide show in the big hall.

'I simply can't wait to see Miss Tallant's face when she opens her drawer tomorrow and that spider runs towards her,' said June, in rather a loud voice.

Freddie giggled. 'We're going to find a spider in the gardener's shed,' she said. 'A big, fat one, with thick, hairy legs.'

'Ugh!' said Susan, giving a shudder. 'I can't say that I'm awfully keen on spiders myself. It will be funny to see how Miss Tallant reacts, though. And it will jolly well serve her right for trying to spoil our meeting the other day.'

'When are you going to play the trick?' asked Felicity. 'Monday morning? Jolly good.'

The four moved away then, to join Pam, who raised her eyebrows and said, 'What's this? Hatching a plot?'

The four girls looked at one another, and Susan said, 'Shall we tell Pam our secret? Let's, for we know we can trust her.'

Quickly, June explained that they suspected Bonnie of telling tales to Miss Tallant, and of their plan to catch her out.

Pam listened intently, her expression very serious. At last, she said, 'I simply can't believe that Bonnie is on Miss Tallant's side.'

'None of us wants to believe it, Pam,' said Felicity, earnestly. 'I know that Bonnie has some funny ways, but I honestly believed that she was completely straight. But if you had seen her in the library with Miss Tallant, you would agree that her behaviour was most suspicious.'

'Hush!' hissed Freddie. 'She's coming over.'

Bonnie joined them, saying excitedly, 'Susan, I have some super ideas for costumes. I've made some sketches and must show them to you.'

'I'm looking forward to seeing them,' said Susan, forcing herself to smile at the girl. 'Bring them to me tomorrow, if you like.'

'I will,' said Bonnie. 'I say, did I hear you talking about playing a trick on that horrid Miss Tallant.'

'Yes,' said June, winking slyly at the others. 'We are going to put a huge spider in her desk on Monday, but you must promise to keep it to yourself.'

'Of course,' said Bonnie, clapping her hands together in excitement. 'I shan't say a word. Oh, how I shall enjoy hearing her squeal!'

With that Bonnie went back to join Amy, and Freddie said, 'See! Even more proof, if we needed it. What a nerve, coming over like that to try and get more information out of us.'

Pam looked thoughtful, and said, 'I must say, she's a jolly convincing actress.'

'Well, we'll see how convincing she is when she's been well and truly caught out,' said June, in a hard voice. 'And then we will decide how to punish her.'

All of those who were in on the secret were looking forward to Miss Tallant's Drama class on Monday. As usual, Bonnie held the door open for the mistress, receiving a warm smile and a word of praise. June, who was watching Miss Tallant closely, thought that there was a triumphant glint in the mistress's eye as she walked towards her desk. She didn't go right up to it, though, noticed June, but stopped a few feet away from it – almost as if she was afraid that there was something unpleasant in there.

'Sit down girls,' she said. The girls did as they were told and, for a moment, the mistress stood watching them, her eyes hard and cold. They seemed to linger on June, and, at last, she said, 'June, please come out to the front of the class.'

June stood up, her head bowed so that the mistress would not see the little smile on her lips, and walked to the front of the room. Miss Tallant looked her up and down coldly, then said, 'Please open the drawer of my desk.'

June put on a puzzled look, and said, 'Open your drawer, Miss Tallant? But why?'

'Don't ask questions, June,' said the mistress. 'Just do as you are told.'

So June pulled open the drawer, noticing as she did so that Miss Tallant shrank back a little. Then the mistress peered over June's shoulder and said, 'Now kindly remove the spider that is lurking in there.'

'Spider? What spider?' said June, looking so puzzled, and so innocent, that Felicity had to clamp her lips tightly together to stop her laughter escaping.

'The spider that I know very well you have hidden

there,' said Miss Tallant, a triumphant note in her voice.

'Miss Tallant, I would never do such a thing!' said June, sounding so outraged that Freddie grinned. 'Why, the very thought of playing a trick on a mistress is –'

'June, your reputation for playing tricks and jokes on mistresses is well known to me,' interrupted Miss Tallant. 'So please don't waste your breath. I know that you have put a spider in that drawer, and I insist that you remove it immediately. After you have done so, I shall inform you what your punishment is to be.'

'But Miss Tallant, there is no spider there,' said June, looking down into the drawer. 'See for yourself.'

Rather gingerly, Miss Tallant looked. 'It must be hiding in one of the corners. Remove everything from the drawer, June, and put it on top of the desk.'

Obediently, June did so, then at last she stood back and said, 'There is no spider there, Miss Tallant.'

Miss Tallant was reluctantly forced to agree that there wasn't, and she said crossly, 'I believe that you have hidden it, just as you did the mouse. Turn out your pockets, at once.'

June turned out her pockets but, of course, there was no spider, and she said cheekily, 'You're quite welcome to feel in them yourself, Miss Tallant, if you think that I am hiding anything else.'

But Miss Tallant had no intention at all of doing this. If she did find a spider in June's pocket, she would simply die! Yet she couldn't let this wretched girl get the better of her.

Miss Tallant had been reliably informed that June intended to put a spider in her drawer today, and she was going to punish her for it.

'June, you will go to bed one hour early tonight,' said the mistress spitefully, and the fourth formers gasped in outrage.

'You can't punish June without any evidence!' cried Susan, stung by the injustice of this, and Miss Tallant glared at her.

'I can do anything I please,' she said in an icy tone, before turning back to June. 'Put your belongings back in your pocket,' she said. 'Then go back to your seat and we will get on with the lesson.'

Susan opened her mouth to protest again, but Felicity whispered, 'Don't, Susan. You will only earn a punishment for yourself. We are going to have to think of some other way to defeat Miss Tallant.'

So, reluctantly, Susan remained silent.

June, meanwhile, stole a glance at Bonnie's face as she made her way back to her seat. The girl really *was* a good actress, for she looked just as shocked as everyone else. June made up her mind that she was going to tackle her later over her deceit – and, my goodness, wouldn't she give her something to look shocked about! The girl wasn't terribly upset about her punishment, though having to go to bed early was a frightful bore. But she *was* upset by the fact that the punishment was an unjust one. She intended to use her hour of peace and quiet to good purpose, however – in thinking up a way to get back at Miss Tallant!

'Phew!' said Pam, when the girls emerged from the classroom. 'What a lesson! How I dislike that woman.'

'It's so terribly unfair!' cried Susan. 'June is being punished for something that she hasn't even done.'

'Don't worry about me, Susan,' said June. 'The main thing is that it proved our suspicions are correct, and that Bonnie is giving our secrets away to Miss Tallant. Where *is* Bonnie, anyway?'

'Oh, she stayed behind to help Miss Tallant tidy up the classroom,' said Nora. 'But what's all this about Bonnie telling her our secrets?'

'Of course, you don't know, do you?' said Felicity. And she and Susan told Nora, Julie and Lucy what had been happening.

They were very shocked, of course, and Lucy said gravely, 'What are we going to do about it?'

'Speak to her about it, of course,' said June. 'And I vote we punish the little beast by sending her to Coventry.'

'That will be a very hard punishment for her to bear, because Bonnie loves to chatter,' said Julie.

'I wonder if Amy will stand out against the punishment?' said Nora. 'After all, Bonnie is her friend.'

'Well, if she does, then I'm afraid we shall have to send Amy to Coventry, too,' said Susan, her expression grim. 'We'll tackle her in the common-room after tea tonight.'

So, after tea that night, the girls gathered in the common-room.

Susan was sitting with Felicity, Pam and a few others, and she said, 'Well, I vote that we get this whole beastly business over with as quickly as possible.'

The others agreed, and Susan called out, 'Bonnie, can you come over here a minute, please? There is something we need to talk to you about.'

Surprised, Bonnie went over to Susan, who decided that it was no use beating about the bush, and said, 'Bonnie, I need to ask you something. Have you been letting Miss Tallant in on some of our form's secrets?'

Bonnie gave a gasp, and said at once, 'Of course not! What makes you ask such a thing, Susan?'

'She's fibbing!' said June. 'There's no one who can play innocent as well as Bonnie can. And we all know how good she is at acting.'

'That's enough, June,' said Susan sharply. 'The thing is, Bonnie, someone told Miss Tallant the name of the play that we are doing.'

'And they sneaked to her about the mouse that I put in Olive's desk,' said June, who was far too angry to stay silent. 'And we saw her with you in the library on the day of our meeting. She gave you a bar of chocolate.'

'Yes, because she had asked me to do something for her, and said that she would give me a bar of chocolate if I did,' said Bonnie, who had turned pale. 'It was all part of my plan to suck up to her.'

Freddie gave a harsh laugh. 'Yes, but you went a little too far in your plan, didn't you? You decided that you had more to gain from being on Miss Tallant's side than ours.'

'That's a horrid lie!' cried Bonnie, tears starting to her big, brown eyes.

'Of course it is,' said Amy, entering the battle. 'How dare you accuse Bonnie of such a thing?'

'I realise that you want to stick up for your friend, Amy,' said Felicity. 'But we know that Bonnie is the culprit. You see, we let her overhear us talking about June's plan to put a spider in Miss Tallant's desk. And, sure enough, word reached Miss Tallant's ears.'

'But it wasn't me!' protested Bonnie, tears beginning to trickle down her cheeks now. 'I wasn't the only one who overheard you. Sylvia was there that night, and so was Olive. And Pam! It could just as easily have been one of them.'

Of course, the others knew that it wasn't Pam, for she had come up through the school with them and would never dream of such a thing. Felicity couldn't help glancing at Sylvia and Olive, though. Sylvia was looking extremely startled, while Olive wore her usual miserable expression. *Could* it have been one of them? She said to Bonnie, 'All right then, you tell us what this mysterious job was that Miss Tallant asked you to do. Then, perhaps, we will believe you.'

But Bonnie had a stubborn streak, and she pursed her lips, saying through her tears, 'I shan't tell you, for if you were true friends you would believe me, and wouldn't expect me to explain myself to you like this.'

'So you are refusing to tell us?' said Susan, looking grave.

Bonnie's soft, brown curls shook as she nodded her head.

'Don't be an ass, Bonnie!' begged Felicity. 'Just tell us what Miss Tallant wanted you to do, and that will be an end to all of this.'

This time Bonnie shook her head, a stubborn set to her firm little chin.

'Then I am afraid, Bonnie, that we will have to assume that you are the sneak,' said Susan heavily. 'And your punishment is that you will be sent to Coventry. Not one girl in the form is to talk to you, or have anything to do with you, for a whole week.'

Then Amy surprised everyone by putting her arm around Bonnie's heaving shoulders, and saying loyally, 'Well, I am not joining in your silly punishment, and I don't care if you send me to Coventry as well! Come along, Bonnie, let's go somewhere where we can be alone.'

With that, she led the weeping girl from the room and, as the door closed behind them, Susan grimaced and said, 'Well, that was simply beastly, but it had to be done.'

Most of the others agreed at once, but Felicity remained silent. She remembered how Bonnie had played a big part in reuniting Julie with her missing horse, Jack, last term. The girl had certainly proved her loyalty to the form then. And there were several other past incidents when Bonnie had shown that, although she could be rather unscrupulous when it came to getting what she wanted, she was absolutely straight and honest – in her own, rather strange way!

Oh dear, thought Felicity, I do hope that we haven't made a dreadful mistake!

A shock for the fourth form

Several days later Felicity and Susan learned some startling news. It was a pleasant, if cold, afternoon, and the two of them were wrapped up in coats, hats and scarves as they walked through the grounds.

'I shall be glad when Bonnie's period of Coventry is over,' said Susan with a sigh. 'It really is horrible. And it is making things awfully difficult as far as the play is concerned, for I can't discuss the costumes with her until I can speak to her again.'

'Yes, but even when we are allowed to speak to Bonnie again, things will never be the same,' said Felicity thoughtfully. 'For this incident will always be at the back of our minds. It's a shame, because although I didn't like Bonnie much when she first came to Malory Towers, I've grown quite fond of her now.'

'Yes, she has many good qualities, although she has a funny way of going about things sometimes,' said Susan. 'Still, I suppose that no one is completely good, or completely bad. And once Bonnie's punishment is over, we shall all have to do our best to try to forget what she has done, and help her try to make amends.'

Just then, the two girls saw a figure coming towards

them, and both groaned inwardly. For it was none other than Miss Tallant!

'Susan!' said the mistress sharply, as she drew level with the two girls. 'I understand that you took a book about play production from my desk yesterday, without permission. Not a very good example for a head-girl to set her form.'

Susan flushed bright red. She had sneaked the book from Miss Tallant's desk, for she knew very well that the mistress did not like her, and would certainly have refused to lend it to her if she had asked.

She had flicked through it in the common-room yesterday evening, and had meant to put it back on Miss Tallant's desk this morning, before the mistress even realised it had gone. But, alas for Susan, she had completely forgotten about it, and now she could have kicked herself!

'Kindly ask permission before borrowing anything again, Susan,' said Miss Tallant coldly. 'And please bring the book to me in the mistresses' common-room before prep this evening.'

'When I will no doubt be given lines, or some other beastly punishment!' muttered Susan as the mistress walked briskly away. 'Blow! Why didn't I remember to put it back this morning?'

'Susan,' said Felicity, with a frown. 'How did Miss Tallant know that you had taken her book?'

'Well, she noticed it wasn't there, I suppose,' said Susan, shrugging.

'Yes, I know *that*,' said Felicity, a little impatiently. 'But how did she know that *you* took it, when it could have been any one of us fourth formers?'

'Golly, I didn't think of that!' exclaimed Susan. 'Well, there is only one explanation. Bonnie must have been tittle-tattling again. Which means that, even after being sent to Coventry, she *still* hasn't learned her lesson! Honestly, that girl is a glutton for punishment!'

'Half a minute, though!' said Felicity. 'Bonnie couldn't have known that it was you who took the book, for she wasn't there when you took it. I was, and so were Pam and Nora – but not Bonnie.'

Susan thought this over for a moment, then said, 'But she *was* in the common-room last night, while I was sitting there reading it. I noticed that she kept glaring across at me, and thought it was because she was still sore at being ignored by everyone. But, of course, she must have been planning to tell on me to Miss Tallant all along.'

Felicity brooded on this as the two girls walked on. They had almost walked as far as the stables, and could see a slim, red-haired girl patting the nose of one of the horses, who had stuck his head over the stable door.

'I say, there's old Clarissa!' cried Susan. 'Hi, Clarissa!'

The girl turned her head, smiling when she saw Felicity and Susan coming towards her. 'Hallo, you two!' she said brightly. 'You only just caught me. I've just been to see Miss Peters, and was about to go back to Five Oaks.'

'How are things at Five Oaks?' asked Susan. 'Bill all right?'

The three chatted together for a while, then Clarissa

said, 'I met that new teacher of yours in town, the other day – Miss Tallant. We had quite a chat.'

'Really?' said Felicity. 'How did you come to meet her, Clarissa?'

'Well, I was in the little tea-shop, waiting for Bill, and Miss Tallant sat down at the table next to mine. I didn't realise who she was at first, of course, but then we fell into conversation. Very pleasant woman!'

Felicity and Susan exchanged startled glances and, noticing this, Clarissa laughed. 'Do I detect that Miss Tallant is not very popular?'

'She's extremely *un*popular!' said Susan, pulling a face.

She and Felicity went on to tell Clarissa about some of the things Miss Tallant had done, and Clarissa exclaimed in surprise. 'Well, I never! She seemed awfully nice when she was talking to me. And, having a niece of her own here, you would think that she would know the best way to handle young girls.'

'A *niece*!' exclaimed the two girls in unison, completely taken aback.

'Well, that's the first we've heard of it!' said Felicity. 'Who is this niece, Clarissa? Which form is she in?'

'Why, the fourth form,' answered Clarissa. 'Apparently she has just started this term.' Clarissa soon went on her way, leaving Felicity and Susan to stare at one another in horror.

'You know what this means, don't you, Felicity?' said Susan in a very serious tone.

'Yes,' said Felicity, also sounding very grave. 'Either

Sylvia or Olive is Miss Tallant's niece. And whichever one of them it is must also be the person who has been sneaking to her.'

'Which means that we accused poor little Bonnie unjustly,' said Susan, with a groan. 'I feel simply dreadful! Felicity, we must round up the others at once, and call a form meeting.'

'Of course,' said Felicity. 'Wait a minute, though! There are two of the others that we don't want at our meeting – Sylvia and Olive themselves. Whichever one of them is the mysterious niece, she obviously doesn't want anyone to know about the connection. And if we ask straight out she is likely to deny it.'

'Yes,' said Susan, looking thoughtful. 'We need to set a trap for her, just as we did for Bonnie. And this time we need to make sure that nothing goes wrong.'

Susan called a meeting of the North Tower fourth formers in one of the music-rooms that evening. Sylvia and Olive, alone in the common-room, wondered where everyone had disappeared to.

'Perhaps there's a debate in the hall, or a slide show, or something,' said Sylvia, sounding puzzled. 'Though I'm quite sure I would have remembered. Do you know where they can all be, Olive?'

Olive shook her head and hoped that Sylvia wasn't going to chatter all evening. She wanted to be alone with her thoughts.

'They can't be holding a rehearsal for the play,' Sylvia went on. 'Or we would have been invited too. Perhaps they're planning some sort of trick, and don't want to let us in on it.'

Olive's ears pricked up at this. 'Perhaps they are,' she said, sounding more friendly. 'Jolly mean of them to leave us out.'

'Well, they know that I'm not awfully fond of jokes and tricks,' said Sylvia. 'I wish that I was, but I never seem to see the funny side of things.'

'I say! Perhaps they are planning to play a trick on us,' said Olive. 'That would explain why they don't want us involved.'

Sylvia looked extremely dismayed at this, and said, 'Surely they wouldn't be so mean?'

'They probably just see it as a bit of fun, and don't think that it's mean at all,' said Olive. 'All the same, after that business with the mouse, I don't really want to be the victim of another of June's pranks. I vote that we go and look for them, Sylvia, and see if we can overhear what they are up to.'

'That seems rather sneaky, don't you think?' said Sylvia, looking rather uncomfortable.

'Nonsense! They are the ones who are being sneaky, plotting things behind our backs,' said Olive. 'Come on, Sylvia! Imagine how uncomfortable you are going to feel tomorrow, knowing that something may be going to happen to you, but not knowing where or when. Why, you'll be on tenterhooks.'

This was quite true. Sylvia really did find the thought of a trick being played on her quite horrid. So, reluctantly, she stood up and said, 'Very well. Let's see if we can track them down.'

But the fourth formers had hidden themselves well. Susan had chosen a music-room right at the top of North Tower, which hardly anybody used. There was no glass in the door, and once all the girls had filed in, she locked the door behind them.

Bonnie had been most surprised to be invited to this meeting, and had said to Susan, 'I thought you weren't supposed to speak to me.'

'Yes, well, I'm afraid there's been a bit of a misunderstanding, Bonnie,' Susan had said, turning red. 'Amy is invited too, of course. I'll explain it all to you both later, at the meeting.'

Bonnie had shrugged, and said, 'You may not get the chance. I don't know if I shall bother turning up.'

And with that, she had walked off, her little nose in the air.

But curiosity had got the better of Bonnie, and now she was in the little music-room with all the others, waiting to hear what Susan had to say.

'It's awfully cramped in here,' complained Amy. 'And it smells dreadfully musty.'

'Well, I shall be as quick as possible,' said Susan. 'Then we can all go back to the comfort of the common-room.'

'I say, Susan, Sylvia and Olive aren't here,' said Julie.

'They weren't invited,' said Felicity. 'And you will understand why, in a moment.'

Swiftly, Susan told the fourth formers what she and

Felicity had learned from Clarissa, and, of course, there was a perfect outcry.

'I wish I knew which one of them it was!'

'Yes, wouldn't I like to tell her what I think of her.'

'To think that she let us blame poor Bonnie,' said June, who was feeling rather ashamed of herself, for she had been the first to accuse Bonnie. She went up to the girl now and held out her hand, saying forthrightly, 'I'm most terribly sorry, Bonnie. I should have known that you wouldn't betray the form like that. I just hope that you will accept my apology.'

Bonnie stared solemnly at June and, for a moment, the others thought that she was going to reject the girl's frank apology. But then she smiled and took June's hand, and a sigh of relief went round the room.

'We are all very sorry, Bonnie,' said Susan. 'We misjudged you badly, and we will all do what we can to make it up to you. Amy, too, for we sent her to Coventry as well. She was the only one who had the good sense to realise that you couldn't possibly have been the sneak, and she was courageous and loyal in sticking by you.'

Amy, unaccustomed to being praised for these good qualities, found herself turning quite pink with pleasure, and graciously inclined her head.

'Well, thank goodness that is sorted out, at least,' said Felicity, thankfully. 'Jolly decent of you to forgive us, Bonnie.'

Bonnie smiled and said, 'I shall expect you all to make it up to me, though, just as Susan said. You are all to be especially nice to me this term.'

'We shall be,' said Pam, giving the girl a pat.

'Bonnie,' said Freddie. 'What *was* the job that you were doing for Miss Tallant? The one that she gave you the chocolate for?'

'It was nothing, really,' said Bonnie. 'She had torn her skirt, and I mended it for her, because she doesn't like sewing. That's all.'

'But why on earth didn't you tell us this in the first place?' said Julie, astonished. 'It would have saved so much unpleasantness.'

Bonnie's little rosebud mouth set in a stubborn line, and she lifted her chin.

'I was cross,' she said. 'Because you thought I was a sneak. And when I get cross I can be awfully stubborn. I thought that you should have believed me, without me having to prove myself.'

'Well, you were quite right,' said Nora. 'But now, the question is, what are we going to do about finding out which of the new girls is Miss Tallant's niece?'

'We shall all have to put our thinking caps on,' said Lucy. 'June, you are usually good at coming up with ideas.'

June, who had been looking rather thoughtful, said, 'I'm afraid someone else will have to think of something, for I have another thing on my mind.'

'What?' asked the others, curiously.

'I'm going to get my own back on Miss Tallant,' said June. 'I don't know how yet, but I'm going to play the biggest, best trick that I have ever played – on her. If only

I knew what her weaknesses are.'

'Well, we know that she doesn't care for mice and spiders, and things like that,' said Felicity.

'Yes, but we have already used those this term,' said June. 'And I do like to be original.'

'There is something that she is even more afraid of,' piped up Bonnie. 'She was talking to me one day when I helped her to tidy the classroom, and I happen to know that Miss Tallant is simply terrified of ghosts.'

'Really?' said June, her quick brain turning over all sorts of ideas instantly. 'How very interesting!'

'How silly of her,' said Susan, rather scornfully. 'There are no such things as ghosts.'

'Well,' said Bonnie. 'Miss Tallant says that she once saw one. It nearly frightened the life out of her.'

'I believe in ghosts,' said Nora, her eyes big and scared-looking. 'I remember once, when I was little –'

'Tell us another time, Nora,' said Susan, who didn't particularly want to spend the rest of the evening in this cramped, musty little room, listening to ghost stories. 'We really should get back to the common-room now, for it won't be long until bedtime.'

She unlocked the door, and the girls filed out. When they reached the bottom of the stairs, Felicity said, 'Now, we must all behave perfectly normally towards Sylvia and Olive for the time being. We don't know which of them is guilty, and it would be terrible if we accused someone wrongly a second time.'

June appeared to have drifted off into a kind of dream,

and Susan said sharply, 'June! Are you listening? We don't want any accusations flying around until we are absolutely certain which of the new girls is the sneak.'

'Of course,' said June. 'Don't worry, Susan, I've learned my lesson. In fact, I wasn't even thinking about the sneak.'

'What *were* you thinking about, June?' asked Freddie, noticing the mischievous glint in her friend's eye.

June grinned, and said, 'I was thinking about the ghost of Malory Towers.'

Miss Tallant strikes again

Sylvia and Olive had returned to the common-room, having failed in their search for the fourth formers. Olive, in particular, felt very disgruntled. She looked across at Sylvia, and thought what a dreadful chatterbox the girl was. Sylvia had kept up a constant stream of talk throughout the search, endlessly speculating on where the girls could be, what they could be doing, and what form any trick they were planning might take. Olive had soon grown heartily tired of her, and thought what bad luck it was that they were thrown together so much.

Just then the door opened, and the rest of the fourth form poured noisily in.

Sylvia and Olive eyed them suspiciously, but Susan grinned warmly and said, 'Did you think that we had got lost?'

'Well, Olive and I did wonder where you had got to,' said Sylvia. 'It's been awfully quiet in here.'

The girls had already decided what story they were going to tell, and Julie said, 'We all popped down to the stables. You see, Lucy has taught her horse Sandy the most marvellous trick. He can count up to five by pawing the ground with his hoof.'

'Yes, I taught him how to do it in the holidays,' said Lucy. 'And, of course, the others were simply dying to see it.'

'I should have liked to see it too,' said Sylvia, looking a little put out. 'I'm very fond of horses, you know.'

'I didn't realise,' said Lucy. 'If I had known I should have asked you to come along too, Sylvia. Never mind, perhaps I can take you to see Sandy tomorrow.'

That cheered Sylvia up, and she was able to dismiss her worries about the girls playing a trick on her. Julie sat down beside her and asked, 'Do you have a horse at home, Sylvia?'

'No, for we don't have any stables,' Sylvia answered. 'My young brother and sister and I go to a local riding school in the holidays, though.'

'How old are your brother and sister?' asked Julie with interest.

Of course, Sylvia needed very little encouragement to talk about herself, and was soon telling Julie all about her home and family.

Felicity, nearby, turned to Susan and said, 'Clever Julie! She is getting Sylvia to talk about her family in the hope that she might let something slip.'

'Good idea!' said Susan. 'If only we could do the same with Olive, but she will just clam up, as she always does.'

'Perhaps the reason she never talks about her family much is because she has something to hide,' suggested Felicity. 'Like an aunt, who also happens to be the most unpopular mistress at Malory Towers.'

'I wouldn't be at all surprised,' said Susan. 'I must

admit, I feel far more inclined to suspect Olive than Sylvia. Sylvia is so open, and will chatter away about herself to anyone who will listen. Hardly the behaviour of someone who is hiding a dark secret!'

'Miss Tallant never seems to take much notice of Sylvia,' observed Felicity thoughtfully. 'Yet she came down hard on Olive over the mouse trick.'

'Did she, though?' said Susan, frowning. 'She may have just pretended to give her a punishment to throw us off the scent. Bonnie said that when she passed the classroom that morning, Olive and Miss Tallant were just talking. Do you remember?'

'Yes,' said Felicity slowly. 'And I've just remembered something else! That photo that Olive put on her locker. I asked her about it, and she bit my head off. She threw it in her locker, in a fit of temper, and I haven't seen it since.'

'What are you getting at, Felicity?' asked Susan, puzzled.

'Well, it looked as if someone was missing from the photograph,' Felicity said. 'Olive's father had his arm outstretched, as though it were around someone's shoulders, but there was no one there. It was as if someone had been cut off. What if that's it, Susan? What if the person missing from the photograph is Miss Tallant?'

Susan gave a gasp, and said, 'I wonder if you could be right, Felicity.'

'Hallo, you two look very serious!' said Pam, coming over with Nora. 'What's up?'

Felicity told the two girls, and Nora said, 'So, it's

looking more and more likely that Olive is the culprit. I must say, I don't altogether blame her for not wanting to own up to having Miss Tallant as an aunt. I certainly wouldn't, if she was mine.'

'Well, we still can't be absolutely certain that it is Olive who is Miss Tallant's niece,' Susan said. 'And until we *are* certain it might be wise to keep our suspicions to ourselves.'

'Yes, I suppose it would,' agreed Pam. 'Actually, Susan, Nora and I came over to ask when we are going to have our first rehearsal. I know it's only short play, and no one has many lines to learn, but we all want it to be perfect.'

'I was thinking about that myself, actually,' said Susan. 'Mary has finished her song, and very good it is too. So now we are just waiting for June and Freddie to add their jokes.' She raised her voice, and called out, 'Hi, June! Freddie!'

The two girls, who were sitting side by side on a sofa, their heads close together as they talked, looked up, and Susan said, 'How are the jokes coming along for our play?'

'Almost finished,' said June, who had thoroughly enjoyed the task that Susan had given her. Ably assisted by Freddie, she had come up with several very funny lines and jokes to add to the script. Now she said, 'Another day or two, and we should be finished.'

'Excellent!' said Susan, happily. 'In that case, we could hold our first rehearsal on Saturday, if the hall is free.'

There were 'oohs' and 'aahs' at this, and Nora clapped her hands together, crying, 'Marvellous! I simply can't wait to begin. Bonnie, how are the costumes coming along?'

'I have made a start on yours, Nora,' answered Bonnie. 'I found the most beautiful dress in the store-room – all white and sparkly. With a little alteration, it will be perfect.'

'I say, I wonder if that was the dress Mary-Lou wore, when she played Cinderella in the pantomime that Darrell wrote,' said Felicity, her eyes shining.

'I'll bet it was,' said Pam. 'My word, that was a jolly good pantomime. I hope our little play will be as big a success.'

'I'm quite determined that it shall be,' said Susan, and everyone agreed.

'We shall spend every spare moment tomorrow finishing our work on the script,' said June to Freddie. 'For once that is done, there is something else I need to concentrate on.'

'How to get back at Miss Tallant?' said Freddie.

'Yes,' said June, her wicked dark eyes glittering. 'My goodness, I'm going to make her wish that she had never crossed me!'

Freddie grinned, and said, 'So, when is the ghost of Malory Towers going to make an appearance?'

'Not until he – or she – is ready,' said June, grinning back at her friend. 'This trick is going to be more carefully planned than any trick I have ever played. I really do intend to give that horrid woman the shock of her life!'

'Well, your brother is coming to see you at half-term, isn't he?' said Freddie. 'He's always full of good ideas, so perhaps the two of you should put your heads together.'

'The *three* of us,' said June. 'Don't forget that you are coming with us at half-term, because your people will be on holiday. And I may need your help, Freddie.'

'You know that you can rely on me,' said Freddie loyally. 'I would like to see Miss Tallant brought down a peg or two as well.'

And Miss Tallant struck again, the day before the first rehearsal was due to take place. The mistress caught Julie whispering to Lucy, and promptly dished out a hundred lines. 'I have to hand them in tomorrow morning!' groaned Lucy. 'And I was hoping to learn my lines for the play tonight.'

'Look here,' said Julie. 'Why don't I do half of them for you, Lucy? My writing is a bit like yours and I bet Miss Tallant will never notice the difference.'

'Oh, would you, Julie?' said Lucy happily. 'You are a sport! If we do them as quickly as we can, we shall both have time to go through our lines.'

The plan was duly carried out, and once the lines were finished, the two girls sat down together in the common-room and read through their parts in the play.

But they were in for a shock the following morning, when Lucy handed two sheets of paper to Miss Tallant, both covered in large, rather sprawling handwriting. The mistress did not even glance at them, but smiled at Lucy, saying, 'I hope that you did not have to waste too much of your evening on these lines, Lucy.'

'No, Miss Tallant,' said Lucy a little nervously.

'Of course you didn't,' said Miss Tallant, her smile

growing broader. 'Because Julie did half of them for you, didn't she?'

Lucy gasped. How on earth could Miss Tallant possibly know *that*? The girls' writing was almost identical, and even if there *was* the very slightest difference, the mistress couldn't have noticed it, for she hadn't so much as glanced at the pages. There was only one way Miss Tallant could know, Lucy realised suddenly, her lips tightening grimly. The sneak had struck again!

Just then, a small second former walked past the classroom, and Miss Tallant called out, 'Elizabeth! Please go and find Julie of the fourth form, and tell her to come to me at once.'

The nervous second former sped off at once, and then Lucy endured a very uncomfortable five minutes indeed! Miss Tallant sat down at her desk and picked up a book, neither looking at Lucy, nor speaking to her. So the girl had to stand in silence, until a puzzled and rather worried-looking Julie arrived. Miss Tallant laid her book aside and got to her feet, and one look at the mistress's face was enough to tell Julie that she was in serious trouble.

'Well, Julie!' said Miss Tallant, looking sternly at the girl. 'I understand that you were foolish enough to help Lucy with her punishment yesterday evening.'

Startled, Julie looked at Lucy. Surely her friend couldn't have been so foolish as to tell Miss Tallant the truth? But Lucy, guessing what Julie was thinking, gave the tiniest shake of her head.

Miss Tallant spoke again, a smile of satisfaction on her face, as she said smoothly, 'Of course, you must both be punished for such deceit. And your punishment will be that you are both forbidden to take part in the rehearsal this afternoon. Instead you will sit here, under my eye, and write an essay on the importance of obeying one's elders and betters.' The girls stared at Miss Tallant in dismay. Julie actually groaned out loud, and opened her mouth to say something, but Lucy gave her a nudge. There was no point in antagonising the mistress, for they would only end up with an even worse punishment. If there *was* anything worse than missing their first rehearsal! They had been looking forward to it so much, and now they were going to miss it. Not only that, but they had let the rest of their form down too, and all through their own deceit.

'I know that what we did was wrong,' said Julie angrily, as the two girls escaped from Miss Tallant's presence, her instructions to come back to the classroom at two o'clock sharp ringing in their ears. 'But we did it for the good of the play, so that you could learn your lines. The mean beast who split on us to Miss Tallant had no good intentions at all!'

'No,' said Lucy miserably. 'She just intended to cause trouble for us with Miss Tallant – *and* to spoil our rehearsal.'

'Well, she has succeeded,' said Julie, who felt very angry and upset.

Felicity and Susan were angry, too, when the two girls

told them that they had been forbidden to attend the rehearsal.

'What rotten luck!' cried Felicity. 'We can't possibly rehearse properly without the whole cast there.'

'Oh, Julie!' wailed Susan. 'I know that you were trying to help, and did it for the good of the play, but I do wish that you hadn't offered to do half of Lucy's lines for her. There are so few characters in the play, that I really don't know if it is worth carrying on with the rehearsal now.'

Julie hung her head and said, 'I'm sorry, Susan. I wish that I hadn't done it now.'

'It's not all our fault, Susan,' said Lucy. 'The person who sneaked on us is to blame, too.'

'I realise that,' said Susan, looking angry. 'But as we don't know who is to blame, we can't deal with them as they deserve.'

'Were both Sylvia and Olive in the common-room last night?' said Felicity, thinking hard.

'Yes, they were,' said Lucy. 'I remember seeing them.'

'Lucy and I were sitting at the table doing our lines,' said Julie. 'I suppose it would have been easy enough for one of them to peep over my shoulder and see that I was helping Lucy. Bother, why couldn't I have been more careful? Susan, you aren't really going to cancel the rehearsal, are you? Do say that you aren't, or I shall feel even more dreadful than I do already.'

'Well, I suppose we shall have to go ahead with it, as all the others are looking forward to it,' said Susan, still sounding rather disgruntled. 'We shall just have to get someone to stand in for you two, though they won't know the lines, of course. For heaven's sake, do take care not to get on the wrong side of Miss Tallant again, for I shouldn't be at all surprised if she is deliberately setting out to spoil our play, simply because we wouldn't let her be involved.'

Fortunately the rehearsal went smoothly, though Olive was not at all happy when Felicity told her that she was going to stand in for Julie, and take the part of the toy soldier.

'Can't you get someone else to do it?' said Olive, sullenly.

'Everyone else is busy with their own parts, or with jobs behind the scenes, so I'm afraid you really have no choice, Olive,' said Felicity firmly. 'And it doesn't matter if you can't act well, because you're only standing in for Julie. All you have to do is read the lines.'

And with that, Felicity pushed a script into Olive's hands and walked away to check that all was well behind the scenes.

A girl called April, from South Tower, was taking Lucy's part – much more graciously than Olive was taking Julie's – and once the two girls joined the rest of the cast on stage, the rehearsal began.

The three producers sat at the front of the hall, and all of them were very pleased with the way things turned out.

There were a few mistakes, of course. Several of the girls fluffed their lines, and Olive somehow managed to trip Nora up during her dance. She hotly denied doing it on purpose, when Nora accused her of this, but most of the girls were quite certain that it had been deliberate.

Susan gave the girl a scold, and Sylvia intervened, saying in a low voice, 'Susan, there's no point in losing your temper. We can't prove that Olive tripped Nora on purpose, and all we're doing is wasting valuable time.' Then she clapped her hands together briskly, and said in her loud voice, 'Come along, girls, back to your places, please, and let's start the dance again. Olive, you stand further back, then if Nora *should* happen to trip again, you can't be held responsible.'

Both Susan and Felicity looked rather taken aback, and none too pleased at this, but as one of the producers, Sylvia was quite within her rights. And both girls had to admit that what she said was very wise and sensible.

The rest of the rehearsal went without mishap, and at the end of it Susan said, 'Well, that wasn't bad at all!'

'I thought that it went very well indeed,' said Sylvia. 'Of course, the girls aren't word perfect yet, but that is only to be expected.'

Felicity, who felt cheered by how well the rehearsal had gone, said, 'You were very good, too, Sylvia. You handled the incident with Nora and Olive perfectly.'

Sylvia shrugged, and said, 'Well, of course, I'm quite an old hand at all of this, you know. Being a former head-girl, and having produced a play myself, I'm used to being a bit of a bossy-boots!'

But both girls noticed that Sylvia had turned pink with pleasure at Felicity's remark and, as she walked away, Susan said, 'Actually, although she can be dreadfully pushy and bossy at times, I think Sylvia is rather nice.'

'So do I,' agreed Felicity. 'And I know it's a horrid thing to say, but I actually *want* Olive to be Miss Tallant's niece, for that would be so much easier to bear than finding out that it is Sylvia.'

'Yes, I feel the same,' said Susan with a sigh. 'What a beastly business it is!'

'Cheer up!' said Felicity, slipping her arm through her friend's. 'There is still an awful lot to look forward to this term, you know. As well as our play, it will be half-term very shortly.'

'So it will!' said Susan, brightening. 'I had almost forgotten about that.'

She chuckled suddenly, and went on, 'And I must say, I'm rather looking forward to finding out how June intends to pay Miss Tallant back. Whatever she has in mind, I'll bet it's something quite ingenious. And I, for one, can't wait to see Miss Tallant get her comeuppance!'

An interesting half-term

The fourth formers took great care not to give Miss Tallant any cause to punish them over the next couple of weeks. They didn't want anyone else missing rehearsals, so they were polite, well-behaved and worked hard in her classes. But, as Pam remarked in the common-room on the evening before half-term, 'She doesn't seem terribly pleased! Any other mistress in the school would be delighted to teach such model schoolgirls.'

'Of course she's not pleased!' said June. 'She *likes* punishing us, and she's disappointed that we haven't given her any opportunity to vent her spite.'

'Well, Miss Tallant might not be pleased, but I certainly am,' said Susan, beaming round. 'Our play is really taking shape, and the last two rehearsals have gone swimmingly.'

'Shh!' hissed Freddie suddenly. 'Sylvia is coming this way, so don't mention Miss Tallant. Change the subject, quickly!'

At once the girls began to talk about the forthcoming half-term, and Sylvia joined in, saying in her hearty way, 'I simply can't tell you how much I am looking forward to my first half-term at Malory Towers, and to showing my people round properly.'

'It's going to be super,' said Julie happily. 'Lucy's parents aren't able to come, so she is coming on a picnic with my people.'

'And I bet Jack and Sandy will be going along too,' laughed Felicity, knowing that the two girls never went anywhere without their beloved horses unless they absolutely had to. Susan glanced round at that moment, and caught sight of Olive, sitting alone, as usual, a sour expression on her plain face.

'Are your people coming tomorrow, Olive?' Susan asked.

'Yes,' answered Olive, in her curiously flat voice. But she volunteered no more information, and discouraged the others from asking any more questions by immediately burying her head in a book. And she didn't look as if she was terribly excited about seeing her family again, thought Susan. She turned to Felicity, and murmured in a low voice, 'I'm jolly well going to keep an eye on Olive and her people tomorrow. If she *is* Miss Tallant's niece, then one of them may give something away.'

'Good idea,' said Felicity. 'And I suppose we had better watch Sylvia's parents too, for we can't rule her out yet.'

But as it turned out, there was no need to watch Sylvia's parents.

The girls leaped out of bed eagerly on the morning of half-term, even lazy Nora, who hated leaving her warm bed on cold mornings.

'Thank heavens it isn't raining,' said June, pulling the curtains open. 'Otherwise the upper-school lacrosse match would have to be cancelled.'

Ruth Grainger, the games captain, had chosen two teams from the upper school to play an exhibition match for the parents, and June had the honour of being the only fourth former to be chosen.

'Just make sure you play up, June!' called out Felicity.

'Yes, we'll all give you three cheers if you shoot a goal,' said Pam.

'I shall do my best,' said June, in her usual off-hand manner. But the others knew that June was as pleased as punch to have been chosen, and felt very proud indeed, though she would never admit it.

After breakfast, Sylvia was called to Miss Grayling's study, and when she returned to the common-room afterwards, she looked so woebegone that the others felt quite alarmed.

'What's up, Sylvia, old girl?' asked Felicity kindly.

'My parents aren't able to come today, after all,' said Sylvia miserably. 'My grandmother has been taken ill, so they have had to go and look after her.'

The others were terribly sorry to hear this, for they knew how disappointed Sylvia must feel.

'I say, what rotten luck!'

'Awfully sorry to hear that, Sylvia.'

'I do hope that your grandmother isn't seriously ill?'

'No, I think it's just a bad dose of flu, but she's too ill to do anything for herself,' answered Sylvia with a sigh. 'Of course, I quite see that Mother and Father have to go to her, but I can't help feeling upset that they won't be here.'

The kindly Pam gave Sylvia a pat on the shoulder, and

said, 'Cheer up, Sylvia! I know it's awful to have news like this at the last minute, but why don't you come out with me and my people instead?'

Sylvia's face lit up and she said, 'Thank you, Pam. That's jolly decent of you, if you're sure your parents won't mind.'

Since Pam's parents were as good-natured and easygoing as their daughter, Pam was able to reassure Sylvia on this point, and the girl cheered up considerably.

'There are some cars coming up the drive!' cried an excited Bonnie, who was peering out of the window. 'Amy, your parents are here! And June, yours are right behind.'

With an excited whoop, June ran from the room, Freddie – who was spending the day with June's people – right behind her. Amy followed at a more dignified pace, while Felicity and Susan went to join Bonnie at the window.

'I do hope my mother and father aren't going to be late,' said Bonnie fretfully. 'They promised to be here early.'

Felicity laughed, and ruffled Bonnie's curly hair. 'Don't worry, Bonnie,' she said. 'Your parents always keep their promises, for you know how to wrap them round your little finger.'

Olive, nearby, muttered under her breath, 'Spoilt brat!' Fortunately for her, no one overheard, for at that moment Bonnie's father's car drew up beneath the window, and the girl squealed loudly in excitement, before darting from the room.

'Someone else's people are here too,' said Susan, leaning out of the window. 'I don't think they belong to anyone here, though, for I don't recognise them.'

Felicity followed Susan's gaze, to where a man and woman were getting out of a car.

With them was a very pretty, dainty girl of about thirteen, with curly golden hair and big eyes.

'The two grown-ups look vaguely familiar to me,' said Felicity. 'Though I don't recognise the girl with them. Oh, I know who they are! Olive, it's your father and step-mother. I remember them from your photograph. Is the girl with them your sister? How pretty she is!'

'She's not my sister!' snapped Olive, her pale skin turning a dull red. 'She's not related to me at all!'

'Well!' exclaimed Nora, as the girl stomped out of the room. 'How odd!'

'Olive *is* odd,' said Susan in disgust. 'Her behaviour gets more peculiar by the day.'

'I wonder who that girl is,' said Felicity. 'Why on earth would Olive's father and step-mother bring someone who isn't related to Olive to visit her at half-term? It doesn't make sense.'

'Oh, who wants to worry about silly old Olive on a day like this?' said Nora. 'If she wants to act all odd and bad-tempered, let her! But I intend to enjoy half-term.'

The others felt exactly the same, and, as more and more parents arrived, went off to greet them excitedly.

Felicity, of course, was delighted to see her own pretty, sensible mother and her tall, distinguished-looking father, and flew into their arms as soon as they got out of the car.

'Mother! Daddy! How super to see you both again!' she

cried. 'Do come and say hallo to Susan and her people.'

Felicity's parents and Susan's parents knew and liked one another, and the two girls were thrilled when both families agreed to join up and go for lunch together at a restaurant.

But before that, there was plenty to see and do.

Parents had to be shown around the dormitory, common-room and classroom, then there were displays of art and needlework to admire, and mistresses to talk to.

Felicity spotted Olive and her family talking to Miss Tallant, and noticed that the mistress was laughing and joking.

'Hmm, that looks very suspicious,' said a low voice behind Felicity. She turned to see that June had come up behind her, and was also watching the little group.

'Miss Tallant spoke to *my* parents a little while ago, and she wasn't nearly as friendly, I can tell you,' June went on. 'Just look how relaxed and jolly she is with Olive's people, though. But then, I suppose she would be if she is related to them!'

'It does look suspicious,' said Felicity. 'Look, she is even talking to the girl that Olive's parents brought with them, as if she is very familiar with her.'

'Well, it looks as if we have discovered who Miss Tallant's niece is,' said June in a hard little voice. 'All we have to do now is catch her out.'

There was no time to say any more just then, for Freddie came over with June's parents, and the four of them went off together.

So Felicity went to join her own parents, who were chatting with Mam'zelle Dupont, feeling rather troubled.

But it was half-term, and Felicity found it impossible to stay troubled for long. Especially when her mother gave her a hug, and said, 'You're doing marvellously, dear. I have had glowing reports of you from every mistress I have spoken to.'

'Yes, Miss Potts said that she is delighted to have you in North Tower,' added Mr Rivers. 'She told me that it is girls like you who makes Malory Towers what it is, for you bring a wonderful spirit to the school. And I must say, darling, I agree with her.'

Felicity felt as if she would burst with pride! Fancy Miss Potts, the strict head of North Tower, saying that about her. She simply couldn't wait to tell Susan.

The two families went off to a restaurant for lunch together, and had an absolutely marvellous time.

'I don't want half-term to end,' said Felicity to Susan, as the two girls tucked into ice-creams. 'What a super day it's been!'

'Well, it's not over yet,' said Susan. 'We still have the lacrosse match this afternoon, then a scrumptious tea to look forward to, and all of tomorrow as well. Marvellous!'

Bonnie was also enjoying herself, for her parents spoiled her dreadfully, hanging on her every word as she chattered away to them. She was taken to a restaurant for lunch too, and was surprised – and none too pleased – to find that Olive and her family had chosen the same one.

'Is anything wrong, darling?' asked Mrs Meadows, noticing Bonnie's frown.

'Oh, it's just that I've seen someone I don't like very much, Mummy,' said Bonnie. 'That girl at the table in the corner. She's in my form and she's simply horrid. No one can bear her.'

'Well, we shall sit as far away from her as possible,' said Mrs Meadows, patting Bonnie's arm. 'What a plain girl she is. Her sister is very pretty, though. Actually, she reminds me a little of you, Bonnie.'

Bonnie hadn't noticed the other girl with Olive, and she looked across at her table again now, spotting the golden-haired girl. Heavens, could that really be Olive's sister? There was absolutely no resemblance between them at all.

'I shouldn't be at all surprised if she was jealous of her sister,' Mrs Meadows was saying now. 'Perhaps that is why she is so horrid to everyone, poor girl.'

'Yes,' said Bonnie, looking thoughtful. 'I think that you may be right, Mummy.' Bonnie watched Olive's family from the corner of her eye as she ate her lunch. Olive remained largely silent throughout, though Bonnie noticed that her father and step-mother addressed a great many remarks to her. But they were treated to the same one-word answers that the Malory Towers girls always got from Olive. The younger girl, however, kept up a stream of bright chatter, much to Olive's evident displeasure, for she scowled constantly.

Bonnie was in a pensive mood on the way back to Malory Towers, and her father glanced at her in the driving mirror, asking, 'Is everything all right, my dear? You're awfully quiet.'

'I'm all right, Daddy,' said Bonnie, smiling angelically at Mr Meadows. 'I was just thinking about something, that's all.'

Bonnie had been thinking about what her mother had said. Mrs Meadows was rather a silly woman at times, but she had a streak of shrewdness in her nature. And Bonnie felt that her mother might have hit the nail on the head with Olive. The girl made up her mind that she was going to try to talk to Olive's sister – if the golden-haired girl *was* her sister – before half-term was over.

And her chance came later that very afternoon. The two girls found themselves side by side while they were watching the lacrosse match. Bonnie disliked all games, and had only brought her parents to watch so that she could support June.

For most of the watching girls, however, it was a thrilling game, and very close. And June proved that she was worthy of being selected for the team by scoring the winning goal in the last minute. While the rest of the fourth formers yelled themselves hoarse, Bonnie clapped politely and heaved a sigh of relief that it was over. And she wasn't the only one, for the golden-haired girl looked relieved too, and the two girls exchanged sympathetic smiles.

As everyone began to move away, Bonnie fell into step beside the girl and said softly, 'I do so hate lacrosse, don't you?'

The girl nodded in agreement, and said in a soft, childish voice, 'I don't like *any* games. Nor does Olive, really. I think she only brought us to watch to spite me, for she knew that I would be simply bored to tears.'

There was a petulant note in the girl's voice, and Bonnie asked, 'Is Olive your sister? You don't look very much alike.'

'Oh no, she's my step-sister,' explained the girl. 'My mother married her father. He's an absolute dear, but Olive simply detests me.'

'Really?' said Bonnie, opening her eyes wide. 'I can't think why.'

'She's horribly jealous of me,' confided the girl, lowering her voice a little. 'You see, she and her father were all-in-all to one another, until Mummy and I came along. Olive simply can't bear it when he pays me any attention.'

She gave a high little giggle, and went on, 'I must admit I do play up to him at times, just to annoy Olive, for I dislike her every bit as much as she dislikes me.'

'She's not an easy person to like,' said Bonnie, wrinkling her nose.

'No, but it is *very* easy to make her lose her temper,' said the girl, pleased that Bonnie seemed to dislike Olive too, and deciding that she was a safe person to confide in. 'And such fun. I like to get her into trouble, too.'

'What kind of things do you do?' asked Bonnie, thinking that this was a very interesting conversation.

'Well,' said the girl. 'Olive deliberately smashed my

favourite doll once, because we had had a row. Of course, I was dreadfully upset, and told Mummy, who insisted that Daddy punish her. He was absolutely furious with her for being so spiteful, and she was sent to bed without any supper that night. Once she had shown that she had a bad temper and a spiteful nature, it was easy. Sometimes things get broken, or go missing, and somehow poor Olive always gets the blame. No one ever suspects that it is me.'

'I see,' said Bonnie. She would have liked to continue talking to the girl, but at that moment her mother called out, 'Annabel! Do hurry up, dear, or we shall be late for tea.' And, with a wave of her dainty little hand, Annabel darted off to catch up with her mother, and Bonnie's own parents appeared, her father saying, 'There you are, Bonnie! You must have fallen behind. Mummy and I thought that we had lost you.'

Bonnie smiled her sweet smile and tucked her hand into the crook of her father's arm, but her thoughts were racing. No wonder poor Olive was so ill-tempered! What a mean-spirited girl Annabel was. And it was quite clear now why Olive despised Bonnie herself, and Nora. The two of them were very like Annabel in looks, though not – Bonnie hoped – in character.

Well, thought Bonnie, quite astonished. Perhaps Olive wasn't as bad as she was painted after all!

Exciting plans

It was a very busy time for the fourth formers once half-term was over. There were rehearsals for the play, of course, with those girls who weren't taking part working hard behind the scenes. Bonnie and her assistants worked like beavers to produce the costumes, those who were good at art helped paint the scenery, and others searched the school from top to bottom for props that could be used.

Then there were school lacrosse matches coming up, and many of the girls were practising hard in the hope that they would be chosen to play.

June and Freddie were full of exciting plans too. They had come back from half-term their eyes alight with mischief, and when Pam had said, 'Oho! What are you two up to?' the two had shaken their heads and replied aggravatingly, 'Wouldn't you like to know!' But they did share one of their plans with the others, in the common-room one evening. Sylvia, who had a sore throat and had gone off to see Matron, was not there. Neither was Olive, who had been called away by Miss Williams over the matter of some poorly written work.

'Gather round, everyone!' cried June. 'With Sylvia and Olive out of the way, it seems as good a time as any to tell you that I intend to hold a midnight feast on my birthday next week, and you are all invited.'

There were 'oohs' and 'aahs' as the fourth formers exchanged excited glances.

'A feast, how thrilling!'

'Yes, we haven't had one in simply ages!'

'We will all bring something, of course, June.'

'Thanks,' said June, beaming round at her friends. 'Mother and Father have given me some money to get what I like, but it won't be enough to feed everyone, so if all you others can bring something, that will be a big help.'

'Jolly decent of you to invite us all, June,' called out Nora.

'Well, that's the thing,' said June. 'I'm *not* inviting all of you. Sylvia and Olive must be kept in the dark for now, for I don't want either of them running off to tell tales to Miss Tallant.'

Then she grinned, and added, 'Actually, that's not quite true. I *do* want the sneak to go to Miss Tallant. But I want to make sure that she tells the *right* tale.'

'What are you planning, June?' asked Felicity.

'I can't say just yet,' said June. 'For Freddie and I haven't quite thought it all out yet. But as soon as we have come up with a way to trick Miss Tallant and her beastly niece, I shall let you know. Personally, I am almost certain that Olive is the culprit.'

Several of the girls murmured in agreement, and everyone looked most surprised when Bonnie piped up, 'I feel rather sorry for Olive.'

'Bonnie, dear, are you feeling quite well?' asked Amy, looking at her little friend in surprise.

'Yes, perhaps you ought to pop along and see Matron, too,' said Nora. 'You're delirious.'

'Nothing of the sort!' said Bonnie. 'It's just that I happened to speak to Olive's step-sister, Annabel, at half-term. And what she told me put quite a different complexion on things.'

'Do tell us,' said June.

So Bonnie told the fourth formers what she had learned from Annabel, and very shocked they looked when she had finished.

'What a mean little beast Annabel sounds!' said Susan, in disgust.

'Poor Olive!' said Pam, her ready sympathy stirred. 'It must be quite dreadful to take the blame for everything that goes wrong, and to know that you are innocent.'

'I daresay it must have seemed to Olive that there was no point in being good and well-behaved,' said Susan, shrewdly. 'So she decided that if she was going to be treated as a bad girl, then she might as well become one.'

Suddenly Felicity snapped her fingers, and cried, 'Of course! The person who is missing from Olive's family photograph isn't Miss Tallant at all! It's Annabel!'

'Yes, that makes sense,' said Susan. 'And to be quite honest, I can't say that I blame Olive for wanting to cut her out.'

'You may be right,' said June. 'But all the evidence still points to Olive being Miss Tallant's niece. And, whatever problems she may have at home with her horrid little step-sister, it doesn't excuse her behaviour towards us.'

'I agree with June,' said Nora. 'I do understand Olive's behaviour a little better now, and I know why she has such a down on Bonnie and me. But, even though I feel sorry for her, the fact remains that we can't trust her.'

Felicity, who had been looking thoughtful, said, 'The best possible outcome of all of this would be for Olive herself to own up that she is Miss Tallant's niece. It would make us all think better of her if she told the truth, and then we could let her know that we felt proud of her for doing the right thing.'

'Marvellous idea!' cried Julie. 'And once we had praised her up a bit, Olive would surely start to feel more confident, and she might find the courage to tell her father about the mean tricks Annabel has been playing.'

Most of the fourth formers thought that this was a very good idea indeed, only June looking rather doubtful.

'If you are all agreed, I will go along with it, of course,' said June. 'But *not* until after the feast, for I'm sure that we are all looking forward to that and we can't risk having it spoiled.'

'That *would* be a terrible shame,' said Lucy. 'I really think that we will have to leave Olive out of it, you know, girls.'

'Yes, I suppose that we better had,' said Susan. 'June, you said that you were working on an idea to trick Olive and Miss Tallant, didn't you?'

'Yes,' answered June. 'If it works, it will keep Miss Tallant nicely out of the way while we enjoy our feast, *and* it will teach Olive that sneaking can sometimes backfire on the sneak, so we shall kill two birds with one stone.'

'That sounds super,' said Susan. 'And once the feast is over, we can all set to work to make Olive own up, and try to set her on the right track.'

Just then the common-room door opened, and in walked Olive, wearing her customary sullen expression.

At once all the girls began to chatter about something else, while Olive sat down in a chair, looking miserably at the returned work that Miss Williams had given her.

Kindly Pam went across to her and said, 'Bad luck, Olive. Those sums that Miss Williams gave us this morning were awfully difficult. I found them quite hard, and I'm not too bad at maths. I say, perhaps I could help you with them?'

For a second it seemed as though Olive was going to bite Pam's head off, but, looking into the girl's friendly, open face, she saw real kindness there and it warmed her. So Olive swallowed her pride, and said, 'Thanks, that's awfully kind of you.'

'Good old Pam,' said Felicity, as she saw the girl sit down next to Olive and begin to patiently explain how best to do the rather complicated sums that Miss Williams had set. 'She really is a decent sort.'

'Yes,' said June. 'Just so long as her decency doesn't carry her away. We don't want Olive turning over a new leaf until *after* the feast!'

Naturally, the feast became the main topic of conversation for the fourth formers. There was a big cupboard just outside the dormitory, which the girls used as a hiding place for all their food. It had a key, which June kept in her pocket at all times so that no one could pry and find the hidden goodies.

The girls were allowed to go into town in their free time, as long as they went in pairs, and June was forever going to the cupboard to hide packets of biscuits, tins of sardines, and bottles of lemonade that one girl or another had brought back with her.

Amy, who had a great deal of pocket money, bought a simply enormous box of chocolates as her contribution to the feast, and she handed them to June when she and Bonnie returned from town.

'Gosh, thanks, Amy!' said June. 'These look simply gorgeous! I'll run up and pop them in the cupboard now, before tea.'

June did so, then she locked the cupboard carefully and slipped the key back into her pocket, before turning to go back downstairs. Then what a shock she had! For Sylvia was standing behind her, and it was quite clear that she must have seen the contents of the cupboard.

June could feel herself turning red, but said breezily, 'Hallo there, Sylvia.'

'Hallo, June,' said Sylvia, her eyes alight with curiosity. 'I say, what on earth is going on? Are you using that cupboard to store food?'

June thought quickly and said, 'Yes, but please don't say anything to anyone, Sylvia. The South Tower girls are planning a feast next week, and they wanted somewhere to store the goodies where their matron wouldn't find them. She's a real nosey-parker, you know, always snooping round, and she's far stricter than our Matron.'

Fortunately, Sylvia, who had never met the placid, good-humoured matron of South Tower, accepted this readily, and said, 'Oh, of course. I shan't say a word.'

June breathed a sigh of relief and went off to tea, catching up with Freddie just as she was entering the dining-room.

'I say!' she whispered. 'I've just had a jolly close shave with Sylvia.'

And, quickly, she told Freddie what had happened.

'That was quick thinking, June,' said Freddie admiringly.

'Wasn't it just?' agreed June, with a cheeky grin. 'And it's given me an idea. How would you like a walk around the grounds before tea, Freddie, old girl?'

Freddie, seeing the gleam of mischief in June's eyes, said at once, 'If I agree, will you tell me what you're up to?'

June nodded, and said, 'Quiet now! Here come the others, and I don't want to let them in on what I'm going to do until I have it all worked out properly.'

It was a chilly evening, and, after tea, the two girls put on their hats and coats, June fetched a torch, and off they went, out into the garden.

'Where are we going?' asked Freddie, curiously.

June glanced over her shoulder, to make sure that no one was around, and said, 'We're going right over in the corner, by South Tower. There is a small gap in the wall there, just big enough for someone to slip through, which leads down to the beach.'

'Is there?' said Freddie, surprised. 'I didn't know that!'

'Hardly anyone does,' said June. 'It's almost completely overgrown by the ivy that hangs down the wall, so it's invisible.'

'Go on,' said Freddie, now very curious indeed.

But June said, 'No, I'll wait until we get there before I tell you what I mean to do. It will be easier to explain if you can see exactly what I mean. Thank heavens that it's a cold evening, and nearly everyone is indoors. No one will be able to see what we are up to.'

But someone *was* about! As the two girls approached the wall, they spotted plump little Mam'zelle Dupont a few yards in front of it.

'Blow!' said Freddie. 'Whatever is Mam'zelle doing here? She likes to be all nice and cosy indoors in the cold weather. It's not like her to take an evening stroll.'

Mam'zelle was well wrapped up in a thick, heavy overcoat, a long woollen scarf around her neck and a fur hat pushed firmly over her neat roll of hair. She was looking a little perplexed, but her face cleared when she saw the two girls, and she cried out, 'Ah, *mes filles*! How happy I am to see you both. You may help me in my search.'

'What are you searching for, Mam'zelle?' asked June.

'My brooch,' answered the French mistress, looking rather unhappy. 'I lost it this afternoon, and now I come to look for it.'

'How can you be sure that you lost it *here*, precisely?' asked Freddie.

'I came this way earlier with Mam'zelle Rougier,' explained Mam'zelle Dupont. 'And I distinctly remember her remarking on how unusual my brooch was shortly before we reached this very spot. Then, when we entered the school, she cried, "Why, Mam'zelle Dupont, your brooch – it is gone!" And so it was – quite vanished. I retraced my steps, but there was no sign of it, so I must have dropped it in the undergrowth here.'

'But, Mam'zelle, why didn't you search for it then, when it was still light?' asked June. 'You don't have a hope of finding it in the dark, especially as you don't even have a torch with you.'

'There was no time then, for I had to teach the third formers,' said Mam'zelle, looking agitated. 'And I see that you have a torch, *ma chère* June. You will switch it on and help me find my brooch, yes?'

Well, this wasn't what the two girls had planned at all, but they couldn't very well say no to the French mistress, so June switched on her torch and played the beam over the bushes that grew next to the wall. Suddenly, her sharp eyes spotted the gap in the wall that she had spoken to Freddie about, and a wicked idea came into her head.

'Here, Freddie,' she said. 'You hold the torch for a bit, and I'll hunt around in the bushes and see if I can spot Mam'zelle's brooch.'

Then, unseen by the French mistress, she winked at Freddie, who wondered what on earth she was up to.

Keeping one eye on Freddie and Mam'zelle, June picked up a stick and poked around in the bushes, then cried, 'I think I see something sparkling – over there!'

Freddie and Mam'zelle both peered in the direction that June had indicated and, quick as a flash, June darted through the little gap in the wall, disappearing from their view.

'I see nothing!' complained Mam'zelle. 'Do you, Freddie?'

'No, not a thing, Mam'zelle,' answered Freddie. 'June, where exactly did you say it was?'

Both she and Mam'zelle Dupont looked towards the spot where June had been standing – but she had gone!

'*Tiens!*' cried Mam'zelle, giving a little start. 'What has happened to June?'

Quick-witted Freddie realised at once what had happened, and distracted Mam'zelle by saying, 'I think I see your brooch down there, Mam'zelle.'

And once again, poor, unsuspecting Mam'zelle, who never seemed to realise when she was having her leg pulled, obligingly turned her head, allowing June to emerge from her hiding place.

'Haven't you found your brooch yet, Mam'zelle?' she asked, and the French mistress spun round sharply, crying, 'There you are, June. Where have you been?'

'Why, nowhere, Mam'zelle,' answered the girl, her lips twitching humorously. 'I've been here all the time. Isn't that so, Freddie?'

Freddie nodded, and Mam'zelle fixed June with a stern

stare, before shaking her head and crying, *'Non! Méchante fille!* You are trying to trick your poor Mam'zelle, once again! I saw you, over there by the wall. I looked away for a split second, and you disappeared – poof!'

'Mam'zelle, I really think that the poor light is making your eyes play tricks on you,' said Freddie, so gravely that June wanted to burst out laughing. 'June most certainly did not disappear.'

'Of course I didn't,' said June. 'You know, Mam'zelle, tricks take quite a lot of planning, and I didn't even know that I was going to bump into you, so I couldn't possibly have prepared anything.'

This gave Mam'zelle pause for thought. She knew how carefully June worked out her tricks, and the girls had come upon her quite by chance. So, she was forced to agree that, in the gathering gloom, her eyes had indeed deceived her.

'And still I have not found my brooch,' she said, rather forlornly. 'It is a very special one, for my nephew gave me it for my birthday.'

Freddie, who, like most of the other girls, was very fond of Mam'zelle Dupont, felt sorry for her, and said kindly, 'Look here, Mam'zelle, why don't you go indoors and get warm? June and I will carry on looking for your brooch, and we will come and tell you if we find it.'

'Ah, you are indeed good, kind girls!' cried Mam'zelle, quite forgetting that, a few moments ago, she had accused June of tricking her. The thought of going indoors and sitting before a roaring fire, with a mug of hot cocoa, was so pleasant that she could almost have hugged the two girls.

June was less pleased, though, and said rather crossly to Freddie, 'Why on earth did you volunteer us to find Mam'zelle's brooch? It's getting jolly cold now, and I was looking forward to sitting in the common-room for a bit, now that we've done what we came for.'

'I know, but poor old Mam'zelle looked so miserable,' said Freddie, who was much more soft-hearted than her friend. 'The brooch must be around here somewhere, so if we hurry up and find it we'll still have time for a sit down before prep. Besides, after the trick you played on Mam'zelle, I think that the least we can do is help her.'

June grinned at this, and said, 'Yes, I suppose you're right. Did it really look as if I had vanished into thin air, Freddie?'

Freddie nodded and gave a shiver, 'It was quite creepy, actually, the way you suddenly disappeared and then reappeared again.'

'Good,' said June. 'I was hoping you would say that, for I intend to give Miss Tallant the fright of her life! Let me tell you what I am going to do.'

As the two girls talked, they began to hunt for the missing brooch. In a very short time their efforts were rewarded. Freddie gave a cry and yelled, 'I've found it! My word, won't Mam'zelle be pleased?'

Mam'zelle was highly delighted when June and Freddie took the brooch to her, patting the girls on their shoulders.

'Ah, you may be bad sometimes, but you are good girls

at heart!' she cried, beaming at the two girls. 'I only wish that there was some little reward I could give you.'

'There is, Mam'zelle,' said June promptly. 'You can let the two of us off French prep for a week.'

But even big-hearted Mam'zelle was not that generous, and she wagged her finger at June, saying, 'Now you try to take advantage of me! One minute you are good, June, and the next you are bad again! I do not know whether I am on my heels or my head with you! But I shall not forget the favour that you and the dear Freddie have done me, and you may be sure that I shall think of something I can do to repay you.'

A trap is set

And Mam'zelle was as good as her word, for a few days later, when the girls were at tea, the French mistress produced the most enormous chocolate cake, which she placed in the centre of the fourth form's table.

'Heavens, Mam'zelle, that looks simply delicious!' said Nora. 'What have we done to deserve this?'

'You have June and Freddie to thank,' said Mam'zelle, cutting the cake into big slices. 'They found my brooch the other day, and I promised them a reward.'

'Jolly decent of you, Mam'zelle,' said Freddie.

'Yes, thanks, Mam'zelle,' said June. 'Though I don't see why the others should share it, for they did nothing. Really, Freddie and I should have half each.'

Of course, June was joking, and the others laughed as Mam'zelle handed round slices of cake, Lucy saying, 'Good show, June and Freddie! Mam'zelle, you should lose your jewellery more often, if this is what happens.'

'I say, June!' said Sylvia, who was sitting beside the girl. 'Speaking of cake, that was a fine, big fruit cake that I saw you put in the cupboard this morning. My word, the South Tower girls must have enough food to feed an army.'

'Sh! Keep your voice down, Sylvia!' hissed June. 'Do you want Mam'zelle to overhear, and spoil the feast for the South Tower girls?'

'Sorry, June,' said Sylvia, lowering her voice and looking rather sheepish.

But Felicity and Susan, on the opposite side of the table, had heard Sylvia's remark and were puzzled by it. What on earth did Sylvia mean about the cake that the two of them had bought being meant for the South Tower girls' feast?

They caught up with June after tea and asked her about it.

'Sylvia caught me stowing some food in the cupboard,' explained June. 'I told her that the South Tower girls were having a feast to throw her off the scent. And I'm going to make sure that Olive thinks the same. Then whichever of the two girls is our sneak is sure to tell Miss Tallant.'

'So she will be thrown off the scent, too,' said Susan. 'And we can have our feast in peace, because Miss Tallant will be over at South Tower on a wild goose chase!'

'June, what a super idea!' laughed Felicity. 'I would love to see Miss Tallant burst into South Tower to spoil the feast, only to find the girls tucked up in bed. How foolish she is going to look!'

'That is going to be the least of Miss Tallant's problems,' said June, with a wicked grin. 'Just wait and see what I have in store for her!'

'June, do tell!' begged Felicity and Susan.

'I shall tell you, but not now,' promised June. 'I have

something else to do at the moment. Has anyone seen Bonnie?'

June eventually found Bonnie in the dormitory, where she was brushing out her curly hair in front of a mirror.

'Bonnie,' said June. 'Thank goodness I've found you.'

Bonnie looked round at the girl in surprise, and said in her lisping voice, 'Is something the matter, June?'

'Not exactly,' answered June, sitting on the edge of one of the beds. 'But I need you to do something for me. I want you to help me set up this trick that I'm going to play on Miss Tallant.'

Bonnie clapped her hands together in glee, and said, 'Goody! Just tell me what you want me to do, June.'

'Well, Bonnie,' began June. 'I know that you talk to Miss Tallant a lot, and I want you to tell her a little story – all about the ghost of Malory Towers.'

'Ooh!' said Bonnie, thrilled, her big eyes growing wide. '*Is* there a ghost at Malory Towers, June?'

'Not as far as I know,' said June, grinning at Bonnie. 'But we are going to make Miss Tallant *think* that there is! Next time you have a chance to speak to her in private, Bonnie, I want you to tell her that you woke up in the middle of the night and went to look out of the window. And you saw a pale, ghostly figure over by South Tower.'

Bonnie was so excited that she couldn't speak, but she nodded vigorously, and June went on, 'Tell Miss Tallant that it looked up at you watching from the window, then disappeared into thin air.'

'Yes, I can do that, all right, June,' said Bonnie, eagerly. 'Anything else?'

'Yes,' said June. 'I think it would be a good idea if we were to make up a tragic story about a young girl who died at Malory Towers many, many years ago, and whose spirit is said to haunt the school.'

'We could say that she died by falling off the cliff!' cried Bonnie, struck by sudden inspiration.

'Brilliant!' said June. 'Yes, I see it all. She quarrelled bitterly with her sister, and was so upset that, one dark, stormy night, she ran away. But the wind was so fierce that it blew out the lantern she carried with her and, in the pitch darkness, she stumbled off the cliff.'

'Oh, the poor, poor girl!' cried Bonnie, looking as if she was about to burst into tears.

'Ass!' said June, giving her a shove. 'It's only a story, remember!'

'Yes, but you told it so convincingly, June, that I felt quite moved,' sighed Bonnie. 'And I think I know what comes next. The girl's tormented, restless spirit haunts the school, seeking out her sister so that they can make up their quarrel.'

'Actually I hadn't thought of that, but it's very good,' said June approvingly.

'I shall tell Miss Tallant tomorrow that I saw the ghost,' said Bonnie. 'Just to unsettle her a little. Then, the next day, I shall tell her the story of the dead girl. I really think that she will be frightened, June, because of the ghost that she saw when she was younger.'

June, who was far too down-to-earth to believe in ghosts, gave a snort, and said, 'I daresay it was a shadow, or a trick of the light. But it's a jolly good thing that it happened, for it has given us a way to punish Miss Tallant for being so mean to the fourth form.'

Bonnie carried out her part of the plan faithfully, and had the satisfaction of seeing Miss Tallant's face turn white as she told her tale.

'She looked like a ghost herself,' laughed Bonnie, as she related what had happened to June and Freddie.

'Well done, Bonnie,' said June, pleased with the girl. 'And now, Freddie, we must make preparations to carry out *our* part of the plan.'

There was a rehearsal for the play that afternoon, and Bonnie, in her role of wardrobe mistress, was most surprised when June and Freddie came backstage and began showing a great interest in the costumes, wigs and greasepaint that were there.

'I say, June!' called out Freddie. 'This would be simply perfect.'

Freddie was holding up an old-fashioned, white night-dress, and Bonnie gave a squeal.

'Freddie Holmes, if you get dirty finger-marks on that, I shall never forgive you!' she said. 'That's Molly's costume and I have just had it washed.'

'Bonnie, dear,' said June, putting an arm round the girl's shoulders. 'May I borrow it, please?'

'Whatever for?' asked Bonnie, puzzled. 'You have perfectly good pyjamas of your own.'

'I don't want to wear it to bed,' chuckled June. 'You see, Bonnie, I am going to dress up as a ghost, and scare the living daylights out of Miss Tallant!'

'When?' asked Bonnie.

'On the night of our feast,' said June. 'You see, she is going to be under the impression that the South Tower fourth formers are holding a feast, and she will rush over there at midnight to stop it. But Freddie and I are going to prepare a little surprise for her.'

Bonnie was torn. On the one hand, she felt quite thrilled at the thought of the unpleasant Miss Tallant being punished for her nasty ways. On the other, the thought of the exquisite nightdress that she had painstakingly altered to fit Molly becoming damaged or dirty quite filled her with horror.

As though sensing what she was thinking, June said, 'I promise that I shall take great care of it, Bonnie, and if it should become dirty I will wash it myself.'

'Very well,' said Bonnie, at last, handing the nightdress over. 'And just see that you *do* take care of it, June.'

'We could borrow some of this greasepaint, too,' said Freddie. 'The white one would give you a ghostly pallor, June, and we could use this purple one to make dark hollows under your eyes.'

'Good idea!' said June.

'And you could really do with a wig,' said Bonnie. 'For you don't want to run the risk of Miss Tallant recognising you. Try this.'

And Bonnie picked up a long, dark wig, which she put on June's head.

'Marvellous!' said Freddie, happily. 'With the wig and some greasepaint, I really don't think that your own mother would know you, June.'

When the rehearsal was over, June and Freddie ran up to the dormitory with the things that they had found for June's disguise, and hid everything away carefully.

As they walked out on to the landing, June spotted Olive coming up the stairs, and, putting a finger to her lips, quickly pulled Freddie into an alcove. Then she waited until Olive had gone into the dormitory, leaving the door open behind her. Beckoning to Freddie to follow, June went over to the cupboard where the food for the feast was being stored.

Unlocking the door, and opening it with a lot of quite unnecessary noise, June said loudly, 'My word, what a lot of food! Those South Tower girls are going to have a marvellous feast.'

Following June's lead, Freddie said, 'What a pity that we can't join them, for it all looks super. Thank goodness we were able to help them out by storing their food for them. When did you say that they are holding the feast, June?'

'On Friday night, at midnight exactly,' said June, in her clear voice, as she locked the door again.

The two girls walked away, and as they reached the bottom of the stairs, June said, 'Well, Miss Tallant is bound to get the false information now, either from Olive or Sylvia. Everything is working out perfectly!'

Friday was June's birthday, and most of the girls had bought her a little gift of some sort.

Felicity gave her a bottle of bath salts, and Susan gave her an enormous bar of chocolate.

Freddie, who had noticed that June's old purse was looking very shabby indeed, had bought her a new one, while Bonnie presented her with a set of handkerchiefs that she had embroidered herself. The only person who didn't give June a present was Olive, but as June said, 'I didn't really expect anything from her. And, to be honest, I'm quite glad that she didn't give me anything, for I shouldn't have liked to have accepted a gift from someone I don't like, and who I believe to be a sneak.'

'Well, you've had some jolly nice presents, anyway,' said Nora, looking rather enviously at the things June had received.

'Yes, thanks awfully everyone,' said June, smiling round at her friends. 'You've all been very generous.'

'And the best part of your birthday is still to come,' said Freddie, in a low voice. 'The feast tonight.'

'Yes,' said June, looking round to make sure that Sylvia and Olive could not overhear. 'I don't know which I'm looking forward to most – that, or the trick that we are going to play on Miss Tallant.'

Felicity and Susan, standing nearby, *did* overhear, though, and Felicity said at once, 'Is the ghost of Malory Towers going to make an appearance tonight, then?'

'She certainly is,' said June, her eyes sparkling with mischief. 'She's going to appear in the grounds, while Miss Tallant is making her way to South Tower. And then she is going to vanish again.'

'But June, you'll miss your own birthday feast if you are out in the grounds playing a trick on Miss Tallant,' said Felicity, with a frown.

'No, I shan't,' said June. 'Freddie and I are going to wake up before you others, so that I can get dressed up in my ghost costume. And the actual trick itself will only take a few moments, so we shall be back in the common-room with the rest of you in a trice.'

'What a pity that we shan't all be there to see the trick,' said Susan with a sigh. 'I should love to see Miss Tallant's face when she sees the ghost!'

'Well, Freddie and I will tell you all about it,' promised June.

'What about Sylvia and Olive?' said Felicity, looking worried. 'One of them is Miss Tallant's niece, and the sneak, and if she wakes up and finds us out of our beds she is bound to cause trouble for us.'

'Oh, I've thought about that,' said June coolly. 'Just make sure that whoever is last out of the dormitory locks the door behind them.'

Susan gave a gasp, and said, 'June, we can't do that!'

'We must,' said June firmly. 'Probably neither of them *will* wake up and everything will be all right, but I don't want to take any chances. Of course, if they should happen to wake, tomorrow the sneak will probably tell Miss Tallant about the feast, but by then it will be too late. It will simply be our word against her niece's. And Miss Tallant's niece is not going to be in her good books, for having sent her over to South Tower for nothing.'

'That's true,' said Felicity. 'I must say, I'm still not entirely happy about locking the two of them in the dorm, but it would be too bad if the feast was spoiled.'

As things turned out, there was no question of locking Sylvia in the dormitory, for later that day she was sent to Matron by Miss Williams.

'Sylvia will be spending a couple of days in the San,' Miss Williams informed her class that afternoon. 'The poor girl has had a dreadful sore throat for several days now, and she has quite a temperature.'

'Poor old Sylvia!' said Pam. 'I thought that she didn't look very well earlier on.'

Everyone was sorry to hear that Sylvia was ill, but as Lucy said to Julie, 'At least it means that she is safely out of the way now, and won't have to be locked in the dormitory with Olive.'

Most of the fourth formers now knew of the plan to lock Olive in the dormitory while the feast took place, and they also knew that June meant to give Miss Tallant a scare.

Everyone was very excited, and found it hard to keep their mind on lessons that day.

'Nora!' said Miss Williams sharply, in the maths lesson. 'Is your knowledge of the maths that we are doing so great that you can afford to waste time by whispering to Pam?'

'No, Miss Williams,' said Nora meekly.

'Then kindly pay attention to what I am saying,' said the mistress. 'Unless you want to come to me for extra coaching after tea?'

Nora didn't want that at all, so she bent her head over her book and did her best to concentrate for the rest of the lesson.

Bonnie also found her mind wandering in French, but as she was one of Mam'zelle Dupont's favourites, she found it quite easy to talk her way out of trouble.

'*Ma chère* Bonnie, you are restless!' complained Mam'zelle. 'You do not concentrate. What is the matter with you?'

Bonnie turned her large, brown eyes on the French mistress, and said in a sad tone, 'I'm sorry, Mam'zelle. You know how much I love your French lessons, but I am just so worried about poor Sylvia. I expect you have heard that she has been taken ill.'

Of course, Bonnie had not been thinking about Sylvia at all. She had been thinking about the midnight feast, and the trick that June was going to play on Miss Tallant. But Mam'zelle, as usual, was quite taken in, and cried, 'Ah, it is kind of you to be concerned for *la pauvre* Sylvia. But you must not worry your head, Bonnie, for Matron will take the greatest care of her.'

Olive, hearing this, threw an angry glance in the girl's direction. If it wasn't just like Bonnie to worm her way out of trouble! She was just like her beastly step-sister, Annabel, and how Olive detested them both.

Surprisingly, though, no one was scolded in Miss Tallant's class. Julie and Lucy whispered together, and June flipped a paper dart at Olive, but Miss Tallant, for once, didn't even notice, seeming quite preoccupied.

'She was thinking of tonight, I expect,' said June scornfully, once the lesson was over.

'And of how she is going to ruin things for the South Tower girls.'

'What a shock she is going to get!' laughed Nora. 'My word, I simply can't wait for tonight to come!'

The ghost of Malory Towers

Some of the girls found it very hard to get to sleep that night, for they were all thoroughly overexcited. At last, one by one, they dropped off. Susan, who was to be responsible for waking the girls in time for the feast, had set her alarm clock for ten minutes to midnight. She had placed it under her pillow, so that the sound did not disturb Olive. June also had an alarm clock under her pillow, but hers was set for half past eleven. When it went off, she awoke at once, and nudged Freddie, in the next bed. The two girls got out of bed, then put bolsters down the middle of their beds, just in case Matron or one of the mistresses should peep in.

The things that they needed for June's disguise were in a box under her bed, and she picked it up. Then the two girls tiptoed silently from the room, and went into a little bathroom at the end of the corridor.

There, they worked swiftly. Freddie rubbed the white greasepaint all over June's face, then carefully smudged some of the purple around her eyes.

'Golly!' said Freddie, standing back to admire her handiwork. 'You look simply ghastly!'

'Thank you,' said June with a grin.

Then June changed into the long, white nightdress, pulling it very carefully over her head, so as not to get greasepaint on it.

'Bonnie will be simply wild with me if I get it dirty,' she said.

Finally, she placed the wig on her head, smoothing the hair into place, and Freddie said, 'Thank goodness it's not windy tonight. It really would give the game away if your wig blew off!'

But it was a perfectly calm, still night as the two girls crept out of a side door and, under cover of the trees, made their way to South Tower.

There, they crouched behind a hedge, and Freddie whispered, 'It's five minutes to midnight. Do you suppose that Miss Tallant is already in South Tower?'

'No,' whispered June. 'She thinks that the feast is starting at midnight, and she will want to catch the girls in the act. I think that she will appear shortly after midnight. Freddie, I'm going to take my place now. You know what you need to do.'

'You can count on me, June,' said Freddie solemnly. 'Now, off you go.'

June darted over to the wall, slipping swiftly through the hidden gap there and disappearing from view. Freddie, still in her hiding-place, gave a shiver. June really did look like a very realistic ghost, and watching her vanish like that was very creepy indeed! The night was cold, and Freddie hoped that they would not have to wait too long for Miss Tallant to arrive.

But, as June had predicted, the mistress came into view shortly after midnight, looking over her shoulder with many nervous glances as she approached South Tower. Freddie grinned to herself in the darkness. Miss Tallant was no doubt thinking of Bonnie's ghost story, for she was evidently very uneasy indeed.

Freddie crouched down lower, to make sure that the mistress couldn't possibly spot her, then she let out a high-pitched wail. This was both to scare Miss Tallant, and to warn June that their victim had arrived. And the unearthly wail certainly succeeded in its first objective, for the mistress jumped violently, and put a hand to her heart.

'Who is there?' she demanded, her voice quavering.

But no answer came and, with one last, scared look round, Miss Tallant put her head down and strode briskly into South Tower.

With the mistress safely out of earshot, Freddie gave a low whistle, which told June that Miss Tallant had gone inside. Now, all they had to do was wait.

Five minutes later, a red-faced Miss Tallant emerged, escorted to the door by Miss Markham, the stern head of South Tower.

Miss Markham looked even sterner than usual, and her voice carried on the still night air to the listening Freddie.

'I find your behaviour quite extraordinary, Miss Tallant,' the mistress said coldly. 'If you had reason to suspect that my girls were holding a midnight feast, you should have come to me, instead of bursting into their dormitory like that and waking them all up. I don't feel that Miss Grayling will be impressed by your conduct.'

Miss Tallant mumbled something which might have been an apology, then Miss Markham bade her a frosty goodnight, before going back inside and closing the door.

Freddie put a hand over her mouth to stifle her laughter at the mistress's disgruntled expression. The person who had wrongly informed Miss Tallant that there was to be a feast in South Tower was certainly going to get it tomorrow!

As Miss Tallant moved forward, Freddie let out another wail, which stopped the mistress in her tracks. And this was the signal for June to come out. She slid silently through the gap in the wall, standing several yards from Miss Tallant.

And Miss Tallant, rooted to the spot in terror, was too frightened even to scream as she stared at the apparition before her, with its deathly pallor and big, hollow eyes.

June took a small step in the direction of Miss Tallant, who let out a sound between a moan and a whimper, then she turned away and vanished through the gap again.

Miss Tallant remained frozen in horror for a moment, then she let out a piercing shriek, so loud that both June and Freddie had to clap their hands over their ears.

Miss Markham, who had just reached her bedroom, gave a start and quickly made her way downstairs and outside again, where she found a pale, trembling Miss Tallant.

'Good heavens!' cried Miss Markham. 'What on earth has happened, Miss Tallant?'

'A g-ghost!' stammered Miss Tallant. 'I – I saw a ghost!'

Miss Markham, who had long ago sized Miss Tallant up as a rather silly, spiteful woman, pursed her lips. She knew that there were no such things as ghosts, and would very much have liked to give the mistress a piece of her mind. But there was no doubt that the woman had suffered a great shock, for she was as white as a sheet, and was shaking from head to foot. Miss Markham said crisply, 'I daresay that your imagination was playing tricks on you, Miss Tallant. Still, it is quite clear that you cannot return to North Tower in this state. Come up to my room, and I shall make you some hot cocoa, and then I will walk back to North Tower with you.'

Miss Tallant was only too happy to let Miss Markham lead her inside, and as soon as the two mistresses had disappeared, Freddie crept out from behind the hedge, and went across to the wall.

'June come out!' she hissed. 'Let's get back to North Tower quickly, while Miss Tallant and Miss Markham are both inside.'

The ghostly June emerged, her enormous grin making her look even more frightening than she had before, as she said, 'That went well. Did you see her face, Freddie?'

'Yes, but do hurry, June,' begged Freddie, taking her friend's arm and beginning to run. 'The feast will have started by now, and I don't want to miss another minute of it. I don't know why, but this midnight haunting has made me awfully hungry!'

The feast had indeed started, and the fourth formers were enjoying themselves enormously.

Susan had gone round quickly and quietly, waking everyone up and taking great care not to disturb the sleeping Olive. June had given Susan the key to the store cupboard, and she, Felicity, Pam and Nora had got all the food out, while the rest of the girls put on dressing-gowns and slippers and padded down to the common-room.

Then Susan had taken a last look into the dormitory to make sure that Olive was still asleep, before locking the door behind her and following the others downstairs.

Someone had lit candles and closed the heavy curtains, so that nothing could be seen from outside. Bonnie, who was a great favourite with the kitchen staff, had coaxed the cook into lending her some plates and cups, and the girls set everything out on them.

Then Felicity said, 'It doesn't seem right starting until June gets here. It is her birthday feast, after all.'

'Yes, but she did tell us not to wait,' said Susan, eyeing the plates of food longingly.

How delicious everything looked! There was an enormous pork pie, biscuits, tins of sardines and pineapple, cake, chocolate and all kinds of goodies!

'She won't be very long,' said Julie. 'And we shall make sure that there is plenty left for her, and for Freddie.'

So the girls munched away happily, all the time wondering what was happening to June and Freddie.

'I do hope that the trick went well,' said Lucy. 'My

goodness, wouldn't it be dreadful if they got caught!'

'June won't get caught,' said Bonnie confidently. 'She always plans everything so carefully.'

And it was soon seen that Bonnie was quite right, for June and Freddie joined them, and the girls gasped to see June dressed up as a ghost.

Bonnie and Amy shrieked so loudly that Susan had to tick them off.

'Idiots!' she hissed. 'Do you want to wake up the whole of North Tower?'

'Sorry, Susan,' said Bonnie. 'But really, June looks so frightening that I simply couldn't help myself.'

June grinned and said, 'Miss Tallant screamed too – much more loudly than you, Bonnie.'

She and Freddie sat down and began to eat, while the fourth formers clamoured to know what had happened.

Assisted by Freddie, June told them, and the listening girls gasped as June told the tale.

'Well!' said Pam. 'All the years I've been at Malory Towers, and I didn't know that there was a gap in the wall by South Tower.'

'Well, we fourth formers will keep it to ourselves,' said Susan. 'Who knows when we may need to use it again.'

'I expect Miss Markham will be bringing Miss Tallant back to North Tower soon,' said Freddie, tucking into a slice of pork pie. 'But we have nothing to fear, because her room is at the other side of the building, and she will come in at the door over there.'

'Perhaps I should go and wait for her,' said June, with

a smile. 'Just to see her jump out of her skin.'

The others laughed at this, but Susan said, 'I don't think we had better risk any more wandering around. It's jolly lucky that you two didn't get caught outside, June and Freddie, for you know that there is a strict rule forbidding any girl to leave her tower at night.'

'I wonder if dear Olive is still sleeping peacefully?' said Amy.

'She must be,' said Nora. 'Or we should have heard her banging at the dormitory door by now.'

'Gosh, I never thought of that,' said Felicity, looking alarmed. 'What are we to do if she starts banging at the door?'

'I suppose I shall have to go up and unlock the door,' said Susan with a grimace. 'And then I will have to tell Olive why she wasn't invited to our feast, and warn her what will happen if she splits on us.'

But there was not a sound to be heard from upstairs, and the girls finished their feast in peace, until there was hardly anything left. Then they sat around eating the chocolates, finishing the lemonade and chatting idly.

At last, Susan said, 'I suppose we had better clear up now.'

Nora gave a groan and said, 'This is the part of midnight feasts that I always hate.'

'Come on, lazybones,' said Pam, giving her a nudge. 'If we all pitch in, it shouldn't take long.'

So the fourth formers got to work, sweeping up the crumbs, piling up the plates and collecting up the empty lemonade bottles. Lucy put them into a cupboard, saying, 'I'll get rid of these tomorrow.'

'And I will take the plates and cups back to Cook in the morning,' said Bonnie. 'My goodness, my first midnight feast! What fun it's been!'

Everyone agreed to that, as, tired and happy, they tiptoed upstairs. Susan unlocked the door very quietly, feeling relieved when she saw that Olive was still fast asleep and didn't appear to have stirred. Tomorrow, she thought, getting into bed, she would have to try and think of a way of getting either Olive or Sylvia to own up to being Miss Tallant's niece. But, at the moment, she was just too tired to think, falling asleep almost as soon as her head touched the pillow. So did the others, for it had been a very tiring evening and they were quite worn out.

And all of them had great difficulty in getting up the following morning! Olive, who was awake bright and early, simply couldn't understand why the others were so sluggish.

Even Julie and Lucy, who liked to race down to the stables before breakfast to see their horses, couldn't get out of bed. At last, Susan sat up and said, 'Come on, girls, we must get a move on or we shall be late for breakfast.'

There were moans and groans at this, but most of the girls got out of bed and began to get ready. Only Amy and Nora stayed put, but they always hated getting up anyway.

'I don't want any breakfast,' muttered Amy, turning over and closing her eyes. 'I would much rather have an extra hour in bed.'

'Amy, it doesn't matter whether you actually *want* breakfast or not, you must put in an appearance, or Miss Williams will come looking for you,' said Felicity. 'And if she finds you in bed, it will mean an order mark against the whole form.'

'The same goes for you, Nora,' said Pam to her friend. 'Do get up.'

'I can't!' wailed Nora. 'I feel sick.'

'Well, it jolly well serves you right for eating six chocolate biscuits,' said Pam, bending her head close to Nora's, so that Olive could not overhear. 'Do come along now!'

At last everyone was ready, and the girls trooped down to breakfast. They cast several interested glances Miss Tallant's way, for all of them were curious to know how she was feeling after her ordeal last night.

She looked very pale indeed, and there were dark circles under her eyes, as though she had not slept well.

June noticed too, with satisfaction, that her hand shook slightly as she picked up her cup of tea. She pointed this out to Freddie, who said, 'Serves her right. At least she won't be snooping around at night in future. I shouldn't be at all surprised if she is afraid to leave her bedroom now!'

None of the girls ate very much breakfast, for they all felt full from the feast the night before, and one or two of them really did feel sick. Mam'zelle Dupont, at the head of the table, looked quite concerned when Nora refused to eat her toast, saying, 'Ah, *la pauvre*! You are sick. You shall go to Matron immediately.'

But Nora had no intention of doing this, for Matron had a knack of knowing when a midnight feast had been held, and kept a bottle of especially nasty-tasting medicine for anyone who complained of feeling ill afterwards. So, to put Mam'zelle's mind at rest, the girl nibbled at a corner of her toast and sipped a cup of tea.

It was as the girls were leaving the dining-room that Miss Tallant approached them and snapped, 'Olive! I want a word with you.'

The listening fourth formers noticed how the girl turned pale, and stammered, 'But Miss Tallant, I have to take some work to Miss Williams.'

'Come and see me immediately afterwards,' said the mistress, a cold, angry look on her face. 'And please don't keep me waiting!'

Olive went off to find the work that she had to give to Miss Williams, looking very unhappy, and the others exchanged glances.

'Well!' said June, raising her dark eyebrows. 'I'll bet you anything you like that Miss Tallant is going to give Olive a scold for sending her on a wild goose chase last night.'

'Yes, I think you're right,' said Felicity. 'It looks as if Olive is her niece all right. And I wouldn't like to be in her shoes when she faces her aunt!'

'I've been trying to think of a way to get her to own up,' said Susan. 'But I really can't.'

'Well, let's have a try in the common-room later,' said Pam. 'And if she won't admit to being Miss Tallant's niece and sneaking on us, then we will just have to tackle her about it, I'm afraid.'

As it was Saturday, there were no lessons, but a rehearsal for the play was scheduled for the afternoon. And several of the girls thought that it would be a nice idea to go and see Sylvia.

'Let's pop across to the San now,' said Felicity to Susan. 'I think that there is a bar of chocolate in the common-room, left over from the feast. Perhaps if we take it to her it might cheer her up a bit.'

'Good idea,' said Susan. 'I feel a lot happier about visiting her now that we know for certain that she isn't the sneak.'

So the two girls went into the common-room to fetch the chocolate, then went along to the San. But they were in for a shock!

Miss Tallant's niece

'Hallo, girls,' said Matron to Felicity and Susan, as they entered the San. 'Come to see Sylvia? Well, she is feeling a little better today, and I daresay a visit will cheer her up.' They found the invalid sitting up in bed reading a book, and looking rather down in the dumps. But she brightened when she saw her visitors and put the book aside, saying in a rather croaky voice, 'Do come and sit down! You can't imagine how marvellous it is to see you. Matron is a dear, but –'

'But she can be awfully bossy at times,' Felicity finished for her, and Sylvia smiled.

Susan handed her the chocolate, for which Sylvia was extremely grateful, then the three girls chatted. For once, Sylvia was quiet, letting the other two do most of the talking, as she had been ordered by Matron not to strain her throat.

Susan began to tell the girl about a trick that June was planning to play on Mam'zelle Dupont the following week, but she realised that Sylvia's polite smile was becoming rather strained, and said, 'Of course, I forgot! You don't like jokes and tricks, do you, Sylvia?'

'I know it makes me seem frightfully dull and

boring, but no, I don't,' Sylvia admitted.

'It seems very odd to me,' said Felicity. 'I don't think I've ever met anyone who doesn't like jokes and tricks before.'

'Well, it's because of something that happened when I was younger,' said Sylvia.

'Did someone play a trick on you that went wrong, or hurt you?' asked Susan curiously.

'No, it was *I* who played a trick on someone else,' was Sylvia's surprising answer. 'And it went terribly wrong.'

'What happened?' asked Felicity.

'Well, I played a trick on my aunt,' said Sylvia. 'My father's younger sister. You see, we live in a big, old house, and my aunt always used to complain that it gave her the creeps. Though it never stopped her coming to stay with us! I love the house, and I became fed up of hearing her criticise it, so one night I decided that I would *really* give Aunt Aggie the creeps!'

'Whatever did you do?' asked Susan, quite unable to imagine Sylvia playing a trick.

'I dressed up as a ghost one night, and ran around in the garden under her window,' said Sylvia, looking rather ashamed now.

Felicity and Susan, with June's trick on Miss Tallant in mind, laughed, and Felicity said, 'Well, that doesn't seem so very bad.'

'Oh, but it was,' said Sylvia gravely. 'You see, Aunt Aggie was so terrified that she fainted, and banged her head as she fell. She was quite ill for a while, and had to stay with us for simply ages!'

'Heavens!' cried Felicity. 'What bad luck. But it wasn't your fault, Sylvia. I mean to say, you didn't harm your aunt on purpose.'

'No, but it quite put me off playing any tricks,' said the girl miserably.

'Yes, I can see that it would,' said Susan. 'Did you own up?'

Sylvia shook her head unhappily. 'I was too afraid,' she said guiltily. 'My aunt has quite a temper, you know, and would have been terribly angry with me. Awfully cowardly of me, I know.'

'Well, you were younger then,' said Susan, attempting to give the girl's thoughts a happier direction. 'And I'm sure that we have all done foolish things that we are not proud of at some time or other.'

Sylvia cheered up at this, and the rest of the visit passed pleasantly, until Matron came in to throw them out.

'Sylvia must rest for a little now,' she said. 'But she may have more visitors later, if some of the others would like to come.'

It was as the two girls were making their way to the common-room that Felicity suddenly stopped dead in her tracks.

'Oh, my gosh!' she cried.

'What's up?' asked Susan, looking at her in surprise.

'I've just remembered something,' said Felicity. 'Bonnie told us that Miss Tallant is afraid of ghosts because she saw one when she was younger.'

'Yes?' said Susan, a puzzled look on her face.

'And Sylvia dressed up as a ghost to frighten her aunt!' exclaimed Felicity. 'Her *aunt*, Susan! Don't you see?'

Light dawned on Susan, and she gasped. 'Olive is innocent, after all. *Sylvia* is Miss Tallant's niece.'

'Which means that Sylvia is also the sneak,' said Felicity grimly. 'Susan, we must tell the others at once.'

But while Felicity and Susan had been visiting Sylvia, a quite dreadful row had broken out in the common-room.

It started over a very little thing indeed, as big rows often do. Nora, not realising that Olive was standing behind her, had stepped back and accidentally stood on the girl's toe.

'Gosh, I'm awfully sorry, Olive!' Nora had said at once. 'I do hope that I didn't hurt you.'

'Well, you did,' snapped Olive, who seemed to be in a blacker mood than usual since she had been to see Miss Tallant. 'Why on earth can't you look where you are going?'

Nora tried to apologise again, but Olive cut her short, an unpleasant sneer on her face, as she said spitefully, 'For someone who thinks that she is *so* graceful, and *such* a marvellous dancer, you're terribly clumsy, Nora. I don't know what Susan and the others were thinking of, to let you play the fairy, for you simply aren't up to it, in my opinion.'

'Well, who cares tuppence for your opinion?' said Pam, roused to a rare show of temper by this. 'Keep it to yourself, Olive, for no one else wants to hear what you have to say.'

There were murmurs of agreement from some of the listening girls, and Olive flushed angrily. But she turned away and said no more. Things might have calmed down, if June and Freddie had not walked in at that precise moment. Sensing an atmosphere, June asked at once, 'What's the matter?'

'It's nothing,' said Nora quickly, for she had no wish to prolong the argument and just wanted to forget all about it. But Amy, who disliked Olive intensely, had other ideas, and said in her haughty way, 'Just our dear Olive causing trouble again – as usual.'

Olive turned on Amy at once, crying, 'How dare you accuse *me* of causing trouble, you horrid little snob! Nora was the one at fault, for she stood on my foot – and I wouldn't be the least bit surprised if it was deliberate!'

'Don't be ridiculous!' said Bonnie, entering the fray. 'I saw the whole thing, and it was quite obvious that it was an accident.'

'Well, you would stick up for Nora, wouldn't you?' scoffed Olive, towering over little Bonnie. 'For you are both exactly alike! Spoilt, silly, pretty little dolls!'

Then Olive folded her arms and stood with a smirk on her face, waiting for the foolish little Bonnie to burst into tears.

But she was disappointed, for Bonnie, very angry indeed, stood up to Olive, saying, 'Well, I would rather be a spoilt, silly little doll than a plain, jealous sneak! For that is what you are, Olive. And I know why you are so jealous of Nora and me, for I spoke to Annabel at half-term.'

The colour drained from Olive's face, and she hissed, 'You had no right to speak to her! No right at all!'

'I have the right to speak to anyone I please,' retorted Bonnie defiantly. 'I understand why you dislike your step-sister, Olive, I really do. I understand why you needed to cut her out of your family photograph, as though she didn't exist. But please don't take your loathing of her out on Nora and me, for it is nothing to do with us, we don't deserve it, and we don't appreciate it!'

'One up to Bonnie!' murmured June, who had been watching the scene with enjoyment. So had the others, and how they relished seeing Olive look so taken aback. There was a great deal more to Bonnie than met the eye, and Olive had found out the hard way!

Now June decided to take a hand, and she stepped forward, saying smoothly, 'Do you have any other relatives that you don't want us to know about, Olive? An aunt, for instance?'

Olive looked extremely puzzled, and said, 'I don't know what you mean.'

'Oh, I think you do,' said June. 'You see, we know all about you and Miss Tallant. We know that you have been sneaking to her, and letting her in on our secrets. What do you have to say about that, Olive?'

Olive had nothing at all to say, for she was completely speechless. But guilt was written all over her face, and she was quite unable to look any of the others in the eye. At last she opened her mouth to speak, but the only sound that came out was a little sob, and the girl ran from the room.

Olive almost knocked over Felicity and Susan, who were outside, and when Susan called out, 'Hi, Olive! Whatever is the matter?' she didn't even look round, but ran up the stairs to the dormitory.

'Well!' said Susan to Felicity, in astonishment. 'What do you suppose that was about?'

Felicity, who had glanced through the open door of the common-room and seen the grim faces of the fourth formers, thought, with a sinking heart, that she knew. She turned to Susan, and said gravely, 'I have a horrible feeling that we are too late.'

Susan gave a groan and went into the common-room, Felicity behind her.

At once June, aided by Bonnie, Nora, Pam and Amy, launched into an account of what had happened.

When they had finished, Susan groaned again, and said, 'June, I do wish that you had waited!'

'Why?' asked June, surprised and none too pleased. 'Olive was never going to own up, and as a row had already started I thought that this was the best time to tackle her.'

'But it wasn't, June,' said Felicity, looking very troubled. 'Because, you see, we have discovered that Olive is *not* Miss Tallant's niece. Sylvia is!'

There was a shocked silence, then everyone began to speak at once.

'Surely not!'

'That's impossible! I can't see Sylvia as a sneak.'

'Olive looked so guilty – it simply *must* be her.'

'And she didn't make any attempt to defend herself.'

'Well, perhaps she felt too shocked and upset to retaliate,' said Susan. 'But there is no doubt at all that Sylvia is the culprit.'

And, quickly, she told the fourth formers what she and Felicity had learned.

'I suppose it *must* be Sylvia, then,' said Pam. 'Though I'm very surprised, I must say.'

'Blow Sylvia!' said June, angrily. She felt very guilty indeed for having accused Olive unjustly, and was wishing that she had held her tongue. 'If only you had come back a few minutes earlier and told us this, Susan and Felicity, everything would have been all right.'

'Well, you can hardly blame us!' said Susan crossly, for she felt very angry with June herself. 'The fact is, that you had no right to say anything at all to Olive. As head of the form it was my duty, but, as usual, you had to take the lead, and go in all guns blazing, without thinking things through.'

June flushed angrily. She felt annoyed with herself, and annoyed with Susan. And the reason she was annoyed with Susan was because everything she said was perfectly true.

June was honest enough to admit that to herself. She *did* always have to take the lead in things. And this wasn't the first time she had caused an awkward situation by accusing someone unjustly.

Nora spoke up for her, though, saying, 'To be fair, Susan, all of us thought the same as June. We were all absolutely convinced that she was the mysterious niece, and had been sneaking to Miss Tallant. And the chances are, if June hadn't accused her to her face, one of us others would have.'

'That's very true,' said Bonnie, nodding solemnly.

'Yes, we were all feeling sore with Olive, because of the row she had started,' said Julie.

'So really we are all to blame.'

'No,' said June suddenly. 'I am to blame. Susan is quite right. I shouldn't have tackled Olive as I did. Speaking out of turn seems to be one of my biggest faults! Each time it happens I tell myself that I will think twice before doing it again, and then I go and jump in with both feet!'

'Well, at least you have the courage to own up to it,' said Felicity, admiring June for being honest enough to admit to a fault.

'Yes, but owning up to it isn't enough,' said June, ruefully. 'I need to do something to make amends. I shall go and apologise to Olive, and I will tell her that we know now that she isn't the sneak.'

Susan was a little doubtful about this, for, while she appreciated June's efforts to make it up to Olive, she wasn't sure whether the girl would accept the apology. And if Olive gave June the cold shoulder, June might flare up again, and then another quarrel would break out!

Felicity, seeing the doubt in Susan's face, said, 'I know! Why don't we all go and speak to Olive? Although she isn't the sneak, she hasn't done very much to make us think well of her, so really it's no wonder that we suspected her. But we can go to her now and tell her that we want to wipe the slate clean and give her a chance to become one of us.'

'Jolly good idea, Felicity!' cried Pam. 'Come along, everyone, let's go up to Olive now.'

So the fourth formers trooped upstairs and into the dormitory, all of them feeling rather virtuous about their decision to try and befriend Olive.

Alas for such good intentions! When Susan opened the door and the fourth formers filed in, Olive was nowhere to be seen.

'Oh!' said Susan, rather disappointed. 'She's not here. She must have come downstairs while we were talking in the common-room.'

'Perhaps she has gone for a walk in the grounds, to clear her head,' suggested Lucy.

'Yes, that's probably it,' said Julie. 'Oh well, we shall just have to wait until later to make amends to Olive.'

'There's something else,' said Freddie, looking rather serious. 'We shall have to tackle Sylvia about her behaviour.'

'Yes, I had already thought of that,' said Susan, looking rather gloomy. Bother, now there would be yet another row, and another girl sent to Coventry. She had just been getting to like Sylvia, too.

'Well, Matron said that she will probably be back in class tomorrow, so we will deal with her then. And June . . .'

June held her hands up, and said at once, 'I know, Susan! I shall leave it all to you.'

Where is Olive?

Olive did not turn up for rehearsal that afternoon, and the girls didn't see hide nor hair of her. When she failed to turn up for tea, Susan grew rather alarmed.

'I say!' she said to Felicity. 'You don't think that Olive's done anything silly, do you?'

'Whatever do you mean?' asked Felicity, startled.

'Well, it just occurred to me that she might have run away or something,' said Susan.

'Surely she wouldn't do such a thing?' said Felicity, shocked. 'Besides, where would she go? We know that she is not happy at home, so it's very unlikely that she would have gone there.'

'That makes it all the more worrying,' said Susan, with a frown. 'If she had gone home, at least we would know that she is safe.'

Pam, who had overheard this, said, 'Steady on, Susan! We don't *know* that Olive has run away. Why, for all we know she may have come back and be up in the dormitory now.'

So, after tea, Felicity and Susan, along with Pam and Nora, went up to the dormitory once more. But there was no sign of Olive.

Looking very worried indeed, Susan marched across to Olive's locker and pulled it open.

Some of her personal belongings were gone, and when Felicity took a look inside the girl's wardrobe she could see that some of her clothes were missing too.

'Oh, my word!' gasped Nora. 'It didn't seriously enter my head that she really *had* gone. Now what do we do?'

'We must report it to Miss Williams,' said Susan gravely. 'At once, for there is no time to lose!'

But Miss Williams was out, so the girls went to find Miss Potts, the head of North Tower.

She listened to their story with a very serious expression indeed, then said, 'I must inform Miss Grayling immediately. You girls had better come too, in case she needs to question you.'

So, all feeling rather nervous, the four girls followed Miss Potts to Miss Grayling's study.

The Head called to them to come in, in answer to the mistress's sharp knock, and saw at once that something was wrong.

Quickly, Miss Potts told Miss Grayling what had happened and the Head listened, her expression grave. Then she said, 'Do you girls have any idea at all where Olive may have gone?'

'None at all, Miss Grayling,' answered Susan. 'I only wish that we did.'

'Then do you know of any reason why she might have run away?' asked Miss Grayling.

The four girls looked at one another, and Miss Grayling

said, 'If you know something, it is important that you tell me, for it might help us in finding Olive.'

So Susan told the story of how the fourth formers had discovered that Miss Tallant had a niece at Malory Towers, and of how she had been sneaking to her aunt.

'We all thought it was Olive,' said Susan, rather miserably. 'And one of the girls accused her to her face. But now we know that we were wrong, and that Sylvia is Miss Tallant's niece.'

'Yes, she is,' said the Head. 'I was aware of it from the first, but at the request of both Sylvia and Miss Tallant, I kept it to myself. Both of them felt that they would be able to settle in better if no one was aware of their relationship. But we shall come back to that in a minute, for I must telephone the police at once, so that they can search for Olive.'

Miss Grayling dialled the police station and held a hurried conversation with the person at the other end of the telephone, before replacing the receiver and turning back to Miss Potts.

'Could you organise a search party of any available staff to search the grounds, please, Miss Potts?' she asked. 'The police will be here shortly, but I really don't feel that we should waste any time.'

Miss Potts nodded and left the Head's study, and Miss Grayling looked at the girls in front of her.

'Now that I know the search for Olive is in hand, let us go back to the question of Miss Tallant,' she said. 'Am I to understand that Miss Tallant has been using her position of authority to find out what you fourth formers have been up to?'

The girls looked at one another a little uncomfortably. For some of the things they had been up to were things that they did not want Miss Grayling to know about. The midnight feast, for example, and some of the tricks that June had played.

Miss Grayling saw the doubt in their faces, and smiled to herself, for she had been Head mistress at Malory Towers for many years, and guessed a little of what was going through their minds.

'I am not asking you to reveal any of your secrets to me,' she said. 'I merely want to know how Miss Tallant has been conducting herself, so that I can deal with her accordingly.'

Felicity spoke up, saying, 'Miss Grayling, it is true that Miss Tallant has found out things about the fourth form that she could not possibly have known unless she had someone spying on us. And some of us have been punished because of the things that she has found out.'

'I see,' said the Head, her face very serious. 'And yet, I find it very hard to believe that Sylvia is a sneak, for she has always struck me as a rather honest, forthright girl.'

'Yes, that is what we thought, too,' said Susan. 'We were most awfully disappointed in her when we discovered the truth.'

'But can you be sure that you know the whole story?' asked Miss Grayling. 'Just because Sylvia is Miss Tallant's niece, it does not necessarily follow that she is the one who has been giving away your secrets. In fact, the impression I received was that Sylvia and her aunt were not close at all.'

The girls looked at one another in surprise. They had been so certain that Miss Tallant's niece and the sneak were one and the same!

'Miss Grayling,' said Pam. 'Do you think it is possible that Olive *could* have been the sneak, after all? She looked awfully guilty when she was tackled, and didn't attempt to deny it.'

'It is possible,' said the Head. 'But I think the first thing to do is speak to Sylvia, so that you can be certain it is not her.'

'Will you go to her now, Miss Grayling?' asked Susan.

'Certainly not,' replied the Head. 'The police will be here at any minute, and my immediate concern is to find Olive. I am going to leave it to you, Susan, as head of the fourth form to speak to Sylvia. And I trust that you will use all the tact and wisdom that I know you possess.'

'Of course, Miss Grayling,' said Susan, feeling awfully proud that the Head thought she was tactful and wise.

Suddenly Nora, who had remained silent up until now, said, 'Miss Grayling, I think that there is something else you should know. Bonnie spoke to Olive's step-sister at half-term, and it turns out that the two of them dislike one another awfully, and there have been dreadful problems between them. I don't suppose that that has anything to do with Olive running away, but I thought I would mention it.'

'Thank you, Nora,' said Miss Grayling. 'That could prove very useful.'

Just then there came a tap at the door, and a maid announced that the police had arrived, so the fourth formers left the Head's study and went to join the others in the common-room.

There was great consternation when Susan announced that Olive had run away.

'How dreadful! I wonder where she has gone?'

'It's an awfully cold night! I do hope that she will be all right.'

'The police will find her and bring her back.'

'Well, let's hope so.'

The only person who remained silent was June. How terribly, terribly guilty she felt! If only she had held her tongue, Olive might be here now, safe and warm. Instead, she was out goodness knows where, alone in the dark and the bitter cold. If only, she, June, could make amends somehow! But perhaps she could! The others were all preoccupied discussing Olive's disappearance and, unseen by them, June slipped from the room.

'I wonder if Matron would let me speak to Sylvia tonight?' said Susan. 'It is quite early, and I bet she is still awake.'

'Why don't you ask her?' suggested Felicity. 'I'll come with you if you like.'

So the two girls went along to the San, where Matron greeted them by saying, 'You two here again? I had no idea that you were such close friends with Sylvia.'

'Matron, we need to speak to her quite urgently,' said Felicity. 'It really is terribly important.'

Matron looked at the watch that was pinned to her crisp, white apron, and said, 'Very well. You may have twenty minutes, no more.'

Sylvia looked surprised, but very pleased, to receive a second visit from Felicity and Susan, saying, 'Hallo, there! This is a pleasant surprise.'

'Well, I hope you will think so when you hear what we have come to say, Sylvia,' said Susan. 'You see, we know that you are Miss Tallant's niece.'

'Oh,' said Sylvia, turning red. 'Well, I suppose I should have known that it would be impossible to keep it secret forever. Perhaps I should have told you all myself, at the start, but I didn't want anyone to know that I was related to her.'

Felicity and Susan noticed the distaste in Sylvia's tone, and Felicity said, 'Don't you like her, then?'

'Of course not!' said Sylvia, in surprise. 'Do you?'

'No, but she's not my aunt,' said Felicity.

'Just because you are related to someone doesn't mean that you have to like them, you know,' retorted Sylvia. 'Aunt Aggie has always been spiteful and vindictive. Even my father dislikes her, and he is her brother! They haven't spoken to one another for years. I half-expected him to take me away when I wrote and told him that Aunt Aggie was a mistress here, but he knew how much I liked it at Malory Towers, so he said that I could stay. My aunt and I bumped into each other on our first day, and – as she dislikes me every bit as much as I like her – we agreed that we would both keep quiet about being related. I told Miss Grayling, of course, for it didn't seem quite right to keep it from her.'

Felicity and Susan exchanged glances. Sylvia was being so frank and open about things, that it was harder than ever to believe that she was the sneak. Susan cleared her throat, and said, 'Sylvia, there is something I must ask you, and I do hope that you won't take offence.'

'Heavens, whatever can it be?' asked Sylvia, looking rather alarmed.

'You see, we found out some time ago that Miss Tallant had a niece in the fourth form,' explained Susan. 'And we knew that it had to be either you or Olive. And then we realised that Miss Tallant had someone in the form spying on us and reporting back to her. So we put two and two together . . .'

'And decided that the niece was also the spy,' said Sylvia, looking rather hurt. 'Well, Susan, I can assure you that I am no sneak! And even if I was, Aunt Aggie is the last person I should tell tales to!'

There was such conviction in Sylvia's voice that both girls believed her at once.

'Well,' said Felicity heavily. 'It looks as if Olive must be the culprit after all, and that is why she has run away.'

'Olive has run away!' cried Sylvia. 'My goodness, do tell me what happened.'

While Felicity and Susan were talking to Sylvia, June had slipped out into the grounds to look for Olive. She couldn't join the official search party, for Miss Potts would certainly send her back indoors, so she avoided them and hunted for Olive alone. Where *could* she be? June went to the stables, the gardener's shed, and even the changing cubicles by the swimming-pool, but there was no sign of Olive. June shivered. It really was a bitterly cold night and, in her haste to find Olive, June had not stopped to put her coat on.

Perhaps she should try searching *inside* the school, in the store-rooms or attics perhaps. It would certainly be a great deal warmer!

She heard voices – the search party approaching – and hid behind the trunk of a large tree.

'It looks as though Olive has ventured outside the school grounds,' she heard Miss Potts say heavily. 'I'm afraid we shall have to leave it to the police to search for her now. I must go and tell Miss Grayling, so that she can telephone Olive's father.'

The search party went towards the school, but June remained where she was for a moment, thinking hard. Her instincts told her that Olive was still here, at Malory Towers somewhere. And if she could be the one to find her, it would go a long way towards assuaging her feelings of guilt. Suddenly June remembered the old boat-house, down the cliff-path. It was the one place she hadn't looked, and she would be willing to bet that the search party hadn't thought of it either.

Swiftly, the girl ran across the lawn, past the swimming pool, and down the path that led to the beach. And there was the boat-house, unused now and looking very dilapidated.

June knocked on the door and called, 'Olive! Olive, are you there?'

There was no answer, and, after a moment, a dejected June was about to walk away. But then her sharp ears caught a sound – a muffled sob!

Cautiously she pushed open the door of the boat-house. A heap of old sacks lay on the floor, and there, on top of them, sat Olive, crying as if her heart would break.

June was not the most sympathetic or compassionate of girls, but she felt a pang of sorrow for poor Olive, who was obviously in great distress. Now was the time, she realised, to let her sympathy and compassion shine through, to offer help and comfort to this poor, wretched girl. So June walked forward and said, in a gentle tone, 'Come on, Olive, old girl. You really can't stay here, you know. Why don't you tell me what's up, then I'll take you back up to the school.'

'You!' cried Olive, sitting bolt upright, an expression of horror on her face. 'Go away, June! You don't care what happens to me, you just want to be the one to take me back to school to face Miss Grayling, so that all the others will say what a heroine you are!'

June felt her temper rising, but she conquered it and, flopping down on to the sacks beside Olive, said, 'You're quite wrong, you know. If you must know, I feel simply terrible about accusing you of sneaking to Miss Tallant earlier, without any real proof. I'm sorry.'

Olive stared at June, a strange expression on her face.

Then she laughed, rather wildly, and said, 'There's no need for you to apologise. You were quite right. I was sneaking to Miss Tallant.'

June stared at the girl in astonishment. 'But it is Sylvia who's the sneak! We know that now. You see, it turns out that she is Miss Tallant's niece. Are you trying to cover up for her, Olive? And, if so, why? It's not even as if the two of you are friends.'

'I'm not covering up for anyone,' said Olive, dabbing at her eyes with a crumpled handkerchief. 'I don't know anything about Sylvia being Miss Tallant's niece, but I *do* know that she wasn't the one who was sneaking to her. I was. So now you can go away and tell all the others that you were right, and that I am every bit as bad as you said I was.'

'I'm not going anywhere until I get to the bottom of this,' said June firmly. 'Olive, *why* did you spy on us for Miss Tallant? Was it just because you dislike us so?'

Olive said nothing, but merely shrugged, refusing to look June in the eye, and June felt her temper rising again. Olive really was one of the most infuriating girls she had ever met, June thought, with her odd tempers and mean, spiteful nature. Perhaps the best thing that June could do was to haul the girl back up to the school and let Miss Grayling deal with her. She looked at Olive in distaste. And, as she did so, June saw something else. She saw the misery and loneliness behind the girl's facade and, hard-hearted as she sometimes was, felt moved by it. June thought about her own behaviour during her years at

Malory Towers, and did not feel proud of some of the things she had done. Yet she had been given chance after chance to change her ways. Perhaps Olive, too, should be given a chance.

Olive, lost in her own unhappy thoughts, was most astonished when she felt an arm come round her shoulders, and heard June say rather gruffly, 'You're awfully sad, aren't you, Olive? I would like to help you, if I can. Won't you tell me what is bothering you?'

This sudden, unexpected kindness was too much for Olive, who burst into tears again, and said between sobs, 'I can't. I'm so terribly ashamed.'

'Well, we have all done things that we are ashamed of, at times,' said June, patting the girl's shoulder. 'I certainly have anyway! But the thing I have always found is that if I've done something bad, it seems to become more serious, and weigh more heavily on me, if I keep it to myself. A trouble shared is a trouble halved, and all that.'

Olive's sobs quietened a little, as she thought over what June had said. Then, at last, she turned towards the girl and said, 'Very well, I will tell you. I don't suppose it matters much if you hate me afterwards, for nobody likes me anyway!'

June said nothing to this and, after a short silence, Olive began, 'It all started with my step-sister, Annabel. From the moment that she and my step-mother moved in with Father and me, she has done nothing but cause trouble. But because she is so pretty and behaves so sweetly in front of the grown-ups, everyone believes her when she says that I am to blame. I suppose I don't help myself by flying into a rage every time I am accused of something, but I simply can't tell you how horrid and hurtful it is to be blamed for things that aren't your fault all the time.'

'I should jolly well think it would be!' exclaimed June. 'Go on, Olive.'

'Well, at first Annabel and I went to the same day school together, though she was in a different form from me, of course,' said Olive. 'And soon she started making trouble for me there too. Taking people's things and hiding them in my desk so that it looked as if I had taken them, and playing petty, mean tricks and blaming them on me.'

'What a nasty little beast she sounds,' said June. 'I'll bet that you flew into some fine rages with her!'

'I did, of course,' said Olive. 'But that only made matters worse, for everyone would leap to the defence of dear, sweet little Annabel and became more convinced than ever that I was the one in the wrong. Eventually, Father decided that I was too troublesome to stay at home, and he sent me to boarding school.'

June's heart went out to Olive as she listened. No wonder that the girl felt bitter.

'Of course, I felt terribly unhappy and terribly angry,' said Olive. 'I hated being away from home, and thinking of Annabel in my place, being spoilt by her mother and my father, and getting all of their love and attention, while I had none. That made me feel mean and spiteful, and I decided that if I was going to be sent away from home for doing horrid things, then I really *would* do them.'

'So you turned into the person that everyone had accused you of being,' said June. 'Poor old Olive!'

'Yes, but it gets much worse,' said Olive, her voice trembling a little. 'Everyone disliked me so much at that school, mistresses and girls alike. And, when I look back at my behaviour, I really can't blame them. Things came to a head when I accidentally knocked another girl, who couldn't swim, into the pool. It really *was* an accident, June, but because I had behaved so badly all year, no one believed me and I was expelled.'

June gave a gasp and Olive said, 'You're shocked. I knew that you would be.'

'I'm shocked that one spoilt, silly little girl could cause so much trouble for you,' said June in her forthright way. 'And she will go on doing so, if we don't think of a way to stop her, Olive.'

Olive felt warmed by the way June had said 'we', and suddenly she felt a little less helpless and more hopeful for the future. With someone as strong and determined as June on her side, perhaps she would find a way to outwit the sly Annabel.

'But you still haven't told me how you came to spy on us for Miss Tallant,' June said now. 'I'm very curious about that.'

'Well, I was just coming to that,' said Olive. 'You see, Miss Tallant used to teach at my old boarding school, so she knows all about the trouble I got into there, and about me being expelled. Miss Grayling knows too, but she must have seen some good in me, for she agreed to let me have a fresh start here at Malory Towers and promised to keep my secret.'

'Well!' said June, looking quite astonished. 'That explains why Miss Tallant seemed so friendly with your people at half-term. That was one of the things that made us suspect that you were her niece. Now I see that we were quite wrong, and she had already met your people at your old school.' June paused, her expression becoming hard, then went on, 'And I suppose she threatened to give your secret away unless you reported to her on all the fourth form's secrets and wrongdoing.'

Olive nodded miserably, and June's eyes flashed angrily as she said, 'Well, Miss Grayling will be very interested to hear that, and I shall take great pleasure in telling her! Olive, you really are silly! If only you had told us this from the very beginning, Miss Tallant's hold over you would have been broken.'

Olive hung her head, and said in a small voice, 'I couldn't. I felt so ashamed of myself, and I simply couldn't bear to see the scorn on everyone's faces. Oh, June, I started this term with such high hopes! I had made up my mind that I was going to settle down, and make friends, and Father would realise that I wasn't so bad after all, and would let me come home. Then the first person I met on the train was Nora, and she reminded me so much of Annabel that I simply couldn't help being rude to her. And then I found out that Miss Tallant was teaching here, and I realised that there was no point in trying to change.'

'Oh, Olive!' sighed June. 'I daresay one or two of the girls might have been a little shocked when they heard that you had been expelled, but once you had explained everything, they would have understood. And as for Miss Tallant, I feel quite certain that the Head will dismiss her immediately once she finds out what she has been up to.'

'Do you really think so?' said Olive, brightening.

'I do,' said June, getting to her feet. 'And now we had better get you back to the school, for the police are out looking for you, and I expect that Miss Grayling has telephoned your father by now.'

Olive turned pale at this, and gave a groan. 'And he will think that I have caused yet more trouble.'

'Yes, but no doubt he will be so glad that you have been found that you might not get into a row,' said June. 'In fact, I rather think that the only person who is going to get into a row is our dear Miss Tallant.'

Bonnie puts things right

Miss Grayling was most astonished, a few minutes later, when someone knocked on the door of her study, and June entered, followed by a very scared-looking Olive.

After the Head had telephoned the police to tell them that the missing girl had been found, she turned to Olive and said, 'My dear, what on earth made you run away like that? The school has been in an uproar, and your father is dreadfully worried. He is on his way here this very minute.'

'Olive, you must tell Miss Grayling everything, at once,' urged June.

So, haltingly at first, and with much prompting from June, Olive poured out the whole sorry tale.

Miss Grayling listened intently, her brow furrowing as the girl told of the spiteful way her step-sister had behaved. And when Olive spoke of the part Miss Tallant had played in her unhappiness, June noticed with satisfaction that the Head's serene blue eyes grew cold and steely.

'Well, this is a most extraordinary tale!' said Miss Grayling at last. 'Olive, you really should have come to me, or one of the other mistresses, and told us about Miss Tallant's conduct.'

'I know,' said Olive. 'But I thought that you would be certain to believe Miss Tallant's word over mine. Especially as you knew that I had been expelled from my other school for making trouble.'

'Miss Grayling, what is puzzling me is *why* Miss Tallant was so intent on finding out all our secrets,' said June, who had been looking thoughtful. 'Was it just out of spite, or did she have some other motive?'

'I rather think that Miss Tallant wanted to be offered a permanent post at Malory Towers,' said the Head. 'As you know, she is only here temporarily, whilst Miss Hibbert is ill. She has lost no opportunity to point out to me, and the other mistresses, that she thinks Miss Hibbert is a poor teacher and a poor disciplinarian. It must have been a great stroke of luck for her to discover that Olive was here. She was able to use her to find out what you fourth formers were up to, punish you, and earn herself a reputation for being strict and able to keep order.'

'Well!' cried June. 'Of all the nerve! Miss Hibbert is a splendid teacher, a million times better than Miss Tallant. She is just, and fair, her lessons are always interesting, and –'

'Quite so, June,' interrupted Miss Grayling firmly, though there was the hint of a twinkle in her eyes. 'Fortunately I have known Miss Hibbert for very many years, so a few words from a new mistress was certainly not going to change my excellent opinion of her. In fact, I will be telephoning her shortly, to see if she is well enough to come back to Malory Towers before the end of term.'

June and Olive exchanged excited glances. This was good news, and could mean only one thing – the Head was going to dismiss Miss Tallant!

'Now,' said Miss Grayling. 'Your father will be here very shortly, Olive, so I suggest you go and wash your face and hands, and brush your hair before he arrives. Then we need to talk to him about your step-sister's behaviour towards you.'

Olive's shoulders slumped, and she said glumly, 'He won't believe me. Annabel has been very convincing, you see, Miss Grayling.'

'Yes, he will!' cried June suddenly. 'I have an idea! Miss Grayling, may I be excused, please?'

'Of course,' said the Head, looking rather startled. 'Olive, you go as well, and tidy yourself up, then come straight back here.'

Both girls left the Head's study, Olive to go to the nearest bathroom, and June to go to the common-room, where the others were sitting around looking rather gloomy, as they discussed Olive's disappearance.

June burst in and Freddie cried, 'Where on earth have you been, June? We were beginning to think that you had run away too!'

'I went to look for Olive,' said June a little breathlessly, for she had run all the way to the common-room. 'And I found her. She is with the Head now.'

At once the fourth formers besieged June with questions and, as quickly as possible, she told them what had happened. The girls listened in open-mouthed silence, but they had plenty to say when June told them about Miss Tallant.

'Well, I always knew she was a horrid woman, but I had no idea she was that beastly! If only we had known, we might have been able to help poor Olive.'

'And she was scheming to take Miss Hibbert's job from her too! Lucky that the Head is so shrewd, and saw through her.'

'Thank goodness that Miss Grayling is going to dismiss her. Good riddance, I say!'

'Listen, everyone!' broke in June. 'There is another way that we can help Olive. Bonnie, you spoke to Annabel at half-term, didn't you?'

'Yes, you know that I did, for I told you so,' said Bonnie.

'And she told you, quite plainly, that she had deliberately set out to get Olive into trouble, didn't she?' said June.

'That's right,' said Bonnie, nodding.

'Good,' said June. 'Now, Bonnie, I want you to come to Miss Grayling's study with me, and tell Olive's father that. You see, Olive is afraid that he won't believe her, but you are a stranger, and what's more, you don't even *like* Olive, so you have no possible reason to lie!'

Bonnie, looking rather bewildered at the speed with which June rattled all this off, blinked and said, 'Yes, of course I shall. It's very true, I didn't like Olive at all, but as soon as I saw that Annabel was to blame for everything I began to realise that she might not be so bad underneath it all. I shall enjoy telling Olive's father what a mean little beast his step-daughter is.'

And with that, June and Bonnie left the room together. As the door closed behind them, Nora said, 'My goodness, *how* I wish that I could be a fly on the wall in Miss Grayling's study when Bonnie tells Olive's father about Annabel.'

'I'd like to be there when the Head gives Miss Tallant her marching orders,' said Felicity.

'How nice it will be to have good old Miss Hibbert back!'

Miss Grayling was seated behind her desk when June and Bonnie returned to her study, a grim-faced Mr Witherspoon and a tearful Olive sitting opposite her. The interview had not gone well, and Olive's father had brushed aside her explanation that Annabel had been to blame for everything that had gone wrong. Miss Grayling had spoken up for Olive too, but Mr Witherspoon had said gruffly, 'I accept that this Miss Tallant of yours is badly at fault, and I leave you to deal with her as I see fit. But little Annabel is a good girl, and she would never do the things that Olive is accusing her of.'

June and Bonnie arrived outside Miss Grayling's door in time to hear this, for Mr Witherspoon had a booming voice, and, as June knocked at the door, Bonnie pursed her lips.

'Come in,' called the Head, in answer to June's knock.

The two girls went in, and June said politely, 'Please, Miss Grayling, Bonnie has something that she would like to say to Mr Witherspoon.'

Mr Witherspoon looked at Bonnie and frowned. He

was a big, rather serious-looking man, and he said, 'I don't mean to be rude, young lady, but I am here on a very serious matter and I am in no mood for pleasantries.'

Bonnie smiled sweetly at him, and said in her soft voice, 'That's quite all right, Mr Witherspoon. I didn't come here to be pleasant.'

The two grown-ups and Olive looked so taken aback that it was all June could do not to burst out laughing. Mr Witherspoon opened his mouth to retort, but Bonnie spoke first, saying, 'I don't know why you should believe Annabel over your own daughter, but I am here to tell you that Olive is speaking the truth. You see, I spoke to your step-daughter Annabel at half-term, and she boasted to me that she has been doing mean tricks to get Olive into trouble.'

There was a note of doubt in Mr Witherspoon's voice now, as he said, 'Are you sure that you're not saying this to get your friend out of trouble?'

'Olive isn't my friend,' said Bonnie. 'She has been mean and horrible to me since the day we met, because I remind her of Annabel. But I'm not like Annabel at all inside, for I don't lie. And, now that you can see that I have no reason at all to be nice to Olive, I hope that you will believe me.'

Mr Witherspoon looked completely dumbfounded by this, and Miss Grayling said, 'Thank you for coming and telling us this, Bonnie. The two of you may go now.'

June and Bonnie turned, but Mr Witherspoon got to his feet and said, 'Just a minute! I'd like to thank you as well, Bonnie. You're a very outspoken and courageous young lady. And my Olive may not have been very nice to you, but you have been a good friend to her today. And you jolly well put me in my place too! Now I can see that I'm going to have to make things up to Olive, otherwise I shall have you after me again!'

'Bonnie, you were simply splendid!' said June, once they were outside in the corridor. 'Olive should be very grateful to you, and if she isn't, then I, for one, will wash my hands of her!'

But Olive was grateful. Very grateful indeed! She came into the common-room an hour later, her face glowing with pleasure, looking so happy that the others could hardly believe she was the same girl.

She stood on the threshold for a moment, smiling shyly round, then, spotting Bonnie, she made straight for her, and gave the surprised girl a great big hug.

'Bonnie, I simply can't thank you enough!' she cried. 'Everything has come right, and it's all thanks to you.'

Bonnie smiled and said slyly, 'I didn't do too badly for a silly little doll, did I?'

Olive flushed and said, 'I could kick myself for calling you that. I take it back, and I apologise. Please say that you forgive me!'

'You're forgiven,' said Bonnie. 'But only if you tell us what happened with your father.'

'He was quite overcome with remorse,' said Olive. 'And simply couldn't apologise enough for doubting my word and believing Annabel all the time. He is going to talk to my step-mother when he gets home, and Annabel is in for the scolding of her life tomorrow.'

'Well, she certainly deserves it,' said Susan. 'I just hope that she learns something from it, and changes her ways.'

'She had better, for Father said that he isn't going to stand any nonsense from her,' said Olive with a grin. 'And the best of it is, that I am to go home when term ends, and go back to my old day school.'

'Well, I like that!' said Pam, in dismay. 'You've just changed for the better, and gone all friendly and jolly, and now you tell us that you're leaving!'

'I daresay you will all be glad to see the back of me,' said Olive rather gruffly. 'I can't blame you, for I've been quite unbearable.'

'Yes, you have,' said June in her usual blunt manner. 'But at least we know that there was a reason for it. And we don't want you becoming unbearable again, for this new, happy Olive is much more likeable than the old one, and she is the one we want to spend the rest of the term with.'

'Hear, hear!' cried Felicity.

'Thanks awfully,' said Olive, looking quite pretty now that she was smiling and her eyes were shining with happiness. 'I promise that I shan't go back to my old ways.'

'Well, we're jolly glad to hear it,' said Nora, who had also suffered badly from Olive's rudeness.

Olive remembered this now, and said, 'I owe you an apology too, Nora, and you, Felicity, and . . . oh, it will probably take me the whole night if I apologise to everyone one by one, so I'll just say a great big SORRY to you all!'

The others laughed at this, and Olive said, 'I say, Miss Tallant was walking towards Miss Grayling's study when I left. I shouldn't be a bit surprised if she's packing her bags this very minute.'

A great cheer went up at this, and Felicity said, 'What a day it's been! But Miss Tallant leaving will just round it off perfectly.'

The Christmas concert

'Come along, everyone! Places, please!' called Susan.

It was the afternoon before the end-of-term concert, and the fourth formers were having a dress rehearsal for their play.

'Doesn't everything look splendid?' said Felicity happily.

'Yes, the scenery looks absolutely super,' said Sylvia.

'And Bonnie has done a marvellous job with the costumes,' said Susan. 'I don't see how our play can fail to be a hit.'

'It's going to be a wonderful ending to the term,' said Felicity. 'At last everything seems to be going right for us. Olive has changed her ways and become one of us now, Miss Tallant has gone, Miss Hibbert is back and everything is working out perfectly!'

Miss Tallant had left Malory Towers the morning after Olive had run away, and the fourth formers had watched her go from their common-room window.

'Good riddance!' Freddie had said with satisfaction.

'Yes, she is undoubtedly the most unpopular mistress Malory Towers has ever had,' Felicity had said. 'I, for one, won't miss her.'

Sylvia, released from the San by Matron, had added,

'Now perhaps you can understand why I didn't want to admit that she is my aunt. I feel quite ashamed to be related to her. Especially now that I know how she treated poor Olive.'

Olive had clapped Sylvia on the back and said, 'There's no need for *you* to be ashamed, Sylvia, old girl. It wasn't your fault.'

Miss Hibbert had taken a keen interest in the fourth formers' play, but unlike Miss Tallant she had not pushed herself forward or tried to take over. Instead, she had let it be known that she was willing to help if she was needed, and had remained in the background.

'Because Miss Hibbert is a jolly good teacher,' Susan had said. 'And she understands that we are going to learn far more if we do this for ourselves.'

Now the actors trooped on to the stage, and the three producers felt a thrill of pride.

There was Lucy in her teddy-bear costume and Julie, dressed as the toy soldier. Little Molly looked very sweet in her white nightdress, while Pam, wearing a grey wig and an apron, made a very convincing old lady. As for Nora, she looked very pretty indeed in her fairy costume, and Bonnie fussed round her, arranging the skirt and making sure that the wings were in position.

At last everyone was ready, and Susan called out, 'Righto, we are going to do the whole play from beginning to end, so I hope that everyone is word perfect. Olive, are you ready, just in case anyone forgets her lines?'

Olive – a cheerful, friendly Olive – had volunteered to

act as prompter, and was sitting in the wings now with her script at the ready.

'I'm here, Susan!' she called cheerily.

And the rehearsal began. It wasn't *quite* perfect, for Julie tripped over during the dance, Pam forgot one of her lines and Mary, at the piano, dropped her music on the floor and lost her place. But the most worrying thing was Molly. She knew all her lines perfectly, and didn't make any mistakes, but she had been suffering from a sore throat and her voice was little more than a croak.

'Oh dear!' said Felicity, sounding very worried. 'I wouldn't be surprised if Molly lost her voice altogether by tomorrow.'

'Don't say that!' begged Susan. 'Why, if that happens we shan't be able to perform our play, for no one could possibly learn all of Molly's lines and take her place at such short notice.'

'I'm sure that she will be perfectly fine,' said Sylvia, trying her hardest to sound optimistic. 'Why, I had a sore throat myself just recently, but after a couple of days in the San I was as right as rain.'

'But we don't have a couple of days,' said Felicity. 'Our play is tomorrow!'

But, as the day wore on, poor Molly's throat became steadily worse, until she could hardly speak at all, and after tea Miss Williams came to the common-room, with bad news.

'Girls, I'm awfully sorry, but I have just heard that Molly has been taken to the San. Miss Grayling has telephoned her parents and, as it is the last day of term tomorrow, they are coming to take her home in the morning.'

There was consternation at this, of course. Everyone felt terribly sorry for Molly, for they knew how much she had wanted her mother and father to see her perform. But they were also very concerned about their play.

'June, you must do it!' said Felicity. 'You have a better memory than anyone in the form, and if anyone can learn the lines in time you can.'

'I might have a good memory, but I couldn't possibly learn all those lines in time,' said June, quite horrified. 'What about asking Molly's friend Harriet? I know that she helped Molly to learn her lines, so she must know them very well.'

'Yes, but Harriet can't act for toffee,' said Sylvia. 'And she's far too tall to play a little girl.'

'Yes, the costume would never fit her,' said Bonnie. 'And I don't have time to make another.'

'Then what is to be done?' asked Felicity in despair. 'We have all worked so hard on this play. We simply can't abandon it now.'

'There's no question of abandoning it,' said Susan, a determined note in her voice. 'Olive, you will have to play the part of Amelia.'

'Me?' squeaked Olive. 'Oh, Susan, I couldn't possibly!'

'You must,' said Susan. 'You know the part, for you have been acting as prompter. And you're only slightly taller than Molly, so the costume should fit you.'

'But we don't even know if Olive can act,' pointed out Sylvia.

'Well, we'll soon find out,' said Susan. 'Olive, stand up and do the scene where the fairy doll comes to life, with Nora.'

Rather reluctantly, Olive got to her feet, and she and Nora acted out the scene. Olive was very hesitant at first, and her voice shook. But gradually she became more confident, and proved to the others that she wasn't a bad little actress at all.

'We're saved!' cried Felicity joyously, as the little scene came to an end and the others clapped. 'Olive, you'll be marvellous.'

'I don't know that I will,' said Olive, turning pink at the applause. 'I mean to say, it's one thing to act out a little scene in here, in front of you others, but it will be quite different standing up on stage in front of an audience full of parents and mistresses and doing a whole play.'

'The whole form will be in your debt if you do it, Olive,' said Susan.

'Yes, and think how pleased and proud your father and step-mother will be when they watch you playing one of the leading roles,' said Pam.

'And it will be one in the eye for that nasty little Annabel,' said Bonnie. 'She won't like the fact that you are the centre of attention, for once, and not her.'

Olive laughed at this, and said, 'Well, it seems as if I have three very good reasons for doing it. And, apart from my nerves, I can't think of a single reason to refuse.'

Of course, the fourth formers were thrilled to hear this, and everyone gathered round Olive, patting her on the back.

'Good show, Olive! You've really saved our bacon.'

'You'll be absolutely super, you'll see.'

'Yes, you'll bring the house down.'

'And perhaps we can fit an extra rehearsal in tomorrow morning,' said Felicity. 'Just so that you feel more confident.'

Just then the bell went for bedtime and Susan said, 'Come along, everyone. We all need to get a good night's sleep, for we have a very busy day tomorrow.'

And it certainly was a busy day! There were no proper lessons, for the three top forms were busy with preparations for the show. The lower forms felt very happy to have a free day, and spent their time peeping into the hall to watch last-minute rehearsals, and getting under everyone's feet.

'Silly kids,' said Susan rather loftily, after she had sent two giggling first formers packing for laughing at Lucy in her teddy-bear costume. 'Righto, let's try that scene once more.'

Lunch and tea that day were very makeshift affairs, for the kitchen staff were fully occupied with the sumptuous supper that they were preparing for the parents that evening.

'Bread and jam,' said Nora in disgust, at the tea-table. 'I say, Bonnie, where did you get that cake from? No one else has a piece!'

'I slipped into the kitchen and Cook gave it to me,' said Bonnie, with her angelic smile. 'I told her that I was simply *starving* and felt quite faint.'

'Trust you to get your own way, Bonnie!' said Olive. But she was laughing, and there was no bitterness in her voice, as there would have been a short while ago. Once again, the girls marvelled at how much she had changed.

'I feel quite sorry that Olive will be leaving tomorrow,' said Felicity to Susan. 'She really is a good sort now that she has settled down.'

'Yes,' said Susan. 'It seems funny now to think that none of us were keen on the two new girls when they first started. But both of them have turned out fine.'

'Yes, Sylvia even seems to have found her sense of humour now that her aunt has gone,' said Felicity. 'Do you know, she actually told me a joke yesterday!'

Susan laughed, and said, 'She'll be playing tricks on Mam'zelle Dupont before we know where we are.'

At last it was seven o'clock and time for the concert to begin. The parents had already arrived and taken their seats in the big hall, along with the mistresses and the lower school. The fourth formers sat with them for the first part of the concert, for they were on last, and they watched the sixth formers perform their Christmas readings.

'Awfully boring,' murmured Amy to Bonnie. 'I'm surprised the parents haven't fallen asleep!'

The fourth formers clapped politely as the reading drew to a close, then, as the fifth formers walked on to the stage, they slipped quietly from their seats and went backstage, to prepare for their play.

Bonnie darted about all over the place, making sure that everyone looked as perfect as possible, while Amy had graciously agreed to help with the hair and make-up. The three producers dealt ably with attacks of last-minute nerves, keeping everyone's spirits up, while the actors themselves muttered their lines under their breath, quite determined that they were not going to forget a single word.

At last the last bars of 'Silent Night' faded away, the sound of clapping could be heard, and it was time for their play to begin. The scenery was already in place, and the actors walked on to the stage.

There were gasps of delight from the first and second formers as they stared at Nora, dressed as a fairy, Lucy sitting on the floor in her teddy-bear costume, and Julie, standing to attention as the toy soldier.

Then Olive, as Amelia, appeared, looking rather shy and scared, but when she spoke the play's opening lines, her nerves seemed to disappear.

Miss Grayling, in the front row, glanced across at Mr and Mrs Witherspoon, smiling to herself when she saw the proud looks on their faces. Mr Witherspoon looked as if he was about to burst! Beside them sat a scowling Annabel, who didn't seem to be enjoying the little play at all!

But Annabel was the only one, for the rest of the audience enjoyed it enormously, and agreed among themselves that it was the best part of the concert.

'Everything is going marvellously,' said Felicity to Susan, as the two of them, with Sylvia, watched from the wings. 'Olive is giving a splendid performance.'

'I knew that she would,' said Susan happily. 'And Nora looks lovely.'

'I say, look at Mam'zelle, in the second row,' whispered Sylvia. 'She's thoroughly enjoying herself!'

Nora and Olive were acting out one of the humorous moments in the play that June and Freddie had written, and the audience were laughing very loudly. But no one laughed louder than Mam'zelle, whose cries of mirth made heads turn in her direction.

'Dear old Mam'zelle!' said Felicity fondly.

Then came the song and dance routine, which almost brought the house down, and at last the play was over. There was silence for a moment, then clapping and cheering broke out from the audience, and, thrilled, Susan said, 'They liked it! They didn't cheer like that for the fifth and sixth formers.'

'They more than liked it – they loved it!' said Felicity happily.

'Yes, I think we've done a jolly good job as producers,' said Sylvia. 'If I do –'

'IF YOU DO SAY SO YOURSELF!' chorused Felicity and Susan, then the three girls burst into laughter.

The cast took another bow, then the curtain came down and everyone ran off-stage, as the applause died away.

'We had better help them get changed, then we can go and join our people for supper,' said Susan. 'I'm jolly hungry, for lunch and tea were pretty poor.'

June and Freddie were also backstage, helping to hang up the costumes as the girls who had acted in the play got changed.

'I think that we can count that as a success,' said Freddie happily.

'Yes, and that is largely due to you and June,' said Felicity. 'The jokes that you wrote made everyone laugh.'

June seemed unusually quiet and pensive, and Susan asked, 'Anything wrong, June?'

'No, I'm just rather sorry that this term is almost at an end,' said June with a sigh. 'It hasn't all been good, but on the whole it has been fun. Next term won't be, for we shall all be studying for School Cert. And after that, we go up into the fifth. No tricks, no jokes, and no feasts then! We shall have to go all serious and dignified.'

'Well, we have a couple more terms in which to learn to be serious and dignified,' said Felicity with a laugh. 'And I daresay we shall find other ways of having fun. My sister Darrell and your cousin Alicia certainly did.'

'Yes, that's true,' said June, brightening a little. 'Alicia was as bold and bad as I am when she was younger. Yet she turned into a good, responsible top former. But she kept her sense of fun too, and that is what I want to do.'

'You will,' Felicity assured her. 'I can't imagine a serious, sober June!'

'Home for the hols tomorrow!' said Susan happily. 'What fun it will be, and the concert was a simply super way to end the term.'

'Yes,' said Felicity, with a contented sigh. 'A marvellous way to say goodbye to Malory Towers.'

And now we must say goodbye to Malory Towers too, for the moment, but we will come back when Felicity and her friends are in the fifth form.

Don't miss the next Malory Towers story ...

Enid Blyton

Malory Towers

Fun and Games

Written by Pamela Cox

There's tension in the fifth form – Millicent
keeps arranging orchestra rehearsals to clash
with June's tennis matches. But the girls
soon find there's more to worry about when
belongings start disappearing from dorms.

Look out for more classic school stories from

ST CLARE'S

Schooldays at St Clare's are never dull
for twins Pat and Isabel O'Sullivan
and their friends.

There's mischief at St Clare's!

More classic stories from the world of

Enid Blyton

The Naughtiest Girl

Elizabeth Allen is spoilt and selfish. When she's
sent away to boarding school she makes up her mind
to be the naughtiest pupil there's ever been! But
Elizabeth soon finds out that being bad isn't as
simple as it seems. Thre are ten brilliant books
about the Naughtiest Girl to enjoy.

Enid Blyton

is one of the most popular children's authors of all time. Her books have sold over 500 million copies and have been translated into other languages more often than any other children's author.

Enid Blyton adored writing for children. She wrote over 600 books and hundreds of short stories. *The Famous Five* books, now 75 years old, are her most popular. She is also the author of other favourites including *The Secret Seven*, *The Magic Faraway Tree*, *Malory Towers* and *Noddy*.

Born in London in 1897, Enid lived much of her life in Buckinghamshire and adored dogs, gardening and the countryside. She was very knowledgeable about trees, flowers, birds and animals. Dorset — where some of the Famous Five's adventures are set — was a favourite place of hers too.

Enid Blyton's stories are read and loved by millions of children (and grown-ups) all over the world. Visit enidblyton.co.uk to discover more.